THE UNDEAD UNDONE!

White lightning sizzled through the smoke, burning it away. Arms thrust wide, black cape outspread like the wings of some monstrous bird, red eyes burning in a dead-white face and fangs shining . . .

Teleri took one look at the vampire and gasped. Then she burst out laughing.

I *told* him to lose that Batman T-shirt.

Praise for
Esther Friesner's Devilish Trilogy—
Here Be Demons,
Demon Blues, and
Hooray for Hellywood:

"A hell of a lot of fun!" —Jane Yolen

"Marvelous . . . absurd . . . a lot of fun." —*Locus*

HARPY HIGH

ESTHER FRIESNER

ACE BOOKS, NEW YORK

HARPY HIGH

An Ace Book / published by arrangement with
the author

PRINTING HISTORY
Ace edition / October 1991

ISBN: 0-441-31762-6

Ace Books are published by The Berkley Publishing Group,
200 Madison Avenue, New York, New York 10016.
The name ''ACE'' and the ''A'' logo
are trademarks belonging to Charter Communications, Inc.

PRINTED IN THE UNITED STATES OF AMERICA

10 9 8 7 6 5 4 3 2 1

Prologue

SAVING THE WORLD from the dark horrors is never easy. With indigestion, it's impossible.

Gorm of the Shining Helm swallowed the last bite of his pastrami special and belched moodily. "By Glyph and Garfrang's prodigious eructations!" he swore to anyone fool enough to share the same table with him. "Low, yea, lower than that have I, Gorm of the Shining Helm, fallen when it so chances that I demand my victuals sliced lean, and so it is not done." He slammed his fist down hard on the table, upsetting his companion's bottle of Diet Dr. Brown's cream soda. "By Ordan and Sifwa and all their illegitimate offspring, I will take mine sword in hand and cleave mine negligent host from chops to chine!"

So saying, Gorm of the Shining Helm rose from his place, on havoc bent. In his good right hand was the fiery Sword of Tagobel, in his left a damning scrap of pastrami fat, and in his heart uncharitable thoughts. These were all directed at the unsuspecting little bald man who stood just beyond the narrow doorway linking the Back Room with the outer world. Muscles rippling, thews bunching and unbunching like well-oiled springs, Gorm of the Shining Helm strode forth, terrible in his wrath.

Or nearly strode forth. "Sit down, asshole," said Perseus, grabbing Gorm by the scruff of his flaring cape and giving him a winged sandal where it mattered.

After he caught his breath, Gorm of the Shining Helm called upon a round dozen of his exotic gods, but his heart was not in it. The litany of maledictions soon dribbled away to a series of *sotto-voce* personal remarks concerning the morals of his assailant's mother. "Who hath died and made *him* a demigod?" he muttered, slitty brown eyes shooting curare darts at Perseus. " 'Tis a free mythos, by Caspid! Verily, I know my rights."

"If you knew squat from squalor, moron, you'd realize you can't leave the Back Room," Perseus replied. He looked smug about it, or perhaps it was just the effect of owning a classically perfect nose.

"Why can I not?" Gorm countered. His own nose was nowhere near Perseus' in perfection. Back Room rumor had it that Gorm had acquired the Shining Helm solely because no other piece of military headgear in his world had a nasal long and wide enough to hide nature's whimsically excessive bit of olfactory design.

" 'Why can I not?' " Perseus turned Gorm's question into a brat's whine. To the Back Room at large he declaimed, "He wants to know why he can't leave the Back Room!"

From more than two-score throats the merriment bubbled and rasped and clicked and chittered forth, filling the Back Room with a broad spectrum of laughter-as-she-was-spoke across the Participating Worlds. Not all the throats so occupied were human, and a number of them sprouted in committee from a single collarbone.

When at last the common mirth subsided, Gorm was pelted with answers:

"Because your presence on the Outside would upset the Legendary Balance!"

"Because the Guardians would have it so, and we are not to question the Guardians!"

"Because thou art a soldier in the ranks of heroes, miserable hound, and it behooveth a soldier to ask not!"

"Because with the death of the culture that spawned you, you lack sufficient anchoring to the actuality matrix underlying the Great Mythos, and you would devolve to a minor folk song as soon as you set one foot out of the Back Room!"

"Because Perseus will whup your ass if you try!"

"What's the matter? You wanna go somewhere you gotta *pay* for the food?"

And last, perhaps most conclusively: "You wanna wreck it for the rest of us, helm-head? You screw with the Mythological

Continuum and maybe you set off a core archetype meltdown strong enough to launch us spang into Doomsday. Me, when that happens, I got an appointment to have my bowels riven by Lord Jaguar. You think I'm in some kinda rush for that? Siddown and shuddup before *I* whup your ass.''

Never a master of the quick riposte, Gorm of the Shining Helm knew when he was outgunned. Obediently he sank back into his place at the table, putting away the fiery Sword of Tagobel, which slid into its sheath with a pathetic little hiss of expiring flame. He threw the scrap of pastrami fat to Zasu and Zisi, his faithful hounds, and watched them slaughter each other for it.

Gorm shook his head. It didn't matter whether Zasu ripped out Zisi's throat or Zisi tore through Zasu's entrails. Both dogs were in permanent self-resurrection mode. Five seconds after their guts stopped steaming in the middle of the floor, they'd be back to normal, tails wagging and tongues lolling idiotically, two of the stupidest legendary beasts ever to slip into a storyteller's repertoire.

Dog blood spattered all over the Shining Helm, which did *not* have an automatic self-clean feature built right in. Gorm sighed. Another afternoon shot over a can of metal polish, and no guarantee that Zisi wouldn't lift his leg against the Shining Helm while it dried. Heroic immortality never seemed longer than when he had to deal with the mutts. How he yearned for the Great Call to come, the prophesied moment of supreme trial that would fully test the storied valor of Gorm of the Shining Helm!

Gorm of the Shining Helm had not built his career on second thoughts, but one of them occasionally managed to sandbag him at a lucky moment. This particular second thought dealt him a healthy wallop at the base of the skull and reminded him that if his entire arsenal was the fiery Sword of Tagobel, the Shining Helm, and two dogs with the collective intelligence of muslin, then when the Great Call came and he fought the Mighty and Venomous Serpent-God of Darkness in the upcoming Battle at the End of All Days, he wasn't exactly looking at a walkover.

It was a sobering intelligence, even for a hero with little experience of things sober or intelligent. Gorm of the Shining Helm settled himself more comfortably in his chair, apologized to Siegfried (or was it Siegmund?) for having upset his Diet

Dr. Brown's, and picked at the leftover crumbs of his late sandwich while he waited for the next one to appear. Upset the
Mythological Continuum, with any and all attendant catastro-
phes such an upset might entail? Him? Hardly. So far as Gorm
of the Shining Helm was concerned, Armageddon would just
have to take a number and get in line.

Unaware of the steely doom that had just missed him, Ben
Kipnis hand-sliced another pastrami special for Gorm of the
Shining Helm and belched moodily. This would make it six on
the cuff—not that the bronze-skinned warrior appeared to be
wearing cuffs—and old Gorm looked good for chowing down
six more.

A tendril of stomach acid tickled its way up Ben's esopha-
gus, filling his mouth with a sour tang. "There's no justice,"
he muttered, addressing the rows of pickle jars lining the back
wall. "None. That big yutz wolfs down enough cholesterol to
give Godzilla heart failure, and what happens to him? Nothing.
But *me*! I take a bite—no, a miserable little *pinch* of meat;
lean, even—and I get the woofs from now till New Year's."
He hacked a chunk off the pepper-studded lump of warm meat
with unnecessary violence and slammed it down hard on the
counter.

The tinny bell over the front door gave a feeble jingle. A
gangly kid in a Glenwood High booster jacket came into Feidelstein's Kosher Delicatessen, grinning like a zipper.

"Morning, Mr. Feidelstein," he said cheerfully.

Ben Kipnis thought that Sunday Morning Cheerfulness
ranked right up there with cardiac problems and cancer as the
leading cause of premature death in adults. Unlike the two
latter afflictions, SMC *could* be circumvented by the premature
death of its carriers. He fingered the hardwood handle of his
pastrami slicer, lost in pleasant fancies.

"My name is not Feidelstein," Ben said slowly.

"Huh? Oh. Yeah. Guess I wasn't really looking. Sorry."
The kid didn't look sorry, or even halfway sincere. He was
fumbling in the pocket of his jacket for a crumpled sheet of
notebook paper. "I've got kind of a big order here, Mr.—uh—"
Ben Kipnis was not forthcoming about identifying himself.
The kid shrugged and started reading through the list. Ben
never blinked. With his wisp-ringed head, receding chin, and
mottled jowls he looked like one of those *National Geo-*

graphic pinup iguanas who lolls motionless on a rock, just waiting for the photographer to be fool enough to try touching him. Then . . . *snap*! And not the shutter, either.

At last the boy reached the end of his order. "Did you get all that?"

"Yuh." Ben went back to slicing pastrami, making no move to begin filling the kid's order. He was just loading a dipperful of kraut onto the layered cold cuts when the kid caught wise.

"Uh . . . I didn't order that."

"No?" Ben didn't bother making eye contact. Lovingly he balanced the top slice of rye at the pinnacle of his creation and jabbed in twin securing toothpicks.

The kid grew flustered. He looked all around him, but saw no one else at or near the counter, not a soul seated in the attached dining area, no takeout slip posted near the wall phone. Who had ordered the sandwich over which the deli man labored so lovingly? Was he taking care of his own lunch? So early?

The kid stared right at the halfway-open door to the Back Room and saw nothing but wall.

Ben permitted himself one tight, humorless smile, relishing the kid's bewilderment. Let him wonder! The deli man rationed his expressions with care, as if Providence had given him only so many to use in a lifetime. *And don't come crying to Me for more later if you spend all your smiles in one place!* Gorm's pastrami special was done, but now it was that big bazoo's turn to cool his heels. Ben enjoyed the thought of keeping Gorm dangling almost as much as he liked messing with this kid's head. He couldn't very well carry the sandwich into the Back Room with a witness present, could he? Not without violating the *very* strict instructions his brother-in-law Sam Feidelstein had left behind, just before he and the missus boarded the plane for Orlando.

Tough toenails, Gorm. The thought wrung another miserly smile from Ben's thin lips. *You can just wait.* Ben Kipnis fancied himself a superb manipulator of more than cold cuts.

Timothy Alfred Desmond watched as the deli man set the mysterious sandwich aside and filled his order with the unhurried efficiency of a great concertmaster conducting Beethoven. The meat-slicing machine set up a hypnotic *continuo* that underscored the whole of the *Opus for Brass, Wood-*

winds, and Stuffed Derma. White paper parcels piled up atop the glass showcase with the speed of a well-played *pizzicato* passage. Plastic tubs crammed with potato salad, cole slaw, and pickles struck more ponderous bass notes as Ben Kipnis built toward his climax. At last a sleek whitefish chub, splendid in smoky golden armor, was unceremoniously yanked by the tail from its nesting place and slapped into a brown paper winding sheet, the crescendo of the Desmond family brunch order. It was all very stirring.

"Cash or you got an account?"

"Uh—cash." Tim dug a roll of bills out of his jeans pocket and peeled off several twenties. Ben's eyes got big. His mouth hung open like a Bismarck herring. The kid looked so nervous with all that cash that Ben examined each bill minutely to be sure it was the genuine article. Where did a punk kid like that come by so much mazuma? Ben could guess: Drugs. Where else? But hey, if the little bastard wanted to sell crack and buy corned beef, who was Ben Kipnis to stand in his way? It wasn't his kid and it wasn't his store and Sam Feidelstein didn't pay him enough to mind anybody's business but his own.

Ben rang up the sale and shoved the change at Tim along with two crammed-full brown bags. "Have a nice day." Funny how close it sounded to *Go to Hell and say I sent you*.

With his lone outerworld customer safely gone, Ben Kipnis brought Gorm his postponed pastrami special. As he entered the Back Room, he thought he felt a cool draft blowing across his ankles. That was ridiculous, of course. The shimmering walls of the Back Room were passageways where no wind blew. Any drafts would have to come blowing *in*, through the Back Room's only connecting doorway to the outerworld.

Something small, black, and hairy raced across the black and white linoleum tiles, giggling madly. Ben thought he saw it, but when he turned his head, it was gone. Placing the sandwich platter before Gorm of the Shining Helm, he asked, "Say, did you see anything go zooming out of here just now?"

Gorm ignored the question in favor of one of his own. "You call this pastrami lean?"

"Lean enough for what you pay," Ben Kipnis grumbled.

"You say something to my pal?" Siegmund (unless he was Siegfried, after all) was the only hero present who could work up a really mean drunk on Diet Dr. Brown's cream soda. He stood up and flexed his muscles aggressively.

Ben was unimpressed. "I said did he see something from in here go running out there?" He jerked his thumb toward the open doorway to the Outside. "Something small and ugly."

Siegfried (or Siegmund) made a crude personal remark about the contents of Ben's breeches, which set the whole Back Room to roaring. The deli man made a disgusted sound. *Heroes . . . all just a bunch of overgrown barrackroom trash.* Aloud he said, "Okay, fine, forget I said anything! I'll be up front if you need me."

A second shape—uglier, hairier, and measurably larger than the first—scuttled across the tiles and through the outerworld portal just as Ben left the Back Room. This time he was a whole lot more certain that he'd really seen it. And so? He shrugged. *He* wasn't about to chase it; not with his condition. He'd done his part; he'd told those big-deal hero *machers* in there about it. If they didn't act, was that Ben Kipnis' fault? When he went to work for his brother-in-law, had anyone told him he'd have to baby-sit the Balance of the Mythological Continuum between heating up potato knishes?

Ben returned to his post behind the counter and tidied up. His back was turned to both the Back Room door and the door leading to the street outside Feidelstein's Kosher Delicatessen. More than once he thought he heard shrill cackling laughter whisking past behind him. More than once he glimpsed the images of successively larger figures reflected in the rows of gigantic pickle jars.

He ignored them all. Paying attention wasn't in his job description.

When a paw the size of a pizza fell heavily on Ben Kipnis' shoulder and dug in hard with a set of ivory claws, he sat right up and took notice, but by then it was much too late.

1

Why I Want to Go to Princeton

"TIMSY, DAHLING, YOU look *mah*velous!" A gust of expensive perfume, a rush of green sequined silk, a rustle of white maribou plumes, and Teleri of Limerick was back in my arms again. I tried to welcome her to our humble apartment, but an open mouth gathers a payload of loose feathers, especially when your once-humble family banshee has gone Broadway on you with a vengeance.

Teleri's initial assault ended with a quick brush of her cheeks to mine—"Kiss-kiss, Timsy dahling!"—and a lightsome spring out of my embrace, the socially Correct Thing having been done. She fanned herself with slim white hands. Master Runyon, her agent-cum-*luchorpan*, looked on bemused. I wasn't born yesterday, even if some of my school pals have started a campaign to get me named Most Likely to Buy a Sahara Desert Tanning Parlor Franchise. I could tell that Teleri wasn't having an attack of heat prostration; she just wanted to make damn sure I noticed that the neckline of her gown gave her about as much upfront coverage as a pair of green sequined suspenders. I plucked some stray maribou feathers from my tongue and tried to think about baseball.

There was no room for debate: Teleri of Limerick had dropped more than her brogue on her climb up the ladder of show business.

To think it was less than a year ago she'd gotten her start, too. I guess they're right, what they say about America. Where else can a modest domestic spirit go from keening over the coming deaths of her assigned kindred to warbling the praises of Ed Kaplan, the Luggage King? ("Bet yerself a pot o' gold, we will not be undersold.") And that had only been the first step.

I peeled the last white plume from my mouth, feeling like a henhouse fox, when Mom came up behind me. "Tim! Where are your manners? Why don't you ask Teleri in?"

"Uh . . . You wanna come in?" God, I'm suave. All that self-possession and nowhere to go. I've often told myself I'm wasted on Glenwood High. After such a gracious invitation, what could the poor dazzled banshee do but say:

"I'd *adore* coming in, Timsy, but you're blocking the doorway."

I was, wasn't I? It's hard for one brain to hold onto self-controlling thoughts of bunts and base hits while managing gross motor skills at the same time. I did a fast backwards shuffle and made my level-best attempt at a bow. "Enter freely and of your own will," I said.

Teleri's eyebrows lifted. "*Where* did you pick up *that* line, dahling? It sounds like something *straight* out of one of those sick-making old horror films. *Too* tacky for words."

"I am *begging* your pardon!" A hostile snort came from the puny excuse for a chandelier that hangs over our punier excuse for a dining room table (Or should I say dining *area* table? In our unpretentious little Brooklyn *pied à terre*, separate rooms for separate functions are at a premium. Hey, I don't even take the bathroom for granted!).

Teleri took a pair of hesitant steps over our threshold, the better to eyeball the snappish lighting fixture. "Who is dying and making you film critic, hah?" the chandelier wanted to know, its frosted glass bowl jiggling with so much indignation that crystal pendants tinkled.

There came a ruffling sound like someone trying to speed-read the whole Sunday *New York Times* and a raggy dark shadow fluttered from the chandelier to the floor not a yard from where Teleri stood. I jumped back into the living room; I knew what was coming.

Thick gray smoke swirled up from the point of impact. Teleri gave an affected little scream, hand over mouth, the better to show off how long her nails had grown, how perfectly polished to a pearly sheen. She was immediately seized from behind by strong arms, made muscular by years of wrestling shoe leather and swinging a golden hammer. Though shorter than

her by a head, Teleri's agent, Master Runyon, wasn't about to
let anything touch his meal ticket.

"What is this unseemly display of pyrotechnics, which I am
assured violates at least seven EPA regulations?" he demanded. The *luchorpan*—better if less correctly known as lep-
rechaun—had traded his T-shirt and jeans for a spiffy suit, but
nothing could purge that good old New York nasal twang from
his voice. "Cease and desist," he insisted, "lest I be persuaded to kick some butt as needed."

Mom rushed in, coming right through the thickening smoke.
We all heard a nice, meaty thud inside the smudge and an irate
squawk, but it didn't faze my mother. She's got a sixth sense
when it comes to doping out a social situation about to escalate
to lease-breaking proportions, and she'll do whatever it takes
to nip it in the bud. Like she always says, when your entire
career-path is managing a McDonald's in Flatbush, you don't
need landlord problems topping it off.

"*Dear* Master Runyon," she burbled, seizing the feisty luchorpan's work-toughened hands. "I'm so happy you and Teleri could join us for brunch. It's been much too long. Is that a
new suit? It's very becoming. Now, this time I made sure to
get plenty of salami for you. Have you ever forgiven me for all
that corned beef and cabbage I served you last time?"

All this came tumbling out of Mom's mouth accompanied
by the most charming smile in the world. Not once did she act
like it was weird to have black things come flapping out of the
light fixtures and turning into pillars of smoke on the dining
area floor.

Master Runyon is a gentleman, in his way. He raised one of
Mom's hands to his lips for a kiss. "Not at all, doll," he said.
"You will not have been the first to have erred on the side of
ethnic overenthusiasm. Leave us merely consign said fawks
pass to the toxic waste dump of history, and proceed with all
due amiability." He tipped her a wink and on a hopeful note
added, "Hebrew National salami, I trust?"

Mom wrinkled her nose at him. "You got it."

They were proceeding into the living room arm in arm—the
whirling smudge still puffing up strong, if now ignored—when
Teleri yelped again. "Runyon, ye miserable great spalpeen, are
ye touched or mere simple? Will ye leave yon rising stink to
burn down this wretched bothy round our ears, so long as ye're
served what sausage ye fancy?"

Ah. Blood will tell, but stress makes blood shout its fool head off. "Welcome back, Bridey Murphy," I remarked to my banshee.

I should've known better. For one thing, Bridey Murphy was a close personal friend of Teleri's (but that's another story). Teleri was livid. The first time I crossed her, I wound up looking at the world through toad-colored eyeballs—mostly because she turned the rest of me into a real croaker. It didn't pay to get her mad.

Fortunately for me, Teleri's temper was so focused on her unheeding agent that my wisecrack wasn't even going to get ten per cent of any homemade havoc she chose to wreak.

" 'Twas in the gutter that I found ye, and 'tis in the gutter I'll drop ye so fast as to make yer head spin, ye vile excuse fer a scoundrel! Makin' off wi' ten per cent o' me dear earned pay, and what's the return I get? Leavin' me t' be smothered alive by as huge a swirl o' soot an' stench as ever I seen this side o' Pittsburgh!"

The still-steaming mass of ashy air uttered another exclamation of outrage. Maybe it had friends in Pittsburgh. Anyhow, Master Runyon took his client's abuse with continued equanimity. Mom had him seated on the couch and was plying him with chopped liver, Ritz crackers, and Dr. Pepper. We Desmonds pride ourselves on our sophisticated palates.

"Do not needlessly excite yourself, doll," he instructed Teleri. "I surmise that if this phenomenon were at all dangerous to yourself or others, our delightful hostess here would be passing out instead of passing liver. No, really, not another cracker, doll; it gives me gas." This last directive was addressed to Mom.

"It's okay, Teleri," I said softly. "Honest, Master Runyon's right. There's nothing to be afraid of. It's just that Yaroslav's—well—a little slow."

"Slow!" White lightning sizzled through the smoke, burning it away. Arms thrust wide, black cape outspread like the wings of some monstrous bird, red eyes burning in a dead-white face and fangs shining, Yaroslav was his own sinister *na-na-na-NAAAAHHHH*!

Teleri took one look at the vampire and gasped. Then she burst out laughing. I *told* him to lose that Batman T-shirt.

"What?" Yaroslav jammed his hands on his hips and turned to me for moral support. "First she is calling my cultural her-

itage tacky, now she is laughing at me? This is what? Old
bimbo folk custom?''

Good thing Teleri was still guffawing too loudly to pick up
on that ''bimbo,'' but that scrap of luck didn't help me placate
Yaroslav. I knew from past experience that he was a sensitive
soul, fully capable of going into and maintaining a snit that an
old time movie queen couldn't top. His petulance was only
annoying; the real problem was that the side effect of Yaroslav's sulks was a thirst so monstrous that already it had brought
him near the brink of violating his own code of good-guest
etiquette, viz.:

1. Bring a gift.
2. Show up for meals on time.
3. Offer to help with the housework.
4. Don't drop wet towels on the floor.
5. Fit into the family's normal routine.
6. Do not drink the host.

Ever since the vampire had moved into our cozy little home,
my grand Purpose of Life had split itself precisely down the
middle, like an obsessive-compulsive amoeba:

1. Get into Princeton.
2. Do not allow yourself to be imbibed by Yaroslav.

That was why the vampire's mental and emotional well-being
were so important to me. Call me old-fashioned, but the only
teeth I want nibbling at my neck belong to the lovely and
approachable T'ing Hau Kaplan.

Master Runyon became my unwitting ally in the struggle to
make Yaroslav feel good about himself as a person. From the
couch he called, ''Teleri, sweetheart, you would be well ad-
vised to let up some on the jollity. Apart from the fact that you
are grossly insulting a party who appears to be one of the
Desmonds' personal associates, you may also be giving your
career an oblique knee to the family bee-jowks. If you make
too much with the ha-ha, such humorous exuberance might rob
your golden vocals of some of their more mellifluous qualities.
Need I remind you that we have us an appointment after
brunch, at which you hope to glom the part of the nightclub
canary on one of them daytime dramas?''

"Saints preserve—I mean, oooh, silly me." Teleri cut herself off in mid-snicker. Blushing prettily, she turned to Yaroslav. "Dahling, I do apologize. Pre-audition jitters. *Too* rude of me. So charmed to meet you." She tendered him her manicured paw.

Yaroslav folded his arms across his chest and looked down his nose at her. It was a good nose for the job, beaky and sharp. The rest of him was cut from the same austere and angular mold. Most vampires I've seen in movies are thin—except for "Papa" Lugosi—but Yaroslav's anorexic. Tall enough to call Christopher Lee "Pee-Wee," he looked like someone had strung his limbs together out of blackboard chalk. Cheekbones you could cut cheese with? Heck, on Yaroslav's cheekbones you could sliver off microscope slide samples. If he would've had the traditional black widow's peak coming down in a V on the center of his forehead, it would've been too much. Nature agreed. Yaroslav had the thickest head of naturally curly blond hair since Shirley Temple was a tot.

"Madam, charmed I am not," he informed Teleri coldly. "Insults! This is all I hear since I get out. This I must bear? Never. I spit on your apology. I spit on your excuses. I spit on your—"

From the bathroom an anguished wail made Yaroslav pause before he could Say It With Saliva any further. Ilya Mikulovich, my Mom's *bannik*, came barreling out of the bathroom, wringing his hands and howling a string of Russian imprecations.

"Ai, Yaroslav, is this how you act to the guests of my dear lady? With filthy talk of spitting on this, on that? You know how messy it gets? Then who has to clean? The vampire? *Nyet!* Is the bannik gets stuck holding the fuzzy end of the borscht!"

In case you haven't caught on by this time, my home life is not likely to make us a good prospect as a Neilsen Ratings family. If the fact that we have banshees and luchorpans dropping in for brunch doesn't sway the doubters, or the palpable presence of a live-in Russian bathhouse spirit and his visiting haemoholic cousin doesn't convince the scornful, then I have one last piece of hard evidence to submit. Very hard evidence. It's propped up in my Mom's bedroom closet next to my baseball bat.

It's the crystal wand whose powers I wield in my exalted capacity as Grand and Puissant Champion to the Fey.

I just wish I knew whether to list that under Special Interests or Extracurricular Activities on the Princeton University admissions form.

2

You Can Pick Your Friends

"TIM, MIGHT I be havin' a word wi' ye?"

Teleri was troubled; I could tell. She was talking normally instead of gushing. It took a lot of self-possession for her to maintain that phony Attack of the Glitzoids accent, and it had been flickering in and out of earshot all through brunch. This made it difficult for me to follow most of the Faerie gossip she'd brought along. It's hard to pay attention to the substance of a conversation when the speaker's voice keeps shuttling between the Auld Sod and Trump Tower.

"Sure," I said. We were seated on the sofa, having dessert. I was wedged between Teleri and Yaroslav, who had maintained his frigid stance of wounded dignity all through brunch with such dedication that everyone else unanimously elected him Unchallanged Ass-pain of the Year by secret Australian ballot. "Where do you want to go to talk?"

That was a poser, all right. Like I said, Mom and I don't have much elbow room to start with. I don't even have my own bedroom. The living room sofa pulls out into my bed, and my stuff is stowed catch-as-catch-can all over the apartment. This doesn't make for much privacy, except in the bathroom, and ever since Ilya Mikulovich showed up to stay, not even there.

Teleri patted my hand. "Follow me lead, acushla." Clearing her throat, she stood up and announced, "*Dah*lings, this has been simply *delicious*—*such* tasty nummies, where *do* you buy your cold cuts? They are simply *out* of this world—but if I don't take an eentsy-weensy walkies to settle my tum-tums, I just *know* I'm going to go whoopsie any minute now, naughty me."

"Wait, I'll go with you!" I exclaimed, seizing the cue. I leaped to my feet and sailed out of the apartment with Teleri before anyone could object or volunteer to join us.

I figured we'd go downstairs and let Teleri spill her guts while strolling back and forth on Flatbush Avenue. There's no better guarantee of privacy than a big city street, especially in New York. No one wants to know your business, on the chance you're one of those nice folks who swap glassine envelopes full of pretty white powder for wads of dirty ol' green paper. And you'd better not want to pay too much attention to anyone else's business, in case *he* happens to be in the swap trade I just mentioned. Can *you* say "assault weapons"? Sure you can.

Teleri didn't figure on waiting to hit the street before we got down to it. As soon as the elevator door slid shut, she flicked the STOP switch. "There, Tim; this'll do," she said. She surveyed the bare, slick gray walls of the elevator with satisfaction. Then she threw her arms around my neck and kissed me hard.

I pushed her away, but how far can you push a determined female when the two of you are confined to a space less than six-by-six? I was dumbfounded. I mean, I'd gone this route with Teleri once before, long ago, when the banshee first burst into my life and nearly ruined it by keening for my approaching death at all the wrong moments.

(Not that there's a *good* time or place to hear that you're scheduled to buy the ranch Real Soon Now, but it's that much worse news to hear in the middle of a tricky baby-sitting job or while you're trying to sweat through your Scholastic Aptitude Tests.)

Back then, Teleri made a unilateral decision to make my last days on earth as pleasant as possible. She thought to accomplish this by sharing my bed, uninvited. She's very beautiful: long blond hair, wonderful green eyes, slender white limbs—not the ghastly white spaghetti old Yaroslav's made of, but long, delicate arms and legs radiant as moonlight. Her voice is enchanting, her only flaw an intermittent tendency to smell a tad—well—briny. She can't help it; there's a little water sprite in her blood.

She made it real clear she wanted me. I made my reaction equally clear: I just said no. Honest. And no, despite the inch-thick file my guidance counselor has on me from those days, I am *not* out of my mind. I just think scoring belongs in football. Gee, I'm noble. It makes great cover for the fact that having a centuries-old and wise beauty like Teleri hot for me scared me spitless.

After that first rejection I thought she'd taken a permanent hint. Now here she was again, attempting to count my fillings sight unseen. It didn't matter that I had aged some since her last lip-blitz, having become that paragon of sophistication, a senior at Glenwood High. Her full frontal assault tactics had lost none of their power to petrify me.

Well . . . maybe *petrify* is the wrong word. How embarrassing.

I got my hands on her forearms and was able to wrench myself free. I swear, her mouth made a loud, hollow *schlorrp!* sound straight out of that golden cartoon moment when Daffy Duck pulls a plunger off his face. We leaned back against opposite corners of the elevator car, breathing hard. I felt as if I'd just broken off a meaningful relationship with a lamprey.

The worst thing about it was, I'd enjoyed it. I wanted more. This wouldn't be a bad thing, in and of itself. Healthy impulses, the hot blood of youth, a banshee having no irate father to hunt me down and kill me no matter what Teleri and I did, the clearing up of some really stubborn zits, etcetera, etcetera. Only there was another factor involved: T'ing Hau. Or so I told myself.

"Teleri, stop!" I gasped. "Are you crazy? Is *this* why you wanted to get me alone? You know I can't—uh—can't—you know."

"Can ye not?" The banshee looked concerned. "Ach, me poor lad, an' ye so young t' be stricken juiceless!"

"I am not! I mean, I *shouldn't*. It wouldn't be right."

Teleri's mouth curved up like a cream-filled cat's. "Not at first, perhaps, but we might work on it." She took a step nearer, lashes lowered, eyes smoky.

I made a grab for the STOP switch, but she was the quicker. Her hand seized mine in midair and guided it around her waist. Her other hand did a two-fingered tip-toe up the buttons of my shirt, then descended more slowly by the same route, unbuttoning it as it went. When I stopped her one button away from my belt buckle, she giggled.

"Is it shy ye are yet, Tim, me darlin'? Wi' me? Sure, and

after all we've been through, 'tis uncommon odd t' have ye play the shrinking violet. What's stole yer hunger fer all the joys I could give ye? Ye want 'em bad, I know. Yer words say one thing, but there's more truth in the tale yer flesh would be telling.''

"You leave my flesh out of this," I protested, rebuttoning madly. "I'm—whatchamacallit—spoken for.''

Her fingers paused and hovered, her face frozen in awe before such a declaration of unimpeachable moral fiber. I had the little minx on the ethical ropes.

Then she burst out laughing.

"Bespoke, are ye?'' She wiped a telltale tear from her eye, though I knew damn well she wasn't crying out of sorrow. "Well, then it's free of all me attentions I'll leave ye, until such day as ye prove t' be as willin' as ye're winnin', lad.'' She sighed and shook her head in just the way my weird Aunt Mariah does when recounting the adorable way one of my little cousins tried fitting the budgie into the blender. You know: *Isn't that cute? Kids do the darndest things!*

Cute! I was a Glenwood High senior. Cute was anathema to us. If you wanted to socially ruin a rival, you spread the word that he still packed an Artoo-Deetoo/Cee Threepio notebook. If you flat out wanted him *dead*, you planted Care Bear stickers inside his locker. And if you fancied driving a stake through his heart afterwards, you stuck a plastic Smurf to his desktop with Crazy Glue just before Sex—I mean, Health Ed.

Before I could squawk, Teleri decided to cut her losses on the romantic front and get back to the real reason she'd lured me out of the apartment. "Tim, we must talk. 'Tis troubled I am by yon creature as I find sharin' yer roof.''

"Who, Yaroslav?" I made a helpless gesture. "He's okay, doesn't take up much room, hangs out in the chandelier mostly. Kind of a dork, but—''

" 'Tis a foul beast that walks th' night an' drinks th' precious blood o' th' livin'! Ye can't tell me otherwise. I've seen reruns o' *Dark Shadows*!''

She really was upset. Maybe that recent surge of hormones—or the supernatural analogue—was just a covering device. Teleri had always been beautiful, and from what Master Runyon told us over brunch, she was en route to being wildly successful. What did someone like her want someone like me for? *Emotional stress makes people do bizarre things,* I told myself. It was the easiest explanation to believe.

Now I knew where I stood. Job One was putting my banshee's mind at ease. That, in turn, ought to douse her carnal impulses with ice water; I hoped. "Listen, Yaroslav's what you said he is. So what? He's a vampire, but not a very *good* vampire. Did you see how long it took him to go from bat to human form? Most of his victims can make their exit while he's still cute 'n' fuzzy from the waist up. We're not dealing with the Baryshnikov of bloodsuckers here. Heck, he can still go out in daylight! Only the big-time batboys have to shun the sun."

"Is that so?" Teleri regarded me with understandable suspicion. "And on whose word do ye have that?"

"His," I admitted. "Backed up by the fact that he arrived on our doorstep at high noon two weeks ago Sunday, a day with about as much cloud-cover as the Mojave, if memory serves. He showed up in one piece, not as a pile of ancestral dust."

"*Ancestral,* forsooth! Whose ancestry will ye be claimin' fer him? Ye'll not be sullyin' the reputation of honest domestic sprites by lumpin' us together wi' such trash as yon midnight footpad. This would be the first I ever heard of a vampire sharin' th' honorable place of such good folk o' th' hearth as *hinzelmänner* an' hobgoblins, *lutins* an' brownies an' piskeymen!"

Teleri's fair complexion paled to a sickly talc-white. She was shaking head to toe, and her voice had gone shrill. What was the matter? Was she that afraid of a minor league leech like Yaroslav?

I took her into my arms, not thinking of consequences. I just wanted her to stop shaking. "He's Ilya Mikulovich's cousin, Teleri, and Ilya is Mom's bathhouse *domovoy.* You know as well as I do that the *domoviye* are just as domestic as all those other spirits you mentioned."

"I know what I know." Teleri's eyes were squeezed shut, her hands in fists by her side, her jaw clenched. She was a one-banshee billboard for I WILL NOT SCREAM, INC. "And what I know is that, cousin or kipper, a vampire's no creature o' th' holy hearth in any family's home." She opened her eyes a sliver. Green fire probed mine. "Did he chance t' mention at all, where he'd sprung from and how it was he happened t' seek out yer premises specific as a place o' shelter?"

If he had, I'd remember it. You don't just forget your first interview with a vampire. "Sure," I said. "He told us it was all part of the Ethnic Magnetism principle. He was attracted to our place the same way it worked with Ilya, on account of Mom having so much Russian bl—so many Russian ancestors. You remember: All the domestic spirits who escaped the Leeside were drawn to their own kind of people."

How could Teleri do other than remember? We'd shared most of those wild first days of the great Leeside Liberation. If you don't know what the Leeside is, trust me: You don't want to find out firsthand. If it were anyplace nice, the Powers That Be would never have used it as a place of exile. Banished to the cold lands were all the beings of myth and magic that set foot on American shores, accompanying the human immigrants.

Poor things, they learned too late that they were a little bit of the Old Country that wasn't wanted in the New World. Early Americans could handle the concept of Frying in Hell Forever a whole lot better than the idea of tricksy spirits livening up the house and occasionally making the master thereof look like a horse's ass. Puritans always do prefer damnation to humiliation.

Fortunately, the Puritans weren't the only ones settling America.

Unfortunately, the rest of the incoming crew was just as close-minded about harboring the Fair Folk when it's even money that the Fair Folk are more whimsical than a college admissions committee, and twice as likely to catch you broadside with a cream pie when you least desire it.

From the very first, the motto of the New World was "Save Face." You can't conquer a wilderness, carve out an empire, or steal the original owners blind if the sounds at your back are snickers instead of huzzahs. Not to say that laughter didn't have its uses, in the right hands. Newcomers to our shores quickly caught on that adherence to the old ways—including belief in the Fair Folk of whatever nation—was definitely *un*American and worthy of over/under double-barreled scorn.

No one wanted to be laughed at—no one ever does. Everyone wanted to be one hundred per cent American. If putting out a pan of cream for the brownies made your neighbors mock you, or pity your antiquated way, well, you quit. But how did you make the misgivings quit, the persistent swarm of second thoughts that echoed the old tales of misfortunes befalling those who neglected the care and feeding of Faerie?

Simple logic: I have nothing to fear if there is nothing to fear. Ergo, if there are no *duendes*, no *kami*, no *follets* or *kobolds* or *lares*, then I have nothing to fear. Can you disbelieve something out of existence? Maybe not entirely, but how many members of the First Congregation of Marduk have you met at the shopping mall lately? The Fair Folk battered at the doors of a million rapidly closing minds in vain, and were finally swept into the chill reaches of the Leeside lands forever.

Until the leak, that is.

We never did find out where the original hole in the Leeside barrier was, or how it happened to wear through. We just discovered a whole lotta Faerie goin' on all of a sudden. The little spirits were back, the wee folk that clung to hearth and home, helped out with chores and didn't ask for more than the odd saucer of milk or Big Mac in return. They'd had a long, sad exile, with nothing to do but survive. This wasn't always easy. The Leeside harbored nastier aspects of the Otherworld; hungry ones.

The folk of Faerie were glad to be free, and eager to get back to work. Age-old traditions dictated that they must serve the mortals with whom they shared the world. There were certainly enough humans around in need of household help, and pleased to get it for free. Better yet, a lot of the old prejudices against magic had lifted since the sixties. There would be no going back to the Leeside. There had better not be. The future looked grand.

Grand it was, for folks whose background was fairly uncomplex by American standards. The returning Fey gravitated into service with those mortals whose ancestral cultures had first named the various breeds of spirits. If you were mostly Irish-American, you attracted banshees and *phoukas* and the odd luchorpan (the *really* odd one when you count Master Runyon); German-American and it was poltersprites or *wichtln* or a beaming *hinzelmänn*. That was what Yaroslav meant by Ethnic Magnetism.

But what about the *other* Americans? The people who really were proud products of a Melting Pot society? The guy with the British last name, the French grandma, the Cuban father, the Dutch great-great-grandfather, the Chinese mother, the—? You see what I mean. The Fey lived to serve, they *had* to serve, and if several of them were equally drawn to a single mortal they were willing to *fight* over who got to serve him. If there was anything left of him *to* serve after he'd been the turf for their private war.

Even though Teleri knew all this, chapter and verse, she still looked unconvinced. My grip on her arms tightened. I wanted to shake that dubious expression right off her face. "Hey, what does it matter where Yaroslav came from or why he's with us, anyway? The fact is, he's here and we've got to adjust. What's one more domestic sprite?"

"That again!" Teleri's eyes flashed. "He's no sprite, domestic or otherwise, by anyone's reckoning. Monster he is and monster I'll be callin' him, and monster he'll be until th' end o' days! Ach, Tim, Tim me love, will ye not *see*? The Leeside's done with lettin' the wee folk go. Wherever that breach is, 'tis a small one no more. 'Tis torn it is, else stretched out o' all knowledge. Greater shadows are slippin' through it into yer fair, unknowin' world."

I pooh-poohed all of Teleri's alarms. You would've heard me actually utter the sound *pooh-pooh* if not for the fact that someone in the building was pounding on the closed elevator doors. I took the chance to release the STOP button and the car rode up to admit Mrs. Emmeline Mandel.

"Good afternoon, Mrs. Mandel," I said.

Mrs. Mandel lowered her three pairs of Army Surplus false eyelashes, looked down her designer nose at Teleri's flaunted cleavage, and sniffed haughtily. In that one sniff she managed to convey her evaluation of Teleri as the living embodiment of the "bimbo" listing in Roget's *Thesaurus*. Mrs. Mandel had pretty high standards for a woman with a lifetime subscription to the *Enquirer* and three sons who were the pee-wee equivalent of the Hell's Angels' K-9 Corps of pit-bulls.

Teleri and I rode the elevator down to the lobby level, where Mrs. Mandel got off, then up to my floor again. As I slipped my key into the lock, I said, "Now knock off this stuff about Yaroslav being a monster. There's plenty of hearth-folk who've done more harm than household chores. Remember the changeling troubles? He's just trying to—"

The door flew open. Yaroslav stood before us, eyes shining the color of fresh blood. A trickle of same oozed from the corner of his mouth. He had ditched the Batman shirt for a starched white dickey that perfectly complemented the full black-tie outfit he now wore. His cape flapped out with a rich rustle of stiff black satin.

"Goot *eeee*vening," he intoned.

Behind him, on the couch, Mom lay very white and very still.

3

What Big Drumsticks
You Have, Grandma

I HEARD TELERI gasp—a tiny, terrified sound. I just stood there, mouth hanging slack, eyes growing wider and wider as my mind called up every escape-script possible and found them all lacking a last page. No amount of fast talking was going to alter the evidence. Teleri was right: Yaroslav was a monster. Fat lot of good hindsight does anyone.

I started towards the couch, but Yaroslav whipped one caped arm up to bar my way. "Do not trouble yourself," he said in the voice of a road-company Rasputin. It was thick with a generic Balto-Slavic accent close kin to Hollywood Southern on the authenticity scale. Every word rumbled up from deep in his chest and slithered around the room looking for small rodents to eat.

"Get out of my way," I snarled. I could feel tears pricking the corners of my eyes. Pure rage was all I had to burn them off. "Let me see her, or—"

"Or what?" He had a smirk oily enough to lube a Greyhound bus.

Teleri pushed past me to glower at the fiend. "Step aside, ye verminous low rapscallion, else it's a stake through yer worthless heart as ye'll be praying fer! Let the boy through, I say, and tell me what it is ye've done with me own agent as well! Where is he? What have ye done with Master Runyon, ye murderous lump o' bat turds?"

"Teleri, doll!" Master Runyon's familiar twang sailed over

the top of Yaroslav's outflung cape. There was a visible tussle behind the thick satin, the raising of the black garment's hem, and the luchorpan peered up at us.

"Cease this untoward brouhaha, if you do not mind," he directed. "It is not in our best interests, nor those of our unfortunate hostess, to engage in repartee of the more wounding and personal nature with Mr. Yaroslav here. Far be it from us to do aught save assuage the gentleman's dignity, the fact that I dearly desire to wreak grievous harm upon his butt notwithstanding."

"Fine advice ye're doling out this day!" Teleri snapped. She seized the luchorpan by the collar and hauled him out from under Yaroslav's figurative wing. Teleri towered over Master Runyon, and what she hauled out she held high. In ordinary circumstances, I should've seen him dangling on tip-toe just an inch or two above the floor.

The last time my life enjoyed some *ordinary* circumstances, I should've had them bronzed. Master Runyon didn't dangle on tip-toe because he no longer had any toes to tip. His feet were likewise AWOL all the way up to the ankles and a shade beyond. I wondered aloud at this phenomenon.

I believe my exact words were, "Holy sweet Jesus H. Christ amen, where in hell are your goddamn *feet*?"

Teleri and Master Runyon looked down at the same time. The banshee shrieked and dropped him. He landed as if his feet were still there. It was more than somewhat disconcerting to see him hovering a little above the ground on the rounded stumps of his calves. If not for the fact that his classy trousers were ripped ragged, revealing what was left of his legs below the knee, you'd have thought he was just the victim of some movie Special F/X wizard on a rampage.

"Mercy on us all." Teleri wrung her hands. "What is it he's done t' ye, darling Master Runyon? By all holy, I swear there'll be a payment for it, and out of his hide I'll take it with me own hands!"

Of all the emotions Master Runyon might have shown at that moment—fear, pain, sorrow, helplessness—he chose *Whoops, looks like I forgot to zip up my fly* embarrassment.

"Teleri, it is like I asked you very civilly before: Do not get your shorts into a sheepshank. And please, do not address Mr. Yaroslav with other than courtesy, for the sake of your own continued well-being."

"How'd he *do* that to you?" I demanded, pointing at Master Runyon's vanished extremities with a trembling finger. "I thought all that vampires could do was drink blood; *mortal* blood. Now you want me to believe they eat *feet*? Off a luchorpan?"

Master Runyon raised an eyebrow, which considering the height of his brow was quite an ascension to watch. "If you conclude that my present condition is the result of Mr. Yaroslav's violent intervention, permit me to tip you wise. You most egregiously wrong the unhappy geek. Rather than attempting to persecute him on two counts of podiatric larceny and one of maternal entrancement, grand, you ought to be apprised of the fact that this poor schmo is more sinned against than sinning. Is that not an accurate assessment of our situation, colleague mine?" He turned his eyes to Yaroslav.

Scorn curled Yaroslav's lip and disdain sat upon his brow, just a little below those golden Kewpie-doll curls. The vampire whipped one side of his cape up so that it covered the lower half of his face and growled an unintelligible reply. He looked like a punk Goldilocks. Still muffled, he stalked off into my mother's bedroom. He paused once on the threshold, jerked his chin up, and declaimed, "Follow freely and of your own will." Then he slapped the cape back over his nose and resumed stalking. The door creaked shut behind him, the hinges groaning like a cranky bear, even though they'd done their work silently as long as we'd lived there.

I didn't follow, not immediately. As soon as the way was clear, I raced to the couch and grabbed Mom's hand. It was white, but warm. Her chest rose and fell with a slow regularity and when I held a cupped hand near her mouth, I felt the breath come and go. She was alive. Once I registered that fact, I checked her neck; clean. No pair of puncture wounds—neat and tiny or large and jagged, depending on which horror writer tickles your fancy. Yaroslav hadn't touched her. Then what—?

"She came in while the two of you were out taking your constitutional," Master Runyon said at my shoulder. "She even rang the doorbell, in the manner of a real *mensch*. This should only go to show you the deceitful nature of appearances. This world is rife with illusion. Reality is subjective. Life is but a dream."

"Merrily, merrily, merrily," Teleri muttered. "And what is it ye're trying t' tell us? What ill-begot *she* is this? A *weisse frau*? A *cluricaune* gone to the bad? If 'tis boggart or *bauchan*, then this is the first I ever heard of 'em being o' th' fair sex.''

Master Runyon dismissed her recitation of some of the commoner kinds of house-sprites likely to work wickedness. "Doll, those suspects whom you are so freely fingering are strictly small potatoes. A world of difference exists between spoiling a churn full of butter and putting a lady out of commission for a thousand years of shut-eye.''

I don't know which went wider, my mouth or my eyes. "A *thousand years*?" I stared at Master Runyon, then back at Mom. Her face was serene, her lips slightly parted. I squeezed her hands and rubbed them hard, then slapped them. No response. I patted her cheeks, softly at first, then harder, until I slapped her across the face without thinking. Her head lolled with the blow and her cheek reddened, but beyond that, nothing. I had my hand ready for a second try when Teleri intervened.

"Hold off, Tim lad," she said. I heard her voice catch. " 'Tis only hurt her ye will, and little good ye'll gain. 'Twould be better were we t' hear out Master Runyon, fer there's more evil afoot beneath yer roof this day than ever ye fancied.''

I collapsed beside the couch, knees clutched close to my chest. I hugged myself hard to keep from crying, I was that scared. This was deep magic, and if there's one thing I don't much like anymore, magic's it.

Everyone who says how great it would be if we'd shake off this cold mech 'n' tech age and recapture the old magic never caught a glimpse of enchantment's dark side. People complain that we pay for every scientific advancement with a loss—the telephone cost us privacy, the car destroyed the air and turned America into a network of cookie-cutter malls and parking lots—but they don't think of the flip side. They say "magic," and right away they see themselves as revered and wise wizards, elfin princesses, and bold warriors armed with enchanted blades that do everything from cook Cajun style to work out your income tax.

They don't know. They think that if they had magic, it would be like living in a print of Disney's *Sleeping Beauty* without the evil fairy who turns into a dragon. Magic can lend this world a lot of loveliness, but it claims its price. Nothing comes free. Just ask me; I had my life saved by magic. A mere elf-child wove me back together when I'd been torn apart. Great, huh? No hospital bills with charges listed for fifty-dollar aspirins, right?

Just another life given to pay for mine. Just my father's.

Magic isn't something you can deny, if you're born to it. I was, lucky me. Magic cost me my dad, once upon a time. Now it looked like it was going to take my mother as a second payment.

Master Runyon slid down the couch to sit Indian-style beside me. It looked really weird, seeing him in his familiar shoe-maker's pose, but footless. The luchorpans are famous throughout Faerie for the fineness of the footwear they make. *The cobbler's children have no shoes,* I thought, *but get a load of what the cobbler doesn't have!* Sometimes you try to make yourself laugh to keep from crying.

"Buck up, pal," the luchorpan said, giving me one of those glancing knucklers-to-the-jaw that are supposed to be the last word in man-to-man chumminess. I hate them second only to the way Aunt Mariah tries to twist a raw hunk out of my cheek when she pinches it. She reminds me of the witch in *Hansel and Gretel,* testing to see whether I'm plump enough to eat yet. "Take comfort from the fact that you are not alone in facing this crisis. I guarantee you my personal support, in whatever capacity, throughout the current beef."

My laugh was short and dry. "You didn't do so hot for yourself. How are you going to help Mom or me?"

"Timothy!" Teleri was scandalized. She hunkered down beside her fey agent and put protective arms around him. "Have ye no more sensitivity than a stone?"

"Never mind, doll, never mind." Master Runyon removed her hands from his shoulders. His ancient eyes regarded me with indulgence. "The kid is upset, as why should he not be? It is not in the normal order of things to return from a brief stroll to find your mother doing the Snow White thing. Surprise is not without its unnerving effect, causing the victims thereof to eschew more habitual reactions, temporarily. Alas, sometimes temporarily is all it takes for our opponents to cosh us one on the bean while we are attempting to recover our wits. So it was with yours truly, I greatly fear."

"Taken by surprise, were ye? There, there. It's happened to many o' yer betters as well."

"Too true, too true," Master Runyon admitted. "When you go to the door, expecting to admit a doll of your own extraor-

dinary attractions—to say nothing of a splendid pair of hooters—''

"Away wi' yer honey-talk!" Teleri simpered.

"—and instead you come nose-to-eyeball with one of the
least pulchritudinous beezers ever to be seen off a bottle of rat
poison, then knocked for a loop is the least of it. And while I
was thus knocked, the crone in question took advantage of me
in the manner you now behold." He indicated his missing feet.

"But what about Yaroslav?" I demanded. "Wasn't he in on
it with this—this crone?"

Master Runyon denied it. "I stand as witness that the poor
moop neither knew nor wished to know the aforementioned
hag. Mr. Yaroslav has confided in me his reflective disability—
that is, his peepers strain themselves in vain to see himself in
mirrors—but he still knows ugly when it leaps out at him. One
gander at her, and he yelped like a scalded producer. He even
attempted to transform himself into a bat and fly for help, but
the unprepossessing bag zapped him in mid-switcheroo. She
left him as you late beheld him." The luchorpan sighed.

"And Ilya?" I asked. I couldn't imagine Mom's bannik
abandoning ship, even in the wake of such a horrendous invasion. A shell of dread formed around my heart. There was
no sign of the bathhouse sprite anywhere in the room.

"He is the previously cited hag's prisoner." Master Runyon's shoulders slumped. "After she did for Mr. Yaroslav and
me, she rolled right into this apartment like she owned it. Your
mother attempted to reason with her. To this end, she had
fetched a baseball bat from yonder coat closet. A doll of great
spirits and resource, your mother." You could see admiration
shining in his eyes. "The crone merely took the time to remark
that a one-handed grip is more versatile before sending her to
dreamland. That was when Ilya burst out of the bathroom and
made his big play." The luchorpan stared at the floor. "The
sorry little bazoo never had a chance. Squeeze-bottles of Mr.
Bubble are of little virtue against the powers of darkness."

"This crone . . ." I spoke the words slowly. "Where is she
now?"

"Gone." Master Runyon stated the obvious. "No sooner
had she dealt with the bannik but she appeared to sense your
return. She vanished of her own volition, conveying Ilya with
her, although she did pause long enough to impart the infor-

mation that she might be reached through the offices of our Mr. Yaroslav, should anyone wish to do so.''

I looked at the bedroom door through which Yaroslav had stalked betimes. ''You bet I wish.'' I started to my feet.

Teleri latched onto my arm and nearly yanked me back to the floor. ''Don't go, Tim! *Crone*, Master Runyon calls her, crone and hag beside! Can ye not tell now that my warnings spoke ye true?'Tis a witch she is, a sorceress o' blackest dye, a monster like yon soul-drinker within.'' She glowered after the absent Yaroslav. ''Master Runyon may talk himself blue; I'll still not be believing that th' wicked vampire's anything other than a monster in league wi' monsters, and they th' scum o' th' Leeside!''

''Now look,'' I said, definitely removing Teleri's hands from my person. ''It doesn't matter what Yaroslav is; not now. What does matter is that he's the only way we'll find the witch who's done this to my mother, and once we find her—'' I broke off the thought and held out my right hand, concentrating. A long, slim, twinkling shadow crystallized into solid form in my cupped palm, my mark of office as Grand and Puissant Champion of the Fey.

Once it had been a wand. I still think of it that way, although it was now a mutant child of wizard's wand and warrior's blade. The honed edge of a legend's castoff sword grinned against a core of blue-flaming crystal. How it came to be mine, how it went from wand to weapon, those are tales I've told. The price I mentioned magic took from me? This sword, this wand, was part of the return I got along with my life. Now all I had to do was be worthy of it.

I led the way to the bedroom door, Teleri a shadow of green and gold glued to my back, Master Runyon stumbling after. He could walk as if he still had feet, but when he looked down and faced his loss, apparent reality overruled the real thing. He tripped because he felt obliged to. I used the wand to poke the door open wide. When I made it move, the hinges didn't so much as whisper.

The bedside lamps were on, the blinds drawn. Yaroslav lay on the bed, legs together and arms crossed on his chest. His eyes were closed. I eyed the wand, wondering whether to try its mettle as a stake. Naaah. If Master Runyon was right, I'd just be killing an innocent victim. Anyway, didn't it have to be a wooden stake? Like they serve in the school cafeteria?

"So you have come."

I jumped. The vampire's eyes were open, staring right at me. I wondered if he could guess what I'd been contemplating.

"If you attempt to kill me, you shall never find her," he said. Well, that answered that. He sat up slowly, then levitated from the mattress. The bedspread wasn't even wrinkled to show where he'd been lying. In the two weeks we'd had our sanguinary house-guest, I never saw him move half so elegantly. Apart from having tortoiselike transformation skills, Yaroslav was a bit of a klutz.

From midair, he made a graceful touchdown on the bedside rug. His cold eyes measured each of us; they lingered on my wand. "You will have to leave that behind when you enter *her* presence," he informed me.

"Fat chance."

The vampire raised his palms, empty of responsibility. "As you wish it. Then you shall not see her." He folded the cape around him like a bat's wings, and in an instant a small, black creature was fluttering before my eyes. The blinds flew up, the bedroom window with them. Afternoon sunlight poured through the fire-escape bars and touched the bat, but that didn't faze it. Apparently some things remained unchanged. Without a single cheep or chitter, the little beast flew toward the open window.

"Wait!" I cried, swatting after it with my wand. The window closed, but the new Yaroslav didn't fly into it snout-first like the old one might have. Instead he did another of those eye-blink transformations and turned to regard me with quiet distaste.

"If you seek to hold me back, I shall remind you that the cracks around the windows are sufficient to permit me passage, should I elect to take the form of mist. Likewise, in the body of a black hound, I may easily burst through something so fragile as glass." His eggshell eyelids lowered. "I assume you have changed your mind and are ready to accept her terms." He held out his hand for my wand.

Teleri stepped between us. "I'll have th' guarding o' that, ye piddly leech." Her chin was getting that tight look, like a baby's fist. I hoped Yaroslav wouldn't want to argue with her.

I was lucky. "Who holds the weapon is immaterial," the vampire said in a way that implied Teleri was less than immaterial.

I passed the wand to the banshee. She was still mad as a peeled hedgehog at Yaroslav, but when she looked at me, her eyes were perilously moist. "Don't," I whispered. "I'll be fine." Aloud I addressed the vampire: "Can we go now, or do you want to search me for any other weapons?"

"That task will not be necessary for me." He let me get a good view of his back as he stared the window open again. He couldn't have expressed contempt better if he'd had it spelled out in neon tubing on his cape. In human form, he floated out onto the fire escape and bid me follow.

It was weird climbing *up* a fire escape, weirder to be accompanied by a slowly levitating vampire in full Lugosi get-up. I hoped no one in any of the apartments above ours was looking out the windows as I passed. Our place didn't give on the street, but shared the view of a grungy alley with a row of identical apartment buildings on the other side of the block. I guess no one was looking out a window over there either, or else no one cared. Hey, it didn't look like I was en route to burgle their place, right?

And if they spotted Yaroslav, ten to one they'd decide that discretion was the better part of not winding up in the Giggly Ward. Tell a cop you saw a caped man flying up to a roof? Yeah. Right. You bet.

So Yaroslav and I made it to the top of the fire-escape ladder untroubled by intervention. He hovered nearby as I slung my legs over the parapet, one after the other, then alit beside me on the tarry roof.

There isn't much to say about the roof of my apartment building. It's not like in those great old movies, where people used the rooftops to congregate and socialize when the weather got hot, or set up clotheslines and hung their laundry out to dry. Air conditioners, electric fans, and clothes dryers took care of that. Nothing broke the monotony of the vast, sticky black landscape except some pipes, a door to the emergency stairs, some butts and some bottles and some other recreational leftovers. . . .

Oh yeah, and the yellow and green cottage on chicken legs that was pacing back and forth, clucking angrily to itself. Or did I forget to mention that?

4

Glasnost

"HE IS HERE, madame," Yaroslav announced. "I have brought him."

The chicken-legged house paused in its pacing. The front turned towards us, and I got the unmistakable impression that the two unglazed windows were staring at me. Trim white curtains with ball fringe don't look much like eyelids, nor does a row of terra-cotta flowerpots on bright green windowsills resemble pupils, but the feeling of being watched remained. The cottage shifted from one leg to the other. Yellow claws the size of sabers scratched at the tar as if searching for worms or insects. For the first time in my life, I became concerned about making a good impression on real estate.

Then, somewhere behind the lacquered green door with its bright brass handle, a decision was made. The house settled down to brood, the scaly yellow legs folding up neatly beneath the foundation. The bottom of the cottage still couldn't touch the rooftop of my building, but now I had a fighting chance of reaching the doorstep if I jumped high enough.

This proved to be unnecessary. The door opened and Ilya Mikulovich appeared behind a thick red roll of something wet and fuzzy. He gave it a push and it unscrolled of its own accord, coming to rest fully extended, its pointed end aimed right between my feet. The smell of moldy oatmeal and rice gone bad hit my nose. Ilya himself lumbered down the strange carpet to meet me.

It was very sad to see Mom's bannik reduced to this. There was a silver dog-collar around his stocky neck, and a chain attached to it that ran back into the cottage's shadowed interior. He refused to meet my eyes, but I could feel his pain and humiliation. He was one of the kindliest spirits I'd ever known, whose only desire in life was to see to it that his people enjoyed the frequent pleasure of a nice hot bath. He didn't deserve this treatment.

"Please to follow," he mumbled, head low between his shaggy shoulders. I tried to reach out and stop him, to tell him not to worry, to let him know I was just happy to see that he was alive and whole. An icy hand stayed mine.

"You mean well," Yaroslav said in one of those muted voices born of fear. "But do not. My cousin bears this better than I hoped. If you can give nothing but sympathy, it will break his heart."

"I can give more," I replied, imagining the powers I could command and direct with my wand. Even all the way up here, I could call it to my hand with a thought. My fingers began to curl around the hilt I meant to summon.

Yaroslav's nails were needles whose pain unfocused my thoughts long enough for him to say, "Do not be a fool. For your mother's sake, if not my cousin's. *She* will destroy him, and leave the spell of sleep inviolate. Some things are worse than death; this I know."

My fingers relaxed. I knew he wasn't lying, and something in the way he spoke of his captive cousin, the bannik, made me realize that Master Runyon had been right on the money as well when he absolved the vampire from all blame in what happened to my mother.

"You're right," I told him. "I'm sorry." I offered him my hand. "I'll go by what you say from here on in. Friends?"

He regarded my hand dubiously. "Friends . . ." He repeated the word. "No. For me, never. None." He compressed his mouth to a bloodless line. "We must not keep *her* waiting."

I walked behind him up the spongy red ramp about halfway to the door before I realized what it was. I haven't seen too many chicken tongues, and even now I'm not really sure they're that color or that shape or feel that springy, but it's the thought that counts. Brunch did a salmon-leap in my stomach and flooded my throat with acid. It was pure good luck I didn't have a more violent reaction.

I was in such a hurry to get my feet off that creepy carpet

that I walked faster, pushing Yaroslav aside in my rush and even leapfrogging over Ilya, who stood in the doorway awaiting us. As soon as I had my sneakers on solid floorboards, I let out a deep breath of relief, propping myself up against the big clock beside the door.

"Dun't touch that, you feelthy cossack!"

A sofa in high heels and a platinum-blond wig body-checked me away from the clock. Only in mid-flight did I realize it was really a woman. I staggered into a spindly candle-stand and sent it crashing, taking a chunky porcelain vase of roses with it. Neither the vase nor the roses survived the impact.

Shrill screams filled my ears as I lay among the shards and petals. "Aie! Look how he comes into a person's home! Like a rhi-*no*-seer-roos, he comes! Like a blind bool! Like a Stealth bomber! See what he does to my bee-yoo-tee-fool vase, my vonderfool flowers!"

I looked up from where I lay, trying to see the speaker's face. The cottage was brightly lit with a score of old-fashioned oil lamps, their spherical bowls painted with softly glowing roses. Besides these, there were candles of every shape, height, and color burning in gilded wall sconces, floating in brass bowls of water, flickering in crystal candelabra. With all that light, you'd think that I'd be able to see what my attacker looked like. You'd be reckoning without the fact that all I could see from the floor was bosom.

Incredible. Tucked and sewn into a shimmery blue dress was frontage that needed to be measured in ells, not inches. Comparisons failed me. Dolly Parton's image would never recover its place of reverence in my mind. Here was nothing short of a force of nature, a thunderhead of endowment, mammaries that needed their own zip code. I wished I had a hat to remove. I stood in the presence of true greatness.

Actually, I sprawled, but you get the idea. As Master Runyon would say, a splendid pair of hooters.

I gaped. Next time you see a toddler get his first look at a seven-layer wedding cake, you'll see the same expression. Part of it's just plain shock, part's greed, and the rest is a heartfelt conviction that he intends to conquer the *whole thing* or perish in the attempt.

The famous words of George Leigh Mallory boomed in the part of my mind not necessarily connected to intelligence, and decreed: *Because it's there!*

"Uh—" I said. It always takes my mouth a while to catch up with my brain.

" 'Uh'?" the vision echoed. "*Uh* is not making excuse! *Uh* is not bringing back my vase!"

"I—I'll pay you for another one." It was the best I could come up with.

The summits of my delight tilted down toward me, an avalanche of blue cloth and white flesh. At last I could see her face.

I wondered whether Mrs. Mandel knew she had a sister living in a chicken-legged cottage up on the rooftop? The two women could have been twins, except for the bosom, which carried enough independent weight to make them triplets and still have something left over. There were certain minor differences of hair color and style between the ladies, but the basic model was the same. The most salient difference, b.e. (bosom excepted), was that when this lady looked at me, she smiled.

"Ooohhhh. Is very *young* man, yes?" She primped her piled-high cloud of platinum hair and got one fuschia fingernail snarled in the rayon morass. It took her a few contortions to work it free without dislodging the wig entirely. She jammed an escaping wad of nondescript brown hair back under the netting. Acting as if nothing had happened, she batted her eyelashes at me so hard, my hair was stirred by the breeze. "And young men, it is not always that so well coordinated they are, no?"

"No," I admitted. I picked up one of the bigger chunks of smashed vase and feebly offered to hunt down a replica.

"Dollink, what kind silly talk this is, a fine, strong, handsome young man like you to be wasting time shopping for naughty little bric-a-brac? *Nyet!* Nyever! Is too painfool to contemplate. Is to bring tears to my eyes and the wrenching grosp of sorrow to my heart." She clutched at her bosom—no easy play, that—and flung her other hand to her brow. She wasn't just suffering, she was *Soffering*! I knew about stuff like that; my English teacher made us read Dostoevski.

She did it very well, staggering around the room until she reached a huge divan covered in shiny red satin. Upholstery met upholstery with a deafening boom as she threw herself across it, weeping gustily. Prone, her bosom lost a lot of its fascination for me. In visual competition with her beer-barrel waist and generous—even spendthrift—hips, it dwindled in status from Eighth Wonder of the World to How Come She Can Still Stand Up Straight?

The spell of mammary madness broke just in time for me to recall my mission. I stood up slowly, careful of the sharper fragments of vase, and approached the divan.

"Ma—Madame," I began, figuring it was safe to address her in the same style Yaroslav used. "Madame, I'm here about my mother."

The tears ceased. The sobs that had been making her body look like the Andes trying to samba stopped dead and cold. Her electric blue eyeshadow actually gave off sparks as her deep red mouth writhed into something between a wolf's grin and a weasel's snarl. She raised one fat white hand and snapped her fingers, thick with dirty diamond rings. The bits and pieces of the shattered vase flew together, the roses dove back into their proper place, the little table righted itself, and the restored container set itself neatly down.

"There," she said, glaring at me. "Done. I freecking hate housevork, but for you, dollink"—her tongue passed hungrily over her lips—"*anny*thing." She sat up and patted the satin beside her. "Now come, is to sit beside me and telling me all about it."

I balked. She saw, and her eyes narrowed. "Master Timothy, you would do well not to thwart Madame." Yaroslav was a cool breeze at the nape of my neck. "Not at present." The vampire gave me a discreet shove in the direction of the divan.

"That is much better," said Madame as I settled myself gingerly at her side. Her pudgy fingers did a coy tip-toe toward my hands, which I quickly linked behind my head, pretending to yawn and stretch. Either she got the hint or she figured there'd be plenty of time to resume her little goo-goo games later. "Now, is handsome young man telling nice Baba Yaga all about nasty, horrid, terribool problems with his mamma, yes?"

"Baba Yaga?" I repeated. The name sounded familiar.

"Is to call me Baba, dollink," she gushed, snuggling closer. One arm of the divan wedged between my ribs as I leaned away. She tittered and sidled nearer yet. "Vhat is the matter, boychik? Is not hearing of Baba Yaga?"

It came to me then—the name, the cottage on chicken legs, the whole enchilada (or should I say, the whole blin?). Back in seventh grade, my music teacher played us Moussorgsky's

Pictures at an Exhibition. In a desperate attempt to have some of the music sink through our brains' protective outer layer of rock 'n' roll, he used slides to illustrate the different movements. One of these was a colored woodcut of the house of the old Russian witch Baba Yaga. I remembered it, feathery underpinnings and all, as well as the sketch of the witch herself, flying through the air in a mortar. Then Bambi Gottfried shrieked that Lamar Wilson was trying to feel her up under cover of the darkened room, so I never did get to see whether the witch in the picture had a wig on too.

"So," said the witch. "Vhat is? Maybe puss has your tongue? So quiet, you are!" She seized a healthy pinch of my cheek between her fingers and gave it the Aunt Mariah treatment until I howled. "Is not to fear telling Baba nossing!" The gold charm bracelet on her wrist clanked like an anchor chain. "Is nossing I vould not do for so handsome a young man."

Hope flashed in my heart—dumb, I know, but I've always been an optimist. "Then you'll take the spell off my mother?" I asked.

Baba Yaga puckered her lips at me. "Certainly! Certainly, dollink. If it is making you hoppy, I am doing it—"

"Gee, thanks. I thought this was going to be hard."

"—*evan*tually." She studied her claws. "Is saying maybe in sixty, seventy years, yes?"

After I got tired of screaming and swearing, the witch laid aside the bottle of nail enamel with which she'd been occupying the time, and said, "So, he is impatient, my boychik. Spell of sleep is to be lasting a thousand years, but from goodness of my heart I am offering to reduce it so much. This is good enough for him? Is not! Is vanting Mamma awake queeck-queeck, very American, horry op and rosh, get ulcer, drop dad, *then* you are hoppy, yes?"

I made myself breathe deeply. "Yes," I replied.

"Hokay." She blew on her wet fingernails and swung her hand languidly back and forth. "You are vanting somesing, *I* am vanting somesing. If you are giving me vhat it is I vant, then I am waking up Mamma vhenever you like." Her puffy cheeks crinkled up in a cunning smile. "Is deal?"

"What's a deal?" I wanted to know. On the sly, I glanced at Yaroslav and Ilya, but the two of them remained immobile at their posts, the vampire guarding the door and the bannik minding a monstrous silver samovar. Neither one let his face betray any knowledge of his mistress's plans.

"So suspicious?" Baba Yaga's overplucked eyebrows rose. "I do not ask of you anysing impossibool. Not even somesing naughty!"

"What do you want from me?"

She clicked her tongue. "All I am vanting is frandship. You know how to be frandly, yes?"

"Whose friend? Yours?" I began to nibble my lower lip nervously, just to keep from adding, *And how* friendly *are you gonna want me to be*?

Baba Yaga's laugh pealed out like a great cathedral bell. "Silly boy! Soch thoughts!" She shook her head. "No, is not reading them; is plain to see them on your handsome face. You think Baba Yaga can use her magic to force nice boychik like you to do *thot*? Is never work. All, all of Baba's magic, must answer to Rule of Feleeceety."

"What rule?"

"Fe-*lee*-cee-ty." She tried to take a second chunk out of my cheek but I was too fast for her this time. She pouted. "Is meaning that spells do only vhat seems most appropriate. Vhat is fitting, suitable. Because you are not naughty-naughty boychik by nature—*damn!*—is no magic of mine could ever force you to behaving like that. Would not be *fitting*."

Now I was worse than confused. "What was so damned fitting about what you did to Ilya?" I demanded, pointing at the chained bannik.

"He is liking to serve and he is liking hot vater." The witch shrugged. "He is still serving vith planty hot vater. Vhat could be more appropriate?"

"And *him*?" My finger swung around to Yaroslav.

"He is wampire. My spell is only making him better one, turning into bat, into mist, into hound of hell, more easy. Is not making him turn into leetle beetsy bonny rabbit. If is vorking, don't deeck around vith it."

"Well, how about Master Runyon? He's a cobbler! Why did your spell steal his feet if your magic can only do what's *suitable*?"

The witch remained unruffled. "Vas very suitable. This Ronyon is not cobbler; *vas* cobbler. Is now agent." Her dimples looked like thumb-holes in dough. "This time, *I* take ten per cent."

5

What Are Friends For?

MONDAY MORNING, JUST before my first class of the day, and I couldn't get my locker shut. It had happened to me before, but never for this reason.

"Hi, Tim. Need any help?"

I turned from my grunting, sweating, cursing efforts to see my adored T'ing Hau leaning against the row of lockers opposite mine. She was looking as lovely as ever, but where once she'd been aloof to me, now she was warm and friendly and passionately in l—Well, not that. Not yet, but I was working on it. You know what an optimist I am.

Ordinarily, I would have been ecstatic to see her, and I would've let her know it. Since the start of senior year, we'd been considered to be a "couple," with all the rights and privileges pertaining thereto, including the right of my good-gang buddies, the Rawbone Kings, to ask me questions about her fit to make a gynecologist blush. T'ing would've killed me if she could've heard the sly, nudge-nudge, wink-wink, tell-all-tell-nothing answers I gave them, but a guy has to get along with his friends, right? Even if it means sort of lying about your girlfriend.

Never mind all that, thanks to my current circumstances I was about to risk T'ing's wrath over nothing worse than a stubborn locker. "Go away!" I snapped at her. "I can handle this fine without you."

Her smile shattered and fell into a look of surprise and annoyance. "I only wanted to help—" she began.

"You want to help, get to class. If old Jarhead's patrolling the halls, he's likelier to spot two people than one.'' ''Jarhead'' is our student body's affectionate nickname for Mr. Jared Alden, our beloved vice-principal and Cerberus for all seasons. Gosh, we're fond of him.

Now T'ing wasn't surprised anymore; just annoyed. ''So what if he does spot us?''

''So you'll get a slap on the wrist and I'll get detention, that's what! Everyone knows Jarhead's soft on girls. I don't need him on my case, not after last year. If it's just me in the hall after the bell rings, I've got the chance he'll overlook me, but with you hanging around, and dressed like *that*—''

That, as the saying goes, done it. T'ing's dark eyes flashed and the blood of warriors flooded her cheeks. ''If you don't like how I'm dressed, you don't have to look at me!'' she shouted. Flicking her long, black braid over one shoulder, she flounced off to class.

I let out a slow stream of air before giving the recalcitrant locker another bash.

''Hey!'' came the voice of protest from within. ''Slack off. I bruise easy.''

I opened the door a crack. Two small red eyes glowered at me from beneath a horned brow. The smell of well-aged gym clothes and forgotten peanut butter sandwiches was joined by the reek of old straw and, well, what you usually find in old straw when said old straw is spread on the floor of a dairy barn. You got it right the first time.

''Quiet,'' I directed. ''You're going to ruin everything if you make too much noise.''

''I will not!'' My guest snorted and pawed the locker floor, sending spurts of textbooks and looseleaf papers cascading out. As I desperately shoveled them back in, he continued his complaints. ''You're just picking on me. I know how to be quiet *and* unobtrusive. Why won't you let me out? How am I ever going to learn anything about this world if I spend all my time wedged into this portable slice of Hades? Aw, c'mon, Tim''— my captive guest went from bluster to begging—''I promise no one will even know I'm here.''

I searched the acoustic ceiling tiles for an inspired way to tell him. I found none, no surprise. ''Look, Krito, I explained this to you a hundred times: New York City law clearly states that from the hours of seven A.M. to four P.M., Glenwood High is a no-minotaur zone. You want to get us arrested or what?''

Krito snuffled. "I don't want any trouble. You go ahead. I'll just wait in here. Alone. In the dark. It doesn't bother me. Who'd care if it did?"

Self-pity is always hard on the audience, but when it's coming from a half-man, half-bull, it gets downright pathetic. I've always been a nice guy, a soft touch, a sucker. Case in point? I'd ripped a rear seam in my best pair of gym shorts just so Krito would have something to wear that would cover his nakedness and accommodate his tail. After making that great a sacrifice, I couldn't take the idea of the minotaur all by his lonesome in my locker for the whole school day.

But what choice did I have?

"Krito, if I let you roam the school, someone will see you." I hoped the beast would see reason and let me off the hook.

"No one noticed me all the way here this morning," he pointed out.

"That was different. That was a public street. People in New York survive by not noticing anything that happens in public."

"Ah! And this is a *public* school," the minotaur riposted. A bull's face isn't supposed to be capable of holding a Cheshire cat's grin, but he managed, imagining he had me on the ropes of Pure Logic. In a smug singsong he rattled off, "A: No one in New York notices what happens in public. B: This is a public school. Therefore, C:—" Oh, he was enjoying this. "All men are mortal!" His grin winked out as he realized his mistake. "No, uh, I mean *therefore* all men are Socrates. No, no, just a second, I know I've got it now. Therefore, Socrates notices nothing—Oh, *Hades*!" He kicked the inside of my locker a hard lick with his hoof.

"Work on it," I suggested, and got the locker to close.

"Talking to our personal possessions, Mr. Desmond?"

I didn't need to turn and see who was speaking to me. I didn't even need to recognize his voice. An icy draft blew down my spine from the human glacier that stalked the halls of Glenwood High. Mr. Alden had found me.

"Good morning, Mr. Alden," I said, praying for swift justice. If Krito suddenly came up with the proper ending for his syllogism, he'd start clamoring for attention by banging my locker silly. I didn't want to have to explain the mysterious phenomenon of the self-banging locker to Glenwood High's vice-principal.

Not that I'd have to explain Krito himself. Even if I flung

open my locker and shoved Mr. Alden into it nose first, he'd never see the minotaur. My initial introduction to the workings of Leeside magic taught me that there are two kinds of people: those who see the world as it is and those who see it as they've been told they're supposed to. The former types can see the Fey, if there are Fey to be seen. The latter can stare down a dragon's gullet and decide it's the entrance to a new heavy metal club because *everyone* knows there are no such things as dragons.

Mr. Alden belonged to the latter bunch. He'd pick up on the effects of magic—heck, magic had given him an impromptu ducking in the school swimming pool last year—but he'd never see the critters who were magic's cause. He wouldn't let himself see.

Right now, he was looking at me with that Humor the Feebleminded expression he reserved for students too wimpy to do more than take it. "Morning, Mr. Desmond?" His pale blue eyes opened in mock surprise. "Why, so it is! And *what* a morning! Too nice to spend in a stuffy old classroom, don't you agree? But of course you do. Or else, what would you be doing here when the bell rang ages ago? Now do tell: What jolly little plans do you have in store for yourself this morning, instead of attending classes? The composition of a fugue? The illumination of a Latin manuscript? The final experiment to create a cure for cancer? You mustn't be selfish. I'm dying to know."

Quietly I counseled myself to be patient. Mr. Alden, I reasoned, was just doing his job. He was being a king-sized prick about it, but Glenwood High was no picnic to police. We're a good school, which means automatic weapons haven't shown up in plain sight yet. Still, we have our livelier element. The time that Mr. Alden, single-handed, stopped the big combination food-fight, book-swap, riot, and dirty-dancing competition sponsored by the Rawbone Kings will live forever in the annals of higher education. He got out of it with minor creamed-rutabaga burns and a hickey from Crazy Nadine Dunlop.

I kept telling myself that sticks and stones could break my bones but snotty sarcasm would never hurt me. If I wavered for even a minute, I knew I'd do something I'd regret. The wand of the Grand and Puissant Champion of the Fey packs a sizable wallop, and comes to its master's call at a thought.

Tying Mr. Alden's ears in a knot and making him run down the school corridors painted purple while clucking like a chicken was the least of my temptations. Baba Yaga didn't care if I used my powers, so long as I didn't use them around her.

Thinking about the witch gave me the strength to bear Mr. Alden's caustic harangue. Baba Yaga was the living lesson of how unattractive magic can be when it's used to answer its master's every selfish whim.

At last old Jarhead ran out of steam. "If you are *quite* done wasting my time, Mr. Desmond, *might* I persuade you to put in an appearance in your class of the moment?" I let him know that would be just peachy with me and skedaddled before he could launch into another lecture.

Mr. Richter didn't even glance my way as I slunk into my seat in A.P. Spanish class. In all his years of trying to beat the *imperfecto del subjuntivo* through solid cork, he's learned to save his energy. T'ing had the seat next to mine, but not for long. I no sooner sat down than she gathered up her books and moved, despite the scene she knew it would make. Mr. Richter just watched her maneuver and rolled his eyes to heaven, then went back to grilling us on the major rivers of *España*.

When the bell rang, I leaped after T'ing, hoping to get in some heavy groveling. Just because I didn't want her to get involved with my current troubles didn't mean I wanted to lose her.

"T'ing, I'm sorry if I snapped at you before. I've been under a lot of pressure at home. There's my application essay for Princeton I still have to write, my SAT results aren't back yet, my financial aid, my—"

"Your mama," T'ing said coldly. Like they say, little did she know. She kept walking.

"Hey, if it makes you feel better, Jarhead caught me anyhow. He didn't dock me, though, so I guess I was wrong about him just letting girls off easy. I'm sorry I was such a jerk, okay? What can I do to make it up to you?"

That fetched her up short. She spun around fast enough for her braid to lash me one on the arm. "You can stop treating me like a doll, for one thing! Yeah, one of those stupid wooden dolls with the heads that bob up and down, side to side, depending on which way you tap them. What happened near the lockers isn't the only thing wrong, Tim. When I called you up last night, why did you hustle me off the phone? Why didn't you call back like you promised?''

Why not? Because when she called there was the little matter of a contract signed in blood—mine—drying on the coffee table while a blowzy Russian witch informed me of the new duties I'd just assumed.

''—and not even an apology for that, this morning; just snap! and you take my head off for asking you a civil question. Then you think it's all fine because you say you're sorry? No way.'' She whirled away from me and marched on.

I chased her all the way to her next classroom, babbling more apologies, entreaties, promises to reform. It didn't do me any good. By the time we reached her destination, I was no nearer her good graces and two flights away from my own class. The bell caught me on the staircase to the second floor.

So did Mr. Alden.

''Well, well, we meet again, Mr. Desmond.'' He slicked back an invisible lock of his thin blond hair, for lack of a handlebar moustache to twirl. ''This is becoming rather a tradition, wouldn't you say? Like delousing the dog every spring. Do you have a watch?''

''Yes, sir.'' I showed him my wristwatch, wondering how he was going to turn this fact into a gut-skewering comment.

''Working, too. My, my. Lack of a functioning timepiece not the reason for your chronic tardiness, then?'' His voice became extremely Harvard, and his slitty blue eyes twinkled as merrily as the edge of a guillotine blade.

''No, sir.'' Inside, I told myself I would not necessarily be a happier person if I used my magic to make Jarhead strip buck-naked and slide down the banister. Well, maybe a happier person, but not a *better* one.

''Hmm. Well, since it doesn't seem to be very good at indicating class-time, why don't you see if you can get that watch of yours to measure one hour's worth of detention for you after school today?''

''Yes, sir.'' My gut chilled. Baba Yaga would be expecting me back at her place as soon as school got out. I didn't think the witch would be any more tolerant of tardiness than Jarhead was. I couldn't afford to have her mad at me. There were too many things we needed to settle up between us that weren't covered in my contract.

"Good. Run along, then." Having done his duty, Mr. Alden turned to go back down the stairs.

Something long and thin materialized at ankle-height across the fourth step up from the bottom. I saw it the second after I heard Jarhead scream and witnessed him do a fine cartwheel into the fire doors. Raucous laughter echoed up the stairwell and nimble hands with filth-encrusted fingernails hastened to reel in the silk bowstring.

Lightly scummed teeth glittered greenly at me from beneath trailing black moustaches. A face only a mother sea slug could love, if bribed, solidified at eye-level, followed by a stocky body redolent of horse, dog, goat, and maybe yak.

"Greetings, revered wussy! You had sex with my honored granddaughter *yet*, or all these months you lying about being gelded?" He made a grab for my crotch, just to check.

Yang was back.

6

. . . and Influence People

"So you're a minotaur." Yang's nostrils flared as he breathed deep of Krito's distinctive aroma. "You remind me of my honored mom."

The minotaur stretched his hamstrings and tugged the brim of his New York Mets cap a little lower over his eyes. "Minotaurs don't have mothers," he said. He was still sulky, even though Yang had prevailed upon me to release Krito from durance vile, cut the rest of the school day, and spend it on the lam with these two model citizens. Between Krito's being slow on the uptake, Yang's brainless bravado, and my own lack of better judgment, we had the collective intelligence of mashed okra.

"No mothers?" Yang was fascinated.

"No females," the minotaur elaborated. "You can't be half-man and half-bull and anything *near* feminine."

"No females of any kind? What do you do for—?"

"—sex," I finished for him, somewhat wearily. With Yang it was always the same drill.

"—clean clothes," he finished for himself, and scowled at me.

Yang is a Mongol. In his earthly life, he was one of the better scowlers the horde produced. During the invasion of China he managed to scowl seven individual villages and an entire subprefecture into submission. At present, Yang belongs to T'ing Hau in the capacity of ancestral spirit. You can't get any closer to hearth-and-home than being blood kin, however many generations removed.

When the rest of the domestic sprites made a break for it through the Leeside leak, Yang was right behind them. He didn't even stop to pack a change of dogskins. That should give you further confirmation of how delightful the Leeside is, if it frightens off a Mongol.

"Clean clothes?" The minotaur yawned and scratched himself heartily through my now-ruined gym shorts. "I don't wear clothes, usually. And I don't have sex." He helped himself to another slice of broccoli pizza.

"No shit?" Yang stabbed his own slice with a jade-hilted dagger and sat back, plucking off clumps of broccoli and flicking them at the metalheads playing the Double Dragon machine. They started for us, leathers creaking, chains clashing, and spiked straps bristling. Then they got a good look at Yang and asked us very meekly whether we had change for a dollar, please sir, thank you.

I gave them four quarters and yanked Yang back down into our booth so hard he launched a glob of half-chewed mozzarella. "Pay attention, O Yang the Occasionally Putrid—"

"*Occasionally!*"

"—because I'm only going to say this once: I've got a job to do and Krito's it. I'm supposed to get this monster accustomed to life in the outer world. I've got to be his"—the word curdled on my tongue—"*buddy*. I've got to give him the friendly show-around and make sure he learns how to make it on his own. The sooner I do that, the sooner Baba Yaga releases my mom from the sleep of a thousand years; that was the deal we cut. You said you wanted to help me? Fine. But I want it perfectly clear that T'ing is *not* to be part of this and you are *not* to screw us up with your usual brand of high jinks. Got that?"

At first Yang looked pissed, which is never a pretty sight on a man who, in his lifetime, terrified half the populace and all the livestock of Asia. Then anger cooled into scientific curiosity. "How come you don't want my honored granddaughter in on this, Tim? She's no coward, and I know she would want to help her man. All the women of my tribe do this, or we trade them for a new saddle." Something clicked in his head (probably a stray beetle). "Hey! I get it! You need a new saddle!"

I'd dealt with enough of the D'uhhh People in banks, service stations, civil service offices, and shopping malls to garner lots of experience pounding sand down a variety of mental rat holes. Therefore it wasn't all that bad trying to explain things to Yang for the uku-billionth time.

"I don't want T'ing in on this because it's dangerous," I said. "Baba Yaga is—" I glanced nervously at Krito, who appeared to be chewing his cud.

"Oh, go on, say what you like about Baba." He made a gesture of encouragement. "Can't stand her, myself. She's not helping me out of the goodness of her heart. A: All witches are selfish. B: Baba Yaga is a witch. Therefore C: Baba Yaga is a pain in the hindquarters. There's plenty of payback in this for her, never fear. Stupid cow."

With the minotaur's blessing, I returned my attention to Yang. "She's a witch," I reiterated. "A powerful one. Not all-powerful—her magic can only work according to a weird set of rules, but she's had centuries of practice getting it to give her what she wants. My wand's strong enough to give her spell-casting a run for the money, but I can't use it against her. She's the only one who knows how to revive my mother, and she'll only do that if I cooperate with her."

"This is understandable." Yang took a bit of 'za and spat broccoli into my Coke with deadly accuracy. "But why no T'ing?"

"Baba already has one person I love in her clutches as a bargaining chip. I'm not about to let her get her hands on another."

Yang bellowed with laughter, mouth still crammed full of pizza. It wasn't a sight I'd soon forget. Then he started to choke and our waitress (clearly a Fey-sighted lady) did the Heimlich Maneuver on him. After he thanked her, he suggested that next time they had sex it would work better if they traded places.

After that, we ate the rest of the pizza while strolling down Flatbush Avenue. Our progress was about what I expected: No one who saw us, saw us. That's what I thought, anyhow. I caught a couple of dubious stares aimed at Krito, but the folks giving the minotaur the chary eye didn't seem to see Yang. See one supernatural creature, see 'em all, was the way I thought it worked. Either you had the gift or you didn't.

I had other stuff to occupy my mind. Yang was gung-ho to help me out of my predicament, but most of his suggestions for improving situations came from hands-on experience in the pillaging line.

"Why can't I burn down the McDonald's?" he demanded.

"Because that won't solve a thing. I covered Mom's absence from work today and they got someone to sub for her as manager, but what about tomorrow?"

"If I burn it down and sow salt on the ruins, they won't open it tomorrow." Yang beamed at his own simple brilliance. "I could cut off the head of the substitute manager and display it on a pike, too. No extra charge."

"No." I was very firm. "Covering Mom's absence isn't the biggie. Collecting her salary is. We need money, Yang. I don't know how long Baba Yaga's going to keep Mom under that sleep spell, and in the meanwhile, bills will come due, the rent will have to be paid, I'll have to buy food—"

"She eats in her sleep?"

"She doesn't eat; I do."

"How about—you know?" Yang raised two fingers and looked a little embarrassed. Maybe civilization was rubbing off on the Mongol. In earlier days he would have dropped trow and illustrated his query right out in the middle of the street, without bothering to ask for the Little Barbarians' Room.

"That neither. She doesn't do anything but lie there. Yaroslav helped me move her into her bed last night. Teleri's minding things in the apartment, answering phones, doing a pretty good imitation of Mom's voice if anyone calls, and saying she's got the flu." The thought of Teleri's loyal service gave me a pang. "She missed her big chance to audition for a part in a soap opera on account of this. Master Runyon's livid."

Livid wasn't the word. I never saw someone with no feet stomp around an apartment that loudly before. While he ranted, he let slip that he and Teleri weren't exactly flush with ready cash either. *"You know how much a rag like she is presently flaunting sets a guy back? Have you perchance priced any of the other accoutrements necessary to the upkeep of a high-class warbler's public image? We are not talking nickel-and-dime, here. We are speaking of frequent outlays of the humongous kind. We are casually letting drop the fact that some people I could mention are in the process of scraping the bottom of the fabled luchorpan's crock o' gold, which certain other people who shall remain nameless seem to think is bottomless."*

"Money . . ." Yang grew pensive. "You need money."

"*Legal* money!" I specified. I knew Yang.

The Mongol slapped his trousers. "Ha! Perfect. I, Yang of the Conspicuously Wisdom-Enriched Brain, have the answer. I will help you get money, much money. *Legal* money." He showed what he had of a mouthful of ochre teeth. "No thanks will be necessary. A small virgin will do." Having given me his wish-list, he vanished.

Krito nodded at the empty air where Yang had been. "Not a bad idea," he said. "I wouldn't mind a virgin myself."

"I thought you said you don't have sex," I pointed out.

"I don't. I eat 'em. Seven youths and seven maidens every seven years. Nice work if you can get it. They've all got to be stainlessly pure, you know, or they repeat on me like Greek fire. Although to tell you the truth"—he lowered his voice and spoke to me out of the corner of his mouth—"it's been so long since I've had a decent meal that I'd be willing to munch a few that've had some impure thoughts. Truly has Anacharsis written: 'Pizza is no substitute for virginity.' "

"*Who* wrote *that*?"

The minotaur's ample muzzle twisted into a *does it matter?* expression. "Maybe I got it wrong. Like I said, it's been a long time." His nostrils twitched abruptly and he stared at me with new interest. "Say, Tim, you wouldn't happen to be a—?"

"Virgin? Me? Ha! That's funny. Funny? Hilarious! Ridiculous! Not for years. Not for *ages*! Kicked out of first grade for—I'd rather not talk about it. *Me* a virgin?" I laughed hysterically and tried to stop shaking.

Krito slowly shook his horned head from side to side. "Just asking. Normally I can smell a virgin a mile away, but this place, this *air*—!" he snuffled up a deep breath and let it out in a barrage of sneezes. "Horrible. I can hardly smell a thing. No wonder my appetite's off."

Quietly I gave thanks for air pollution and the yellow-green skies of New York.

Krito and I returned home. Before going up to the roof to make my progress report to Baba Yaga, I stopped by the apartment to check on Mom while Krito went on ahead via the emergency stairs. Mom lay peacefully sleeping in her own bed with Yaroslav in bat-form hanging upside down from the bedside lamp. He fluttered across the room to perch on my shoulder.

"Greetings." His voice still sounded like a three-way mating of Karloff, Price, and Lugosi, underscored by a ghostly arpeggio of *Phantom of the Opera* organ music.

"Greetings yourself. Where's Teleri?"

"She and Master Runyon were constrained to depart. A previous engagement that would brook no evasion. Something about an advertisement for His Royal Highness Edward."

"Oh, you mean Ed Kaplan, the Luggage King. Yeah, Teleri's got an ad campaign contract with him. So you've been watching things here?"

"I have." The vampire made it sound solemn enough to be funeral duty. I glanced nervously at my mother.

"How is she?" Mom's face was placid. She smiled in her sleep. At least the witch hadn't condemned her to a thousand years of nightmares.

"Well. And your mission? It is close to being accomplished?"

I tried to shrug, but Yaroslav drove his talons into my shoulder. I guess he didn't like an antsy perch. "I'm making some progress. Krito's a good pupil. I feel kind of sorry for him, though. Once he's ready to take off on his own, he's going to starve to death. Do you know what minotaurs eat?"

"Virgins."

"And pizza. But if he needs the virgins for essential nutrients, he won't last long. Not unless he leaves Brooklyn."

"That is, I believe, the whole purpose behind Baba Yaga's scheme, Timothy. The creatures of the night who emerge from the Leeside desire to recapture the full scope of their ancient kingdom. To be confined to Brooklyn . . ." He flapped his wings the way a man might turn his hands palm up, at a loss. "A temporary inconvenience which *you* must help them overcome as swiftly as possible."

I cocked my head at the little bat. "Why do you say *them*, Yaroslav? Why not *us*?"

The vampire's glowing red eyes dimmed. I never saw a bat look ashamed before. (I never saw a bat at such close quarters before, either, and it's a learning experience I'd have passed up gladly.) "It is so. I am, as are they, of the monstrous breed of spirits. There is no help for it, or hope of change. But for me, neither was there ever any choice."

He released his grip on my shoulder and flittered over to Mom's easel. My mother's quite the artist—or was. Whenever she had a spare moment—and she didn't have too many of them—she'd paint. Her work tended toward the superrealistic. She liked to put anomalous pieces of reality together into a joker's giant jigsaw puzzle, taking most of her models from photographs. Way the heck before the Leeside sprang its smallest leak, my mother was painting the impossible person in the unimaginable situation. Juliet in a leather halter-top tugged the safety pin that dangled from Romeo's ear lobe as they kissed on the balcony in front of an Elvis poster. The late Liberace rode into town on a rhinestone-studded Harley, right behind the rest of Brando's gang in *The Wild Ones*, Marilyn Monroe riding pillion. A grizzly bear in a ringmaster's suit presented the leaders of East and West shaking hands while riding unicycles on a circus high wire.

I looked at the interrupted work currently on the easel. A wizard with the bearded face of Art Carney was studying the document offered him by a horned and tailed devil. It looked like a direct take on Faust, until you caught the contract to be a ream of computer printout and spied the pocket-protector in the wizard's robe. The devil wasn't the usual either. His goatish lower body was topped with a midway barker's peppermint-striped blazer, and a straw boater was balanced on his horns. He held a cardboard mask of Nixon's face behind his back while offering his intended client a sleek black quill pen with a cartoony blob of blood hanging from the tip. A Happy Face grinned vapidly from the gory driplet.

"You like it?" I asked the bat. Instead of replying, Yaroslav flew straight for the window, turning to mist and seeping out through the cracks around the sash at the instant of impact. I had to admit it, he was getting good at being a creature of the night. When he got good enough, would he have to stay in his coffin during daylight hours? I wondered where he was keeping that little item of personal furniture, but not half as much as I wondered whether Baba Yaga would give the poor guy sufficient warning to hide from the sun when the time came.

I opted for climbing up the fire escape again. Krito was waiting for me at the top, with Yaroslav a misty presence around the minotaur's head. The witch's house spotted me right away and came prancing up to meet me. Strolling up the tongue still gave me the minor heaves, but by now I knew I could depend on Baba Yaga to be up to something so outrageous inside that I'd be too shocked to stay nauseated.

I wasn't wrong. This time my eyes were assaulted by the sight of the buxom witch going at full throttle aboard a stationary bicycle. That was bizarre enough without her having outfitted herself top to toe in electric pink-and-yellow skintight exercise togs.

"Tim, dollink, come in, come in!" She raised one green-nailed hand from the handlebars to beckon me. The witch's sweat smelled like melted marshmallows and yogurt. "You are here to see me feel the burn, yes?"

I bit my lower lip. Watching a lady of her physical attributes work out was like witnessing two wombats wrestling in a pillowcase. Fortunately for my mental and emotional hardwiring, she decided to let the burn feel itself for a while and stopped pedaling.

Unhappy little Ilya was right there to hand his mistress a towel. It broke my heart every time I saw the little bannik. Shaggy as he was, I could still tell how thin he was getting. Under all that thick brown hair, he was wasting away with sorrow, and I couldn't do a thing about it.

"So!" Baba Yaga flopped down on the ugly red satin divan and indicated for me to do likewise. "Now, is to telling me how my Tim he is doing with teaching my dear, dear friend Krito the—how do you say them?—ropes?" She regarded the minotaur, her heavy-lidded eyes lingering hungrily over certain parts of the creature's mixed anatomy. "Yes, Krito is telling me first whether you are doing good, Tim. This is best, no?"

The minotaur came forward and bowed awkwardly to the witch, doffing his Mets cap. "Lady, it's been better than I hoped. This new world is as vast and complex as you warned me. The pull of the Leeside is still strong—"

"But of course! It is an evil place and you are an evil being, so it pools, it *pools*!" She engaged in an invisible tug of war with the Leeside. "What could be more proper to the great Rule of Felicity?" Baba Yaga looked pleased with herself. "That is why it is our dollink Tim's job to teach you to *belong* to the ways of the outervorld as completely as once you belonged to the ways of the Leeside. When this happens—poof!— the pool of the Outside, she cancels the pool of the Leeside and no longer will you be confined to *this* dreary corner of the vide vorld."

"Good," Krito said, "because from what I gather, finding a virgin around here is going to be—"

"Soon!" Baba Yaga threw her arms wide, almost knocking over the tray of drinks Ilya Mikulovich had dutifully brought for us. "Soon there shall be no barriers, no confinement! The wall crumbles, the Guardians sleep. There is a vorld for us to take back at our pleasure. All that we must do to sever the Guardians' spells is to become so much a part of the Outside that they cannot tear us from it if they try. Our roots will have run too deep for that. To this end—*education*!" She smacked her fist down on the little lacquerware table beside the divan. It left a dent the size of a teacup.

"Education is good," Krito agreed. "The place where Tim spent most of his day is devoted to it."

"This place . . . you were educated there as well, Krito?" Baba Yaga looked very interested. I didn't like it.

"No, I had to wait until he was done for the day. I did overhear some fascinating tenets of this world's dominant philosophy while confined to his—locker—right, Tim?" I nodded. "As Socrates would put it, 'I know nothing except the fact of my ignorance, and that if I do not get rid of these zits before my date Saturday night I am going to die.' "

"Marvelous." Baba Yaga leaned nearer, her eyes shining. "Is to illuminate whole of life, such philosophy, yes? And this you are learning only by being kept locked up?" She tapped her fingertips together. "Think! Think how much more you are learning when Tim is taking you out of locker and letting you to spend whole day roaming institute of such vonderfool learning."

"Now hold on right there—!" I started up from my place, but the witch still had the other barrel primed, loaded, and aimed straight at my gut.

"—and think how much the *others* vill learn there too."

"What others?" I asked.

7

Student Bodies

THE WORST KIND of walls that can close in on you are invisible ones. No matter how much elbow room and breathing space I had around me, the events of the past week left me feeling like I was slowly sinking down into a bottomless pit of day-old oatmeal.

Monday afternoon's little tête-à-tête with Baba Yaga ended with the witch's imposing bosom about an inch from my eyes and her nougat-gooey voice informing me, "But of course you will be happy to doing this leetsle-beetsy favor for me, dollink, no? Because if not"—her eyes, how they twinkled—"is hot day in Novosibirsk before your mama sees *Today* show again."

Tuesday I spent in bed. When I had Teleri mimic Mom's voice and call me in sick at school, it was no lie. The thought of what Baba Yaga wanted me to do had me floored, literally. Next to this new, improved assignment, shepherding a minotaur was a breeze.

Wednesday I spent relearning how to walk. Every time I thought about the raw materials awaiting my attention on the rooftop, I walked into another wall. Krito came down, took one look at me, and let me go to school on my own. Even minotaurs can have mercy. No word came down from above, not even a fly-through by Yaroslav. Either Baba Yaga was being patient, or she'd forgotten about our Monday chat.

Thursday she proved that she hadn't forgotten one damn thing. I woke up and went in to check on Mom, only to find Baba Yaga herself stretched out on the bed beside her. Her taste in lingerie was a black and scarlet undercoating of *Rocky Horror Picture Show* with a plaid topping of flannel bathrobe.

"Oho, dollink, so early we are getting up this morning, like good leetle boys." She rolled onto one hip, a veritable Cleopatra on her royal garbage barge. "Is perhaps you are ready today to begin project we are speaking of Monday? Hmmm?"

"Uh-huh. I mean, uh-uh." I tried to get the old mental cogs whirring up to speed. We were the only ones in the apartment. Though Teleri had offered to move in and mind Mom on a pretty permanent basis, I'd turned her down. Every time I recalled the banshee's hard-sell come-on in the elevator, I got nervous, and nervous always leads to stupid, for me.

"What is this?" Baba Yaga feigned shock. "Is *uh-huh* or is *uh-uh*? Which is? Is not nice to toy with one who only wishes best for you. Is only teensiest favor I am asking. You tell me, 'Baba, this is big job. Large! Hoomongoose! Baba,' you say, 'I am needing time to plan.' So good! Time I give you. But how much? Is to taking five-year plan and stoff it. Five *day* plan, fine."

"Five . . . days. From today?" I was playing for whatever leeway I could get.

"Silly boy," said Baba, and ticked off five days from the Sunday she'd first appeared. "Like the fellow is saying, dollink, is to be moving it or losing it." She stared meaningfully at my mother's sleeping face.

Friday didn't so much roll around as roll right on top of me. I forgot what it was like to take a deep breath without fighting for it. There was no hope, no help, and no sign of Yang the Unreliable since Monday. Teleri wanted to do something for me, but what the witch had in mind didn't fall within her territory. I was on my own.

So you can see why I wasn't in a playful mood when I ducked into the school gymnasium—just to catch a little time out—and a roll of toilet paper came flying down from the rafters to bounce off my chest.

"Hey, Tim! Howzit going?" My old traveling buddy and— yeah, I guess I'll have to say it—friend, Neil Fitzsimmons, grinned down at me from his perch. He was balancing on Ibrahim Carter's ample shoulders, both of them wearing their Rawbone Kings gang jackets. Together they had managed to t.p. the gym from floor to ceiling and were finishing the job by garlanding the basketball hoops with long, pastel-pink streamers.

I was astonished. The Kings never went in for wussy stuff like t.p.ing parties. Wrapping their victims head to toe in duct tape and storing the bodies in the janitor's closet for later consumption—now *that* was their normal level of good, clean, wholesome fun. Mostly, though, their group imagination was limited to beating the crap out of anyone they felt like.

"What the hell are you guys doing?" I asked. With all I had on my mind already, I didn't need the Rawbone Kings behaving out of character. It upset the natural order of things, screwed the yin-yang balance of the universe, and made my head hurt.

Neil slid effortlessly to the floor and came over to slap me on the back. "Just a little high spirits, Tim, my man. Ain't that right, Ib?"

"What he said," said Ibrahim. He sank a few baskets with open rolls of Charmin while we chatted.

"Yeah, just a little surprise for the Gargoyles when they come in here for the game on Saturday. Janitor's already done this room, not likely to come back until it's time to open the doors for the game tomorrow, and whaddaya think's gonna happen then?"

Ibrahim had the answer: "Fit's gonna hit the shan, man."

My jaw had been dropping with such regularity these days that I think I dislocated it on that one. " *'Fit's* gonna hit the *shan'*? Is *that* what you said, Ib?"

"Yeah." Ibrahim looked at me like I was crazy. "So?"

So nothing. So only here were two of Glenwood High's prize specimens of matriculated pond scum, whose ordinary vocabulary made dockworkers exclaim "Mercy sakes!" and cover their ears, and what were they doing? Working mischief instead of wreaking havoc. Using words that ranked a *tsk-tsk* instead of an *Oh, my God*! Being naughty. Not nasty: naughty.

Carefully, so as not to slip into a parallel universe, I asked these gentlemen of the leather persuasion, "Whose cute idea was this? You lose a bet or what?"

"Wager?" Neil laid a hand to his chest. *"Nous?"*

"C'mon, Desmond." Ibrahim gave me a palsy-walsy noogie. His erstwhile method of physical expression was to slap people in the back of the head and score himself points for any teeth knocked loose or tongues bitten bloody, with a bonus for dislodging eyeballs. Now he shoved a couple of rolls of toilet

paper into the pit of my stomach and encouraged me to: "Party
down, dude."

What could I do? I took the rolls and started t.p.ing with a
bad aim and a phony smile. I was getting too damned used to
having no choices. If I refused, there was the off chance that
whatever esoteric influence was at work on the Kings would
suffer a momentary short circuit and they'd be their old, vicious
selves again. You can Just Say No to a Rawbone King all right;
then you can just say your prayers.

Just so you know, I *am* one of the favored few non-gang
people who can get familiar with the Kings and still be allowed
to live, within limits. Neil and I are close comrades, in spite
of the fact that we began our relationship with him trying to
feed me my math textbook. Through my right nostril. Teleri
showed up and put a definite stop to that. Neil's shock at being
outflanked by a banshee was nothing compared to mine when
I realized he could *see* her. I never expected a throwback like
him to be Fey-sighted, but then too I never expected half the
stuff that happened to me after that. Funny thing is, it happened to Neil as well.

Just because you've gone through passages perilous and hell
on wheels with a guy, doesn't mean you can get away with
anything, especially when he's a Rawbone King. I'd survived
nearly all the way through Glenwood High by watching my
step and not getting anyone's back up. This is wise when the
back is accompanied by an equally hulking front.

So I took the line of least resistance and tossed the t.p. hither
and yon, as directed. My fixed grin stiffened like old mashed
potatoes and flaked away, my mind on other things. Eventually
Neil noticed my glumness.

"Yo, Tim! 'Smatter? You scared we're gonna get caught?
No sweat."

"Yeah, man," Ibrahim chimed in. "We're *seniors*. What
they gonna do to us? Keep us back 'nother year for *this*?"

I couldn't feature any sane public institution holding onto
the Rawbone Kings for a minute longer than legally enforce-
able.

"Nah, it's not that, it's—"

Before I could come up with some lame excuse, Neil decided he had the answer. "Your old lady still on your case?"
God, he sounded so *chipper* when he said that! Rawbone Kings
take a blood-oath on initiation to have their chipper surgically

removed along with their pert, perky, waggish, and droll.
Against all sanity, I felt the compulsion to mentally deck Neil
out in spotless tennis whites and cast him in a Noel Coward
play. And then, as if to confirm my diagnosis that the fabric of
the world's safety-net was fraying out from under me, he said:

"Buck up, Tim. The course of true love never did run
smooth. Let me not to the marriage of true minds admit im-
pediments. Love is not love which alters where it alterations
finds, nor bends with the remover to remove. Maybe she's, you
know, on the rag."

An inarticulate roar burst from my lungs as I seized Neil by
the leather lapels and dragged him into the boys' locker room.
As the doors swung shut behind us I distinctly heard Ibrahim
declare, "Well, for heaven's sakes!"

I flung Neil against the lockers.

All right, I *tried* to fling Neil against the lockers. He out-
weighs me by several loads of muscle and he's taller, too. The
best I could do was make him take a couple of steps backwards
before he straightened the set of his gang jacket and gave me
a hurt look.

"No need to resort to violence, Tim," he said, shooting his
cuffs. Civilization and urbanity dripped from him in large, oily
clumps.

"Neil, what is the *matter* with you?" I screamed in his face.
"The *lhiannan sidhe* get her claws in you again?" The fey I
mentioned is a vampiric sort who likes to prey on poets. Under
all those skins and spikes, Neil has gifts neither the Kings nor
the local constabulary suspect.

"Hardly." Neil's accent kicked off from Brooklyn and was
sailing east across the Atlantic. As he spoke on, I could hear
it drawing ever closer to the shores of Jolly Olde England with
each passing syllable (the occasional linguistic relapse only
made it sound worse). "Haven't laid eyes on the lady since
you so kindly divested me of her company. Fascinating chit,
though. Great tits, no conversa—"

"Neil, do you hear yourself?" I latched onto the front of
his jacket like it was a rappelling line.

"Hear—?" He blinked dull eyes, hovering on the brink of
sentience, but the pull of whatever force had him was strong.
"My dear boy, I haven't the foggiest notion what you're babbling about."

That did it. I slapped him across the face; hard. It was a

backhand stroke with a lot of follow-through, not too bad an
effort if I do say so myself. I might as well have been proud
of it, seeing as how it would be listed as Cause of Death on
the Coroner's certificate.

Neil's fingers scooped up a generous hunk of my shirt, taking a little flesh with them. I could feel all five of my chest
hairs tear loose at the roots. Their death-screams were heart-
rending. I should know: I was having my heart rended. At least
he looked aware again, big consolation.

"Desmond"—Neil's lips curled around each letter of my
name like a python—"have you lost your fucking mind?"

"Yes! Oh, God, yes!" I tossed my head back and laughed
like a maniac, doing an end-zone victory dance that nearly
shook me loose from Neil's grip. "You said it! You actually
said *that word*!"

Neil's fingers unclenched some, in case I got violent and he
wanted to make a hasty break for it. "What the fuck did I
say?"

"*Yes!* Again! You said it again!" I threw my arms around
him and gibbered with joy.

That was when Ibrahim and the rest of the Kings came into
the locker room to see what the fu—what in the name of goodness was going on.

"You know what your problem is, Desmond?" Neil asked
as we sat on the front steps of Glenwood High, a matched set
of Life Bites It bookends.

"My problem is I seem to be devoting my glory years to
getting thrown out of places," I replied. "First it's the Napoli
Pizzarama on Monday, now this."

Neil gave me a bop in the shoulder. "It was a rhetorical
question, asshole. If you think I don't know what that means,
I'll tell you: It means I ask it and I get to answer it, too, so
shut the fuck up. Your problem, Desmond, is that you do stuff
first and try explaining why you did it after it's too damn late."

Oh yeah, right. Great philosophy from a guy who bites the
heads off parking meters.

"I *did* explain, though," I said in my own defense. "I tried
to tell Ib and Brendan and Gaspar about what I heard happening to you, what you were doing, the way you were talking."
I held fast to the belief that anyone else in my position would've
greeted Neil's use of the F-word with as much unbridled joy.

The Kings didn't agree. The sight of me and their leader in a clinch kind of superseded all other evidence and explanations thereof.

"My jacket." Neil moped, pulling pinches of thread from my shirt, rolling them into balls and shooting them at the sky. "They took my jacket."

"Yeah, and you're taking my shirt. Lay off!" I pulled away before my left sleeve was reduced to fringe. Neil was in one of those reflective, unreasonable moods common to poets. He just reached out, clamped onto the back of my neck, and yanked me back into a convenient position for him to continue unraveling the material. Maybe it was his way of dabbling in deconstructionism.

"Desmond," he said at length, having made a complete circuit of my cuff so it looked like cole slaw. "Desmond, I'm gonna give you the benefit of the doubt on this one. You and I, we've gone places together regular dudes couldn't survive: the elfin high court of Lord Palamon, the Leeside lands—"

"—the Kaplan wedding at Rosemont Manor last year," I supplied.

"If you say something's out of whack in the world, I'll buy it. Not without proof, though. I don't remember nothing about talking like some Brit wimp and playing whoopsy-daisy with a lot of toilet paper in the gym. Neither do the guys. That's not our—their style." He sounded wistful when he spoke of his recent forced abdication from Rawbone royalty.

"You want evidence, you go back and see how the gym looks!"

"How it looks now don't prove nothing about who made it look that way, and you know it." He folded his arms, waiting for me to do better.

What was one more non-choice in my life? I looked him in the eye and nodded. "Okay. You want proof something screwy's seeping out of the Leeside again? I'll give it to you. *On one condition!*" I risked jabbing a finger near his nose. "Once you see it, it stays between us. Nobody else gets told."

"Not even T'ing?"

"*Especially* not even T'ing!"

Neil shrugged. "No problem. I can keep my mouth shut."

I took him back into the school and opened my locker, then bowed him into it. He studied the narrow, smelly space dubiously, but past experience had taught him that the laws of the physical universe are up for grabs where things of the Fey are concerned. He ducked his head and wriggled in. I hurried after.

They were waiting for us on the other side, in the annex Baba Yaga had so thoughtfully provided. There was nothing in the Rule of Felicity to countermand her conjuring up a little additional space at the back of my locker. She just borrowed a cup of spare area from a galaxy that wasn't using it at the moment. I was mighty glad there was so much room, because with these tenants, distance really lent enchantment.

"Hi," said the minotaur, a greeting echoed by a roly-poly blue *oni* demon, a trio of frost-giants, and some big geek in a sweatshirt reading PHILISTIA: LOVE IT OR LEAVE IT. The four dragons just growled and snorted while the chimera forgot he was housebroken—*again*. And these were just the ones we could see clearly, standing in the front rank.

Remember what Neil promised? About keeping his mouth shut? He lied. One gawk at my new "pupils," and I couldn't get him to close his mouth for three whole hours.

8

We've Only Just Begun

"No." NEIL LAID his head down on the Formica tabletop and pounded it rhythmically with his fist. "No, no, no, no, no, no, NO!"

"Hey, Neil, shhhh, okay?" My eyes darted to all corners of the Napoli Pizzarama, expecting to see the joint's resident one-man goon squad, Gene Roselli, emerge from the shadows to boot us out. It didn't matter that the Pizzarama's stark fluorescent lighting effectively killed anything resembling shadows: Gene brought his own. Then he skulked in them.

For once, my luck decided to be decent. Gene was in the back room, performing unspeakable acts on pepperoni. Neil got to finish out his tantrum in peace. When he was quite done, he lifted his head and said, "How did I ever let you talk me into *this* mess?"

"I didn't talk you into a thing," I reminded him. "It was Goliath's idea. Can I help it if he took a shine to you? You oughta be flattered."

"To death," Neil assured me. "Desmond, you know the truth about what I am. You tell me whether it makes sense for a Philistine to take a shine to a poet."

I sipped at my Coke and considered. "Maybe he's a Philistine in ethnic affiliation only. They can't all have been conformist clods and proud of it."

Neil pulled a long face. "Maybe."

"Whaddaya mean, 'maybe'? Come on, not every Vandal went around chopping the nose off the Sphinx."

"No, the rest of them were too busy spray-painting graffiti

on the pyramids. Listen, Desmond, I didn't ask to be shang-haied aboard your little ship of ghouls, but since I'm tagged It, I'll play. What do we have to do?''

Inwardly I rejoiced to hear Neil's surrender to the inevitable. Many hands make light work, and all that. If I could get Baba Yaga's crew of horrors processed twice as fast, I wouldn't complain. ''Basically, Neil, we're the monsters' answer to Ellis Island. Our job is to get them naturalized. They've been gone a long time from the Outside, and things have changed. Once they feel they know the world well enough again to make it on their own, they'll be off.''

''Off to do what?''

''Oh, you know: Astound; terrify; curdle the blood; cause the flesh to creep; make you shit in your pants; give Stephen King continued employment. Stuff like that.''

''That's all? You telling me that gang of snaggletoothed bad dreams in the back of your locker are going to be happy just jumping out at normal people and shouting 'Boo!'?'' Neil's fingers laced closed around his own soda. ''You seen the teeth on some of them? Tell me they're just for show.''

I couldn't, of course. I've never been a convincing liar. The thing about monsters is, they're such a motley crew you can't generalize about them. Sure, Krito the minotaur was philosophical about the lack of on-site virgins, but how many of his cohorts were half so circumspect? Dragons aren't noted for being fussy about their meat, and even the dragons seemed antsy around the chimera. Then there were those in the throng who couldn't pronounce the names Tim and Neil, but had no trouble at all referring to us as 'num-nums' and 'din-din.'

I told myself that it wasn't my job to worry about what the monsters would do once we'd gotten them adjusted to the outer world. Hey, it wasn't like they'd be something that new for humans to handle. The time of the Leeside exile wasn't all that long ago, was it? People had coexisted with dark horrors before; we could remember how to survive a shared world again.

Couldn't we?

''This stinks worse than deep chimera-doo,'' Neil muttered. ''You got any idea how many monsters are waiting for us to give them rehab training?''

''You were in the locker; you saw. You can count noses the same as me.''

''The ones that *have* noses. But what makes you think that

group's all there is? What's to stop the witch from giving us a new batch of returnees to process after we finish with the first lot?''

"She said—"

"—what? A promise? From a *witch*?" Neil shook his head, wondering at my innocence.

"Oh," I said. On reflection, it did seem kind of a fool's game, trusting Baba Yaga to keep her word. She was the worst possible combination of terrorist and opportunist imaginable, and the scariest part was she didn't even have a healthy fear of the IRS to keep her in line.

"No, Desmond, this won't do. We go along and do what she wants, she'll just want more. You took World History, right? You got, what?—a B?"

"An A," I admitted.

"Yeah, well even with the lousy C-minus I pulled down, I still remember what happened with Hitler and Chamberlain. Dumb-ass didn't think about what happens when you try to appease some fuckers. Good thing he got outa the diplomacy racket and started making all those miniseries. You and me, we're no Dr. Kildares; we're gonna *do* something."

"Oh sure we are. And what about my mother?"

"Relax. You got my word she'll come through this all right. She's an okay lady, and I'll look out for her. Now if it was my old man sleeping for a thousand years . . . Hmm. Desmond, you think maybe I could cut a side deal with Baba Yaga about that?"

(Neil's affection for his father would be a whole lot healthier if Mr. Fitzsimmons senior didn't like to play handball so much. The thing is, he also likes to use Neil's face as the court.)

I distracted Neil from thoughts of having his father frogified, or whatever, at least for the moment. "You got something specific in mind for us to do that'll sidetrack the monsters and keep Baba Yaga in the dark until we can spring my mom?"

Neil tilted his chair back and stretched his arms high, fingers linked. He looked smug as a cat with a pitcher of cream. "Tim, my friend, you're talking to the man who engineered the secret videotaping of the faculty Christmas party. Or how do you think I managed to get a passing grade out of Ms. Alexinsky for English Lit.?" He clicked his tongue. "Where in hell she found a red-and-green suede miniskirt . . . and those propellers!"

I cut in on his sartorial reminiscences. "The plan?"

He winked at me. "What size shirt do you wear, man?"

I lowered the wand slowly, staring into the cracked mirror all the while. Incredible. I'd engineered the whole process, witnessed it while it was being carried out, mastered the magic that had effected the change, and I still couldn't accept the results. It was too much for my mind to handle.

"Gimme," said Neil, reaching out for the wand with the scrawniest arm I ever saw—pitiful, really. Too bad it was mine.

I passed it to him. "Easy does it." My new voice boomed in my ears. "Only take it by the pommel or it'll cut you bad." He gave me the thumbs-up sign and accepted the sword-encased crystal wand as cautiously as you please. Somewhere under the faded ANTHRAX T-shirt stretched to the limit across my—his—chest, I felt a pang of loss. "Take good care of it, Neil."

"Like it was my own." What a weird sensation, to see yourself winking and know it wasn't all done with mirrors. Neil laid the wand down and wrapped his—my—jacket around it before cramming it into my backpack. Then he checked his watch. "Nice goods," he said.

"Birthday present," I mumbled. I looked at my new wrist. No watch, but a heck of a lot more hair than I was used to seeing. I stole a quick peek down the front of my T-shirt and saw more of the same. Now I knew how the Wolfman felt.

Neil elbowed me aside, or gave it his best shot. There was something distinctly pleasant—addictive, even—about being promoted from Tim the totally Portable to Neil the Immovable (On Pain of Death) Object. From rabbit to rock, not too bad a deal. I played it gracious and stepped aside to let my body's new resident get a look at himself in the mirror.

"Holy shit," Neil said, taking in the full picture. "You really did it. Far fucking out."

"Yeah, not too shabby for a bush-league wizard." For the first time, I had a chest I could puff out with pride. "You ever doubt I could do it?"

"Ehhh." The boy didn't want to commit himself, but honesty has a nasty way of coming out, like zits. "I figured it was worth the risk."

"What risk?"

"Oh, you know, like on *Star Trek*, where someone gets sucked up in the transporter, only it busts when they're halfway there and their molecules get spritzed all over space? Or like in *The Fly*, where Goldblum starts to, you know, sort of drip slimy goo and rot and you name it, it falls off his body, and—''

"Enough, enough, I get the idea!'' Good thing Neil hadn't mentioned all these sticky possibilities before we tried the switch, or I'd have frozen up. Even with success behind me, I'd still have to face the future moment when it was time for us to trade bodies back. I wasn't looking forward to it. "You better get going. Baba Yaga's going to expect a report from me on how well I'm bringing her beastly little buddies along.''

"Chill out, Desmond. By the time I finish outlining my super deluxe extra-cheese-and-anchovies plan for monster mainstreaming, the old hag'll need a snow blower. But she'll be hap-py!''

"She'd better be.''

"Hey! Trust me. If anything goes wrong, I've got just as much to lose as you, now.'' Neil's hands swept his borrowed body. I had to admit it was a comedown, like abandoning Trump Tower for a trailer park, or buying a used Pinto when you've been driving a Maserati all your life.

I made a mental note to save my pennies and sign up for body-building at a health club when this was all over.

Neil slung the backpack over one shoulder and left. I stayed where I was. Why shouldn't I? We'd done the swap in Neil's room. I flopped down on his bed just to enjoy the sensation of having a room of my own for once. It was dingy, raggedy, and it smelled like dead peanut butter sandwiches, but it was the first time I'd been in a room with a functioning door that didn't have a toilet in it, too.

I hope I've led an evil life, because after fifteen minutes of heaven, I was bored out of my skull. I told myself to get moving. Neil had gone to uphold his part of the pact; I had my own duties waiting. Baba Yaga's strength lay both in how much she knew about me and in how little I knew about her. One clue to her weaknesses would've been a godsend; one hint as to how far her powers stretched would've made my day. She, on the other hand, had known enough about the powers I commanded as Dread and Puissant Champion of the Fey to neutralize them straight off the bat. Did she also know about some of the equally powerful allies I could call on?

The witch was no one's fool. She had too many other cauldrons to mind for her to keep me under constant surveillance, but that didn't mean she wouldn't cast the occasional long-distance glance my way. Neil and I had switched bodies so fast, it was a pretty safe bet she'd missed seeing it happen, but seeking out my old friends in the field wasn't something I could do in an eye blink. It needed time, and it wouldn't do to have Baba Yaga spy me while I tried to enlist troops to my cause.

So while Timothy Alfred Desmond going down a dark and sinister alleyway might arouse Baba Yaga's suspicions, Neil Fitzsimmons doing the same thing was no big deal. With someone who looks like Neil, you figure dark and sinister alleyways are his life.

The portal was right where I remembered it, just past the garbage cans, a big metal door with black enamel paint peeling off it in huge flakes. I didn't have my wand, but I hoped they'd let me in anyhow. They owed me, in there.

I laid my cheek against the cold metal and whispered an alien name through the crack: "Lord Palamon . . . Lord Palamon, it's me."

At first, nothing. Then I thought I felt a breath of cool air scented with lavender, a hearty relief from the stench of rotting trash and vintage urine surrounding me. The door began to glow at every edge, the blackness changing from opaque metal to the midnight depths of a beckoning tunnel. I took a step forward. Either it was all an illusion and I'd mash my nose against what was still there, or I'd make like a cartoon character and walk right through.

Neil's nose survived. Better than that, it lived to experience a heady gust of rare perfumes, pungent incense, a wealth of fresh flowers, and the mouthwatering aroma of baking bread. The darkness ebbed faster the further I went, until at last I emerged into a huge, high-ceilinged chamber.

Crystal bowls heaped high with rainbow-colored coals shed a delicate light over golden marble floors and blue silk rugs. Tall and graceful beings robed in pure white satin shot with silver glided back and forth between columns of pink tourmaline and pearl. At the far end of the great hall stood an ivory throne, its arms and legs banded with emeralds, its back inlaid with luminous enamels until it resembled a gigantic peacock feather. A lone figure sat upon the steps of the throne, coaxing the plaintive music of the Fey from a silver harp.

It was awesome, breathtaking, a spectacle of elfin elegance and beauty fit to ravish all mortal senses.

It wasn't a damn thing like I remembered Lord Palamon's totally tacky court to be. Where was the juke box? Where were the elf-vixens in their string bikinis and wet T-shirts? Where were the minstrels in their Hawaiian shirts and pompadours, singing "Louie, Louie" in close harmony while they kept the beat by flicking their switchblades? Where was the turquoise Thunderbird convertible that formerly served as Lord Palamon's throne of choice? For that matter, where was Lord Palamon?

As I stood there, bewildered and off balance, the aimlessly wandering Fey appeared to become aware of my presence. By ones and by twos they drifted towards me, eyes bright and burning, until I was most subtly ringed by a throng of sharp, staring faces.

The harpist from the throne steps was in the forefront among them. Even as he peered into my eyes, his fingers continued to call music from the harp strings. Abruptly he stilled the instrument and set it down. The others deferred to him absolutely as he addressed me in a liquid, mellifluous tongue unlike any human language I'd ever heard.

"Huh?" I said. "You, um, wanna run that by me again?"

I guess he didn't. Something went *snick* between his tapering fingers and I was eyeing the business part of a switchblade for the split second before he jabbed the point up against my throat.

At least I knew I was in Lord Palamon's court after all. Some things just never do change.

9

Downunder

"ALL I'M ASKING is to speak to Lord Palamon," I gurgled. "You know, Palamon? Your natural lord? Too-veddy-veddy upper crust British accent? Set of teeth like a pure-blooded palomino? Father of Lady Eleziane, cute kid, used to be a changeling?"

My captor snarled a whole fresh bunch of words that rippled up and down the musical scale but remained untranslatable. Curiouser and curiouser, as a fellow underground traveler used to say. On my previous visit to the elfin high court, everyone spoke English; British English in all its glorious variations of accent and dialect, but still something I could understand if I put my mind to it and pretended I was trapped in an episode of *Masterpiece Theatre*.

Body English, however, always scans. The harpist exerted a wee bit of extra pressure on the blade at my throat, and right away I knew that he wanted me to shut up and move. You bet I did.

We moved through corridors and chambers cut to the same standard of discreet luxury as the great hall. Opulence was perfectly balanced with the best of taste. Nowhere did I spy a single hint of Lord Palamon's former excesses, the too-liberal use of cloth-of-gold, the glut of extraneous gemstones. It was like picking up a copy of *The National Enquirer* and finding that it had been rewritten, cover-to-cover, by the staff of *The New York Times*.

With every richly appointed but tasteful room we traversed, my uneasiness grew. The elvenfolk we passed reflected the

same overruling hand of elegance, and not merely in their
dress. Where once I had seen denizens of Faerie in a diversity
of heights, shapes, and appearances, now every elf I passed
was supremely tall, exquisitely slender, with silky golden hair
cascading down his back, and eyes that held the secrets of
moonlit water.

By and by, we reached a portal that led into a garden. Tame
white deer with Disney-animation eyes raised dripping muzzles
from pools of fragrant nectar. Butterflies big as looseleaf bind-
ers flapped and danced on brilliant yellow sunflower heads the
size of manhole covers. Here and there I saw others of the
glimmering Fair Folk weaving garlands of roses to hang around
the necks of the chubby bear cubs and frolicsome wolflings
that gamboled like squirrels at their feet. Maidens clad in diaphanous white drapery piped tunes on rosewood flageolets
while spring lambs capered and cherubic faerie children sang
in merry chorus, tra-la.

I could literally feel my blood-sugar level rising into the
danger zone the longer we lingered. One of the lambs came
tripping o'er the greensward to gaze up at me. The animal had
Liza Minelli eyelashes and pastel pink fleece. I didn't need any
extra urgings from my keeper's knife to make me walk faster
through the gardens. By the time we reached the gate to the
forest, he had to jog in order to keep pace with me.

I slowed down some when we hit the forest. Something about
a deep and ancient woodland tends to inspire awe in mortal
souls. The gold-leafed trees climbed shafts of sunlight until
their tops were lost to sight above me. Tiny purple flowers
strewed the grass where no dead leaves had fallen, and luminous green moss enfolded the towering trunks in a velvety
embrace.

My guide had me go straight on through the woods until we
came into a clearing. The sound of gently splashing water was
the only thing to break the silence. It came from a fountain
carved of smoky stone, the figures of beasts and faerie folk
looking almost alive, despite the patches of blue-green lichens
clinging to them. The water poured freely from the tilted am-
phora of a regal stone elf-maiden in the fountain's midst, its
flow augmented by the two smaller streams that trickled from
her unseeing eyes. Up to the lip of the fountain the waters rose,
then slipped over through a narrow sluice. This sent them into

a tiled conduit that led at last to a reflecting pool as perfectly round and golden as the sun.

It was fortunate for me that I wanted to get closer to that wondrous pool, because my friend with the switchblade had the same idea. Still blabbering at me in that incomprehensible tongue, he shoved me so near the basin's brink I almost put my foot in it. He then put his free hand on my shoulder and pushed down hard.

Once he had me on my knees, he used the same direct method to make me bow my head. I had nothing to look at but my own reflection in the golden pool. I guess that satisfied him; he withdrew the knife and I got the feeling he withdrew himself as well. I didn't try turning my head to see, just in case, but even with no proof one way or the other, I couldn't shake the sensation of being alone.

It didn't last. As I stared into the smooth face of the water, I heard a whispering sound. Across the pool, a second face glided into sight. Summer-bright hair crowned with a diadem of starry diamonds framed a face too fair to be human, almost too beautiful to be elfin. Whether I died for it or not, I had to look up.

"Welcome, seeker," she said. Her reflection hadn't exaggerated her beauty. As hungrily as I gazed at her, she didn't see me. Her eyes were focused on a vision hers alone. Gusts of snowy plumage frothed around her face, trailed from her sleeves. Her green gown billowed and clung at the slightest motion of the slim body beneath. When the hem moved, I saw that the only covering on her white feet were sandals of braided violets.

I wanted to speak, but my tongue was a strip of dry leather in my mouth. A swarm of those mammoth butterflies from the garden came into the clearing and lit on her outstretched arms, purring like Persian kittens. A distant, reedy melody of flute music threaded its way around her, and the sound of artful hands plucking the strings of a lute. The golden trees began to shake, and through the sparkling tumble of their leaves a unicorn emerged, his horn a triumph of light. His advent was accompanied by the murmurous strains of a string quartet and a muted fanfare of trumpets. A hidden choir raised a wordless paean of glorious harmony.

I found my voice just as the singing and dancing nymphs came on, banging their timbrels in tandem with the panpipeplaying bunny rabbits. I found it, but I didn't have any idea what to do with it.

Not so the lady of the glade, who jammed her hands on her hips, screwed her face into a scowl Yang would've loved, threw her head back, and howled, "DADDY!"

"Yes, yes, just coming. What's all the pother, then, eh?" Lord Palamon bustled into the clearing, shooing the nymphs aside and chivying the musical bunnies out from underfoot. He was dressed in the same high style as his subjects, but when he yanked the hem of his robe to avoid one of the unicorn's little gifts, I saw a pair of blue rubber zoris on his feet. Like I said, some things never change, and for once I was glad of it.

"Daddy, I thought we agreed that you were going to cut it short right after you cued the flute music." The lady thrust a hand between her legs and kilted up her trailing skirts. Her bare legs were a healthy brown just above the ankles, and I could see where the pale basecoat and powder whitening her feet had smeared.

"Now, now, precious, I've just been giving the scriptures a bit of a glimmer, and I *think* you'll have to agree that I've found lashings of textual evidence to support these few, ah, improvements I've tossed in, what?"

The lady was not convinced. She stomped over to confront Lord Palamon, using the principle of a straight line being the shortest distance between two points. This as-the-crow-flies route took her right through the middle of the golden pool. The spray she kicked up soaked me head to foot. It was my own fault: It wouldn't have happened if I'd had the presence of mind to get up off my knees.

I couldn't, though. The spectacle of that superlatively lovely elf-maiden mad as a wet hen—and just as wet—had me flabbergasted. Too, she'd said something that latched onto the back of my brain and commenced gnawing.

"You can show me proof from your so-called scriptures until the pages fall out," she snapped. "It won't change a damned thing. You know very well that you're the only one here who's gone so clear mad on those books that you've turned your whole life upside down. Why did you have to turn everyone else's life on end, too? For the love of Lugh, Daddy, it's only a *story*!"

Lord Palamon lifted what there was of his chin. "How sharper than a serpent's tooth, and all that rubbish. Is this the thanks a sire gets for trying to raise his child as befits a proper elf-princess? No more of these dashed hodgery-podgery Yank doings, but a fey court run the way a fey court should *be* run. Harrumph! And if I've had the jolly good fortune to find a—a perfect spiritual and practical guide as to how we ought to be living our lives, I'd think you ought be deuced grateful for it instead of rounding on your poor old pater like this."

The lady clapped her hand over her eyes. "It is a sto-ry," she enunciated in that patient way which always means there is no patience left. "A story written by a mere mortal, no less. How you expect a paltry human being to have the last word on how we Fey should behave, I'll never know. Look at all this!"

She flung out one arm to indicate the clearing, the enchanted woodland, and the palace beyond. "This is all Lord Hogbane's fault. The old poop insisted we humor you, go along with your latest mania until you got tired of it and found a new toy. Well, maybe you're not tired of it yet, but I am! I am sick and tired of slouching around this miserable forest, waiting for your flunkies to bring me any geek they can catch who doesn't know the setup, just so he can be awed and startled by my exquisite beauty and my astonishing gift of prophecy."

Lord Palamon colored up a nice, juicy red. "My dear child, never did I think to hear such blasphemy from your lips. Break, break now my heart! Come, gentle Death, and wrap me in your caul. Out, out brief candle—"

"Die or get off the pot, Daddy," the lady said.

"Daddy?" I finally recovered my English-language skills. "Did I hear you call Lord Palamon your daddy?"

"You did unless you're deaf," the elf-maiden shot back at me. "Is it any of your business, bozo?"

I stood up from the pool's brink. "Lord Palamon, it's me!"

The elf-lord squinted at me closely, then dipped a hand into the pocket of his royal robes and fished up his monocle. Screwing it in, he brightened at once. "So it is! Well, well, my dear, *dear* chap, such a treat! How long has it been, then? Too bally long, I'll be bound. Why, you're looking utterly top-hole. Outer world agreeing with you all right, eh?"

The lady sidestepped to whisper in my ear, "He doesn't remember you from a boggart's buttonhole, but he's too proud to admit it. Go along with him for a bit, okay?"

I nodded tersely. Lord Palamon was going on at length about how pleased he was to see me once more and what fine fettle

I was in, so he couldn't hear me hiss back at the lady, "Suits me. Can I at least tell you who I am so you can maybe slip it into the conversation, for your father's benefit? I've come a long way with a real problem."

"My pleasure to help you, but save the intros. I do remember who you are. It's good to see you again, Tim." Surreptitiously she squeezed my hand.

"You know who—?" I touched my face, but my fingers still encountered Neil's borrowed features.

The lady had a pretty laugh. "The pool reflects only truth. I saw your real face while you were kneeling beside the water."

"Oh, yeah. So did I, come to think of it. It just didn't register."

"It's easy to forget you're wearing a mask," the lady said. "Can we keep it our little secret? I promise not to let it get in the way of whatever help you've come for, and I'd really like to have a hole-card to pull on Daddy. If I can prove to him he's not right all the time, maybe I can wheedle him into seeing how wrong he's been, trying to force all Faerie into this book-born charade of his."

"Deal." I looked at the lady more closely. I had plenty of time to make a proper job of it. Lord Palamon had finished his speech of personal welcome and was now fairly launched onto a sea of oratory concerning the grand old elfin traditions of hospitality. Dwarfs figured heavily in the text, God knows why. The longer I looked at her, the deeper one nagging thought sank its teeth into my gray matter.

"You said it was good to see me *again*?"

"Mm-hm." The lady's lips curved into adorable dimples. She was enjoying this. "And yes, I did call Lord Palamon 'Daddy.' Want another hint? Care to buy a vowel?"

"No." It was disbelief, not refusal.

"Yes." Her dimples deepened. "Hello, Tim. You'll never know how good it is to see you again, but I'll do my best to show you." She put her arms around my neck and kissed me.

"Eleziane!" Lord Palamon sputtered and fumed, but the lady had a liplock on me she wasn't about to break. When she let go, it was to give me some air, not to obey her father. The Supreme Seigneur of the Fey vented all the sound effects of a choleric teakettle as he gave his child a formal dressing-down.

He had uttered his fifteenth "demmed bad show" when I interrupted the tirade. "How can she—? She isn't—*That's* Eleziane? But she was just a baby last year! A child! You used her as a changeling for Brittany Izanagi. Now she's—"

"Quite." Lord Palamon huffed. "Blame myself, ekshally. Young pups grow so fast. Three hundred years pass in a twinkling and poof!—childhood's done. Should've used the time I had to breed proper manners into the gel. Sad, very sad. Lacked expert advice, I did. Never would've had her grow up half the hoyden chit she is if I'd come by *this* excellent *vade mecum* earlier on."

He extracted a thick, leather-bound book from somewhere in his robes and passed it to me for inspection. "Chap's got the how-to of it down pat—to a science, really. Could be said to apply to grown folk as well as the little nippers. Never too old to profit from his words. Doing my level best to have all of us make up for lost time by following his teachings. Sacred duty, rather."

"Who wrote this?" I asked, hefting the intricately tooled volume. "Dr. Spock?"

"Oh, I say, that *is* a good one! Spock? Haw! Never did catch the fascination for that show, m'self. No, no, my dear fella, this isn't any of your bally sci-fi nonsense. This"—reverently he opened the book in my hands to the title page—"is the meaning of life itself!"

I had to admit, it was the classiest edition of *The Lord of the Rings* that I'd ever seen.

10

Tolkien Heads

"IT'S NOT LIKE it was a *bad* book," I murmured by way of comfort to my dining partner.

"It's a *good* book," Eleziane returned quietly as we sat at the high table. "But it's just a *book*. And even so, it wouldn't be so dreadful if only Daddy would stop mucking about with the text as it's written. *Interpretation*, he calls it; *improvement*. Just look at all that." She indicated the massed Fey before us. "Would you call that an improvement?"

Her eyes saddened as she surveyed the feasting boards crowding the length of the great hall. It was like looking out over a sea of dandelions blooming on the snow. Every elfin head shone golden, every tall and slender body was clad in white raiment. You couldn't tell the players without a score card; you could hardly tell one sex from the other. Even the servants were lissome, lovely clones.

I had to agree that Lord Palamon's new and improved look-alike court had a stultifying effect. "His interpretation of what elves should look like?" I asked. "What's he got, a bulk-rate deal with Clairol?"

"His decision, based on the—he insists on calling them the scriptures, for pity's sake. He got a walloping great crush on the one female in the story who's a big blonde, and never mind how many others are described as having dark hair, blond elves are *it* for Daddy."

She scooped up a gob of syrupy red glop from the silver trencher we shared and licked it off her fingers noisily. "Ugh," she remarked. "I could live with the whole Malibu elves thing, if Daddy hadn't insisted that his perfect *scriptures* had an obvious Shakespearean subtext. Next thing you know, he's instructing the kitchen staff to serve us nothing but thirty-one flavors of *Midsummer Night's Dream* nectar. 'Where the bee sucks, there suck I.' Sucks is the word.''

I had to sympathize. The thick liquid in our goblets was just as bad. The very air dripped sugar crystals. I felt my teeth crumbling with every breath I took. "Why did you let him get away with this? I know that Palamon's Supreme Seigneur by courtesy only. Your father's an all right guy, for an elf, but he's not what I'd call leadership material. How many heads could he lop off if you all refused to play?''

"As I said, our chief minister, Lord Hogbane, suggested we go along with the mania. *He* claimed it would keep Daddy from moping and sulking in his rooms when he had to be out performing his ceremonial functions. *I* think Hogbane really backed the plan so that he could change his physical appearance without being accused of vanity.''

I remembered Lord Hogbane from before. He looked more gnome than elf; a dried apple had fewer wrinkles, and more personality. You couldn't fault him for wanting to change all that.

"*He* said it wouldn't make any real difference in our lives,'' Lady Eleziane continued grimly. "He's not the one who has to rot in the forest all day, worrying what new idiotic interpretation our natural lord's going to put on a nice, simple story. That's the problem with imitators: They ape the classics and come off like a bunch of classic apes.''

"So why don't you call a stop to it?''

"Me?'' Eleziane rested her chin on her palm. "Too many of the old aristocracy are just as ugly as Lord Hogbane, under normal conditions. This kind of democracy suits them fine. One squeak of objection from the younger Fey, and they'll band together and *reason* with us, if you get my drift.''

"Ouch?'' I suggested.

"Binding arbitration,'' she said, "with real ropes.''

"I wish there was something I could do to help.'' I meant it.

Eleziane's smooth brow creased in thought. "Maybe there is.'' She cupped her hand around a whisper.

The feast progressed, one gummy course after another, the courses interspersed with entertainment. Lord Palamon's subterranean showbiz savvy was likewise drawn from his beloved "scriptures." His interpretation thereof dictated that one clutch of identical elves come into the center of the hall and sing a lilting tra-la-la, followed by an identical faerie consort who warbled hi-lee-hi-lo. The smash hit of the evening was the madrigal ensemble, who had their hey-nonny-nonnies and tu-whit-tu-whoos dead on. As far as I'm concerned, syllabic singing belongs strictly with doo-wop backup groups, but these elfin ensembles all lacked lead singers. I found myself thinking of the Osmonds with genuine longing. My kingdom for an actual set of lyrics, even something by the B-52s!

At last the feast ended with heaping bowls of berries for dessert. I had a handful halfway to my mouth when Eleziane stopped me. "Want to bust a tooth?" I looked; the berries were solid gold. "Those are party favors, not dessert," she whispered. "Go on, help yourself to a couple. Don't get too greedy, though. Greed doesn't go with Daddy's new aesthetic *gestalt*."

"Say what?"

"It doesn't match the drapes and it makes him cross. No elf-guest in the *scriptures* ever pillaged worth a damn. Try pocketing too many of those pretties and he'll sic his muscle squad on you to recover the assets and pound some manners through your skull—strictly on the Q.T., of course."

"All in the name of Art," I mused. "I've heard that the critics can be murder." I returned nearly all the golden berries to the bowl and made a big deal about showing everyone at the high table that I'd only kept three.

Lord Palamon rose from his high-backed throne and motioned for silence. A baby spotlight fell on him, bathing his face with the amber-filtered light of cunningly staged benevolence. A quartet of dueling harpists struck up a slightly out-of-sync *continuo* to accompany his speech. His subjects obediently turned their eyes to him and assumed smiles of deep contentment as he spoke on and on; and on. And on.

I wondered how they did it, until Lady Eleziane tugged at my sleeve and covertly directed my attention to the bench of elves nearest us. Silent, efficient zippers peeled down the backs of the shining white robes, but didn't stop there. The skin beneath was itself split and through these narrow emergency hatches all the Fey came tumbling out in their original forms. Cautiously, under the towering cover of their abandoned shells, they hid behind predetermined angles of the feasting tables and got out decks of cards, dice cups, and Monopoly boards with which to while away the time until their noble lord might fully empty the royal gasbag.

"Rat on them and die," Eleziane counseled me.

Nothing was farther from my mind. If Lord Palamon's people wanted to escape their lord's besotted jabber of quests and dragons, dwarfs and trolls, they had my support. Obsessions are never pretty. I speak from experience. My best friend, Larry Perlmutter, once dragged me to a Star Trek convention.

I waited until Lord Palamon had to stop for breath and leaped to my feet. "A boon, noble lord!" I cried. "Aid for the West! The ancient evil stirs, the ancient pledge must now be paid!"

"Oh ah?" Lord Palamon made fish mouths at me. "What's all this, then?"

"Go on," Eleziane growled. She gave me a surreptitious prod in the ribs. "This is your chance, *and* mine. Don't louse it up, or you'll answer to me."

The wrath of the Fey was something I'd sampled a little too much to take lightly. Eleziane was just out of childhood—three hundred years of it—but I wasn't taking any bets about whether she could still throw a tantrum if thwarted. Was I going to give our plan anything but my best shot? Silly question.

I stepped around the edge of the high table and knelt directly before Lord Palamon. My ears caught a faint scrabbling sound behind me, probably the truant Fey slipping back inside their cookie-cutter bodies to watch.

"My lord, you know me." I lifted my eyes to the Lord of the Fey, who was still trying to make his blobby lower lip respond to direct mental control. "I would not come into your realm if not on a mission of the utmost urgency. In the kingdoms of men they sing of Lord Palamon's wisdom, which supersedes even this, your most open-handed hospitality."

"Ah, yes? Thanks awfully. Beastly good of you to say so, old man." Lord Palamon might gobble up the fluent forsooth-verily's with a spoon, but when it came to replies, he remained firmly entrenched on the playing fields of whatever elfin Eton. "Mission, eh? What sort?"

I hoped I'd got Neil's face looking solemn and portentous enough before I declaimed: "A quest."

Lord Palamon jumped in his seat and clapped his hands together. "Oh, I *say*!" His eyes sparkled with tears of joy, and his voice broke with the force of that same emotion. Next to him, Tiny Tim on Christmas Day was jaded. "And this—this quest of yours, dear boy, it's not—? It couldn't possibly be—? May I dare to hope it is—?"

"It is." I licked lips gone suddenly dry. "The ring."

I was going to hate myself in the morning.

"Would you stop looking behind you every two steps?" the lady Eleziane snapped. "No one's following us."

"I sure hope not. I'd hate to be the one to explain to your father why you stuffed your traveling duds into that dumpster back there."

The elf-maiden dismissed my fears. "You couldn't expect me to schlep around Brooklyn in a gown like that." She patted her blue-jeaned thighs, very pleased with her new look. "Don't worry; I've got plenty of other regal robes at home. My closet's just lousy with samite *schmattes*."

"I believe you. But did you have to deep-six the diamond crown too?"

Eleziane giggled. "Can you imagine the look on the garbage man's face when he upends the dumpster and catches a glimmer of *that* little *tchotchke*? Either he'll figure it's a fake, or he'll try to pawn it and get every cop in New York down on him like white on rice. Won't that be a scream?"

Evidently so. I reminded myself that the Fey had a sense of humor markedly different from that of normal human beings. The only thing that came close was a Rawbone Kings knock-knock joke contest. They whammed on your locker to get the right sound effect, and if you didn't laugh loud enough they repeated the joke, this time using your head to get a better *knock-knock* resonance.

"I still don't feel right about this," I told her.

"Oh, pooh. Lighten up, Timmy." She threaded her arm around my waist and rested her golden head on my shoulder. "All you have to do is remind me to bring home *some* odd bit of junk jewelry or other for Daddy when all this is over. You know, 'the meed and guerdon of the quest fulfilled,' or whatever b.s. he wants to hear."

"I feel funny about tricking him."

"Hey, do you want my help or not? One hand washes the other. You've bought me a little vacation from propping up the oak trees and droning over that *meshuggene* pool of prophecy, and I'll use all my powers on your side against this witch-bitch. You do want my help, don't you?''

I had to admit I did.

"So what's the problem? If you're that afraid of Daddy, remember: He doesn't know it's you. If he gets mad at anyone, it'll be the incredible hunk you borrowed this bod from. And chill out, he won't do a thing to Neil. Daddy never holds poets responsible for their actions, especially not poets that the *lhiannan sidhe's* ever had her claws in. Once you survive a liason with a fairy mistress, it's like getting permanent diplomatic immunity, so Neil's bacon's safe, and yours—? Safe as you and I keep it. How will Daddy ever find out it was Timmy Desmond pulled the old ring scam on him if we keep our lips buttoned?''

"Veeeeeery simply," said a cool, drawling, familiar voice that set each hair on Neil's body on end. "I will beeeee the one to tell him.''

Icy fingers touched the lobe of my right ear and made every fiber of me burn. I turned, and through a blood-red haze I saw a cloaked woman with pupilless, silver eyes. The street vanished, with all its traffic. Even Eleziane disappeared. There were only two breathing beings left in the world. The woman slowly parted her cloak; beneath it she wore nothing but her own pale green skin. She came closer, naked feet dancing over the cracked concrete of the sidewalk. I could scarcely hear the words she spoke through the pounding in my head:

"Deeeeear love. Did you miss meeeeee?''

I couldn't talk. I could only stretch my arms out to her. Her body melted into mine and I crushed her against me, desperately afraid that someone might try to tear her away. She tilted up her head and let me stare into those uncanny eyes where lightnings darted and cold stars died.

I hardly felt the fingernail that glided down the side of my neck and opened the vein.

11

Ladies, Please Remove Your Heads

My consciousness ebbed quickly, the light of day draining from the sky. Buildings swam from hard-edged rectangles to gray blobs as a pair of soft, greedy lips fixed themselves to my neck. Cool hands stroked my chest and clung around my shoulders. If anything else happened to me, I didn't know or care. I was lost to the world, and happy to be lost. I gave myself up entirely to the heady pleasure filling me, unable to recognize that it was in truth another mask of emptiness.

And then, the jarring sensation of the pressure at my neck was abruptly torn away. "Um?" An indistinct sound of puzzlement and irritation in my ear, followed by the vulgar noise of someone with a mouthful of liquid spritzing it all over creation. "What is thisssss? This taste I do not recognize at all! Who in all the Leeeeside are you, skin-steeeealer?"

"I—I'm really—" Silver eyes seared the stammered excuses from my lips. I was gazing into the face of fury. All at once I understood, with an icy certainty, that there are ways and ways of dying and I had forfeited the gentlest for the most savage. Pale lips curled back to reveal razor sharp teeth. Nothing surrounded us but shadows. The street, and all chance of rescue, had vanished behind walls of greenish ice. I could just make out the vague shapes of people, street lamps, and storefronts behind the watery green barricade. *Frozen in place,* I thought. *Frozen in time.*

"Did you not heeeear me, boy? Who are you, to come creeeeping in among the Faerie court in borrowed skin? False one. Deceeeeiver. What have you done with the one I truly love?''

I knew her. We had met before. She had almost been the death of Neil Fitzsimmons, and the wild jealousy she inspired in him had almost been the death of me. She was Andraste, the *lhiannan sidhe*, the fey woman whose lawful prey was poets. Then, it was Teleri's intervention that had banished her. Now I faced her alone, in a place that my crawling skin remembered, even if my mind hadn't accepted it yet.

"If you mean Neil, he's safe," I told her. *Safer than I am,* I thought. "Not that it'll make any difference. You're not getting him back."

''Am I not?'' The fairy mistress's voice dwindled deliberately until each word was a cloying whine. "And who shall keeeeep him from meeeee? You know his love is for meeee alone. Has any other sheeee laid claim to his heart since weeee were parted?'' Her fingers like long blades of new grass pushed back the bronze fall of her hair. Deceptive warmth kindled in her pupilless eyes.

Although it hurt me to admit it, she told the truth. Neil hadn't exactly been burning down Glenwood High with any romantic conquests since our return from the Leeside last year. He'd taken plenty of ribbing about it from his fellow Rawbone Kings until he did some selective head-bashing, but even when it wasn't talked about, the situation remained the same.

"Ah! No neeeed to speak, skin-steeeealer. I reeeead the answer in your face. Banned I may beeee from supping at that sweeeeet fount, for I may reclaim none of my lost loves unless they come back into the Fey kingdom willingly. Still, I will hold his heart captive. Unless heeee may find an earthly love, then unto the end of days heeee is mine.''

She flexed her fingers, and tiny sickles of bone gleamed keenly from the tips. "In whatever shell of flesh heeee now walks, heee shall not escape the longing for meeee. Heee shall return, in time. A shame to destroy so pretty a dwelling as this, where once heeee dwelled, but in the end, it shall not matter. The longing shall drive him back to meeee, and the soul of him I shall possess utterlyyyy.'' She tilted her head toward me, the silver of her eyes frosting over to purest white. "This skin of his you have taken without my leeeeave, steeeealer, it shall make you a more than worthy tomb.''

I closed my eyes and turned all my concentration inward,

sending out the call. Wherever it was, the wand and sword conjoined that made me Dread and Puissant Champion of the Fey, I summoned it to me. With that weapon in my hands, I had nothing to fear from Andraste. It was only a matter of fetching it.

A small matter; a matter that remained unrealized. My mind held its picture so clearly that I could see the subtle patterning of metal along the sword's edge, visualize my breath fogging the central core of crystal. My hand held nothing. I opened my eyes and saw only Andraste's face.

"Sssso. *That* is who you are. If seeecrecy is what you wish, you must learn not to shout so for what you want. Oh, but my apologieees, lord." She dropped me a curtsey, at once graceful and taunting. "I did not know my deeeear one had traded shells with such an exalted personage. Why does our own Champion come so seeeecretly into the court of the fey? Shall that beeee the price of your life, the gift of such a small bit of knowledge?"

The *lhiannan sidhe* drew the wings of her cloak tightly around her naked body in an ostentatious display of false modesty. "You may speeeak at any length you like, lord. Our counsel shall beeee undisturbed. None of my folk come back into theeeese lands of their own freeee will, nor anything belonging to them. Call and call as you will for your little play-toy, it shall not come to you heeeeere."

Colder than any fear, colder even than the ice walls separating me from the outer world, cold as heart's loss came the realization of where the fairy mistress had conveyed me.

"If this . . ." I spoke slowly, unwilling to make my predicament more real by naming it. "If this is the Leeside, why can I still see—?" I gestured at the figures beyond the frigid barrier.

Andraste's grimace could have been a smile, if sharks smile. "I could lie, and tell you that you still behold the world weee left beeecause it is my pleasure that you do so. But I leeeave lies as birthright to mortal men. Weeee stand near one of the Leeeeside's boundaries with the waking world, and such transparency is meeeerely this particular barrier's natural propertyyyy."

She turned her shoulder to the wall of ice and I thought I saw her shiver. "I have as little love for theeese lands as any of my kin, but I find their shelter a great conveeeenience for conducting uninterrupted business. Therefore I choose to keeeep my guests as neeear the Leeeeside border as I may. Eeeeasy it is for any of the Fey to enter again theeese cold lands, but to eeeemerge again—Ah! That reeequires more.''

"A mortal," I said. "Or a touch of mortal blood." *Like Teleri has,* I thought. My banshee began her life as a human girl. Still, I recalled, there was no way for a full mortal to control where you emerged on the Outside. Something had to pull you, an attractive force of magic. The last time I'd torn free of the Leeside with my friends, we'd wound up at the wedding of T'ing's sister Daniela. You don't get that many Kaplans under one roof without generating enough—I don't know, call it kinfolk gravity—to tug in the *Queen Elizabeth II.*

When the Fey wanted out of the Leeside, they had to find their way to the same tiny tear in the border that had allowed their escape the first time, unless they had a mortal along for the ride. Mortals for fuel and the Fey for steering was how I figured it.

"Mortal blood." Andraste repeated my words with a true epicure's relish. "You should know, deeear Timothy, that I of all have the leeeast trouble acquiring the neeeedful touch of mortal blood. Temporarily." Her eyelids lowered until two slits like white-hot knife blades seemed to cut into my flesh. "Tell meeee why you wear my Neeeeil's disguise, and I shall take what I reeeequire mercifully.''

"And after . . . you'll let me go?''

"There will be no 'after'.''

"Then kill me; or try. You won't get anything more from me but what you can take.''

The *lhiannan sidhe's* teeth were incandescent in the Leeside shadows. "Will you play the fool, then, and strive against me? If you hope for rescue, you dreeeam. *Sheee* will not come, Lord Palamon's delicate, spoiled daughter. The night terrors that haunt her since last she came into theeeese lands are legend. How sheee made her sire's halls echo with her waking screeeams!'' I could see Andraste's tongue tasting delight from every word. "Oh no, lord, *sheee* leeeast of all will venture into theeese lands.''

A wind I could not feel lifted the wings of her hair, sent it streaming back like a river of bronze fire. Her white eyes darkened to a whirlwind's dirty gray as she closed on me. "So you seeee, foolish man, you are onlyyyy mine.''

A bulky shape at the end of a long tether came swinging through the green ice wall and caught the *lhiannan sidhe* square in the side the head. Andraste squealed and staggered. The weapon vanished into the Outside, only to come sweeping back on the return stroke. This fell short, the fairy mistress having lurched out of range, but it was only a momentary setback. Ice exploded in a glittering fragmentation of emerald crystals as the lady Eleziane came hurtling through, a terrifying battle cry on her lips:

"*Who's* spoiled, you sonnet-sucking little tramp?"

Andraste's surprise lasted long enough for Eleziane to land a couple of additional blows with her tethered bludgeon. Dazed but still in the battle, the *lhiannan sidhe* recovered enough to slash through the long strap. Freed, the weight at its end went soaring right for me. I put up my arms to shield my face and got a bruised elbow for it. Looking down, I saw the ruins of Eleziane's pink leather shoulder purse, the attached Madonna photo-pin a battered memory.

Disarmed, Eleziane was still an enemy to fear. Her entire body sizzled with escalating magics, her face was contorted with rage. For her part, Andraste crouched like a cornered animal, her own native sorceries crackling from hair to naked feet.

Right then I knew that when these ladies made their move I didn't want to be anywhere nearby. Heck, I didn't even want to be in the same universe. My eyes darted all around, seeking someplace to hide, but this sector of the Leeside was flat, featureless, and barren. I eyed the barricade, now fully healed of Eleziane's abrupt entry. I could try breaking though, but there was no guarantee as to where I'd come out. What was there on the Outside to pull me through? My mother? But she was asleep, and what if one of Baba Yaga's minions, willing or not, was keeping watch? I couldn't risk that: the scrutiny, the explanations, the chance of losing all the advantages I'd borrowed so far to a single missaid word. Present safety would have to take a back seat to the success of future plans.

The ladies were circling each other now. Purple sparks wreathed Andraste's head, green fireworms slithered up and down the length of Eleziane's arms. The air around them held the pocketed pressure of a thunderstorm about to break. My skin tingled in the electrifying atmosphere of pent magic.

And then Andraste said, "You do reeealize, do you not,

milady, that weeee are most eeequally matched in matters of high sorceryyyy?''

"And if we are?" Eleziane gritted, never taking her eyes from the *lhiannan sidhe*.

"Well, then there shall beee no victoryyy won heeere for either of us, and the yeeears will roll on, Outside.'' She spared me the smallest glance, to ensure that Eleziane took her meaning.

If Eleziane didn't, I did. Time passed differently in the Faerie lands, and that included the Leeside. If these two went at it hammer and tongs, by the time I got out of this place, Mom's sleep of a thousand years might have reached its natural conclusion. Also, I'd have missed the application deadline for Princeton.

I could always try making a break for it. I might have to. As I took a sideways step nearer the barrier, one of Andraste's captive ropes of enchantment leaped out, one end collaring my ankle, the other plunging deep roots into the ground. I was caught.

"Well, milady?" The *lhiannan sidhe's* eyebrows lifted. "Shall weeee pay our debt in coin other than sorceryyyy?"

Eleziane's decision was quick to come. She held up her hand as Andraste mirrored the gesture. All the massed potency of magic they commanded gathered into two whirling balls of power that rose high above their heads, banished to the Leeside's unwholesome sky. The fetter binding my ankle went with them. Thus disarmed, the ladies faced each other.

In my heart, I dearly hoped that whatever code of honor bound the tribe of Faerie in battle, it was an unbreachable one. In Glenwood High, when girls fought, it was always ten times as vicious and twenty times less fair than when two guys went for the throat. *They're women of the Fey,* I told myself. *Our rules don't apply. Honor's more important to them. They're nobler, purer of purpose, more high-minded—*

"Die, bitch!" Eleziane shrieked, and leaped for Andraste. She managed to yank out two fistfuls of silky bronze hair and rake her cheeks bloody before the *lhiannan sidhe* kicked her where it counts.

I hope I never have to witness a battle like that one again. The clawings, the cursings, the kickings, the knee-drops and rabbit punches and ear-gnawings, were enough to scare the entire World Wrestling Federation off the turf. Andraste showed herself to be undisputed mistress of the Indian burn and the flying *ninja* noogie, but in the end it was Eleziane's spike-heeled boots that won the day.

"Come on, you can stop it now," I suggested, ineffectually trying to drag my champion off her fallen foe. "You don't kick someone who's down."

"Why not?" Lord Palamon's delicate daughter replied, getting in a few more good licks. "When they're up, they kick back."

I exerted moral force on her, pointing out that such behavior was unworthy of a highborn elfin princess. She just shifted her angle, tired of booting Andraste's ribs. I had to chuck the moral force bit and simply bench-press the Faerie hellcat before she scored a conversion point using the *lhiannan sidhe's* nose for a football.

"Put me down!" she screamed. "She's not dead yet!"

"And she's not going to be." I was firm. "You don't need a murder rap dogging you."

"I'll get off." Eleziane squirmed and thrashed like a gaffed sailfish. I gave thanks for Neil's borrowed muscles; I could never have held her, in my own body. "I'll just tell Daddy I discovered she was a servant of the Dark Lord in disguise."

"And what if Daddy's got a new hobby and doesn't care if she's the Dark Lord's personal massage therapist? He's not God's gift to aesthetic stability, you know. You could be grounded for an epoch. Let her go lick her wounds. We've got business Outside that won't wait."

Reason prevailed. Eleziane's struggles subsided enough for me to put her down. She tucked back her disheveled hair and gave the defeated *lhiannan sidhe* a haughty sniff. Then she raised both hands to the heavens, and the two balls of temporarily exiled power came homing in. One she held to her breast where it melted back into her, the other she let drop on Andraste.

"She'll be healed before you can say *Thomas the Rhymer's a tone-deaf blowhard*. Satisfied?" I nodded. "Good. And now, *get me out of here*!"

Shuddering and weeping, the lady Eleziane collapsed into my arms.

12

Mother's Helper

"I DO APPRECIATE what you did for me, Eleziane," I said, daring to reach across the table and cover her dainty hand with Neil's huge paw.

"No, you don't," she countered, tears streaming from her eyes. "You of all people should know how much it cost me to go back into the Leeside, but you don't care."

"Why? How can you say that? What have I done?"

"That." The elfin princess disengaged her hand and pointed at the pizza between us. The anchovies pointed back.

As I nimbly plucked little hairy fish out of the La Brea Mozzarella Pits, I explained to the lady my ignorance of elfin high court tastes.

"It is more than a matter of taste, Timmy."

"Don't call me *Timmy*. Your father calls me Timmy and I hate it. So if it's not taste that makes you throw a cat fit over anchovies, what is it?"

"We are the Seely Court," Eleziane instructed me, a tad haughtily. "Or what passes for the Seely Court on these forsaken shores. We don't *do* anchovies. Or lima beans. Or Brussels sprouts. Or head cheese. Or—"

"Broccoli?" I prompted.

She made a face at me. "Okra. Such noxious substances remain the purview of the *Un*seely Court, to which belong all evil sprites, night grims, boggarts, bugbears, tax assessors, and stinky cheese."

"Your little playmate back there strikes me as the perfect candidate for the Unseely Court," I said, jerking my thumb vaguely in whatever direction. Since I meant to indicate the capricious location of the Leeside, it didn't much matter where I pointed. "How come Lord Palamon allows a monster like Andraste to hang out with the Good Folk?"

Eleziane looked at me as if live mice blowing bagpipes were dangling from my ears. "Can you mean that, Timmy?"

"I'm only saying this one more time: *Don't* call me Timmy."

"Can you mean to include my own sweet sister among the horrors of the Unseely?"

"Your *what*?" It was my turn to examine her face for minstrel mice. "I hope you mean that figuratively."

"My elder sister," Eleziane maintained. "By blood."

"And lots of it." Well, I assumed that would explain why the two of them had shown such determination to rip each other's spleens out and use them for tennis balls. If elves had spleens. Sibling rivalry is never a pretty sight.

A nasty thought struck me. "Say, Eleziane, since your sister's a *lhiannan sidhe*, that doesn't mean that you're—?"

She laughed away the question. "Silly. Of course not. I just *hate* poetry." She studied Neil's body closely. "I must hand it to Andraste, though; this is not the sort of shell I would associate with poetry. Mayhem, yes, and pillage on the grand scale, but she always claimed that Homer made her skin break out. When our task is done, and you are back in your own skin, I shall have to seek out this Neil and ask him to recite one of his works for me."

"I thought you said you hated poetry."

"Tastes can change, or be changed. To live," she replied, idly running a fingertip over Neil's knuckles and giving me a case of goose bumps, "is to learn. One must stretch one's cultural horizons, or one is in jeopardy of being stuck propping up Daddy's latest fad until Doomsday."

Eleziane would never make a good poker player. I could tell just by looking at her face that she wasn't merely interested in having Neil stretch her cultural horizons. For some reason, I found this knowledge profoundly irritating.

"If that's all you want to meet him for," I said, rather testily, "I can save you the wait. I know all about Neil Fitzsimmons' poetic works."

"Do you?" She had turned his hand over and was pretending to trace the lifeline, all the while sending screaming purple wake-up calls to every cell of my borrowed body.

"Limericks," I said. To her inquiring look I added, "Neil

knew the verses to every dirty limerick ever written, and he made up a few that would've incinerated paper on contact. Want me to recite one? Several? Ahem. 'There once was a lady name Joy—' ''

"No, thank you." Frost laced Eleziane's refusal, but a least she stopped playing tickle games with my hand. She was so put out with me that she picked up a slice of anchovy 'za and chowed down on it without thinking. Also without complaining.

"Ever'thing okay over here, lady?"

Eleziane and I looked up at the sound of that voice, like the scraping of a gravel pit. Gene Roselli stood over our table, wringing the neck of an innocent dish towel. I've seen baboons bare more modest sets of choppers. Gene's smile jacked his jaws apart a good three inches, but it was never a purely friendly expression.

"Everything's just fine," I told him, my mind attempting to give his the subliminal hint *Away. Go. You. Now.* Telepathy only works when you've got both sending *and* receiving apparatus, though.

"I wasn't talkin' to you, Fitz." Talking to me? Hey, he wasn't even looking at me. He ran a hand through his short crop of glossy black curls and fixed his glittering eyes on Eleziane. More specifically, on the scoop-necked front of her tanktop. Gene Roselli was a man of few interests—two, to be exact, and the bigger, the better.

"Delicious," Eleziane answered around a mouthful of 'za. She then tried to ignore her smitten admirer.

Gene has one of these healthy self-images impervious to any amount of negative input or gentle hints to go drop dead. When he dies, it's likely that someone will have to do a mercy-killing on his ego afterwards. *Dead? But we've got a date tonight!* He tucked the dish towel into the waistband of his apron and sat himself down at our booth, giving me a smooth body-check with his hip to encourage me to move over.

"So, you new around here?" he asked Eleziane.

"Hardly." Her mouth tightened up. A wise man would've read this as a warning that he was Excess Baggage, Not Wanted On Voyage.

You'll notice, I said "a *wise* man." Gene had a physique that made Neil's look puny, but he'd overinvested in sinews and body hair and neglected to make even minimal deposits in a brain trust. As far as he was concerned, he was God's gift to women, and heaven help any heretics out there.

"No kiddin'? So how come I never seen you in here before?"

"Perhaps I only came in while you were at Obedience School."

"Cute," Gene said. Stung, he turned his attention to me. "This how you teach your woman t' talk, Fitz? A guy tries t' be p'lite an' he gets his fuckin' head bit off?"

"She's not my woman, Roselli." It wasn't the most heroic defense of a lady fair ever uttered, but you have to remember that I hadn't been in Neil's body long enough to visualize myself as big and strong. In my mind, I was still Timothy Alfred Desmond, wimp or shrimp, depending on who was describing me. My main survival techniques against the Rosellis of the world were the same that had served the early mammals so well in the ages when dinosaurs ruled the earth:

1. Run.
2. Hide.
3. If caught, play dead and pray.
4. If that doesn't work, try to talk your way out of it.
5. Wait for the big lizards to do something stupid and get themselves killed.

"Not your woman, huh?" My simple declaration restored a lot of Gene's bounce, even if it did buy me a cold scowl from Eleziane. He hooked his paws over her side of the table and hauled himself nearer to his heart's desire. "So, babe, howzabout it, huh? You an' me. I can get outa here in two shakes; my old man owns this dump. C'mon, I'll take you places."

"Oh." Eleziane's scowl melted into a terminal case of Bambi-eyes. She batted her eyelashes at supersonic speed and laid two fingers on Gene's meaty fist. "*Would* you?"

"Yeah, sure, you b—"

Gene stopped. More to the point, he choked. Seated beside him, I had the best view, and what I saw iced my blood. A thin disc of orange light materialized just beneath his chin and encircled his neck so that he looked like John the Baptist after Salome got *just* what she asked for from Daddykins Herod. Below the glowing platter, his body remained motionless. Above, his face went from olive to deep crimson and began to swell. His eyes bulged like two hard-boiled eggs, his cheeks pooched out into perfect beefsteak tomatoes, his ears turned the rich brown of porcini mushrooms, and every vein inflated until it resembled spinach linguini.

It's very difficult to feel terrified and hungry at the same time. I managed.

"Eleziane, stop!" I cried. "You'll kill him."

"That was the rough idea. I think I can get in a few more artistic refinements before he croaks, though. Brains dribbling out the ears—? Mmmmmno. Too retro. How about—?"

"*I told you to* stop *it!*" I clenched my fists, and in the darkness of our booth, something long and sharp suddenly twinkled with its own inner light. My fingers tightened around a familiar hilt.

Eleziane saw, and her eyes widened. "My lord, forgive me. I forgot myself. It shall be done at once, as you command." A wave of her hand and Gene was released from her spell. He sat there with his hands around his neck for some time.

"Holy shit, what happened?"

I slipped my Champion's sword under the table before he could see it and threw my arm around his shoulders, buddy-buddy. "Sad, Gene. Very sad, very common accident. You got a piece of 'za stuck in your throat and I had to perform the Heimlich Maneuver on you. Saved your life. I think that's probably the saddest part of all."

Gene was not disposed to believe me. "What the fuck you talkin', Fitz?" The companionable arm I'd thrown around his shoulders, he threw right back. "I never eat nothin' offa your—"

"Gene," I said mildly. "Gene, Gene, Gene. If it wasn't a piece of 'za, why else were you choking? People don't just gag on thin air."

He couldn't argue with that. "Yeah, but . . ."

"Unless they're total geeks." I smiled. "Might as well face it, you just happened to bite off more than you could chew."

"Uh, yeah. I guess." He slid out of the booth, still regarding Eleziane and me dubiously. "Thanks, okay? I owe you one. See you." And back he slithered into the fetid ooze that spawned him.

Eleziane laughed. "Well, my lord, you're a bit slow on the draw, but in the end you show the true colors of a Dread and Puissant Champion of the Fey. You made that slug go away without resorting to death. A unique and innovative technique, but one which I doubt will ever catch on among the majority of my people."

"If your folks want to stay on the Outside, they'd better learn a smidgen more diplomacy. So if you'd followed through and killed him, then what? Vaporize the body? People still notice when someone's not there. The results would be, shall we say, a little too much adverse publicity for the Fey."

"I know." She toyed with her half-eaten slice, making a gooey cat's cradle out of the mozzarella. "I vow I will never do that again, my lord." A spark of mischief glinted in her eye. "Unless you want me to."

"That I doubt." I checked my watch and only then remembered Neil didn't have one. He'd scored a nifty Rolex as a gift from Andraste way back when, but I hadn't seen him wear it at all, this year. Either he left it at home for safekeeping—although who at Glenwood High would be fool enough to try ripping off a Rawbone King?—or else his old man had appropriated it. The latter seemed likely. Mr. Fitzsimmons senior had a rep as being the Anti-Ward Cleaver, and one of the few people alive Neil actively feared and hated.

None of which helped me figure out the time. "You know what time it is, Eleziane?" I asked. Then I reminded myself where we'd come from and I added, "And what month?"

The lady was amused. "My lord, do you suffer from amnesia?"

"No, I suffer from a case of ingrown Faerie. The last time I entered your father's realm, I came out about a couple of months late for all my appointments. The normal passage of time's not exactly chiseled in stone for you people." I'll say it wasn't. The last Eleziane I'd seen had been a preschooler, and this one looked like a prom queen. The thought of proms depressed me. It was entirely possible that I'd paid for my latest sojourn in the Faerie lands by missing my own senior prom.

Eleziane just shook her head over mortals and their little ways. "It's still March, if that's what you mean, but just barely—the thirtieth. As for the time—" She consulted her own watch and announced an hour scarcely at all removed from the one I had chosen for my descent into Lord Palamon's domain.

"How come—?"

"I thought it would please you, my lord." Eleziane looked even more charming when she was putting on a front of false modesty. "As a princess royal of the Fey, it lies within my powers to select the hour at which I may emerge from my sire's kingdom. It's awfully convenient, especially when I've got a beauty parlor appointment.'' She lowered her lashes and waited.

She waited about five minutes before snarling, "That *would* have been a nice time for you to say, 'O my lady Eleziane, *you* don't need a beauty parlor!' ''

"Sorry. I was just thinking about your talent.''

"Hmph. First time I've heard it called *that*.''

"I mean for bringing people out of the Faerie realms at whatever time you like.''

"A royal prerogative,'' she said rather stuffily. "And subject to the usual paradox injunctions and retroactive intervention tariffs, as stipulated in the case of *Tortoise vs. Achilles*. Which means if you want me to take you back in time to head off Baba Yaga at the pass, as it were, no can do. I'm only enabled to bring you out of Daddy's kingdom at any moment *subsequent* to your entrance. See?''

I saw. At least I wouldn't have to worry about time running away from me in the real world while I chewed the fat with the Fey.

Chewing the fat reminded me of Baba Yaga. "What other powers do you have, Eleziane?''

"Oh, scads.'' She ticked a few off on her fingers. "Levitation, fire-making, the breeding and domestication of will-o'-the-wisps, the utter annihilation of creeps like that ape who was just bugging us, insider trading without tears, the simultaneous creation of softer hands and harder nails, clean teeth and fresh breath, long-lasting yet natural-looking hair color, the ability to brew beer that both tastes great and is less filling—''

"Could you make us both invisible and go into Mom's room and wake her from the witch's spell?''

The princess royal of Faerie took this scheme under personal advisement. Pensiveness sat upon her lofty brow, and the gathered arcane wisdom of centuries. After due and solemn consideration of my petition, the highborn lady of the Fey spoke:

"Okey-dokey,'' she said. "Let's give it a try. I mean, what've we got to lose, right?''

Right.

13

But She's Got a Great Personality!

"YOU KNEW IT was a mistake," said Yaroslav as he hung by his heels from one of the rafters in Baba Yaga's cottage.

"Honestly, I thought it was a good idea at the time," I replied, looking him right in the eye. This was easy. In the three seconds immediately following Eleziane's attempted coup, the witch had lashed out at the elfin princess with what looked like a remote control television channel changer. It was no such thing, and I got caught in the sorcerous backwash to prove it. When the flashing blue and orange lights died, Eleziane was gone and I was upside down, swinging back and forth from the ceiling like a smokehouse ham. That was how the vampire found me.

Yaroslav hadn't tried to munch on me yet, and my dearest hope was that he'd keep up the good work, despite my too-suggestive posture and helpless position. I tried to keep up the conversation, just in case he started getting peckish.

"Is—is *she* around?" I asked. I tried to get a little axial twirl going, the better to see if anything or anyone important (read: dangerous) was lurking behind me, but whatever the bonds holding my ankles fast, they wouldn't let me play gyroscope, just pendulum.

Yaroslav folded his arms across his chest. For some reason known only to vampires, his cape defied the law of gravity and clung to his topsy-turvy body like a lover. Fortunately for me, as a non-vampire, Neil liked tight clothing. I'd lost enough dignity without the added minus of having my wardrobe falling all over my face.

"She?" the vampire repeated. "That would depend. Which *she* do you mean?"

I motioned him nearer, making hush-hush motions at the same time. At least my arms were loose, for all the good that did me. Yaroslav sidled along the beam, like a parakeet on its perch, dislodging a bunch of drying herbs that dangled between us. Powdery yellow flowers tumbled down, invading my nostrils. I sneezed violently, loud enough to make a mockery of any further attempts at confidentiality.

"Where's Baba Yaga?" I demanded, as soon as I got my breath back.

"Oh. *That* she." A little *frisson* rippled the vampire's cape. "She was not amused by your—how did she term them?—high jinks. You, she has obviously immobilized, to be dealt with at her later pleasure. As for the girl—" Yarsolav released a long, melancholy breath. "Poor thing. Poor, poor thing. So beautiful. So young. So tender."

"Oh my God, she didn't *eat* her?"

"No." Yaroslav sounded depressed. "She did not."

"Then what—?"

"Ah! *There* you are, my leetle dollink!" A blast of My Sin perfume roared into my already weakened sinuses. Baba Yaga looked even worse upside down than rightside up. Live and learn. She was wearing a hostess gown that must have been made out of the tackiest wallpaper ever imagined: crimson velvet curlicues and scarlet dragons on a ground of red watermarked satin. I stared, speechless, at the rhinestone-embellished shoes she wore, a hideous cross between Cinderella's glass slippers and fuzzy pink bunny scuffs.

Yaroslav flipped himself down from the rafter and into a low bow at the witch's feet, all in one slick move. "Madame, I regret to inform you that I have learned nothing from this interloper. I await your displeasure."

Interloper? I thought. *Why didn't he call me by my proper name? And why is the witch's gaze now resting on me so thoughtful, so appreciative, and yet so thoroughly devoid of recognition?* A glint of hope gave me a *Hello, sailor* wink out of the unending darkness. *Could it be that she doesn't know who I—?*

The witch wiggled her fat fingers at the pentitent vampire and sailed past. As soon as her back was to him, I caught the look he sent me. Plain as plain it said: *Shut up or we're both dead. You won't like it. I should know.*

Oho. So *he* knew who I really was. How? Probably the same way Andraste did. The shell might be Neil's, but what counted inside remained mine. The *lhiannan sidhe* had needed to get a mouthful of my blood before she realized what was what, but Yaroslav was a connoisseur. If he were a wine-fancier, he'd be one of those who can tell you type, vintage, country of origin, vineyard, and whether the vintner had dandruff, all just by inhaling the bouquet from one decanted splash.

He knows, but she doesn't. And he's not going to tell her! I had a small advantage back; miniscule, but better than nothing.

Baba Yaga bent over to regard my face. "Well, and who is it we have here my leetle blintz?" Her fingers gave Neil's biceps an appraising pinch. "So beeg, so strapping a young man to come barging into a poor old lady's home, no invitation, no knock-knock, just you and *rude* leetle tramp you go booming around with, *such* uncouth. Does our mama know what kind of beembos you run with, ha?"

"Yes, ma'am. No, ma'am. Sorry, ma'am." I rattled off. "We didn't mean any harm, ma'am. Just, y'know, getting some kicks. I mean, we see this place, okay? And it's, like, up on this roof on chicken legs, y'know? So my old lady she's, like, 'Oh wow, let's check it out,' and I'm, like, 'No way.' But she calls me a chicken, y'know, and that, like, makes me totally crack up an' everything because this place is, like, built on *chicken legs*, okay? So I'm, like, laughing and everything and she's, like, 'Come *on*, you turkey,' which is *really* funny on accounta there's these *chicken* legs, y'know, and *turkey*, *chicken*, get it? And we're sorry and we won't do it no more and you're not gonna call the cops on us, are you, lady, huh, please?"

Not bad, if I do say so myself.

The witch smirked. "Who do you think you are playing for a *kulak*, boy?"

Oh well.

"I know you," she went on. My heart sank, which considering my position meant that the poor abused organ had to fight gravity. "You are one of *his* friends, yes?"

"Uh—ma'am?"

"Why else"—her plump hands described a dancer's graceful twist of the wrists, and a crystal-hearted sword gleamed across her palms—"would you be so equipped?" Her eyes slid slowly down my body. Cats purr just the way she did, usually when they've got a mouse tail or a tuft of canary feathers sticking out the side of their mouths. "Frandship . . . Is wonderful thing, no? Timmy, he is lucky to be having loyal frand like you. Is forbidden him to come into my presence with this—this peeg-steecker—so he is trying to, how you say, circum-navigate conditions I set."

"You mean *circumvent*," I muttered, then realized that Neil wasn't a likely member of the Vocabulary Constabulary. "Or circumcise," I added in a hurry.

"Whatsever." The witch didn't much care. She took hold of my sword by the hilt and set it down a safe distance from herself.

I suppose I could have sent the blade a mental summons and had it slice me loose, then fly to my hand, but my memory of Baba Yaga's excellent reflexes was still painfully clear. In the lightning-fast instant when we burst into the chicken-legged cottage and Eleziane shot her bolt of enchantment, the witch had managed to throw up a protective barricade and at the same moment take out the lady of the Fey. Add to this the fact that Eleziane had made both of us invisible—supposedly—before our abortive assault, and you can see just how damned good Baba Yaga was.

Eleziane was born to her magics; I was still picking my way around mine. If someone with over three hundred years of experience wasn't swift enough to zap the witch, I wasn't about to take a chance that would definitely blow my cover.

Now Baba Yaga began to pace around me, her hefty hips rasping loudly inside her gaudy gown. "You are more than loyal, boychik; you are brave. Yes, brave, or else merely stu-pid."

"Hey!" I thought it prudent to protest. Neil would've wanted it that way. "Who you calling stupid, lady? I done okay on my SATs."

"To me, this is meaning zeep." She was behind me now, and resting her hand somewhere I wished she wouldn't. "So, is then only being loyal to friend Timmy, coming here as his secret agent, hoping for to surprise poor old Baba Yaga with nasty, mean, long, sharp sword." She clicked her tongue. "Seely boy. Baba Yaga is knowing that Timmy has manny friends. She is knowing that some are being human, some are being . . . otherwise. Like rotten leetle poosycat-faced trollop who is trying to blast Baba Yaga all the way to Irkutsk, she should only hang weeth her head in a pot of borscht.''

"Ma'am? About that trollop—? Errr . . . would you mind, like, telling me what happened to her? I mean, is she, y'know, kinda dead or anything?''

The witch's laughter shook loose another shower of dried herbs. As I sputtered and snorted to clear them from my nose and mouth, I heard her say, "Dead? But, pracious boy, dead would be *merciful*!''

I felt as if an imp with a bent for anatomical mischief had replaced all of my long bones with icicles. "Where is she, then? What'd you do to her?''

Baba Yaga gave me a friendly swat on the rump that set me swinging. "That would be tellink.'' She sauntered around to where I could see her and twitched the tip of her index finger. Immediately I was standing upright, free of my bonds, and uncomfortably close to the witch's wallpapered bosoms. "So much about you I am knowing already, dollink,'' she murmured, lifting her mascara-heavy eyelashes. In Neil's body I towered over her. "Is so leetle I do not know. If you are tellink me what I am wanting to learn, then I am taking this to be sign that you are not so stupid after all. You are tellink me, and I am letting you go free; leetle beetch, too.'' Her moo-cow eyes hardened up in the instant she referred to Eleziane.

"Well, uh, sure, y'know?'' I said, shuffling my feet and trying to look gawky. Neil's body managed to turn my best attempts at awkwardness into jungle-cat elegance, whereas if I'd been in my own shell—Hey, life's not fair. "I mean, whaddaya wanna know?''

"Ohhhh, is not much.'' Her fingers plucked up little bits of my shirt and twined them tight. "First, is to tellink Baba Yaga what name such a fine, beeg young man is having?''

"Oh, okay. I'm Neil Fitzsimmons.''

"Mmmm. Nice. And now is to tellink Baba Yaga how you are getting meexed up weeth elf-beetch, jomping out at poor leetle helpless me, scaring me all to pyieces, not even wiping feets before coming into a person's house, she should only fall into plaster and get turned into lawn ornament.''

So I told her. It was a pretty good story, parts of it taken from actual truth. It's not easy, trying to explain the inarguably hostile act of invisible invasion while doing all you can to place

the blame nowhere. If the government can do it, I can try. The
attack couldn't be "Timmy's" fault, because Baba Yaga might
do something worse to my mom than she'd done already. Neither could it be Eleziane's inspiration, because I still didn't
know how badly the witch had already made her suffer for her
part in it. Nor could it be "my" idea. I was too close to the
witch to chance making her mad at me. Neil would want to
get his body back in one pyiece. I mean *piece*.

When I was finished, Baba Yaga wore the glazed expression
of someone who's just been listening to an Official Spokesper-
son explain the trickle-down effect.

"Well, well, well, that is being as it might, dollink," she
said, struggling to appear as if she'd followed my every word.
"Is not important how nice boy like you is getting handed
fozzy end of lollipop. Elfs! Always they are theenking that they
can outwit Baba Yaga! Even"—her voice dropped dangerously
low—"when we are living together in Leeside." A hunted look
touched her eyes when she mentioned those grim lands, but
she cast if off quickly.

"You see, my leetle cabbage, elfs is elfs, and they are having magic, true. Is good magic, strong magic, but is not like
my magic." She looked really proud of herself. Her bosom
swelled to dangerous proportions.

"Your magic's too strong for them, huh?" I asked, trying
to back away. The back of my knees hit the edge of a chair
and I sat down whether I wanted to or not. The witch closed
in. Now I knew how a driver feels the instant the air bag in-
flates in his face.

"Strong?" she echoed. "Is hardly the word, strong. Is like
to comparing apples and watermillions. Elfs, they are merely
creatures of the hearth, speerits that dwell close to mortal men.
Respect, yes, there is respect people are feeling for the mischief they can work. But there is no fear. That is beeg difference."

"How does fear come into it?"

Baba Yaga snickered as she ran her hands through my hair.
"Soch innocent!" She lifted my face and lowered her own
until I could smell the reek of her breath. Pickled herring played
a key role. We were so close that I felt her lips brush mine as
she spoke. "Leetle boy, is to telling: Do you fear Baba Yaga,
yes? No?"

I tried to answer. Part of me insisted that I tell her no, just to show her she couldn't push me around. *Villains always appreciate a worthy foe,* ran the argument. Another part of me insisted that I say yes, and tell her what she wanted to hear. *There's nothing wrong with buying off the enemy, and this is a cheap price to pay.* And down in the center of my soul, where the truth had gone to ground, lay the unvoiced desire to scream, wet my pants, and run like all hell and part of Newark were after me.

"I thought so," said the witch, well satisfied. She let me go.

"I didn't say nothing!" I objected.

"Was no need. Is sometimes no answer being loudest answer of all." She shrugged, splitting both shoulder seams. Sheer force of internal pressure kept the dress up, thank goodness. "In the home, in the creatures of the home, there is no fear. Fear is belonging to the outside places, to the dark that is waiting beyond the firelight. Fear is *strong*! Speerits of the hearth, they are like the masters they serve. They cling to the light, they are shunning the shadows. But *my* people, the dark is making us strong, stronger because more feared! Fear is our strength, leetle boy. Those who fear us, they are never being a match for us."

"I guess the elfs—I mean, the elves—they're afraid of you, huh?"

"Shaking in cutesy leetle elf-bootsies. I am despising them. I speet on their puny excuses for magic," the witch said, hawking up quite a respectable gob and rifling it slap on the carpet between my feet. She dabbed at her lips with an embroidered lace hankie. "Never can they hope to be outdoing me. I am Baba Yaga! I am the thunder-witch! I am grandmother to the devil himself!"

She sounded pretty proud of that. I didn't ask to see any baby pictures of Grandson when he was a little tyke, and she looked downright disappointed.

She tucked the hankie back into her cleavage. I thought I heard a gulping sound. "When you are fighting me," she said, looking full of herself, "you are fighting more than the devil's dam. Is to be taking one who can outwit my pracious grandson to defeat *me*! Not whole bonch crummy elfy-welfies. So you see, dollink Neil, while you are being so very brave, so very loyal to your frand Timmy, you would be doing him *beeg* favor if you go now and are tellink him to just go and do like Baba

Yaga wants him to, get job I give him done, no more tricksies, not to bother anymore his elf friends to be helping him. No, no, no. Because *next* time he is trying stupid trick like having his palsy-walsies come bosting down my door, trying to turn Baba Yaga into piroshki—''

Her voice drifted off. She snapped her fingers. Yaroslav scuttled through a low-beamed doorway and returned almost at once. He was leading someone by the hand, someone who wept bitterly in shrill, harsh tones. In the murky shadows of the witch's cottage, I couldn't tell much about the wailer beyond the fact that he—or she—was built like a square. Then Yaroslav brought his charge into the light.

Her face was a perfect circle to partner the perfect square of her body. It looked like the moon, just as pasty white, complete with a pockmarked wasteland of acne craters. Below a nose too small to be a joke, her flabby lips were insufficient to cover the gleaming trove of fillings and braces. Mousey brown hair hung in oily strings past her shoulders. Her eyebrows were too much there, her eyelashes not enough. My nostrils twitched; whoever this girl was, no one had ever taught her that mouthwash and deodorant commercials can sometimes be believed. Her sagging cheeks ran with tears, and when she wiped them with the back of her hand I saw that she was a nail-biter too.

Then I saw the one thing that remained unchanged: her eyes.

''Eleziane?'' The horror and pity I felt reduced my voice to a whisper. The ravaged princess royal of the Fey could only nod before breaking into fresh sobs.

''Like I am saying,'' Baba Yaga remarked smoothly, ''*next* time no more Comrade Nice Guy.''

14

Young Love

BABA YAGA SPRANG the lock on the rooftop door to the emergency stairway. With my wand now in the witch's custody, and with Eleziane shorn of her powers, we couldn't have gained access to the stairs any other way. By no stretch of the imagination were we going to climb down the fire escape, either. Giving us a graceful out was a big favor to Eleziane and me, and don't think Baba Yaga was slow to call that to our attention.

"You are now owing me," was how she put it. Then she tried to pick my rear jeans pocket.

I didn't grin, but I bore it. What else could I do? The witch's spell on Eleziane was just as hermetically tight as the one on my mother. It excluded everything else, including the possibility of Eleziane's using her own magic to reverse it.

"That wouldn't work, anyhow," she gasped as we trundled down one flight of stairs after another. "The shattering of any spell can never come from the one who's been enchanted."

"Why not? Do-it-yourself is all the rage."

She grabbed onto the banister and hung there awhile, puffing laboriously while she glowered at me. "It's the *law*, Tim. It's how magic works. It's—"

"The rules. I know. It's all gotta balance out. I just wish there was something I could do to scoot that balance along. I feel awful about what's happened to you."

"Oh, don't." She put on a brave smile, but three hundred years was insufficient time to make her a convincing actress. "You're not to blame. I should've done my homework, that's all, before I went charging in on Baba Yaga. Speaking of homework, we'd better hustle. Maybe we can still make it to that school of yours before it closes.'' She took a deep breath and attacked the stairs with fresh enthusiasm. It lasted about a flight and a half before she was winded again.

"Maybe—maybe we could get off at the next floor and take the elevator?" she panted.

"Bad idea, very bad. The elevator in this building has more breakdowns than a soap opera star. Hey, lean on me if you want and I'll—"

"You're afraid I'll break it, aren't you." Eleziane wasn't asking a question. "You think I'm that fat."

"Whoa, back off. I never said that."

Her lips compressed as much as they could over all that oral hardware and her still-gorgeous eyes furiously blinked away tears. "You didn't need to." She rumbled on down the stairs without any further complaint.

She was wheezing like an old radiator by the time we reached Glenwood High. It was the only sound I could get out of her. All of my concerned inquiries and helpful suggestions were received with the same dead silence. Only when I mentioned the possibility of contacting her royal father for help did I get a response:

"You really *want* to be a toad?"

That put the old sopping wet blanket on the rest of the conversation pretty neatly until we reached the school.

Glenwood High is what you'd call a "good" school: No on-campus murders yet—homicide conducted on a strictly extracurricular basis—and the drug dealers have the good taste to combine business with discretion. You can still Just Say No and be allowed to live. From the outside, it looks a lot like Independence Hall in Philadelphia, with plenty of red brick and white wood trim. There's even a cupola with a working clock, though the weather vane horse at the top has a case of the blind staggers.

I was glad of the clock; it told me we were still in time for school, although barely. When we reached the bottom of the white stone steps leading up to the main doors, I took Eleziane's hand.

"Hey, calm down!" I told her when she tried to wrench it away. "I said I was sorry."

"No, Tim, *I'm* the one who's sorry. I can't allow you to risk personal contact. Ugly might be catching.'' She repeated the attempt to jerk free of my grasp.

"Come on, enough. I've got a reason. We have to find Neil— the real Neil—and let him in on what's happened. Maybe he's had better luck holding up his end of things than I have.''

"How could he have worse?'' the transformed princess sniped.

"Thanks. That's helping a whole lot.''

"What's that I hear? Sarcasm?'' Eleziane's wiry black eyebrows rose. "A welcome change from pity, anyhow. Think you can keep it up? I've always preferred snotty to sniveling. We'll get along better.'' Her wry look warmed into a genuine smile.

Even with that mother lode in her mouth, it was a charming smile. I felt my own lips mirroring it. "Yeah, maybe.'' A little of the tension seeped out of my body. "Now are you gonna give me your hand or what?''

"In marriage?'' She batted her sparse eyelashes. "Why, Tim, and me a scant three hundred years old. This is so sudden!''

"Just give me the hand. Attached to the arm, okay? We've got to go into the school building to meet Neil when he comes out of his—*my* last class of the day. I know where that is and you don't, so unless you like getting lost, hold onto me.''

Eleziane saw that I had a point. There were no further refusals. Hand in hand we climbed the steps, skirting the blobs of chewing gum and the dead cigarette butts, and opened the great front doors.

Inside, the vast marble lobby was silent and apparently deserted. The bronze bust of Roger Glenwood, nineteenth-century educator and author of *Spare the Rod*, regarded us with solemn eyes neatly pasted over with a couple of Scratch 'n' Sniff Smurf stickers. Tall glass cabinets to left and right were crammed with dusty sports trophies, and one small plaque sacred to those Glenwood High students who had achieved the Roger Glenwood Award for Unremitting Academic Excellence. The last inductee's inscription was dated 1961.

I tugged Eleziane along, wanting to slip into the corridors as quickly as possible. The lobby was too wide-open, too bereft of any possible hidey-holes or coverts to be secure. Beneath this wimpish bosom there beats the heart of a born guerilla warrior, or else a darned thoroughgoing *They can't kill what they can't find* coward. Eleziane wanted to stop and gawk, but I knew we'd better get moving before—

"Yo! You! Yeah, you two. You got hall passes?"

I froze at the sound of that guttural voice behind me, clapping one hand over my eyes. "Great, just great. It's one of the school security guards," I told the darkness. "If I'd had any sense, I'd've sneaked us in by a side door, only *there* we might've run into one of the school aides, and they're worse."

"Worse than *that*?" I heard Eleziane hiss, a twinge of panic in her voice.

"Yeah. School aides never take coffee breaks. They're always *there*. I figured the odds were better for us not to get stopped by anyone if we came in the front way, but—"

"Hey!" The guard's voice grated on my ears. Still deep into the denial phase, I refused to uncover my eyes and confront my accuser. "Hey, you deaf or something? I said show me your passes! And you look me in the eye when I talk to you, you misbegotten son of a socially disadvantaged camel!"

Something cold and sharp insinuated itself under my eye-shading fingers just as revelation hit. I dropped my hand and took in the sight, the sound, the eight-cylinder *smell* that was Yang the Resplendently Emetic.

"You showing me your passes or am I cutting off your ears and seeing what the cafeteria can do with them?" he snarled.

"Yang! Boy, am I glad to see you!" I crowed, and flung myself into his arms.

Mistake. Big mistake.

Some time later I sat warming a chair in Mr. Alden's office while Yang stood by at attention, sword drawn.

"Well, Fitzsimmons, here we are again," our noble vice-principal said. He tilted his chair back and steepled his long, white fingers into a bony triangle. Late afternoon sunlight fell over the sharp planes of his face, making him look like a recently calved iceberg.

"Yes, sir, Mr. Alden," I replied automatically. I wondered how Eleziane was doing. After Yang clapped me in irons—figuratively speaking—he scooped up Eleziane—*very* figuratively speaking—and frog-marched the pair of us down the hall to the blood-soaked lairs of the school administrators. Me, he propelled through Mr. Alden's door and just kept walking, but I never saw what he did with Eleziane. Mr. Alden had begun our little *tête-á-tête* by the time Yang returned, unaccompanied, to give testimony.

Mr. Alden pursed his lips until the sight of that knotted little mouth made me think of a single, sour raspberry afloat in a sea of curdled cream. " 'Yes, sir, Mr. Alden'?'' I didn't much like his snippy imitation of me. "Not just, 'Yuh,' not even a subhuman grunt, but an actual, articulated, *polite* reply? *Mister* Fitzsimmons, are you quite well?''

"Yes, sir, Mr. Alden,'' I reiterated. Then I added, "At least I hope so, sir.''

His chair tipped back an additional five degrees as he clasped his chest in melodramatic shock. I hoped he'd overdo it and fall right on his astonishment, but Jared Alden was an old-line Yankee, the kind who never loses control of his wallet, his actions, or his bowels, in that order.

"*Sir!* This, from you? My, my. To think my horoscope didn't say one word about the end of the world coming today. Not that I don't appreciate the courtesy, Fitzsimmons; you merely have me at a disadvantage. Still, whether or not this apparent step towards civilization is a permanent one on your part, we must deal with the present offense in a detached and rational manner. Isn't that so, Mr. Yang?''

He surrendered the floor to T'ing's Mongol ancestor, who was exploring the stately pleasure dome of his left nostril with one of the vice-principal's pencils. "Huh?'' he responded, looking like a mutant walrus.

"I said, I would like to hear your version of why Mr. Fitzsimmons is now gracing my humble office.''

"Oh yeah.'' He removed the exploratory pencil with a loud champagne-cork report. "I ask him and this fat one for hall passes. They don't got hall passes. Fat one doesn't even have student ID. Then he tries to have sex with me, so I took him here, her straight to the principal's office. Where's my money?''

Mr. Alden nodded his head sagely at every other word of Yang's report, tapping his index fingers together all the while. The rule of selectivity that veiled all or part of the returned spirits from some people's sight must have worked the same way on hearing. Though Yang was dressed to the nines for a Mongol, wearing only the finest fur and rawhide, Mr. Alden had to be seeing the ensemble as a freshly pressed security guard's uniform. Yang's partly shaved skull, twirl of greasy braids, and dangling black moustaches? Knowing Mr. Alden's tastes, he beheld a cleanshaven face topped by one really sharp crewcut. As for the wild warrior's remarks, these too were passing through some kind of cosmic filter that cleaned up grammar, accent, and "have sex with me."

In other words, when Yang spoke, Mr. Alden only heard what he'd expect to hear from a normal guard.

"Just so, Mr. Yang, just so. Thank you, you may resume your post."

"I better get a bounty for this one, koumis-face, or next time the cafeteria serves meatballs . . ." Yang made an unmistakable gesture before he stalked out.

"Have a nice day," Mr. Alden remarked absently to the slammed door.

I was released with a detention, to fall due after school on Monday, and the parting jab that it was nice to see me in school at all, even if I had yet to discover what classrooms were for. Once escaped from Mr. Alden's emporium of biting wit, I made a straight run for the principal's office. Touching base with Neil would have to wait; I couldn't let Eleziane feel I'd abandoned her.

I checked out a hall clock en route to Dr. Oxenstierna's lair. School would be out in five minutes. I was riffling through my fifteenth mental script of Likely Stories to try on our beloved Doc Ox, the better to explain Eleziane's undocumented presence within the halls of Glenwood High, when I saw her emerge from the head office.

She waved at me. She was smiling. She nearly knocked me on my rump in her rush to clasp my hands and say, "Oh, Tim, I never met a nicer lady this side of the Seely Court!"

"Shht! It's *Neil*, remember?" I whispered. In that same midnight-assassin voice I asked, "What happened?"

The enspelled princess was happier than the proverbial unchowdered clam. "She just fixed *everything* for me, that's all. That awful, awful man shoved me into the office, saying how the principal knew how to handle students with no ID. He said I'd have my ears cut off and pickled, and my head chopped off and loaded in a catapult and lobbed across the soccer field at the next big game Glenwood has against Desiderius High and—"

"I get the point and I can name that tune in one note: Yang. I'm surprised you don't remember him. He was in on the ex-

pedition we mounted into the Leeside to rescue you when you
were just a little changeling. Last year.''

Eleziane shrugged her meaty shoulders. "You know how
horrible the Leeside is, Ti—Neil. And I was scared. I guess I
thought he was just part of the scenery. Can we please forget
about him? I want to tell you about this wonderful woman in
there, Ms. Stone.''

She chattered on about how the lady in question had inter-
cepted Eleziane before she could be thrown on the mercy of
Dr. Oxenstierna. No doubt that was a lucky break. Doc Ox is
a Minnesota import with a moral imperative of iron and a
strong sense of justice till it hurts. It must be a leftover from
all those Twin City winters—frostbite builds character. His idea
of mercy is letting you zip up your parka before he tosses you
off the snowmobile to the pursuing wolfpack.

"She just smiled at me and said, 'You're the fifth one of us
today Mr. Yang's apprehended. I'll take care of you, dear. We
must stick together, mustn't we?' And she made me my own
ID *and* gave me a school program, even though it must've been
a terrible strain for her, poor thing.''

"How so?" I asked. I was perplexed. I didn't recall any
Ms. Stone working out of the main office. And what was all
this conspiratorial *We must stick together* stuff? "What kind of
a strain is it to type up a couple of pieces of paper?''

"*Eye* strain, silly. The poor woman has trouble with her
eyes. You've only got to see those horrid, heavy sunglasses she
wears—*indoors*, mind—to know she must have some sort of
awful condition.''

"Yeah," I said. "Awful." I cast a chary glance at the frosted
glass panel of the principal's office. Should I—?

Then the final bell rang and made my decision for me. The
mysterious Ms. Stone would have to wait. I wanted to find
Neil.

I towed Eleziane as fast as she could trot, heading for my
last-period classroom. We had to fight the tide of Glenwood
students, all of them propelled for the nearest exits by the double impetus of end-of-school day, start-of-weekend. Another
good thing about my squatter's rights on Neil's body was that
most of the horde had sense enough to clear a path for us.
Slowing down a Rawbone King can be hazardous to your
health. Alas, many of those who'd normally get the heck out
of Neil's way got a look at Eleziane and halted to gape. There

were remarks—some plain conjecture, too many unkind. She couldn't help but hear. I saw the captive princess stiffen her face to hold back the tears.

At last we hit the hallway I wanted and battled our way salmonwise upstream. "There he is!" I cried, glimpsing the back of my own head at the far end of the corridor. "Thank God he's not playing truant on my time. Tim! Hey, Tim!"

He heard me, and more to the point, he knew enough to respond to a name not his. He paused in front of another classroom, turned, and waved.

"Tim, honey!" T'ing Hau sprang from the open classroom door and pounced on him. He opened his mouth to say something. She closed it for him with a kiss fit to give Mr. Jared No-Public-Displays-of-Affection Alden the quaking hissies.

Hm. Hadn't I been a busy boy.

15

Personal Beast

IF I HADN'T been there myself, I'd never believe it could've happened. But it did. I grabbed hold of my own shirt collar and, over the enraged objections of T'ing Hau and Eleziane, I hauled myself out the nearest side door, slammed myself up against the brick wall of the school, and told myself I was going to beat the crap out of me.

"Hey, man, what's eating you?" Neil touched the back of his head gingerly, brushing off the brick dust. "You nuts or what?"

"Just because I give you my skin, it doesn't mean you get to take over my life!" I hollered. This time, when I seized him, I did it with both fists, hoisting him off his feet to twist in the wind. Nostril-to-nostril I let him know that I was not pleased with what he had done and was going to give him some demerits of the bleed-and-swell kind to remember his offenses by.

Before I could put this plan into action, little hands latched onto my forearm and small feet began to kick at my shins. "You put Tim down, you big jerk!" T'ing Hau lashed out with another kick. This one hit me just above the left ankle.

"Ow," I commented, more for form's sake than to register any significant pain. I resumed my attentions to Neil, shaking him like a wet rag and getting ready to wring him out for good measure.

Then Eleziane was at my right side, saying, "Tim, please, I beg you, let him go."

"*Tim?*" I felt T'ing's negligible assault stop cold as she

goggled at Eleziane. "Who are you and why are you calling Neil Fitzsimmons *Tim*?"

"I'm not calling anyone Tim but Tim himself," Eleziane answered solemnly. "Would you like proof of it?"

"That—would be nice." T'ing shifted her eyes uneasily, not willing to leave a patent nut-case like Eleziane entirely unwatched, even if it meant momentarily breaking visual contact with me. "Okay," she directed from the corner of her mouth. "Proof. Give."

I stood like a soldier making a sworn deposition at a court martial—without letting Neil loose, though—and crisply recited: "Your *formal* introduction to my family banshee, Teleri of Limerick, took place in my mother's bedroom. Your ancestral spirit, Yang the Ravisher of Winsome and Complaisant Draft Animals, was a witness. In the course of this meeting, Teleri transported me elsewhere. We returned accompanied by Master Runyon, the goblin Hobson, and the phouka Donahue, whom I stabled on the fire escape. That good enough for you? Oh yeah, and Neil Fitzsimmons was nowhere in sight when any of this happened, as you yourself know."

"That's right," Neil piped up, still dangling. "I wasn't." To me, he added, "You got her into your mom's *bedroom*, Desmond? Waytago!"

T'ing took a couple of shaky steps away, her eyes wide and focused on me alone. "Tim?" she repeated, feebly. Her gaze flicked from me to Neil and back, then to Eleziane, who nodded. T'ing stepped back further yet, shaking her head. "No. This can't be. Not my Tim. No."

My Tim, she said. I heard her.

I lowered Neil to the ground. He didn't matter anymore—as far as I was concerned, he didn't even exist. Only T'ing was real. Suddenly I realized what an idiot I'd been. When I'd needed her with me most, I'd pushed her away with the self-serving excuse that I was doing it for her own safety. The truth was, I was protecting myself. From what? From her. All the feelings she called up in me had been too overpowering; they made me nervous. So what did I do? What I always did, given the chance: I hid.

Now I knew I was done with hiding. If you do it too well, sometimes you don't ever get found. Then you're alone. It took the threat of losing T'ing to wake me up—even if the person I almost lost her to was me. Why did I need to have someone

else borrowing my skin and stepping into my life to make me
understand how much I cared about her? You can buy psy-
chobabble reasons by the quart to account for it, but I'd say it
just needs one word of explanation: Stupidity. I wasn't going
to let that happen again. T'ing was frightened, upset, unhappy,
and all I wanted was to put my arms around her and let her
know that everything was going to be all right.

Easier said than done. When I tried to embrace her, she
reacted more violently than Yang. "What do you think you're
trying, Neil?" she yelled.

"That's not Neil." Eleziane clamped her stubby hands down
on T'ing's shoulders and forced her to face my shell. "That's
Neil over there; *this* is Tim, I tell you."

T'ing regarded me again, head to foot. "Uh-huh." She
weighed Eleziane with her eyes. "And who did you say *you*
are?"

"I am one who is eternally in your debt, milady, for all the
services of rescue you rendered me in the cold Leeside lands.
I am the lady Eleziane, Princess Royal of the Fey." Here she
tried to drop an elegant curtsey while still holding T'ing fast.
The two of them staggered across the sidewalk and bumped
into the side of the school building.

"Princess . . . Eleziane?" T'ing's hands described in the
air the dainty dimensions of the elfin girl's size when last they'd
met. There was a world of difference between memory and
actuality, all of it too, too solid flesh. T'ing accepted this dis-
parity by opening her mouth wide and screaming for help.

We tried to calm her down; it didn't work. She only squealed
louder and squirmed the more mightily to escape Eleziane's
clutches. Even Neil tried to chill things over, but T'ing didn't
want reasons or explanations or excuses. *Out* and *away* and *far
from here*, those were some of the things she wanted, and she
didn't mind using all the lung-power at her disposal to get
them.

I could have predicted the outcome. First, a crowd of kids
from school gathered to see what was going on. Interfere?
Them? Not on your life. Remember, these were all New York-
ers in training. Either they were too scared to step in, too
indifferent, or they were enjoying the free show too much. The
few adult passers-by who caught sight of our impromptu street-
theatre moved on, fast.

I guess our pickup audience figured that if T'ing were fated to make a successful break for it, she'd manage. If not, it wasn't any skin off their collective butts. *Hey, man, that's not my job/table/lookout/problem.* In my neighborhood they've got a healthy respect for predestination, kismet, *que será, será,* and *Don't get any on me.* I think I kind of disappointed them when I kept making soothing sounds at T'ing instead of trying to separate her from her cash and/or clothes.

But T'ing Hau Kaplan was a woman of resources. One resource, anyway. When Neil and Eleziane and I formed a human box-canyon around her and herded her to the wall, still doing our best to make her stop hollering and *listen* to us, she made her move. Head back, eyes shut, she let fly with a multi-tonal stream of strange syllables. It wasn't magic, just Mandarin, but it had its uses.

"*Awright!* You dog-lickers back offa my honored grand-daughter before I carve out your worthless livers and shove them in your skulls through the eyeholes!"

The crowd scattered. Sword in hand, with a dagger in the other one for backup, Yang strode up and made his presence felt. I jumped out of the way just in time, or he would've made his sword felt on my shoulder.

The Mongol bared his saffron teeth and used his dagger to motion T'ing into the safety of his personal sphere of influence. She must have been really frightened, to cling to Yang so closely. That, or her sinuses were stuffed shut.

"Yang, listen, this is all a big mistake—" Neil began.

Yang spat a glob the size and color of a mature bullfrog. "You bet, yurt-head, and you made it. Alla time I tell my beloved granddaughter not to waste herself on yak-piss like you, but will she listen? Nooooooo. And I'm a man who knows his yak-piss! Still she insists on making snuggy-noses with you. Ha! You tell me you don't want to put her in danger. You tell me you're not gonna tell her nothing about nothing. You tell me to go get a job, earn big bucks, do it *legal*, for shit's sake, but don't say one goddam word to T'ing about it, ha? And then what do you do? *What do you do?*"

Poor old Neil. I bet he was so sick and tired of being yanked by the lapels that he was never going to wear a collared shirt again as long as he lived. In the meantime, Yang jounced him up and down on the pavement, as if he were a balky vending machine that wouldn't cough up the merchandise advertised.

"Wait, stop, halt, whoa, *let go of him, damn it*!" I used all the muscle Neil owned to seize and immobilize Yang's jouncing arm.

The Mongol's flat, black gaze shifted gradually to me. "You wait, asshole. You're dead next."

"Yang, you're killing the wrong guy."

"I am?" He didn't look like it made no never-mind to him, but he did stop playing bouncy-bouncy-ball-ee with Neil. I winced in sympathy as my friend worked on making his teeth stop knocking together. (*Real* sympathy; I'd have to live with those teeth, some day. I hoped.)

"Yes, you are," I went on. In as few words as possible, most of them simple nouns and verbs, I let Yang and T'ing in on the body/self situation as it presently stood. Neil and Eleziane offered their confirming testimony. The second time around, T'ing heard us out more placidly, but serenity should never be mistaken for credulity. When I was through, you could really see the family resemblance between T'ing and her honored ancestor. No matter how much proof we offered, neither one of them looked like they believed us any farther than they could heave the Empire State Building into a head wind.

It was T'ing who decided we were telling the truth at last. "It has to be so," she told Yang. "Not even Tim could have any other reason wacko enough to lie about something like this." She looked from Neil to me and back again, a woman resigned. "So all this time I thought we were getting back together, it wasn't you who wanted me; it was Neil." Her voice caught in her throat. "The joke's on me, but it's over now. We're back to where we were; back to nothing."

I wanted to say something to her—one of those great movie speeches that wipes all past goofs and blunders off the hero's record while at the same time it makes the heroine realize that of course he was perfectly right about everything all along and she'd been a fool not to have believed in him utterly and unquestioningly because nobody else in the whole world is worthy of her love. Then they set fire to each other's lips.

What I said was, "Uhhhh . . ."

Yang stepped in to fill the great silence with his own individual brand of witty repartee. "Screw this. I got paid today. We go to McDonald's, eat a lot, maybe see who can hide the most Chicken McNuggets in his armpits without cracking up, extra points if you do it with barbecue sauce on them. I'll buy." He swatted Eleziane across the haunches and added,

"Finally, a woman I can sink my teeth into! Come on, Princess; you look like your pits are good for a coupla twelve-packs, easy."

As the Mongol himself once said, *When Yang pillages, everyone pillages.* Doing disgusting things with fast food wasn't precisely pillage, but I wasn't going to tell him that. We closed ranks and followed the leader, T'ing keeping as far away from Neil and me as she could without crossing the street.

"So okay, now you screwed up using my body to try and sneak one over on Baba Yaga, can I have it back already, Desmond?" Neil was at my elbow, hanging on like a gecko to a plaster wall.

"What's the big hurry?" I asked.

"Let's just say I didn't much like you trying to pound me into the ground using my own fists for the sledgehammer. Anybody does any pounding with this body"—he poked me in the chest—"it's gonna be the original owner, not no new management. Got that?"

"You don't seem to have been doing too badly with *my* body, Neil." I gave him a meaningful look, then pointed at T'ing to make sure he copied.

"That's what fried your tail?" Neil laughed. "You dumb fuck, that wasn't *me* she was all over; it was *you*. Or didn't you get a taste of what T'ing thinks of Neil Fitzsimmons back when you tried creaming her darling Tim?"

I massaged my temples. "This is giving me a headache."

"You mean it's giving *me* a headache." Neil was having fun with this. God, did I really look that much like a hyena when I grinned? "And I'd like to have it firsthand, so make with the magic wand and let's get this swap happening."

No use trying to hold back the bad news any longer. "The wand . . . is gone."

Yang, Eleziane, and T'ing got a whole block ahead of us while I waited for Neil to come out of his nuclear conniption fit. "What? Gone? How? When?" He kept shrilling interrogatives until I told him the whole story. "You mean I'm stuck in this dump?" he bleated.

"Watch it, that's my dump you're talking about. This is no thrill for me, either."

"*Sure*, it's not." Subtle scorn wasn't Neil's style. He preferred the kind you pile on with a forklift. "Why would *anyone* want to swap a wonderful bod like *this*"—he struck a circus strongman's pose that made me look ludicrous—"for a cruddy wreck like *that*?" He punched me in the stomach with no warning. His fist sounded as if it were striking solid leather and I never felt a thing. "Next you'll be telling me that Donald Trump's dying to move into a trailer park," he concluded sourly.

"Neil, my pal," I said, doing my best impression of a hungry used-car salesman. "Neil, I hear you. You're not happy being me, are you, Neil? You want to be you again all the way, is that right, Neil, old buddy?" I laid a friendly hand on his shoulder. Then I dug in until he twitched. "Well, get this straight, bozo: I'm not jumping for joy living under all this meat, no matter *what* your ego says to the contrary. I'm going to get my wand back, I promise you that, but when I do, you and I are going to have to take a number and wait before I get us traded back where we belong. The first thing I'll use my powers for is transforming Eleziane into her proper shape, and don't you forget it. We can live with ourselves the way we are now, if we've got to, but what Baba Yaga did to her—" I shuddered.

"Oh." Neil was abashed. "See whatcha mean. I guess I was getting kinda whiny about it."

"You know it. Now forget it. Let's put wheels on it, or the only thing we'll get to eat will be Chicken McNuggets *à la* Yang armpits."

We should have been so lucky. Neil and I entered the McDonald's where my mom used to work and looked around for our gang. The place was crammed with the after-school crowd and a lot of traffic from Brooklyn College. Up at the serving counters the bodies were stacked eight deep and ten across. People coming, people going, people looking for a table, people searching for a familiar face—all conspired to confuse us as we searched for T'ing and the others.

"Tim! Hey, Desmond, over here!"

I heard the halloo before Neil did. No matter how good he'd been at playing me, I was still faster at picking up the sound of my own name across a crowded room. I nudged him. "Hear that? It's them. Over there."

He followed me dutifully, weaving in and out between tray-bearing bodies, making a broken-field run through the tables, doubling around a tall stand of potted plants that split the dining area and gave the customers a little privacy.

"There you are, Tim! Howzit going? Who's your friend? We got room? Any friend of Tim's, right, boys? Pull up a chair, man!"

Neil went pale and I must've lost a lot of color myself. It's not every day you come around a corner to see five giants, the shortest of them eight feet tall, all mashed into a booth at McDonald's. Two of them were gnawing on bones big as Thermos bottles. McDonald's doesn't serve anything with bones. All of them wore Glenwood High letterman's sweaters. On closer inspection I saw that the two bone-gnashers wore nothing else. Neil gave me a weak smile and took the last vacant seat in their company. A giant with skin like a "Ski Colorado" poster pounded him on the back in welcome. Tiny icicles tinkled down from the colossus' frosty head. Then he motioned for me to join them, too.

"I—Thanks, but there's no more chairs," I said.

"What, you don't hear?" The one-eyed titan who'd been doing all the talking tossed a Quarter-Pounder into his mouth like a potato chip. "Pull up a chair, I said!"

"I can't. The chairs here are bolted to the floor."

"Tchah!" One-eye dealt himself a stunning blow to the forehead. "Dumb me. No wonder Ms. Fine's flunking my ass in Math. Hey, you! Goliath! You wanna be a Philistine all your life? Pull up a chair for the kid."

The giant thus addressed remained where he was, idly toying with the plastic doohickey from his Happy Meal. There was a muzzy look of bovine contentment on his bearded face.

The cyclops shook his head.

"Stoned again."

He then reached across to the next table and plucked up one of the vacant chairs as if it were a dandelion. The floor groaned and split where he jammed it back in at our table.

"Sit," he said. "Sit and talk. Any friend of Tim's, like I said. What's your name, kid?" His lone eye narrowed. "And don't try giving me that old 'My name is Noman' scam, got it?"

"I'd sooner die," I told him.

"I guarantee it," he replied.

16

Monsters in Action

T'ING HAU HUDDLED on the bleachers between Neil and me and for the twentieth time in ten minutes announced that she didn't want to be there.

"So go," Neil told her. She stayed. "Women."

"If you really want to leave, go ahead," I told her.

"If you stay, I stay," she returned, grim. "I don't know why you insisted on this, though."

"I told you, we found *five* giants sitting in McDonald's and they were all wearing letterman's sweaters. That means they're on one of the Glenwood teams, and the only sport we're actively playing now is this. I've got to see them in action to check out how much disruptive damage they're capable of causing."

"They're giants." T'ing spread her palms. "They grind your bones to make their bread, but aside from that, they're no big problem. Not since Coach put them on a low-carb diet."

"I said *disruptive* damage, the kind where they act up enough to attract the attention of whatever Powers slapped them into the Leeside in the first place. Disruptive damage would blow their cover and wreck this whole operation."

"And that would mega piss off Baba Yaga," Neil concluded. "Which in turn wouldn't do your mom any good."

"You got it." I settled myself more comfortably on the bleachers and found it to be an impossible task. "So here I stay, just to check them out. God knows I wouldn't be here if I had a choice. I hate organized sports."

"Good for you," Neil said. "This ain't them."

He was right. School sports at Glenwood High were in a sorry state. Don't get me wrong—we had the talent. Most of it was hungry talent, kids who saw sports as their only way the heck out of Brooklyn, into college, and, with luck, on to the big time of pro playing. Our trouble was that all the other schools we played against were equally supplied with talent that was just as hungry, if not hungrier, and they all came from neighborhoods where your choices were get out or die.

The result was that the players developed a win-or-else attitude that rubbed off on their non-playing supporters. If their school lost, it was a personal insult to the pride of the entire student body. For most of them, the only thing they had was pride; too bad they defended it in ways no one could be proud of. Sportsmanship and fair play were strictly monitored on the field, but what a kid did on his own time was a strictly eyes-closed matter to the coaches. When I was a freshman, a gang of football players from Desiderius High managed to angle the Glenwood Gargoyles' star quarterback into an after-hours fight at a video arcade. He didn't play for the rest of the season. The next year, he didn't go out for football at all.

I felt a drop of wetness on the back of my hand. April weather can be treacherous. I checked the sky and didn't see a single cloud. Then I checked the playing field and I understood what had happened.

"Sssst. Neil. We all know the cheerleaders are doing warm-ups. You can stop drooling now."

"Sorry, man." Neil chuckled, wiping the back of his hand across his mouth. He leaned forward at such a sharp angle that the lightest push would have sent him tumbling down the bleachers. T'ing looked about ready to give it to him.

"Wow," he said, hugging himself as the pep squad bent, stretched, twisted, and inhaled. Blond, black, brown, and red hair bounced and shone in the sunlight. A dozen sparkling smiles, held in unflinching grimaces of regimented cheerfulness, blinded spectators in the cheap seat. What was Glenwood gonna do? Win. When were we gonna do it? Right now. How were we gonna win? We were gonna fight, fight, fight.

"What a bunch of great broads," Neil sighed. "Too bad they can't fight worth shit."

How sad, but how true. Although our massed battalion of school spirit storm troopers continually promised that we were gonna fight, we were gonna win, we were gonna kick some butt and kick some head and stomp that foe until it's dead, the Glenwood High pep squad was a severe disappointment to the players.

As my old nemesis, Billy "No Neck" Klauser once said, way off the record in the locker room, "Not only don't they put out, the dumb bitches don't even pack razors. How the fuck we supposed to believe they're behind us if they won't try ta cut the other team's cheerleaders in the girls' room any chance they got? Call that school spirit?"

I studied the squad on the field, presently going into their pyramid formation, and tried to imagine any one of them flicking out a blade. Impossible. A nail file, maybe, or a corkscrew. Like I said, Glenwood's a "good" school. We've even got our own preppie population, and the female portion thereof gravitated to and took over the cheerleading empire faster than the Germans ever said, "Poland? *Us?*"

They did allow others to join the squad. *Someone* had to be the bottom row of the pyramid. As we watched, Brooke, Ashley, and Heather did spectacular back-flips before taking their places as the second row up. They were followed by Megan and Summer, whose cartwheels caused spontaneous carbonation in Neil's hormones. Topping the structure was Kirsten, a lady whose blond hair and blue eyes seemingly possessed the mystic power to broadcast the telepathic message: *Of course everyone wants to look like me. Tough luck, losers.* On the field, Jennifer and Tiffany flanked the pyramid, chanting with all they had to the tribal gods of Victory Or We Pout.

"Makes me proud to be an American," said Neil.

"Makes me want to have sex," Yang said, materializing one row of seats below us. He carried a Glenwood High pennant and a box of popcorn. "So, where are these monsters you say are so dangerous? There? I see women, not monsters. Dangerous, though, especially if you let one talk you into trying it Sogdian style the sixth time. The fourth time, the fifth, okay, but the sixth—!" He rolled his eyes and stuffed his face with popcorn to drive off the horrible thought. On reflection he added, "Of course if that butter-hair up there *really* wanted me to try . . ."

"The monsters will be along," I assured him, through clenched jaws. "Neil saw to that."

"What'd *I* do? What'd *I* do wrong, huh?" Neil appealed to T'ing, who to my chagrin took his side.

"You didn't do anything wrong, Neil. You were just doing someone else's job for him." I felt my eyebrows crisp to ash under her glare. "If he doesn't like the way we handled it, he should've stuck around and done better."

"What's this *we* stuff?" I wanted to know.

"*We* is Neil and me. He wasn't ashamed to ask for some help when he needed it."

"Good going, man," I rounded on him. "The whole point was to keep T'ing out of this."

"Hey, what could I do? She caught me having a chat with that minotaur dude. Is it my fault she sees him like he is and starts asking questions? Anyway, she came up with some damn good ideas, so why not use 'em?"

T'ing's smile wasn't friendly, just provoking. "You were supposed to be looking after the socialization of the returning monsters, weren't you, Tim? Show them the way into society, teach them what's what, help them adjust to a world that's changed a lot since their Leeside exile? In short, you had to give them a quick education." She clasped her hands over one knee and let her wicked smile stretch a little wider. "We found the way to educate them efficiently."

"By matriculating a bunch of nightmares at Glenwood High?" I knew it to be so, and too far advanced for anyone to stop it now, but I still couldn't accept what T'ing and Neil had done in the name of efficiency. "Jesus Christ, have you *seen* some of them?"

"I have," T'ing replied. "But I'm not just anyone. You know how it worked with the domestic spirits—it takes something special for a person to see them as they are, or to see them at all. As for the people who can't see them, their minds find acceptable ways to account for any—mmmm—thingies the beasties do."

"She's talking 'thingies,' " I told the heavens. "And when a dragon gets loose and eats somebody, how do we account for *that* 'thingie'? Don't tell me Coach put the Worms on a low-carb diet, too!"

"Don't you mean low cholesterol? Oh, relax, Tim. As soon as we sold the real group leaders on our plan, they agreed to keep the friskier critters in line and out of the way. Dragons!" She laughed. "If you think they were our biggest problem, you've got a lot to learn."

"But where did you *put* the drag—?"

"Shut up, loathsome puddle of cat vomit," Yang suggested, passing me the popcorn. "Here comes the team. I wanna watch, and when bones crunch, I wanna hear."

Bones crunching? With the Glenwood Gargoyles football team, there was always the slightest chance of on-field mangling—all done with the highest respect for the *mens sana in corpore sano* ideal, of course—but this was April. The football Gargoyles had retired for the season. In the spring a young man's fancy lightly turns instead to thoughts of soccer.

I said I don't have much use for organized sports, but soccer's an exception. There's always lots of action on the field, not a lot of time pissed away in huddles. Soccer's a tougher game, too. The cleats are just as mean as for football, but the players don't have seven layers of protective gear to save their skins from a swift kick that "accidentally" misses the ball. Sure, in football you get tackled, while in soccer you're not supposed to touch another player, but when has *not supposed to* stopped a really determined soul?

Remember that Glenwood quarterback I mentioned who got clotheslined at the arcade? He came back as a soccer player and evened the score against the Desiderius team so thoroughly that he got penalized by the ref, benched by the coach, suspended by the principal, and hired by the CIA.

So if Yang wanted to hear bones crunch, he'd get his wish. He just wouldn't get it today.

"Yang, this is only practice. The game's tomorrow," I told him.

"We used to practice," he said. "Me and the horde, alla time practice, practice, practice. Then anybody who survived practice got to go burn China." His belch made the metal bleachers vibrate. "Practice is good, if you can get the bloodstains out later."

I gave up. Yang the Pillager of Whatever He Damned Well Felt Like Pillaging was a hard man to win over in an argument, unless you hit him upside the head a few times. I was debating whether it would be worth trying, or just fun to do, when I heard T'ing cry out, "Here they come!"

The world went knobby-kneed and hairy.

"Did you see what they did?" I howled, stalking up and down in front of the bleachers. "Did you?"

"Yeah," Neil said, his face bright with joy. "Shit, I think

we actually got a chance of burning Desiderius' ass tomorrow, for a change!''

"Is that all you can say? Are you *blind*?" I appealed to T'ing. "You were here, you saw it. Or am I just crazy? Tell me I'm crazy!''

"My pleasure,'' T'ing said. "You're out of your mind."

Yang leaned back, licking melted butter off his fingers, his palms, his forearms, his elbows. . . . "Now *that's* what I call a practice!'' He hooted approval, then sucked flecks of popcorn off the ends of his moustaches.

"They're doomed.'' I shook my head in despair. "One more performance like that and they'll be chunked back into the Leeside so fast, they'll leave scorch marks."

Shaking my head didn't help jar the scenes I'd just witnessed on the soccer field into something more nearly approaching normalcy. I could still see the foot-deep ruts dug into the turf by the two ogres' soil-churning barefoot goal runs. True to the rules of the game, they hadn't touched the ball with their hands at all, not even once. However, my brain was ineradicably printed with the sight of Coach holding a deflated soccer ball that was a lacework of tusk-marks.

The soccer balls weren't the only equipment with which the giants had had a high old time. One goal net was no more than a handful of fluttering threads to mark the many times the cyclops had sent the ball roaring through to score. In front of the other net was a pool of ice that was just now beginning to melt. The frost-giant had done a wonderful job as goalie, aided by the fact that any player who got close enough to score would slip on the ice first.

Goliath hadn't done so well. He kept demanding to take on the opposing team one-on-one, then burst into tears and went home when Coach said any more funny stuff and someone's butt was going to be in a sling.

Home . . . I pondered, watching him go. He wasn't heading back toward the school, where my locker was supposedly the holding space for all of the waiting monsters. *Wonder where else these creatures have to call home?* Suddenly I was hit by a more pressing problem. *Where do* I *go that's my home now?*

I got my answer when the last player departed and my small group split up.

"Catch you at the game tomorrow, Desmond?" Neil inquired. "Maybe a real match'll chill out the big boys."

"I sure hope so." We all started down the street together, but when we came to Flatbush Avenue, Neil stopped short.

"You're going the wrong way," he said.

"What do you mean? I know my way home."

"Forgetting something? C'mere and I'll get you a mirror. *Your* building's this way, but the place Neil Fitzsimmons has gotta sleep is *that* way." He pointed me toward his own address.

Some of the hollow, lost feeling inside me must've shown. T'ing took my hand, and for the first time since soccer practice spoke to me kindly. "It won't be for long, Tim. We'll find a way to get your wand back, and we'll help your mom out, too. But for now, you've got to go along with things as they are." Then she stood on tip-toe and gave me the sweetest, shyest of kisses.

I walked to Neil's place in a dream. The key bungled around in the unfamiliar lock, but I got the front door open eventually. Inside, the apartment was dank and dark, full of the smell of stale beer. There wasn't much in the refrigerator or the kitchen cabinets. I opened up a tin of sardines and couldn't locate a clean fork to eat them with, though I did manage to find the one unmoldy piece of bread in the apartment. It was hard and crumbly, but the sardine oil softened it up so I could chew it. I washed the mess down with half a can of flat Coke from the fridge.

I was stretched out on Neil's bed, staring at the ceiling and wondering whether I ought to go out somewhere to get some real dinner when the front door squealed open and slammed shut. Heavy, stumbling footsteps blundered through the apartment beyond my closed bedroom door. I heard a couple of big, clunky things being thrown down on the kitchen counter— my room lay up against the kitchen and I couldn't miss the noisy thump as both packages whammed into the shared wall. Then I picked up on the softer, no less distinctive pop-and-hiss of a drink can being opened. I was betting it wasn't Seven-Up.

The footsteps barged past my door again. A chair groaned with the weight of a man falling into it. A ball game broadcast blared on. I decided to stay put. I didn't want to come out of the bedroom and have to try fooling Neil's dad into believing

I was his son. The sardines would have to see me through to morning. I curled up facing the wall and tried to go to sleep.

That night, I dreamed of monsters. They grabbed my hands and dragged me down the halls of Glenwood High until we reached my locker with its hidden gate to their domain. They pulled and pushed until they had me wedged inside. Only then did I realize that the gate was gone; cold metal pressed against my skin. I was crammed into the locker so tightly that I couldn't turn my head, I couldn't move an arm or leg, I couldn't even breathe. My eyes yearned toward the light, but leering faces blocked it. Their slavering grins were the last sight I had before they clanged the door shut over me.

The nightmare didn't end there. In the dark, wrapped in the sour, reeking air, I felt the first blows fall. The monsters were pounding on the outside of the locker. The blows fell slowly, rhythmically, with a dull intensity as plodding and loyal as the workings of a machine. I shouldn't have felt a thing, encased in armored walls, but each blow shook my body, every impact carried through the hardest shield I could raise around my soul.

The worst part of it was, I knew that it didn't matter who the monsters held trapped in the locked metal box. It didn't make any difference whether they pounded their sullen, idiot hatreds out on me or on another. I was handiest, that was all. If I survived after they tired they would be back. If I died, they would find someone else. There were plenty of victims to be found.

That was the waking truth inside the nightmare that finally made me scream myself awake.

And awake, I felt the blows continue to fall on my back, on my sides. I heard the tearful, maddened, muttered curses against people whose names I didn't know. The smell was there, a foulness of beer on his breath, of sweat on his body. I cried out, told him to stop, tried to cover myself against the blows, hit back and made him trade the open-handed beating for fists.

I made him do it. That was part of what I heard him say. It was all *my* fault; mine and theirs, the names I didn't know. We made him do this, and he hated us for it. Why did we force him to act this way, when he loved us so much? It wasn't *his* fault at all.

He grew tired, after a while. He sank down onto my bed and stretched out beside me. Soon he was snoring.

I wiped the tears and mucus from my face. I was too scared to move, afraid what waking him might bring on. The inside of my cheek tasted salty. I closed my eyes and concentrated on swallowing sobs. The darkness in the room had a weight all its own, and it lay heaviest across my aching bones. Chilled, willing my shudders to stop, I tried to steal back into the mercy of my nightmare, where all the horrors wore their own honest faces and never excused their evil in the name of love.

17

Smoking in the Boys' Room

"TIM!" T'ING EXCLAIMED when she saw my face. "What happened to you?"

I edged past the last few students in the bleacher row and sat down next to her. "I'm Neil, remember?" I mumbled. The collar on my denim jacket was pulled up as high as it would go, but it wasn't enough to hide the cuts and bruises.

From T'ing's far side, Neil leaned across to grab my hand briefly. He didn't have to ask what had happened. "I'm sorry, man," he said. "Shoulda had you come back with me to your real home, made up some excuse to take the witch off the scent if she stuck her nose in and asked questions. What's the worst coulda happened?"

"The worst is that she'd catch on and that'd be that for any hope of saving my mother, let alone our own hides." I blinked my left eye, testing to see how well it would respond for being swollen halfway shut. "Is it always this bad with him?"

Neil sized up the damage his father had done. "Bad enough. When something makes him start thinking more about the war, it gets worse. I'm the last one he's got left to work on, so he's kinda refined his act. When Mom was still home, and my brother, he didn't have so much *quality time* to give me." He grimaced. "Last time Mom wrote to him, asking for money, I got her return address off the letter before he could toss it. I wrote her about all the great stuff she's been missing since she ran away. I offered to join her, let her know about it firsthand. She never wrote back. That's my mom: Doesn't want to get all selfish and deprive me of one lousy minute of the best home-life this side of *Family Ties*.''

''Where's your brother, Neil?'' T'ing asked softly. ''Wouldn't he take you?''

Neil's laugh wasn't funny. ''They're not so hot on live-in family members at Sing Sing.''

''Neil, when this is over, we're gonna do what you just said. You're gonna come live at my place.'' I meant it.

A sad smile crooked up his mouth. ''Just because we're playing tag with monsters, Desmond, don't mean we have to believe in fairy tales. Shut up and let's watch the game.''

He turned his attention to the soccer field and resisted all further attempts on my part to get him talking about his hellish home. T'ing laid a hand on mine and with her eyes alone told me to let it ride. Any healing or help that Neil needed would have to wait for us to clear the board of greater matters. Part of me agreed; part of me stubbornly insisted that there was no matter greater than stepping in when you knew—how well!—that someone was in pain.

School maintenance had been busy; the churned-up field and the tattered nets were restored to playable condition. A spotty turnout of students from Desiderius High occupied the opposing set of bleachers. Soccer games didn't bring out the rabid school spirit that football did, but the Desiderius Demons fans could still make a halftime trip to the boys' room a life-threatening venture for us Gargoyles boosters, especially if their team was behind.

Speaking of teams, ours wasn't on the bench yet, let alone the field. I looked over toward the high school, where the Gargoyles changed into their uniforms for home games, then asked T'ing for the time.

''Little less than five minutes to one. Why?''

I frowned. ''The game's supposed to start at one and I haven't seen a single one of our players. They should be out doing warm-ups by now. Look, there's the cheerleaders and the ref and the team from Desiderius, but where's our guys? Where's Coach?''

''Not all the cheerleaders are down there,'' T'ing pointed out. ''Kirsten's not, and she's the captain of the squad.''

A missing head cheerleader wasn't much, but together with a whole soccer team being tardy, plus Coach nowhere in sight, it added up to trouble. I stood up. ''Be right back.''

Neil tried to join me. "You think maybe the giants got hungry and—" He didn't bother finishing the thought. We had some bruisers on our soccer team, but I'd seen the size of the bones the ogres had been munching at McDonald's.

"I hope not. I've just got to check. You stay with T'ing."

"Hell I will! Aren't you forgetting something? These big guys have been taking their orders from me—I mean, you. Only I'm who they think is you. Now if you go after them, no way they're gonna know you're you, and if they eat you, what's gonna happen to me?"

I closed both my eyes all the way, ignoring the pain. "You're giving me another one of those headaches. If you come along, will you stop doing that?"

" 'Smatter? Tough guy can't take semantics?" Neil snickered as we slid past an assortment of knees to get out of the bleachers. "Don't look like I just grew an extra head, man. I cracked a book or two in the past four years. It just didn't get noised around too much, that's all. Hell, I even took the SATs this year."

I couldn't have looked more shocked if someone had told me that Dr. Oxenstierna had been caught in a steamy love nest with three trained parrots and a jar of peanut butter. Neil enjoyed it, the rat.

"Want to hear what I scored on them?" he leered. Then he told me.

"You lousy—! You—! You big—! *You did better than me in the* math *section, for cripes' sake?*" Neil just grinned. "There is no God. No, strike that: There *is* a God and He has a warped sense of humor."

I had to shelve the issue of whether or not the Divine allowed punsters into Kingdom Come. First there was the soccer team to be found, preferably uneaten. Trailed by a sickeningly smug Neil, I went into the school building.

The front lobby seemed bigger on the weekend. The whole school felt as if it had grown to several times its normal size. Without the students and teachers to fill it, the building held too many ghosts. The walls and floors could not absorb sound at all. Our footsteps sounded harder and louder, our whispers harsh and blaring. Haunted and hunted, I doubled and redoubled my pace without thinking about it.

"Where—where will we find them?" Neil panted as he jogged to keep up with me.

"We're going straight for the gym locker rooms. Then, if they're not there, we best-guess somewhere else."

"Hey, you want to—want to maybe slow down a sec?" Neil poked me. We were just passing one of the boys' rooms. "I think I heard something in there: Voices."

I pulled up short and listened. He was right. There was plenty of chatter going on inside, voices raised in raucous laughter. I pushed the door open.

A roiling cloud of smoke rushed out and engulfed us in a fog that made pea-soupers look like consommé. I gasped in surprise, then choked as the crud flooded my lungs. It stank of tobacco, but not just from cigarettes.

"Holy shit, what *is* that smell?" Neil gagged.

"Cigars," I supplied, pinching my nose shut and trying to breathe through my cupped hand. "And dope."

"Oh no, man." Neil wasn't buying my analysis. "If that's dope, they oughta burn their dealer. Smells like he's been selling them dog hair, used kitty litter, and shredded tires." His skin went sallow, with white blotches over the cheekbones. "I think I'm gonna puke." Holding onto his stomach, he lurched into the heart of the fog. If he'd have been thinking about it, further *in* was not the best place to go, but when your innards announce they're about to have a Going Out Of Business/Must Vacate The Premises sale, all you think about is where's the nearest john.

Idiot that I was, I stumbled after him. The stench got worse as the smoke got thicker. I couldn't see six inches in front of me. I heard Neil wallowing about somewhere ahead, plaintively begging directions to the toilet. The laughter we'd heard before was all around, a part of the smoke. Now it was purely cruel.

Then I heard Neil kick something substantial—his porcelain Grail by the sound of it. "Thank God!" he cried, and then came the lusty noises of a man actively reviewing what he'd had for lunch; also breakfast.

"Hoo, Gwimcur, think as he's done?" The voice was a knife blade drawn slowly down a chalkboard, and answered in turn by one like swamp-gas bubbles rising through chocolate chip rat pudding.

"Hope not, Skeffins. Hardly 'nough t' go around as is, and me with the thirst of a thousand devils on me."

"Who's there?" I called.

"Yah! 'Nother one." Swamp Gas sounded delighted. "Think as maybe he'll heave, too?"

"Narrrr." Knifeblade wasn't at all optimistic. "If he was a-gonna, he'd've done it 'fore this, Gwimcur. He's got a cursed strong stomach on him and no mistake."

Swamp Gas (or Gwimcur) tittered. "How's about let's see just how strong it is, eh? You all with me, boys?"

A mixed chorus of agreement rose up from a good half-dozen throats whose owners remained hidden in the putrid mist. One among them who sounded surprisingly refined took charge, saying: "I would respectfully suggest that we make a concerted effort on the count of three. Shall this be pleasing you all?"

"Aw, get on with it anyway y' like, Shiko. Yer th' only one o' us knows how t' count anyhow."

"My humble thanks for this overwhelming vote of confidence. Now, if you please: One, two—"

And on *three*, a blast of wind corkscrewed down directly over my head and knocked me to the tiles. Instinctively I covered my head with both arms, but once the gust had me floored, it lost interest. From the floor itself to a height of about two feet was a zone of dead calm where I could crouch in safety and look up to see the wild wind's chosen playground. It roared around the room, scouring the fog from its path. It also had a merry time tearing paper towels loose from the dispenser, rattling stalls and sinks, whisking streamers of toilet paper over and under any obstacles. Below the level of the wind, I caught sight of Neil on his knees in a stall, holding onto the bowl for dear life.

I also saw paws. And hooves. And plump, bare feet that were blue as a Caribbean lagoon.

The smoke was gone; the wind that drove it away followed it into oblivion. I pushed myself up from the floor cautiously, taking in the bent, furry, scaled, and just plain hairy legs that accompanied each pair of those extraordinary feet, then the attached bodies, and last of all, the tooth-baring circle of seven heads. Each one was a visual essay on the topic *What Hideous Means To Me*.

"Greetings," said the owner of the blue feet. He was also that well-spoken mathematical genius who could count to three. Brains aren't everything. Although he was the shortest of the seven horrors facing us, he managed to pack more pure ugliness into less space than any of his comrades. Bulging white eyes rolled in a puff-cheeked face shiny as a brand new Cadillac's flank. Below a smear of tufty-nostrilled nose a pair of tusks protruded upwards. Once they might have been white, but now they were streaked brown and yellow. When he extended his flabby hand to me in greeting, I saw fingernails five inches long crusted under with three-inch layers of smut.

My stomach gave a little jolt, but held its ground. I'd bolted from Neil's home that morning with no breakfast, and the creature didn't look bad enough to make me toss up pure bile.

"Greetings, yourself. Who are you?" I asked.

"I?" The blue monster bubbled with amusement, his paunch quaking. "I am your very humble servant Shiko, *oni* second-class in the legions of Yomi-tsu-kuni." His black lower lip curled away to show off a ridge of razor-sharp teeth no less impressive than the tusks guarding them. "And these are my honorable associates: Gwimcur, Skeffins, Doggo, Ving, Stalker-of-Deadmen, Luthenard, and—Now, where has the *ugly* one gotten to? Ah, well, it is of little moment. Whom do I have the esteemed pleasure of meeting, before lunch?"

He said "lunch" in a dreadfully personal way. I decided it was a good time to drag Neil into the conversation. I had to do it literally. He was still very much attached to the toilet, but I was able to haul him to his feet and prop him up until his legs got their bones back.

"I'm Neil Fitzsimmons," I said. "A very *close, personal friend* of Tim, here. You all know Tim?" I waited for them to express their respect and gratitude toward the person responsible for their smooth reentry into the waking world.

Gwimcur made a long, futtering sound with lips that would leave Mick Jagger feeling underendowed. The others chimed in with their own versions of the Bronx Cheer from Hell.

"What, palsy with old cream-face?" Doggo was as good as his name and lifted a furry hind leg against the bathroom wall, the better to relieve his feelings. Then he barked with laughter.

"*How* close a friend d'you be?" Skeffins inquired nastily. "Little o' this 'n' that, is it?" He sidled along until he was pressed against my leg and turned up large, melting eyes the color of moldy strawberries. "Be wantin' y'self a third partner for't, darlin'?" His offer was immediately hooted down by the others, who reminded the amorous Skeffins that it was not good manners to play with one's food.

Shiko took charge, nabbing Skeffins by one of his drooping ear lobes. Jabbering indignantly in a foreign tongue, the oni dragged the unlucky monster toward the door. The language sounded like Japanese to me, but a true leader's wrath communicates across more barriers than that. Skeffins appeared to understand he'd committed a faux pas, and earnestly begged Shiko's pardon.

"Accepted," the oni snapped. "But for your penance, you may only partake of leftovers."

"You can't mean you're going to eat us!" I hollered.

"Let 'em." Neil leaned heavily against me. "If I'm dead, I don't gotta smell 'em."

"This is a joke, right?" I searched one pair of alien eyes after another and saw no such luck. What I did see was that all seven of them were a solid wall between us and the door. "You're kidding. This is *Timothy Desmond*. You know, the guy who's been showing you the ropes, putting you wise, letting you know the score—"

"It is as you say." Shiko inclined his bulbous blue head with its twin knobby horns. "There has been much showing of ropes, putting wise, and knowledge of scoring. What there has not been is feeding." He took a step forward and his pals did the same.

I took one backwards and yanked Neil with me. "If you eat Tim, Baba Yaga's not going to like it," I cautioned.

"The frustration of desire is the proof of desire's vanity," the oni instructed me. "If my humble act of devouring this honorable person will be the unworthy instrument to set Baba Yaga upon the Eightfold Path, I will be quietly grateful."

He came closer. Pencil-thin ribbons of smoke were beginning to trickle from his ears and nose. His associates were also starting to steam up anew. The more excited they became, the thicker the funk emanating from their various orifices. Neil got a lungful of these fresh exhalations and launched himself back to the sanctuary of the toilet bowl.

Now we know where the smoke came from, I thought. As I positioned myself between Neil and the little monsters, I wished for something—anything—with which to defend us. From the corner of my eye, I saw a round wooden handle sticking up near the back of the toilet. There might be dumber weapons to use than a plumber's helper, but when you're making your last stand in the boys' room at Glenwood High, you don't expect to find Excalibur poking out of the john.

I made a grab for the plunger, swung it around and snarled, "*En garde*, you pack of apprentice plagues!" Then I whonged Shiko straight in the face with the red rubber tip. It was a perfect fit. The oni's furious scream was smothered by the plunger, and not all the clawing in the world would break the suction.

Emitting tiny, shrill sounds like a teakettle with diaper rash, he tumbled away, swinging his head wildly from side to side. He took out Skeffins and Doggo on the outgoing swipe and clobbered Ving, Luthenard, and Gwimcur on the return stroke. The plunger handle sounded a nice, resonating note on impact with goblin skulls. You could almost hear tiny cartoon birdies going cheep-cheep-cheep around their heads.

The first three bugbears so served collapsed senseless on the floor, but Luthenard and Gwimcur were only stunned. Stunned and angry. They leaped for Shiko, maws gaping. Luthenard looked like something cats hawk up on good rugs, only with a set of teeth and claws straight out of the best cutlery catalogues. He also had a saliva-control problem. This was too bad for Gwimcur, whose death-dealing leap takeoff was right in the middle of a big puddle of drool. This is not the best traction, especially on bathroom tile, and the unlucky beast's battle-roar skirled up into a shriek as he went sailing across the floor, face-first into one of the sinks. His nostrils sort of wrapped themselves around the Hot and Cold faucets and there he hung, counting stars. Luthenard laughed so hard, he didn't duck in time as the still-blinded Shiko scored a homerun off the base of his skull with the plunger and retired the side.

Stalker-of-Deadmen put a stop to this by seizing the handle and pulling on it with all his might. Alas for Shiko, this entailed his friend's placing both taloned feet on the oni's shoulders to get leverage. Stalker-of-Deadmen had very long, very keen talons, and when he pulled in one direction, they sank deeper in the opposite one. Black blood puddled up and slid down the oni's chest.

Shiko's scream this time was loud enough to be heard through the plunger. His groping hands clamped around Stalker-of-Deadmen's wrists and tore the creature's paws from the plunger handle. Still yowling, the blue oni swung his buddy three times around his head before letting go. I hit the tiles just in time to miss being clipped by the flying horror. It was a good thing that Neil had recovered enough to crawl away from the toilet. Stalker-of-Deadmen smashed against the back of the stall and ended his flight rump-up in the bowl, where he subsided into a series of peaceful gurglings.

As for Shiko, he ran around in diminishing circles, jerking futilely at the plunger, until at last his efforts were rewarded with a reverberating POP and he was free.

He had exactly time enough to stare at his devastated companions and bellow the Japanese equivalent of "What in the name of Louisa May Alcott happened to—?" when a chunk of plaster as big as the *Oxford Unabridged Dictionary* plummeted from the ceiling and reduced him to a squat blue accordion.

Neil and I looked up.

Eleziane looked down.

"Hi," she said. "I'm the ugly one."

18

Teamslay

"IT'S REALLY A very simple rule to remember," Eleziane said as we walked back to the soccer field. "Roses are red, violets are blue, don't mess with goblins and they won't eat you." She paused, then tacked on the codicil: "As long as you also never eat oysters in months with no *R*."

"You just left them lying there," Neil said. He'd been casting short jumpy glances over his shoulder every four steps ever since we'd closed the boys' room door behind us. His nose twitched, constantly sifting the air for evidence that the seven smelly horrors might be following. "I mean, shouldn't we have tied them up or something?"

"Their friends would only find them and untie them," the Faerie princess replied. "To defeat one of the Unseely in a fair fight is honorable, but to attempt to remove him from combat permanently, while he is helpless, brings down the wrath of all his breed upon you. They're nasty, but they stick together."

"Sounds like what my old man usedta say about unions." Neil jerked his head too sharply and wrenched his neck. "Ow! Damn. So you guarantee we're safe from them?"

"As safe as you choose to be." Eleziane did not smile. We had to slow down a lot for her to keep up with us. "I've been among them since we parted. They have learned much about your world, and knowledge breeds confidence. Many of them have said in open council that they no longer need your services, nor T'ing's. You are fortunate that the few dissenting voices belong to monsters with enough status and clout to protect you . . . for the time being."

I patted Eleziane's shoulder. "Thanks a lot for looking out for us. It's a good thing we've got you to keep an eye on them."

The face she turned to me was cold and expressionless, yet I'll never forget how it stabbed me with guilt. "Where else could I go but among monsters?" she said. "No one else wanted me."

Neil and I stumbled over each other trying to tell her that it had been a mistake, an oversight, a reasonable error. Neil thought she'd come with me or go with T'ing; T'ing and I expected her to do the inverse. All of us believed that a princess of the Fey had somewhere of her own to go, somewhere more worthy of her royalty and power than the humble homes of mere mortals.

Her laugh sounded like a smoker's cough. "And where did you expect me to go, if not with you? Home to my father? Into the invisible palaces of the air? There are none. Tell me truthfully, now: Did you really think that any shelter you might offer to share with me was unsuited to my high rank? Or did you really not care where I went, so long as I took my ugliness anywhere you didn't have to see it?"

Neil and I were silent.

Eleziane tucked a greasy strand of hair behind her ear and showed us a cardboard grin. "Did I offend you? I'm so sorry. Sometimes we of the Seely Court are grievously afflicted with the compulsion to tell the unvarnished truth. Daddy used to tell me tales of the Old Country, when one of his bigwig cousins got her paws on a tuppenny poetaster who called himself Thomas the Rhymer. He was *such* a pretentious bore, even for one of those artsy-smartsy mortals, that Cousin Ysout shipped him back to his own kind saddled with the obligation to be eternally honest." She smirked. "He didn't last long."

"Eleziane, we didn't think that—"

"Oh, forget it, Tim. Done is done." Her beautiful eyes were dry and bright. "As you said, this way I can be of use to you, playing the spy."

"They don't suspect?" Neil asked.

"Not a thing. Nor will they. No one saw me flatten Shiko but you two."

"He might put two and two together, though." I was concerned. "He did wonder where you'd gotten to."

"Don't worry. Being able to count and being able to add

things up aren't the same. If he asks me where I was, I just say 'karma' and look resigned. Shuts him up every time.''

"I don't know," I said. "I'm having misgivings about you staying among them. What if they do wise up and find out who you really are? You shouldn't take the risk for us." *Especially since we didn't give you a second thought,* I added for no other ears but mine.

Eleziane had no such qualms. "You'd better keep me as your eyes and ears among the Unseely. It's an advantage you'll be glad of soon enough. Wouldn't you like to have some advance warning on the day that *all* the monsters decide you're no longer indispensable?"

"Aw, I don't believe it," Neil said. "You get a look at how many of those horrors are on the waiting list to learn how to get on in the outer world? They need what we know and they'll keep on needing it for months, yet; years!"

"Will they?" Eleziane's shaggy brows lifted. "Knowledge spreads in funny ways. You and T'ing have been introducing a few dozen monsters into the school by degrees—"

"A *few dozen*?" I wailed.

"—but the creatures have been coming home nights and passing on what they've learned to those waiting. You can't imagine how many of their ranks have infiltrated Glenwood High without asking your leave. They're ambitious, I grant them that, and the way things are, they have every need to hurry themselves along."

"What do you mean, 'the way things are'?" I asked.

The lady of the Fey was enigmatic. "That's a question for the Three. You'll find them keeping the dragons company down below, but it's not a question whose answer you need to know right away. In fact, if I were you, I'd be in no rush to meet the Three. Not until you're back in your own skin, anyway. They're sensitive, and they take violent exception to what they view as people trying to buck the system. Don't ask me to tell you any more—" She put up her hand, second-guessing me neatly. "I won't."

We crossed the street without further conversation and found the soccer match in lively session. The only vacant seats on the Glenwood-side bleachers were too high up for Eleziane to climb, so we crept into places on the Desiderius side, doing our best to ignore the poisonous looks we were getting and the muted clicks behind us as our sportsmanlike rivals fiddled with whatever hardware they'd brought to boost their alma mater on to victory.

"Just watch the game and don't act scared," Neil whispered. "They can smell fear."

That being the case, I gave them a snootful. It wasn't that I expected one of the goons behind me to start practicing amateur switchblade neurosurgery on any of my exposed vertebrae; it was the spectacle on the soccer field that had me sweating ice.

When you're confronted with disaster, your senses get picky. They refuse to take in the whole picture at once for fear of burning out every Real World Impossibility filtering-cell in your brain simultaneously. Bit by bit, my eyes gently broke the news to me that this was not soccer; this was insanity with matching uniforms.

The first figure I focused on was the referee. The poor man was jumping up and down in place, blasting his whistle, hands clutching his thick clumps of green hair. Then I saw that his hair wasn't green—someone had simply picked up a pie-shaped clod of turf and slapped it down on the ref's head.

While I was debating the possible ways and reasons for someone performing a horticultural hair-transplant, I was privileged to see the whole process in instant replay. The ball came downfield, past the sidelined ref, a panic-stricken Desiderius player in possession. Hot after him came one of the tusk-faced ogres, waving a bench overhead and booming, "FEE, FI, FO, FUM, GIMME THE BALL, YOU SNOT-NOSED SCUM!"

Every stride the monster took sent huge divots flying up from the field to shower the spectators. I got a grassy hunk in my lap and the ref got a second helping of sod right on top of the first. He knocked both of them off, took the whistle from his mouth, and bawled, "Assault with team equipment is strictly against the rules for North American soccer! *Put down that bench, dammit!*"

That was where Coach came in. His sweatsuit was liberally splattered with dollops of soil, but his granite-hewn game-face made it seem like standard procedure for all official personnel to wear portions of the playing field. All he did was cup his hands to his mouth and shout, "You heard him, Danforth. Drop the bench or you're out of the game!"

The ogre harkened to Coach's orders and threw on the brakes, casting up a yard-high mound of dirt in front of him.

Growling and snorting, he tromped to the sidelines and dropped the bench, as ordered. For extra credit, he dropped it on top of the Desiderius High second-string team. The Glenwood cheerleaders went wild.

Ah, the cheerleaders. They were lined up to do their famous pyramid formation, only Kirsten wasn't there. I scanned the stands and didn't see her. Then my eye fell to the Gargoyles' team bench and there she was, sitting on Goliath's knee, clinging to him like a lovestruck lamprey.

"Whaddaya wanna bet he's telling her that size isn't everything?" Neil snickered in my ear.

"Hey, she's not even in uniform!" I was genuinely shocked. Kirsten never missed the opportunity to flaunt her perfect body and stunning face. Mr. Richard Izanagi, the most feared guidance counselor Glenwood had to offer, was once compelled to convince her that most colleges prefer you to write about more conventional Future Ambitions on their application forms than homecoming queen, MTV video jockette, and Princess Di's Worst Nightmare. "What gives?"

I got my answer as the pyramid neared completion. It only wanted one girl to climb the summit and egg on the Gargoyles to clobber the foe. Jennifer and Tiffany took their usual positions to either side of the structure, making no move to usurp Kirsten's place of honor. Was the pep squad pyramid changing its style from Egyptian to Mayan?

Not so. Not one, but *three* uniformed figures came bounding out from behind the bleachers, pom-poms jouncing. All of them had the same long, silky blond hair that was Kirsten's trademark, and bodies that could infuse school spirit into a dead man.

Their faces, though . . .

"Jesus Christ, how many years did *they* get left back?" Neil gasped.

Old? Fossilized. Wrinkles and bags and skin like ride-toughened saddle leather. Chins and noses, eyes and cheekbones, were flinty enough to supply a whole chain of Stone Age K-Marts. The gap of years between their ancient faces and their youthful bodies was an abyss of ages.

No one who saw them seemed to notice anything odd about blond cheerleading nymphs with the faces of hags, except us. Our classmates in the stands cheered mightily for them. I have to admit, they did have some spectacular moves. Splits and jumps, somersaults and cartwheels, they went through all of them like they were flying.

Then they *were* flying. Clay-colored batwings poked out the backs of their letter sweaters. One by one, they rose into the air. The first one up took Kirsten's place of honor at the pyramid's apex. From there she wigwagged her pom-poms like an airfield worker flagging planes. Taking their signal from her, her sisters tore off into the wild blue in close formation. The higher they got, the harsher their voices sounded, until it was like listening to the croaks and caws of scavenger birds.

"Oh, no," Neil said. "Not them. I told them they couldn't come out until they were housebroken. They *promised*—"

"Who are they?" I demanded, shaking him by the arm. "*What* are they?"

"Harpies."

"Oh, sh—!"

I didn't need to say it. From the heights of the sky we heard the hag-faced birdwomen chanting. "Glenwood High don't play no games! Kick some butt and then take names!" Then they swooped down over the Desiderius fans.

Harpies: If you teed off the Greek gods, they sicced a pack of these critters on you. I read about one mythological guy, Phineas, who shot off his mouth once too often to the Olympians. As a result, he was never able to get a square meal again. As soon as the food was on the table, the harpies zoomed in and destroyed almost everything. What they couldn't devour they—This is sort of gross—Did you ever get trapped in the same room with an uncaged parakeet who thinks your head looks *just* like a sheet of old newspaper? Now multiply the parakeet's body-size about a hundred times and you know what one harpy can do to your dinner table, to say nothing of your appetite.

"Dive! Dive!" I shouted, dragging Eleziane and Neil from their seats as the harpies came tearing out of the sky. We moved fast, getting under the bleachers just in time. From our shelter we could hear the sounds of the first bombardment, and the shrieks of the pelted Desiderius students. The risers echoed with the thunder of escaping feet. Several soda cans rolled through, and a lot of empty junk-food wrappers, and some miscellaneous personal effects, but for the most part we were untouched. Overhead we heard the rhythmic impact of the harpies' strafing runs. Then, silence; stench and silence.

I peered out through the slats. The soccer field was empty of everyone except our team. The Glenwood fans were jumping up and down with glee. The ref was in heated confab with the Desiderius coach, who looked like a lobster that'd been tossed into Mount St. Helens. Our coach stood a little apart, looking smug. The clock was still running, but I had a feeling that so was the Desiderius team. The game was a forfeit, pure and simple, favor us.

Neil picked up a crumpled Desiderius High banner that had been shoved through the risers in the panic. Looking very solemn and philosophical, he said, "Talk about the shit hitting the fan."

I punched him in the arm. Very hard.

19

After the Ball Game's Over

THE VICTORY PARTY was the most glorious, giddiest, goofiest bash in the history of Glenwood High. No one could recall the last time the Gargoyles had downed the Desiderius Demons, and certainly not by a forfeit.

"Not even any shakedowns at the Porta-Potties!" Neil exulted, standing on his chair at the Napoli Pizzarama. "Another first! Yow!"

He did an end-zone shimmy, banging his shins against the edge of the table and spilling a whole glass of Coke into Yang's lap. The Mongol stood up, letting both the empty glass and Crazy Nadine Dunlop roll to the floor. Nadine giggled and went to find a dry lap, much to Yang's chagrin.

"Come back! We were going to have more pizza!"

"What, no sex?" Eleziane remarked dryly, playing cat's cradle with the strands of melted cheese caught in her braces.

"No sex," Yang said staunchly. "Not with that one."

"Because of her age? Yang, can it be that after all these centuries you're finally learning discretion?"

"Bugger discretion. I want one of *them*."

He jabbed a thumb at the table where our preppy pom-pom princesses were playing You-Be-The-Wall-I'll-Be-The-Wallpaper with the soccer team. Our former star forward, Glendon Essex, was the only morose face at the feast. He and Kirsten had been an item, once. Now she only had eyes—and whatever else went with them—for Goliath. Glendon didn't look like he had much of an appetite, which was just as well. The harpies had taken a shine to him and gobbled up every slice of 'za he touched before a nibble could reach his mouth. Old habits die hard. I just hoped he ran out of slices before they ran out of room. I remembered what they did to Phineas' food when they'd eaten as much of it as they could hold.

Neil observed the team table, then snorted. "One of them? The pom-poms of passion? You think you can get 'em to notice you, Yang, you're all wet."

"I know this," Yang countered loudly. "And whose fault is that, Sputum of a Gelded Water Buffalo?" His hands swept over the sticky stains on his rawhide trousers. "I need something to wipe this off with. I think I will use the hair of your severed head. Not very absorbent, but tough enough for the really big household tasks."

"Revered Grandfather, do me a favor and try using this." T'ing passed her honored ancestor the paper-napkin dispenser, but he misunderstood her purpose and heaved it at Neil's head. I was glad Neil had good reflexes, or it would've been my skull that got dented. I attempted to explain this to Yang, who was looking for another napkin dispenser.

"Don't be stupid," he snapped. "I'm not going to kill you; just him."

"He is me. The outside of me, anyway, and I'd rather get it back in the same condition I gave it to him."

Yang's nostrils flared, the more energetic hairs within fanning like a peacock's tail. "Good luck on that one."

"What do you mean?"

T'ing's ancestral spirit winked at me. When Yang, Contractor of Ten Thousand Social Diseases and Inventor of Fifty-three More, gave a dirty-minded wink, there was no mistaking it. One twitch of his eyelid carried more prurient content than a lifetime subscription to *Playboy*.

"He didn't," I said.

Yang winked again, dirtier.

"Aw, *no*. That's not fair. I mean, if he—if I'm not a—if the minotaur finds out that—if he really went and—with *my* body, and I wasn't even there to enjoy it? Does that *count*? Hey, Neil!"

Before I could ask Neil just what he'd been doing with bodies that did not belong to him, Billy Klauser hailed him from one table over. This was another historic first, since old "No Neck" hadn't said two nonlife-threatening words to me since I stuck a gerbil in his lunchbox back in kindergarten. "Yo,

Desmond, nice move with the pants! Maybe you're not such a dork after all.''

I grabbed Neil by the waistband as he made a gracious bow of acknowledgment in Billy's direction. "Whose pants?" I queried, forcing him back into his seat.

He shrugged modestly. "Oh, no big deal. Remember when the game was just over and I said I hadda go to the can, only there's someone in the Porta-Potty so I go back into the school? Well, I catch sight of Doc Ox in the next stall over—ain't nobody wears shoes like that but him—and he's got his pants down around his ankles and . . ." He teased the end of the sentence into silence.

"And what? *What?*" I demanded.

"What's with you, Fitzsimmons?" Billy shouted. "Too unpatriotic to give a look up the school flagpole?"

My jaw dropped. "You didn't."

"It wasn't easy," Neil admitted. "Hell to yank 'em off over those clunky wingtips he wears, and him hollering and kicking and carrying on, but I had a little help." He gave a chummy wave to the team table. Goliath sent him a thumbs-up back.

I would have put my head down on the table, only I don't like mozzarella in my ears. "I'm dead. If he got a look at you, I am cold meat. Did he?"

Neil shrugged. "Just a little one when I was out by the flagpole. You know how hard you gotta pull to get something all the way to the top of that thing?"

Mozzarella or no, my head sank. "I might as well stay in this body for the rest of my life."

"Try it," Neil challenged. "When it's time to get the hell out of my skin, I want you to *get*."

Strange to say this, but when Neil took his tough-guy stance I lifted my eyes and looked at him—I mean *really* looked—and saw what a ludicrous picture my outer self made when delivering an ultimatum. My face and body were no more intended to put the fear of God into a foe than a chipmunk was meant to tote an Uzi. They say it's the mark of maturity to be able to laugh at yourself, but I bet they never expected anyone to apply that dictum like this. Through my laughter I watched Neil's face go first red, then white, then mottled with rage, and still I roared on.

I stopped laughing when a cold, heavy hand slammed down on my shoulder. Icy fingers punched through my denim jacket

as easily as if it were made of wet tissue. Five points of un-
believable cold seared my flesh. My shoulder was nearly
wrenched from its socket as I was lifted from my seat and
made to turn around.

"What is the matter, Fitzsimmons? Yew have no school
spirit, *ja*?" The accent was that lilting singsong people associate with first generation Scandinavian-Americans and the
Swedish Chef from the old *Muppet Show*. The hand was the
frost-giant's.

The voice was Dr. Oxenstierna's.

"Put him down, Sweyn," our principal directed. The giant
obeyed. I gawked like a gaffed carp, even if that did mean I
ran the risk of being converted to *lutefisk* by the Norse monster.
It wasn't enough that Doc Ox was standing there talking like
a refugee from the cast of *I Remember Mama*: He was standing
there with no trousers.

"Yoost what are yew staring at, Fitzsimmons?" His frosty
brows rose as a meager smile chilled his lips.

"Um, nothing, sir." I lied like a rug. How often do you get
to see your high school principal wearing a pair of neon pink
and green surfer baggies? And they went so well with his
starched white Oxford shirt, blue tie, and gray tweed jacket.
The frost-giant behind him was wearing an identical outfit,
plus a glaring yellow cap worn back-to-front that proclaimed
him to be a Rad Dude.

"Stare at it somewhere else, then," he said crisply. Turning
his back to me, he faced Neil. "Mr. Desmond, yew are to be
congratyewlated on a remarkable and unexpected show of cre-
ativity in the yewtilization of my personal wardrobe to bolster
student morale. I commend yew. Might I trouble yew to give
me five?"

Everyone in sight had their minds efficiently boggled as they
witnessed Doc Ox put Neil's hand through the contortions of
a power handshake culminating in a whipcrack-loud high five.
Fist clenched, he entreated us to "Party hardy, dewdes," and
walked away straightening the knot in his tie. Sweyn remained,
grinning.

"What did you do to him?" Neil barked.

"Got the man to chill out." Sweyn's teeth were a nasty
double row of icicles. "It didn't take much. A touch to freeze
those portions of his brain which store all stodginess, pedantry,
pompousness, and Ingmar Bergman movies was all."

"And who told you to try something like that?"

"Not you, little master." The icicles tinkled against each other. "I did not wish to trouble you with such a minor undertaking."

"Well, you should've asked."

"Oh, I know, I know!" If Neil couldn't see that the frost-giant was making fun of him, I could. The monster's obsequious manner was a sham, and he didn't care who saw through it. "But since you were so busy with your own project involving Dr. Oxenstierna, how could I have obtained your approval?"

"Okay, but next time—"

"Next time you will be too busy, too." Deliberate malevolence twinkled in the frost-giant's eyes.

Finally Neil caught on. "Hold it right there. As long as you're in my charge, you're not going to start acting up unless I tell you it's all right." He waved a finger at the frost-giant.

Bad maneuver. Sweyn breathed on it and it turned pale blue from the nail to the second joint. Neil jerked it out of range quickly, but I didn't resume normal breathing until I saw the natural color return to my borrowed flesh. If this was how fast and loose he played with my body, it was past time we reversed the swap.

Sweyn went back to his table, where he and his big buddies had a healthy guffaw at Neil's expense. "Yarrr, big boss don't like what ol' Sweyn does to Doc Ox?" one of the ogres taunted. "Awwww, ain't that just too farkin' bad!" He pulled out his lower lip about a yard and dumped his soda into the resulting trough—ice, paper cup, and all.

His pal, the ogre whom Coach had addressed as Danforth, made a tiny mew of revulsion. "Heavens above, Kirkwood, your manners! Were you brought up in a barn?"

"Narrrr. Under a gallows, I was, get of a hanged man's seed." Kirkwood's bare, hairy belly heaved with a five-megaton belch. "Not too bad a breedin', do I say so myself, but precious hell to know where to send a card come Father's Day." He shoveled up another slice of pizza and got most of it into the proper facial opening.

Danforth made clucking sounds through pursed lips. With many an "I do beg your pardon," he extricated himself from his companions and delicately placed a spare chair at our table. As he straddled it backwards, his goatskin loincloth rode up enough for me to see the pristine white tennis shorts he wore beneath.

"*Do* say you forgive Kirkwood his little foibles, my dear, *dear* Desmond," he gushed. Was *this* the monster who had literally benched the Desiderius High second-stringers?

"If you don't, I shall have to grind your bones to make my bread, and I do so hate kitchen drudgery." I guess it was.

Neil was not behindhand in assuring Danforth of his immediate and absolute forgiveness for all Kirkwood's faux pas, past, present, and future.

"Oh, I am *so* glad to hear that. Kirkwood may not be the epitome of refinement, yet I do owe him a measure of solidarity. Ogrehood is powerful. Or it was until all these *foreigners* started pushing their way into the ranks." His clear blue eyes burned as he fixed his gaze on Sweyn, Goliath, and the cyclops, each of whom had at least two members of the cheerleading squad attached to their persons.

"Foreigners?" Neil was nonplused. "I thought you were all pretty much Americans by now. Couple of centuries in the Leeside, doesn't that kinda give you instant naturalization?"

"Or supernaturalization," I provided.

Danforth's distaste swerved from the carousing giants to favor us for a moment. "You sound just like that *dreadful* egalitarian witch person who gave us into your charge. *No* sense of a woman's proper place at all, and not a clue to where to shop. *She* would have us work together, for the greater glory of monsters, fiends, and nightmares everywhere. Together!" Scorn dripped from Danforth's lips. So did saliva. He flicked the latter away with a taloned pinky. "What *would* you expect from a sorceress of *her* background." He lowered his voice and whispered, "Russian. And you certainly know what *that* means!"

"Oooo." Neil nodded his head dutifully. "Commies."

"Dirty, filthy, godless Commies," I added. "Women's libber commies," I appended for good measure.

"EXACTLY!" Danforth's fist drove our table into the floor as if it had been a thumbtack. T'ing and Eleziane screamed, and Yang bared steel. All of us scarcely escaped with our knees intact.

"Watch where you wreck, Face of a Monkey Fart!" The Mongol's sword glittered under Danforth's thickly beringed nose. "Another dog-brained stunt like that and I slice off enough of your lard to build you a little brother."

"Hmm." Danforth looked down his nose at Yang and Yang's sword. "Aren't *some* people bitchy."

"I don't know," the Mongol admitted. "Are they?"

The ogre's hand shot out and closed around Yang's windpipe. All of us were treated to the sight of the redoubtable Mongol warrior disarmed, kicking helplessly in midair. He tried to dematerialize, but Danforth made a slight adjustment to his grip and Yang's wavering outline solidified.

"Ah, ah, ah. I won't *hear* of you going," the ogre said. Coyness didn't suit him. "Not until we clear up a few teensy details. You are ugly, creature, but you are hardly in *our* league. You're one of those tacky little domestic spirits, aren't you?" Through purpling lips, Yang affirmed this. "Well! Just because good domestics are *so* hard to find doesn't give you *carte blanche* to attempt to bullyrag *moi*. Too *arriviste* for words. You won't do that again, will you, dear boy?"

Yang gagged out his unqualified refusal to even think of doing that again. Still the monster kept him dangling.

This proved to be too much for T'ing. "Let him down, you creep!" She found the napkin holder that had missed Neil's head and lobbed it at Danforth's. Her aim was a hundred per cent better than her honored ancestor's. The loaded dispenser made a sound like a large gong being dropped onto a large cement block and got the ogre's attention.

"Young woman, this is a *private* conversation."

"Listen to me, you affected twit, I remember you. I was the one who sneaked you into Ms. Alexinski's Modern American Fiction class."

"*Just* when she was starting the unit on John Cheever." Danforth sighed in bliss at the memory. "Did I tell you it looks like I'll get extra credit for my paper on the novels of Gore Vidal?"

"When I brought you out of Tim's locker, you didn't know the novels of Gore Vidal from *toilet* paper, and now you're messing with my revered ancestor? After everything I've done for you?" She cast about for more missiles, but all she could find was the empty pizza pan. She prepared to use it in the style of an oversized *shuriken*, one of those nasty, sharp metal throwing stars no good *ninja* would be without.

Danforth dropped Yang, but only so that he could pluck the

pan from T'ing's hands and pinch it into a solid aluminum bow tie which he clipped to the front of his letter sweater. He patted her on the head with one huge finger the way he might patronize an endearing infant.

"That was then, darling." He blew her a kiss. "This is now. None of us need any of you anymore. Oh, there may be one or two old stick-in-the-muds who claim there's a trick or two you've yet to teach us about this outer world. Poppycock. Which was *just* the way we worded the consensus report we sent along to Baba Yaga. The old bag may be redder than borscht, but even Commies see the sense in cutting the deadwood from the payroll. You might as well face it, loves"—he tugged at his new tie until the metal groaned—"we're through with you." He went back to the team table, where Tiffany and Megan told him that aluminum was definitely his color.

20

The Coldest Cut of All

I SAT DOWN in the midst of our demolished table and covered my head with my arms. T'ing's comforting presence by my side only made me curl up into a tighter ball. Her efforts to make me face her were useless, though she did get enough of a look at me to tell the others, "He's crying."

They all gathered around, speaking in hushed tones, while the Glenwood High victory bash went on without them. The only voice I missed hearing was Eleziane's. *Of course she'll steer clear,* I thought without rancor. *It won't help her masquerade as one of the Unseely if she shows any interest or sympathy for an afflicted mortal.* I wished the rest of them would take a cue from her. I wanted to be left alone.

"Go away," I mumbled.

"What?" Yang seized me by the hair and yanked my head up. "You say something?" His nose smacked mine as he stared at the tears streaking my face. "Son of a splay-legged bitch, he *is* crying! Hey! You stop that. I'm all right, see? You don't need to cry."

"I'm not crying about you."

"No? Why not? I'm worth it."

"I'm crying about my mother."

My reason for tears made Yang stop and think. The smell of burning yak-chips was unmistakable. "Why you crying for her? She's all right, too. A little cursed with the sleep of a thousand years, but the witch will take care of that once we do what she wants."

"And how are we going to do that now? You don't see, do

you?'' I flung my hand at the giants, who were paying us no further mind. "You heard what the ogre said: They don't need us! They've told the witch so! Why should she release my mother from her curse? We've got nothing left to buy her waking with. The monsters can fend for themselves." I tucked my head back down. "Baba Yaga will leave Mom enspelled forever because I failed her. I'll never again be able to tell her I love her."

I stayed like that for a while, nothing but my own sobs filling my ears. T'ing's gentle touch withdrew and still I cried. I was tired and all hope was gone. Only once I paused, took a breath, and tried to summon my sword. Nothing happened, except that instead of my thoughts pulling the weapon to my hand, my hand felt as if the sword were calling to it from behind a wall of magic it could not pierce. The phantom of Baba Yaga's laughter jangled in my ears until I drowned out the gloating sound of it with sobs.

My misery wrapped me so completely that I don't know how long it was before I realized that I wasn't the only one crying. The sobs were deeper than mine, and louder, more like a behemoth with the dry heaves than a human noise. I should've known right then who was doing it, but I had to look up anyway because sometimes theory is not enough.

I looked. I saw. I was right, but I still couldn't believe it.

"Yang?"

What a sight. The Mongol's moustaches dripped like pine branches in a tempest, his thick lips bobbling madly with every sob. He stopped his blubbering only long enough to wail, "*I* had a mother too, y'know!"

Fresh waterworks surged from his eyes as if he had taps instead of tear ducts. I forgot my own sorrow as I watched the sluice gates open before the flow. Neil performed a little experiment, holding an empty soda glass under the Mongol's left eye; ten seconds later, the glass was full.

"Look at this!" T'ing lifted her sodden sneakers from the puddled floor one at a time and regarded them with disgust. "Honored Grandfather, quit it!"

"I can't!" Yang blubbed. "You never knew my mother. What a woman! Jadwiga the Implacable, they called her. She was a Russian princess before my noble father, Joti, carried her off; that's the way the bard told it who lived to collect his commission from her, anyhow. She gave Father seventeen sons, four daughters, and a knife in the ribs—Well, she *told* him she had a headache!—then she founded her own squadron of raiders, with the blessings of our local khan.'' The tears abated slightly as Yang gave himself over to dewy-eyed nostalgia. ''I can still remember the day she came up with her recruitment motto: 'Join the Cerise Horde and see the world! Then burn it.' And now she's gone, and I'll never see her again, and I'll never get the chance to tell her—to tell her that—''

T'ing hugged him. ''That you loved her?''

''Nahhhh. That I finally found the way to make a man swallow his own nose while it's still attached to his face. No one appreciated technological advances like my mother.'' Yang's filial grief redoubled in a genuine cataract of weeping.

''We've got to stop him,'' I said, watching the pool of tears at our feet go snaking across the floor and out the door of the Pizzarama.

''No we don't.'' Eleziane was at my ear, her voice low and urgent. ''Let him cry. Make him cry more, if you can. His tears may be our salvation. With them, he is the pathfinder we need.''

''Pathfinder? What path? Where to? What are you talking about?''

''Hush. This idea just came to me, and it's a hope for us. Have we any other? Just do as I say,'' the lady of the Fey insisted. ''I'm going ahead. Let him weep at least five minutes longer, then follow. Five minutes, mind! And don't watch me when I go; they mustn't see us leave together.'' She trotted out as fast as her size allowed, her eyes fixed on the fast-flowing streamlet of tears.

''What do you think she's up to?'' I asked Neil. ''I mean, should we do like she says, or is she just nuts?''

''Nuts or not, can we afford to ignore her?'' he countered. ''You heard it yourself, the monsters are breaking free. They say they don't need us for anything, but how much longer before they decide they *do* need us—as one of the four basic food groups. If Eleziane's got a plan—any plan!—it's one more than we've come up with. I say we chance it. Besides, this Mongol wiener tried to brain me with the napkin dispenser and now someone tells me I should *make* him cry? Think there's any way I'm gonna pass this one up, think again, uh-huh, you betcha.''

So we waited. Neil spiced up the five minutes by reminding

Yang of how many times he'd neglected his poor old gray-haired pillaging mother, of the countless nights Jadwiga had waited up for her wandering boy in vain, in the dark, in the yurt, alone. "And did you call? Could you trouble yourself to spend one lousy quarter on the woman who gave you birth? Did you even *try* to let her know you were okay?"

"How could I?" Yang spread his hands.

"He's right, Neil," T'ing put in. "The nearest telephone was, oh, five, six centuries away."

"And who had change?" the Mongol sniveled.

"That's no excuse." Watching Neil's expression, I sure hoped I never looked that prissy when I was in my own skin. "*Some* sons dispatch messengers who whip their ponies into a bloody lather across the steppes so they drop down dead at the threshold of the yurt and—Yurts do have thresholds, don't they?"

"Right past the poles where we display the severed heads of our enemies and hang out the wet wash, yeah."

"Okay, fine. So *some* sons find a way to drop their mothers an occasional note that *doesn't* ask for money. I'll bet your sixteen brothers managed."

"I don't think so." Yang grew meditative. "I killed them all." Suddenly dry-eyed and on the defensive he snarled, "They started it!"

Before Neil could try priming the guilt-pump any further, I proclaimed the five minutes to be over. I did it for T'ing's sake. She was looking really queasy. Neil was *too* good, and I could almost see the specter of T'ing's adoptive mother, Mrs. Kaplan, hovering over his head saying, *Stand up straight. Make your bed. You want to wash your neck or are you planning on growing potatoes back there? Oh, you don't* have *to listen to me; I'm only your mother, what do I know? Just wait. When I'm dead you'll be sorry, only then it'll be too late. I hope you have children of your own some day.* No wonder the girl was writhing.

"Let's go." I pointed to the salt-water rivulet Yang's eyes had spawned. It was presently six inches wide and running strong, though it appeared to grow shallower the further we trailed it.

"How come we're doing this?" Yang wanted to know as we hustled down the block. The stream was becoming more ghostly, the rushing tears fading to little more than a damp stain on the sidewalk.

"Eleziane said to try it," I told him, jogging on. "Said you were our pathfinder, though I don't know what—"

"I can tell you now, Tim." Eleziane stepped out of a storefront to block our way. Beyond her, the tears were thinning to a dark trickle no broader than a pencil point. "What we're after is a path to the Leeside."

Judging by the way all the other people on the street moved away from us, they must've been seeing what looked like the start of a modest gang war. Yang alone, goaded to nail-spitting disbelief and waving his sword to the four points of the compass, could pass for an entire battalion of street-scum.

"Calm down, calm down," Eleziane commanded, her royal bearing coming through in spite of her ungainly new body.

"Calm down my left nut and all his cousins!" Yang squawked. "You're crazier than Kipchak-kissing a bear with the toothache. You *want* the Leeside?"

Neil and I leaned heavily on Yang's shoulders until he stopped spraying foam. "Even if she's got a sane reason for wanting to get back there, this doesn't jibe," I said. Leaving Neil and T'ing to monitor the Mongol's pressure-gauge, I turned to Eleziane. "Why all this with the tears? Getting *into* the Leeside's the easy part. You don't need directions, just a psychological evaluation."

"I don't want to get *into* the Leeside," she replied, making a big, insulting, unnecessary show of patience in the face of dumb questions. "I—*We*—have to find the spot in the Leeside barrier where things are getting *out*."

"Why?" T'ing asked. "So we can lock the barn door after the horses are out, gone for two years, turned into dog food? The damage is done; all the monsters are free."

"Not all." One look at Eleziane's solemn face and you knew that what she said would admit no argument. "You're strangers to the Leeside, compared to me. It's where I was born, where my mother was—" She choked on a word and left it unsaid. "What I mean is, you don't know how many terrors the Leeside holds. I've been among the Unseely, I've taken count, and I can tell you that these who're out now are only the frothing tip of the first great wave."

I shook at the Faerie princess' words. The clamoring crowd of unspeakable beasts in my locker had been too many for me,

and now she said there were more where they came from?
"How many more are there? Where are they?"

"Waiting." Eleziane was grim. "I *hope* waiting in the Leeside, for word from their bolder brethren of how things are on
the Outside. Monsters are basically cowards and bullies. They
like to know beforehand that they're going into a guaranteed
winning situation. As soon as they receive the slightest encouragement, they'll be along, and the hole in the great barrier
is their point of exit from the Leeside. That's why we have to
find it and stop it up now, before the rest of them break
through."

"Also to make sure the monsters we've already got don't
get out again," T'ing said.

"Again?"

"When we push them back into the Leeside." When she
put on a grin that wicked, I had no trouble accepting Yang the
Homicidal Overachiever as her direct blood ancestor.

"Nice theory," I said. "Got any practical ideas for seeing
it through?"

Still looking like a cross between a kitten and a piranha,
T'ing said, "First things first. It doesn't pay to shove them
back into a sack with a hole the size of Cleveland at the other
end."

"Right!" Neil seconded T'ing enthusiastically. *Too* enthusiastically for my taste. Yang's words earlier about Neil's un-
authorized use of my body had me concerned. It takes two to
play an R-rated game of spin-the-hormones. Just who had Neil
asked to join him?

First things first, as T'ing said. Jealousy had to get in line
behind higher priorities. While we debated, Yang's tears were
vanishing. Eleziane saw, and it threw her into a panic.

"*Please* come," Eleziane begged. "The Leeside's a greedy
place, never willing to let us go entirely. If we shed tears in
your world, they seek the Leeside level at last, and the only
way in for them is the hole. We must follow!"

The lady had a point, but I had a question. "What's the
rush? If we lose the trail, you could just cry some and we
follow that."

She glowered at me. "T'ing's ancestral spirit was mortal,
once. I am Fey. Tears—*true* tears—are the birthright of humans
alone." Without more being said, she flung herself back onto
the swiftly vanishing track.

"Hey! Who are you calling human?" Yang shouted, and took off after her, leaving the rest of us to sprint after him.

It wasn't that long a race, or Eleziane never would have preserved her lead. I saw her hang a sharp right and duck into an open doorway, Yang on her heels. I stopped short to check out the name over the door: Feidelstein's Kosher Delicatessen. Oh joy. I could hardly wait to see whether our entrance would get any kind of a rise out of the guy behind the counter. Last time I'd been in to pick up an order, it was like dealing with a tortoise on tranquilizers.

I bet Yang's tears go all the way through this place and out the back way, I thought. *If this is the spot where the monsters came out—and all the domestic sprites before them—you'd think that Old Stoneface would've noticed. Yeah, maybe even opened his eyes more than halfway, for a change. No way could the hole be in here.*

So I jogged blithely into Feidelstein's deli, T'ing and Neil behind me. As I we shoved open the glass door, I thought I saw a "Sorry, We're Closed!" sign out of the corner of my eye and what looked like a broken lock. My best friend, Larry Perlmutter, was an uninvited presence in my mind, a voice that reminded me, *You want a corned beef sandwich today? You crazy? It's Saturday, man. Feidelstein's is never open on the Sabbath.*

But the door *was* open. What can't be, won't be, right? We were well and truly inside the deli before I realized, in hindsight, that if Yang wanted to get *in* somewhere, *in* he'd get. A blade like his could crack a lock just fine. We were probably lucky the lock had given, or he'd have shattered the glass door itself. I glanced around the deli and saw no cold cuts in the display cases, no lights on, and all the chairs in the darkened dining room piled high atop the tables.

"Breaking and entering," I said aloud, and hit the brakes. T'ing and Neil rear-ended me.

"Say what?" Neil rubbed his nose.

"I said, there's no one here. The place is closed. Yang busted the lock, and if there's a silent alarm system, we'd better get the heck out before the cops come."

"No one's here, huh?" Neil jerked his thumb in the direction Yang and Eleziane had had to take, the only other door in the place. It was closed, and the fast-disappearing thread of the Mongol's tears slipped away under it. Closed or not, the sound of many voices raised in anger on the other side was perfectly audible. " 'No one's' being pretty damn loud." As if to emphasize Neil's observation, a heavy object smashed against the shut door. I could almost see the wood bulging under impact.

"Oh, Lord, what's he broken now?" T'ing dashed past us and flung open the door, crying, "Revered Grandfather, whatever you've got, you put it down right this minute!" She was over the threshold before we could stop her.

Neil and I rushed in after T'ing in time to see her, arms folded and toe tapping impatiently, as she confronted her honored ancestor. In the heart of a ring of drawn steel, Yang the Dispenser of Sucker-Punches regarded his miffed descendant with the sheepish expression of a kid caught rifling the cookie jar. In his right hand was his sword, in his left, the throat of a heavily muscled warrior attended by two hysterically snapping hounds. The radiance of the man's helmet was blinding, but obviously it hadn't been enough to stop Yang.

"I was only gonna maim him," he whined. "Maybe."

"Not from the look of things," T'ing said, indicating the victim's table-mates. Their array of edged weaponry was astounding, and all of it focused on Yang. "Put him down."

"But he got in our way! The tears are gone, and now we'll never find—"

"PUT HIM DOWN!"

A voice that rolled with thunder and cracked with lightning shook the walls of the deli. Need I add it wasn't T'ing's? We turned. We stared. And in the ozone-tingling silence, the speaker arose from his dim corner table, shook a wrinkle or two from his wizard's robe, and added in a pleasant tone, "That's really no way to treat a hero."

21

The Good Doctor

"YOU DIDN'T HAVE to drop him quite so hard," the wizard said.

Yang shrugged. "I wanted him to flatten those two mutts when he fell. I did pretty good; one got its stinking head smashed in, and the other's limping, see?"

The wizard sighed. "I fear your best efforts are wasted on Zisi and Zasu, sir. One of the more annoying features of those hounds is that they keep coming back for more. Part of the integrity of the Continuum, you see. Even my most concentrated spells to separate their mythic entity from that of their master have had no effect."

"Why would you want to do that?" I asked.

"That which is no longer linked to the Mythological Continuum can not adversely affect the Balance and is more vulnerable to having its mangy hindquarters kicked all the way to Heidelberg the next time it forgets it is housebroken all over *my* new shoes." Beneath his trim black moustache his mouth twisted with remembered distaste.

I looked at him more closely. "Hey! I think I know you."

"Do you?" Keen blue eyes peered at me, and a small silver mirror appeared in the mage's hand. He held this close to my face, ran a finger over the fog my breath left on the surface, and tasted it. "Pure mortal," was the judgment. "Not even a hint of the demonic, nor the heroic. Are you sure we've met before, lad?" He turned his eyes to Neil. "Now *you* look familiar."

At that word, there came an agitated rustling from the wiz-

ard's robes. He laughed and tugged up the hem far enough for
us to see the pink nose and amber eyes of a flame-colored
kitten. It sniffed at Neil's ankle and turned up its nose in disdain.

"Your pardon," said the mage. "Bungay does not like me
to use the term 'familiar' in a too, well, *familiar* manner with
just anyone. Fortunately, his indulgence may be purchased for
the price of a bologna sandwich. If you will join me . . . ?"
He scooped up the kitten and planted it on his shoulder, then
linked arms with Yang and grandly led the way back to his
corner table.

"I *know* I've seen him before," I confided to Neil as we fell
into line behind the mage and the Mongol.

"You know it," Neil replied. "And he's seen us. Remember
the Leeside, that spooky cottage, your great-uncle Seamus?"

I slapped my forehead as the recollections came pouring
back. Only a year had passed, but experience gained in the
Leeside was usually too frightening, too painful, and best when
soonest forgotten. Yet how could I? My dreams were haunted
by a lonesome hut in the cold lands, and by a meeting that still
burned in my heart, though my mind refused to recall it in any
detail.

I was still able to remember some things about my last visit
to the Leeside, though: I remembered coming to the cottage,
with its shifty-natured doors and windows. I remembered going in and finding Neil waiting for me with Teleri, Yang, and
Master Runyon. I remembered my first meeting there with my
great-uncle Seamus, the "fairy friend" who'd vanished from
his native Ireland without a trace, but the cottage wasn't his.
The true owner's name was clear to see on the aged scroll
above the fireplace. That, too, I remembered.

"*Faust?*" My hand closed around Neil's arm. "*That's* Dr.
Faustus? But—but he looks so different!"

"No so much, my friend." The wizard winked. I'd spoken
almost in a whisper, yet he'd heard. "I may appear younger to
you than when first we met—a trifle, to make wizardry serve
vanity—and you may have observed that I am no longer so, ah,
strikingly attended as before."

That was one way to put it. The Faust I'd seen was served
by a tusk-toothed, repulsive, terminally vulgar creature known
as a boggart. To the shame of the punctilious and proper goblin
Hobson, this particular boggart turned out to be his uncle Cal-

iban. It was a revelation to learn that even among the Fey, you can't choose your relatives, although sometimes you can eat them.

"Yeah," I said. "Where's your old pet ugly?"

"Monstrous, was he not? And where have so many monstrous creatures gone, of late?" Dr. Faustus seemed to shrug away the question, but his eyes burned with full knowledge of what was going on in the outer world. "Pray join me. I think you will find we have much common cause to discuss."

He took his place at the head of the table and indicated where we were to sit. One by one we obeyed, with varying degrees of wariness. Eleziane took the chair farthest from the wizard and glowered at him. I inserted myself in the place between her and T'ing, then waited until Faustus was deep into some jolly remember-whens with Yang before whispering, "What's wrong?"

"Nothing." Her mouth snapped shut. "Only *that* scrofulous moron had to go pick a fight that took up enough time for his tears to dry completely. Now we'll never find the hole to the Leeside!"

"Maybe there wasn't any farther for the tears to flow," I suggested. "Maybe the trail stopped here."

The princess sneered. "*Certainly.* Look around you."

I did. "I never saw so many loincloths in my life. And armor. And swords. Between the leather and the metal, this looks like Central Casting for rock video extras."

"Are you so blind to your brethren, my lord?" Eleziane was astonished. "Can't you sift their nature from the very air?"

I tried, but all I got was a snootful of mixed dog, horse, and human funk. It was enough to gag a polecat.

"Ahhhh!" Eleziane closed her eyes and drank in the miasma. "The breath of heroism! And do you think, O Grand and Puissant Champion of the Fey, that if the source of all escaping horrors from the Leeside were here, that these mighty ones would let the monsters pass unnoticed?"

I gave the assemblage of iron-hatted, iron-thewed, iron-brained titans another once-over. "Far as I can see, they're not paying attention to anything that's not sitting right in front of them on a plate with a side of pickle. Holy crow, don't *any* of them chew with their mouths closed?"

"The privileges of heroism are many," the elfin lady intoned.

"Yeah, I'll bet. Kill a few monsters and who's going to have the guts to make you take a bath after? Don't lump me in with them, Eleziane. Your daddy may have made me Grand and Puissant Champion of the Fey, but nobody's a hero by royal appointment. You heard the doc: I failed the breath test for heroism."

Eleziane lowered her eyes. "I recall a youth who came near to losing his own life for the saving of mine."

"That wasn't heroics; that was just doing what was right. And I had lots of help behind me. Heroes do *not* do teamwork. I mean, look at this bunch! Can you imagine them doing anything cooperative?"

My hand swept the room in a grand, all-encompassing gesture. Instead of Eleziane's reply, however, I heard a familiar whine: "Yeah, yeah, right, I see you, hold on, I've only got two hands, I'm coming." Through the press of overdeveloped shoulders and underdeveloped minds I saw the deli man approaching our table, order pad in hand.

I blinked hard; he looked different. Were Neil's eyes playing tricks on me? The last time I'd come into Feidelstein's, the man behind the counter had seemed smaller. This guy had the same lizardlike looks, the same sparse hair and perpetually downturned mouth, but he bulked in at one-and-a-half times the size of the man I remembered. What gave?

Before I could ask him whether he'd been pumping iron instead of pastrami, he focused on our table and scowled. "What's going on here?" He waved his order pad like an accusation in T'ing's face. "Who are you punks? How'd you get into the Back Room? What'samatter, you can't read?" He pointed to a big sign on the wall that read:

RULES OF THE BACK ROOM

1. Absolutely No Soliciting

2. This is *Your* Mythological Continuum. Please Keep It Clean.

3. Do Not Do Anything On The Floor You Would Not Like Done To Your Mother, Whether Divine Or Mortal.

4. Please Refrain From Ordering Omelettes When Sharing Tables With Any Of Your Fellow-Heroes Who May Have Been Hatched From Eggs.

5. Do Not Bus Your Own Tables. That Is What Ordinary People Are Good For.

6. Be Prepared To Show Proof Of Legendary Heroic Status At Any Time. Apocryphal Texts O.K. 10% Off For Those Mentioned In National Epics.

"See?" The man jabbed the pad at Rule Six. His tone got downright nasty as he added, "None of you look like saga material to me."

"My dear Mr. Kipnis, they happen to be my guests," Dr. Faustus said mildly. "While I, myself, am securely legendary, my heroic status is debatable. Still, you've never challenged my presence here."

"Anyone lives as long as you have in the Leeside gets tapped a hero in *my* book," Kipnis snarled. "I've got no problem with you, but as for these creeps—" He grabbed T'ing's arm and hauled her from her chair. *"Out!"*

"Don't you touch her!"

I was up and on him before my brain had the chance to cut in. My hands closed around his throat as a flood of conflicting input jammed my senses. Through my rage I heard T'ing shouting "Tim, no!", Yang cheering "Attaway, kid! Now bite his ear off!", Neil groaning "Oh, shit," and the wizard murmuring, "So *that's* who—" At the same time I heard that exasperated inner voice of mind sigh, *Well, now you've done it, asshole. Ever stop and think that a guy who can keep a roomful of heroes in line might be too much for you to take on barehanded, even if he does look like a big lizard?* To which I replied, just as my fingers met around the man's neck: *Lizard is right. Hey, man, this isn't skin, these are—*

Then a whip of wizardly robes flickered black before my eyes and the Back Room vanished in a rain of silver comets.

"—scales," I said to a bright blue sky and a lacework of white-blossomed branches.

"Tim, you're all right!" T'ing bent over me, her face haloed by the flowery branches, just like in my earliest fantasies of her. Unfortunately, I always scripted those dreams with me dying nobly in her arms (You know: "Oh, Tim, why wasn't I nicer to you when you were alive? I'm *so* sorry! Let me but kiss your lips this once—Ah! He is dead. Woe is me. Now I will run away to pass the rest of my days doing penance in a convent. I know I'm Jewish, but I'll adjust."). Whatever had happened, I sure hoped we weren't going to follow *that* scenario through. I checked myself for any aches, pains, bumps, bruises, or undesired bloodshed and came up clean. I didn't even feel dizzy when I sat up.

"Where are we?" I asked.

"Central Park," she replied. "I think."

I looked past the grass and trees to the encircling skyscrapers and saw that she was right. Then I heard a sound behind us and spun around quickly.

Arranged artistically beneath the same tree that sheltered T'ing and me were Eleziane, Yang, Neil, and Dr. Faustus. The wizard was feeding the last scraps of a bologna sandwich to Bungay. Yang tried to steal a bite and the kitten clawed his hand open.

I caught my breath. "Whoo! For a second I thought you guys were—"

"Hey, chill it, Desmond," Neil said. "We'd'a been a gang, you'd be long gone. Quit staring."

Quit it? No way. Staring was all that was keeping me vertical. I was getting a good look at Neil's face and doing my best not to keel over.

"Neil! Your face!" I gasped. "It's—it's *your face*!"

"Brilliant." Neil chuckled. "Desmond, you're really on top of things. Now wanna tell us who's buried in Grant's Tomb?"

I grabbed T'ing by the shoulders. "A mirror! Have you got a mirror?"

Before she had the chance to give me the tranquilizing smack I so evidently needed, the wizard was there. "Calm yourself, my friend," he said. "What you suspect has indeed happened, by my arts. Your face and body are your own again." He extended his hand. "Your great-uncle Seamus sends his best regards, Timothy."

Faustus could say what he would, I still ran my hands over my face to double-check. Yes, there it was, back to normal; better. Neil had cleared up my complexion for me. The wizard watched all this with an indulgent smile that I found really obnoxious.

"Thanks," I said, keeping it as curt as possible. "You did us all a big favor, I guess. Why?"

"Tim!" T'ing was shocked by my ingratitude.

Dr. Faustus chose to ignore my hostility. "You suspect my motives, Timothy? This is good. I, of all, know the immortal fallacy of free lunches. Yes, I want something in exchange

from you. That was why I saved your life—all of your lives—
in the Back Room.''

''*You* saved *my* life? From that wimp who's minding the
store for Mr. Feidelstein?'' I had to laugh. ''Come on, he's a
nothing! A wuss! A zero!''

''A fiend,'' said Faustus. ''And believe me, I ought to
know.''

22

Crystal Clear

IT WAS SUNDAY morning and the world was about to be overrun with the assorted horrors of the primeval abyss.

So what were we doing about it? Having brunch at Teleri's place. Hey, it made sense to me.

"No lox?" Dr. Faustus looked from his naked bagel to his hostess, disappointed.

"Whisht! And would ye be havin' me devour me own kinfolk? For sure, 'twas the very Salmon o' Wisdom who dwells in the River Shannon itself whose blood runs in these veins." She plopped a slab of Spam onto his plate instead.

"Which is why the doll occasionally has what we might delicately put to be a problem with causing olfactory offense to those as are not familiar with the Fulton Fish Market," Master Runyon said. "Be so kindly as to pass the lunchmeat, doll."

Teleri made a face at him and pointedly ignored the luchorpan's request. Instead, she bustled off into the kitchen space of her open-plan loft apartment and came back with more orange juice and croissants. She knelt with the tray before Eleziane, but the elfin princess didn't even glance at the lavish feast spread before her. From the moment we'd arrived, she had done nothing but drop herself onto the futon and gaze glumly at her feet.

"Won't yer honor be tastin' a morsel o' this fine fare?" my banshee wheedled. Eleziane only sighed.

"Leave her alone," said Yank, glomming a croissant and slashing it open with his dagger. He jammed half the Spam and twin dollops of mayonnaise and ketchup into the slit. "She wants to lose weight, let her. I think she intends to make herself worthy of my attentions. Hey! Elf-woman! Eat if you want. I'll still have sex with you. A woman without meat on her bones is like a day without slaughter. Being dead, I gotta see enough skeletons."

"You are a disgusting reptile and the abortion of a leprous toad with fallen arches." Eleziane enunciated every syllable perfectly, wintry eyes on the Mongol.

"Okay, your loss." Yang swallowed the last of his sandwich and began doing creative things with a chocolate donut and a glazed cruller.

Eleziane lost it. Could be she'd been brought up not to play with her food, but she slapped the pornographic pastries from his hand and shouted, "Is this all we do? Sit around this miserable hovel and blather while the forces of the Unseely Court call more and more allies to their dark banner?"

"Belay yer grand talk o' banners, when ye've the poor grace t' be insultin' the first dear home that's me own since I left the rath back in Erin. The cheek of it!" Teleri swept the refreshments out of Eleziane's reach in a huff.

Yang looked at his sadly truncated cruller, then at me. "I don't give a shit if anyone says different: Elves do *too* have that time of the month."

"Honored Grandfather, shut up," T'ing instructed him. She tried to reason with Eleziane. "We had to come here, my lady. We agreed yesterday, remember? We tried to reach Teleri and Master Runyon, but we couldn't."

"The doll had another audition," the luchorpan provided. "I think that maybe this one could be a sure shot to the big time. If I may be indulged in a bit of justifiable pride, I would say she knocked the producer on his keister."

"Keister me no keisters!" The lady of the Fey was bitter. "Agreed to this, did we? I was not consulted. The wizard offered what he might do for us, and *he*"—she stood up suddenly and pointed at me—"decreed what we must do next."

"Well, excuuuuse me for taking charge, but I kinda thought that since your own father named me Grand and Puissant Champion of the Fey, it was what you could call a leadership position." My dander was up—my dander was in the *stratosphere*, for God's sake—but my bridling cut no ice with Eleziane.

"Yesterday he told me there was no heroism in him." She went on as if I hadn't spoken at all. "Perhaps I should believe it, or why do we hide here when there is work to be done?"

T'ing stepped in gracefully on my behalf. "You know what you're saying about Tim's not true," she said. I could hear the reins tightening on her temper. I was more than glad she was on my side. "Dr. Faustus told us he has an enchantment that will conceal our movements from all of the witch's far-scanning devices—crystal, cauldron, magic mirror, whatever—but it's a spell he's only got the power to cast once."

"Once in a *while*," the good doctor emended. "As part and portion of my arrangement with the demon, I was only granted access to arcane energies at or below the G-8 level."

"You mean, like, your batteries run down?" Neil asked through a mouthful of jam-thick croissant.

"More or less. I would be able to summon up enough power to repeat the concealing spell in fifty years, give or take. I'd have to eat a lot of calcium, though."

"You see?" T'ing was never happier than when scoring a point in an argument. "Unless all of us are safe under one roof when he does it, Baba Yaga might still be able to find and harm any of our friends left outside. Are you in such a hurry to confront the witch that you'd leave Teleri and Master Runyon unprotected?"

Haughtily, Eleziane disregarded the question. "You, wizard!" Her finger swung around, aimed at Dr. Faustus' heart. "Yesterday you filled our ears with oaths of help, promises, fair words! 'My aid for yours,' you said. 'I shall use my dear-gotten magic to defeat the witch, to undo her every spell, to break her power utterly! Only swear to stand by me in my own seeking, and by tomorrow you will see a great wonder, to your benefit.' Well, wizard, tomorrow has come. Is Tim's mother awake? Is the witch destroyed? Am I given my own shape back again? Have you even begun the incantations that will cast this shielding spell over us all? Or is it only a ploy of yours to buy time against a battle you never really wanted to engage?"

Silence answered her accusations. As we watched, Dr. Faustus carefully folded the napkin in his lap, set it on the glass coffee table, and rose. He was not the figure of sorcerous awe he had been when we first met. Silver-stitched black robes had been exchanged for a crisp navy blazer and powder-blue slacks, yet even without the trappings of his calling he carried authority. He reached into his breast pocket and removed a gold pen, which a simple pass of the hands darkened and elongated into a gnarled wooden staff topped with a rainbow-crystal younger cousin to my own lost wand of office.

"My lady has just cause to take me to task," he said, his voice controlled. "I did indeed make the promises she speaks of, before this kind company parted yesterday, to go our separate ways. Is instant action what you desire, my lady? I can provide. A direct attack against the witch, then? Immediately? Do you believe that will serve us best?"

He didn't have to say any more. Eleziane's anger drained from her face. I could tell she was remembering that an ill-counseled direct attack was just what had gotten her into her present state. None of us had told him this, but still there was a terrible *knowing* in his eyes. All the old legends of Faust showed him as the scholar first, the seeker after hidden knowledge whose research finally showed him how to call up the powers of Hell itself. Good study habits stay with you forever.

"No." The word croaked from Eleziane's throat. She sank back into her place, head bowed.

Now Faustus smiled and took a seat beside her. Speaking gently, he said, "Don't be ashamed, Highness. You fought well." A twist of his wrist, and the staff vanished. In its place, a flawless crystal sphere perched on the tips of his fingers. "Last night, with thanks to my host Fitzsimmons' hospitality, I had the leisure to consult visions of the past. I could not begin to know how my powers might best help you if I were ignorant of what befell you before this."

"It was a mistake." Eleziane wouldn't look at him. "A stupid mistake that I made in my pride."

"Don't listen to her, sir; it was *my* fault," I said, stepping in. "But I guess you know that."

The wizard's calm eyes met mine. "No effort is worthless if we learn from its errors." His pupils shifted to the sparkling ball. It held a flowing picture of Eleziane's direct assault on Baba Yaga, my own brief upside-down captivity, her transformation from elfin beauty to plain-and-chunky schoolgirl. The picture watered away, replaced by a serene image of my mother's sleeping face. A grim Yaroslav stood beside the bed, the bannik Ilya Mikulovich crouched weeping at the foot. How had they come there? The last I knew, they were in Baba Yaga's cursed cottage. Unless . . . Make one prisoner stand guard over another, why not? That was just the sort of cruel, twisty notion that would appeal to the witch's sly mind.

"Not all the hag's captives sleep. These, too, will need our aid," the wizard muttered. "A false step, an attack poorly considered, and although my illusions may be enough to shelter all of you from harm, other innocents are still too close within the witch's reach. I know the workings of her mind: Retribution is her choicest food. Cold, she is, and cruel. Whatever we do, we must give her no opportunity to exact revenge from us or them."

"How do you know her so well?" I voiced the question we were all thinking. "From the Leeside?"

"No." Even Faustus' expression stiffened when I mentioned that dread place. "What Powers be were good enough to keep Baba Yaga's accursed hut far from my humble home. No, Tim, our association goes back farther than that. You see"—he arched his brow mischievously—"I have had some negotiations with the lady's grandson."

"You mean—?" He nodded. "I thought—I thought that when she called herself the devil's grandmother, she was only kidding."

"Bragging. I cannot say whether the title derives from blood kinship or is merely honorific, but I do know that she has a firm connection with more than one of those beings who call themselves devils."

He gazed back into the crystal ball, which still held my mother's image. Her face alone had grown to fill the entire vision. If things had been less tense, I might have wondered why the wizard's eyes got so tender, or why he kept the ball focused on her for so long.

"Devils," he repeated, tearing himself away from her at last. "Surely you know the traditional tale of my dealings with that breed?"

"Mmmmyeah." I was trying to be casual and sophisticated about this. "Something about selling your soul to one of them? Mephistopheles?"

Faustus shrugged. "Names do not concern demons much. They deal in harder practicalities."

"Pretty hard practicality, considering he was supposed to take your soul to Hell. You know, if that's the truth, don't you think you might want to reconsider? I mean, we do need you and everything, but just suppose when we come barging in on

Baba Yaga she's having a visit from that grandson of hers who holds your I.O.U. and—''

Faustus laughed so hard he nearly dropped the ball. "Ah, Tim, there speaks the goodness of heart that makes the truest heroes. No, no, do not fear for me. I do not dread a meeting with the—ha!—purchasing agent you mention. Rather would I welcome it. He is, you see, the goal of my own seeking.''

"What? You *want* the devil to catch you?'' This was a new one.

The wizard let out a long, slow breath. "Do you know the true terms of that famous compact I signed? Wait!'' His hand went up, leaving my response unsaid. "I know that you do not. No one does. Legends always get in the way of actuality. Too many poets have gotten their teeth snagged on that meat, and chewed it past recognition.''

"Well, what's to know?'' Neil asked. "We studied it in English class, one year. There was this demon—Mephistopheles, like Tim said—and you were old—I mean *really* old, maybe fifty, sixty—and he promised to make you young and give you anything you wanted, but he got to take your soul once you'd had it all.'' Neil's brow creased in thought. "You wanted women, right?''

"Women . . .'' This time I picked up on the way Faustus' eyes strayed back to the crystal-captured image of my mother's face. "That much is true—a small part of the truth. Fair women were a part of my desires, and the demon whom I summoned was ready to grant me them, and more. I was to have any material thing I wanted—*anything!*—for as long as I wanted it. He gifted me with the magic of supreme illusion, though illusion itself is not infinite. I doubt he was Mephistopheles, or any of the higher-ranking fiends. We did not get down to personal details like names, that halfpenny prince of Hell and I. 'My name? That would make it too easy for you to find me again,' he said.'' Faustus shook his head.

"Find him? Why would you wanna do something stupid like that?'' Neil inquired.

"And so we return to the prime question! Why? Why, to beg him to take my soul from me, of course. Do not startle so, my friends. Fiends are subtler monsters than mortal poets. By the terms he set, I must live on, all earthly wishes of mine instantly achieved, until I learn the weary lesson of a wearier world. What is life without accomplishments to mark the passing days? And what satisfaction can I ever have from such now, when I need to make no more effort to gain what I want than saying, *Let it be mine*?''

''There's more to being alive than that,'' T'ing said.

''Is there, my child? I never found it, and the centuries have left me tired of looking. Now the one thing for which I search is a nameless devil. I have pursued him over the face of the earth and hunted him through the shades of the Leeside. I only hope that, when I find him, he will not make me beg him too hard to take my soul.''

We gathered around him quietly. His face was young, but his eyes told a truer story. Eleziane placed her chubby hands over the crystal sphere so that my mother's face glowed with a golden light.

''I'm sorry,'' she said. ''If I was restless to have you turn your magic against the witch, it's only because—'' She faltered. ''This body—''

''You feel trapped, do you not?'' Dr. Faustus' soft question encouraged her. She nodded, her lips pressed together hard.

''Sometimes I'm afraid I'll never be free of it again. Yet how long has it held me? How long, compared to—?''

''To me?'' he finished for her. His hands came around to clasp hers. The glowing crystal's light seeped out between their fingers. ''Let it not trouble you, my lady. Soon we shall both be free.''

He turned his head and looked right at me.

I raised a hand to hold him off. ''Now hold it right—''

''—there,'' I said, pointing up at the roof of my apartment building.

Dr. Faustus pulled a small brass spyglass from his jacket and scanned the roof line. ''So. Chicken legs. That is Baba Yaga's house, right enough.'' He spun the spyglass until it turned into an ivory-topped walking stick, and headed for the entrance to the building.

''Whoa! Wait a minute!'' I hung on his arm until he stopped. ''We're partners in this, right?''

''More than partners, if all goes well. Your magic shall be the freeing of me, Tim. It is not common knowledge, but a magician can summon up a living embodiment of the forces of Hell only once in his life. Once''—he pulled a droll face—''is usually enough. We are agreed that when your power is restored to you, you will use it to call upon the very fiend who struck this diabolical bargain with me, and when we have him . . .'' Dr. Faustus closed his eyes and smiled.

"So okay. Don't you think it'd be nice to tell your *partner* what the plan is here? Just to make sure you've still *got* a partner in one piece when this is over?''

"Didn't I already—?'' Faustus scratched his chin. "No, no, that must have been the other young man. Dear me, the years do take a toll. I was positive we'd gone over . . . Well, never mind. All you must do is knock at the witch's door, smile, bring me in and—and—'' He consulted the sky for a hint.

"And—?" I prompted.

"And duck.''

23

Have I Got a Deal for You!

BABA YAGA WAS a witch of such monumental powers that she had been able to defeat a princess royal of the Fey. The massed monsters of the Leeside looked to her for leadership, and I knew that that mob of ghastlies wouldn't follow someone they didn't fear.

Dr. Johannes Faustus was a mortal, but as such he had applied the full vigor of his mind to acquiring the deepest knowledge of darkest sorcery. His wisdom, the lore he had accumulated over centuries of unnaturally extended life, and the outright gifts of magic from his anonymous demon patron all combined to make him one of the most fearsome arcane opponents in existence.

A battle of witch and wizard is not something for the weakhearted to witness. A confrontation of *this* witch and *that* wizard was certain to set the buttresses of reality shaking, crack the foundations of mundane logic, and knock loose a whole lot of plaster besides. I rapped on the door of Baba Yaga's cottage with my heart slowly crawling up my throat. When this clash ended, the security deposit on our apartment wouldn't be worth beans.

Ilya answered the door. He cringed when he saw me. At my back, the wizard's presence hummed and spat with barely restrained mystic potency. The bannik's eyes widened until I was afraid they'd come rolling out of his head. Stammering in Russian, he groveled and scraped away from the door, nervously motioning for us to enter. With a last jabber of Slavic noise, he scurried into another room.

"He says he will fetch the mistress at once," Faustus translated for me. "Sit, Tim. She will be a while." He laid a hand on my shoulder and bright yellow sparks arced and sizzled, blowing me into a painted metal chair shaped like a manicured hand. I hit it with a clang.

Faustus seemed unaware of his pent-up energies. He strolled around the room, crackling with every step as he took in our surroundings. Every now and again he pointed out an especially interesting piece of décor to Bungay, who had come along for the ride in the good doctor's breast pocket. Baba Yaga had shucked all her Early French Cathouse décor for something a lot trendier. Red velvet and plush alike had been devoured by a pack of Southwestern pastel coyotes and buried beneath truckloads of terra-cotta-potted cacti and sage. Bungay remained unimpressed.

"I like what she's done with the place," Faustus remarked, pausing before a Georgia O'Keeffe lithograph.

I didn't. Something was wrong, gravely wrong. Baba Yaga had done trendy things before, but she'd always managed to slide over into tackiness. Not now. "It's tasteful," I muttered. "*Too* tasteful. I don't trust it."

"Trust?" A voice I shuddered to recognize trilled from the recesses of the cottage. "You are fine one to be speaking of trust, my leetle balalaika." Ilya Mikulovich scrambled back into the room, rolling out an incredibly long Navajo rug before him as fast as his squat body could move. It flopped flat at the wizard's feet and the bannik flopped likewise.

Face down, rump up, the poor little spirit announced, "Her Most Exalted Cosmic Wholeness, Bambi Yaga!"

"Did he say *Bam*—?" Before I could check my hearing aid, she entered, and it was time to visit the eye doctor too.

Lordy.

One look at the witch as she now appeared and the entire cheerleading squad would go home and slit their throats. She was tall and golden-haired enough to join Lord Palamon's court, though instead of diaphanous white drapery she wore a hot-pink bathing suit cut up past *there* on her hipbones and down to *there* over her cleavage. It also featured a handy zipper. And rivets. And silver chains. One step off the edge of the pier and she'd sink, causing anything male within a fifty-mile radius to leap into the briny after her, like sex-crazed lemmings.

And you know what? I'd be leading the pack.

She saw me staring, and struck a pose that sent my hormones leaping into a high-impact aerobics routine. Deftly she turned, to let her body assault my eyes from an even more well-rounded angle (Yeah, I know, angles can't be rounded, but we're not talking sane geometry here; we're not even talking, we're just kinda slavering). "Is having to change personal image," she explained. "Wake op and smell the cappuccino. Getting op, getting down, getting fonky. Look, I am even shaving legs!" She flaunted them, long, brown, and slick with oil. "You like?" she asked, batting her eyelashes.

"Gah," I said.

She placed two French-manicured fingers under my chin and gently lifted my jaw until my mouth shut. "Is glad to see me, dollink?" She wore no makeup; she didn't need it.

"Madam, you would do well to leave the boy alone. Do not postpone the inevitable any longer." Dr. Faustus spoke to command immediate attention.

The witch's warmly glowing eyes slued around to regard him. "Oho! Is long time, not much seeing. Welcome, welcome! If is looking for my grandson, you are barking up wrong segment of Mythological Continuum. Last time I am seeing him, you think he is stopping, sitting down to nice hot meal like a civilized fiend, spending any time with his poor grandmamma? *Nyet!* Is just grabbing handful of chocolate chimp cookies, goosing me once with pointy tail, and shouting, 'Bye-bye, Baba! Catch you at Armageddon!' I speet on the younger generation." And she did.

While I was wiping my eye, Dr. Faustus said, "My business is not with him, madam. I come to issue you a formal challenge to a duel of sorcery most high and deadly, in accordance with all laws and statutes, cosmic, federal, local, and legendary pertaining thereto, to wit—"

"Bah!" The witch tossed her mane of champagne-blond hair over one bronzed shoulder. "Always the windbag, Faustus. If you are wanting trouble, hokay!" Unseen forces gathered around the witch, an infestation of the air that I felt to the roots of my teeth. Her thick blond hair lifted from her shoulders and began to stream out behind her. Every bit of chromed metal on her swimsuit sprouted into a spike, glittering evilly. She rubbed her hands together and cackled. A cackle, coming from lips that moist, full, and tempting sounded as inharmonious as a Tyrannosaurus Rex playing Pee Wee Herman.

"Now . . . we fight!"

The chicken-legged cottage shook. Pinfeathers showered

down from the thatch. Ilya groaned and rolled up the Navajo
rug with himself in it. From Dr. Faustus' blazer, little Bungay
uttered a terrified mew. One of the pastel coyotes let loose a
real howl and decorated the floor with a small pastel pile of
something appalling. Three pots of cacti inflated to the burst-
ing point and exploded, sending silver needles lancing everywhere. I yelped and threw myself under a glass-topped table
just as the witch and the wizard closed on each other, doom
and havoc pulsing through the air around them.

It was the end of the world.

"So there is no more chocolate ladyfingers, dollink? Don't
look so glom. Is not end of vorld."

Baba—sorry—*Bambi* Yaga passed Dr. Faustus a plate of zucchini
sticks and urged him to try some. He scowled. I wiped the last of
the chocolate crumbs from my face and tried to look innocent.

"I have not come here to eat." Dr. Faustus crossed his legs
and gave his trouser creases an unnecessary tug. "I have come
to try the mettle of my magic against yours, hag. You should
be grateful. If the Guardians learn of your doings, they will
reduce you to a nursery rhyme!"

"Guardians . . ." The witch's upper lip curled. I detected
nothing but scorn for the Guardians, whoever they might be.

Her snooty attitude goaded Dr. Faustus. "You, madam, have
committed offenses unspeakable against the proper running of
the Mythological Continuum. You have somehow captured the
Guardians' designated doorkeeper, one Benjamin Kipnis, and
replaced him with a fiend of your own nomination, disguised.
That is the only reason that the noble inhabitants of the Back
Room did not notice the parade of ill-formed, misbegotten,
uncanny, and hideous monsters who *you*, madam, have been
introducing illegally, by degrees, to the outer world."

"Notice something? *Them?*" Bambi Yaga laughed. "You
try leaving peeckle off their lunch order, *that* they notice!"

"Madam, you speak of heroes!"

Bambi Yaga blew a Bryansk cheer (or whatever's the Russian
equivalent of the classic raspberry) in honor of heroes everywhere.

"You *will* release Kipnis," Faustus thundered. "And you
will likewise undo all the evil you and your minions have
wrought upon this world. Yes, you will do this, or—"

"Brother. Beetch, beetch, beetch." Bambi Yaga lazily
sucked crumbs from her fingers. "Is been saying same damn

thing ever since you sit down to tea, even when all this is as good as settled alraddy. No vonder you can't get a girl vithout my grandson's help. You don't got no conversation.''

The wizard harrumphed. I just kept on nibbling a cookie and checking out possible hiding places should his temper flare. ''Never mind my social life. I have come to challenge and to conquer, in the name of righteousness and the preservation of the Mythological Continuum. You desire this battle as much as I do. Why do we linger?''

''You know vhy, same like I do.'' The witch let her perfectly tanned shoulders lift and fall languidly. ''Is maybe my fault stupid machine has soch crommy response time?'' She gestured expressively at the softly humming computer terminal in the corner. Just then it emitted a well-bred *meep* and the screen filled with string after string of fiery red characters.

''Ah! Is *finally*!'' Bambi Yaga clapped her hands and danced over to the terminal. While she peered at the screen, Dr. Faustus and I joined her.

''Are you sure this contraption is a legitimate device for the registration and retrieval of occult lore?'' he demanded, sounding rather stuffy about it.

''Do not be giving birth to bovine, hokay?'' The witch tapped in a few more tidbits of input. ''Is saying right there, in black and red, that terms of all duels of sorcery most be properly entered before battle and most respect ever-fluctuating demands of Mythological Continuum. Othervise . . . BOOM!''

''But the parameters of the Mythological Continuum are only described within the covers of certain universally accepted grimoires,'' Dr. Faustus protested. ''Tomes of unquestionable ill repute whose very pages are bound with skins into whose origins a wise man dares not inquire too closely.''

''Mnyah.'' The witch hit RETURN and the screen displayed the message:

```
********************************************
```

THANK YOU FOR USING
HEXSOFT

Ye Compleate On-lyne Resource

For All Your Esotericke Needs

Approved for Use in Settling All Wars,
Battles, Conflicts, Set-tos, Spats, and
Bar Bets For Established and Recognized
Magic-Users
In the Mythological Continuum
(This Incarnation Only)
Fully Guardian-Tested and Recommended

****

"If is making you feel any better"—Bambi Yaga smirked—
"I am using only terminal cover made from skins into whose
origins vise man does not inquire too closely."

Faust folded his arms. "It remains unorthodox."

"Hey, boddy, you the one who loses coin toss. Is meaning
I am in charge of how we make pre-battle arrangements. If *you*
had been winning, then maybe I have to sit down at croddy
slant-top desk, scare op last bottle of indelible B-positive in
the place, obtain parchment made from skin of child, break a
nail sharpening lousy queel pen to write down post-battle
agreement, ha? *This* you would like jost fine, I betcha!"

"Madam, I—"

The witch groused on. "Not even caring that is having to
first *catch* bird for to plock tail-feathers for making queel pen.
And not jost some damn goose, baby! Handwritten documant
of soch importance most be written with tail-feather of roc,
and you got maybe some idea how hard is getting to pin one
of *them* down? Beeg, overgrown torkeys with brains of learning-
disabled budgie, and every one of them sleepery like vater-
melon seed. You think I like waste time, track down dumb
roc, maybe have stupid bord *seet* on me?"

"Well, far be it from us to leave you between a roc and a
hard place," I remarked.

Witch and wizard both glared at me. I twiddled my thumbs and
whistled at the ceiling, all the while looking pure and free of guile.

"Faustus," Bambi Yaga said slowly, "maybe I am being
hasty. Is moch to be said for contract written on parchment
made from skin of wise-mouth kid, *nyet*?"

To his credit, Dr. Faustus waxed eloquent in his reasons for
not turning my hide into stationery. He ended by saying, "In-

deed, I see the advantages of using this—ah—device for our purposes. Who are we to stand in the way of progress, of technology, of—?"

"Yeah, yeah, yeah. Now sharrup so I can be getting Boris Bytenov here"—the witch patted the terminal lovingly—"to run through menus, *da?*"

"Well, hurry it up," Faustus said sharply. He did not like having his oratory cut off so summarily.

"*Da, da,* is not to get shorts in knot. First ve are having to register pre-agreed-upon concessions depending on outcome of duel. Cannot be having agreement saying that if you win, something happens that completely opsats vorld. You know, like if you win, is no more vaneela ices cream."

"I wouldn't mind that," I mumbled.

"Me neither," the witch concurred. "Most sansible magic-users are being chocoholics. I speet on vaneela. But vhat can you do? Vaneela is also wital part of *Reality* Continuum, can neither be sorcerously created nor destroyed, espacially not as part of post-duel agreement. Magical duels most only affect *Mythological* Continuum. Even mageecians having to bear up, live with vaneela. Othervise . . ." She raised an admonishing finger.

"Boom. I know." Dr. Faustus inclined his head. "So be it, then."

"Good. Hokay, everything is looking to be in order here. We got leeftoff." She hit another button on the keypad and a long, yellowed, red-writ parchment document spewed out of the attached laser printer. "Sign."

I grabbed Faustus' wrist as he was taking out his pen. "Don't you think you oughta read that first? I mean, you've been pretty free and easy about putting your name on all kinds of non-kosher contracts before this, and look where it's gotten you."

The magician just looked at me. "Don't let appearances deceive you, Tim. I seem young, but my eyes are not what they were. I thought I might leave the reading of fine print to you, since the document requires your signature as well, to make it valid."

"My—?"

"Teemothy, dollink." Bambi Yaga was behind me, her breath hot in my ear, her hands doing piano exercises all over my chest. "I am *devastated* to be needing you to sign away so moch, but vhat can I do? A girl is needing to defand herself. And you *are* a recognized magic-user, no?"

"Not without my wand, I'm not," I grumbled. The witch's attentions planted colonies of invisible ants under most of my skin.

"Is that all? Is wanting wand? So take!" She pushed away from me just as my right hand felt the return of my long-absent sword hilt. I couldn't do anything but stare, glad to have it back, surprised it had been so easy, more surprised that I'd missed my elfin mark of office so much.

"Taking a chance, are we, madam?" Faustus was pleased to be ironic.

"Tchah. Is—how you say?—bagatelle. I can defand mysalf against all dollink boychik can do with wand, and I am still holding onto his mamma, you betcha. He is using it to work magic against me, I am sending his mamma beddy-bye forever. Maybe longer."

I studied the witch. "You look different," I said, "but you're still the same underneath."

She laughed, this time without slipping into the faux pas of a cackle. "Is different *world*, Teemothy, but is same underneath. Smart girl is moving with the times. Highest achievement of black sorcery is to compel veectims to do things that are against better nature, things they vould not normally do, and at same time *conwince* them that doing soch things is all their own idea and for the bast!"

She snapped her fingers. The computer vanished, replaced by a big-screen television with state-of-the-art VCR system attached. The news was on, one of those all-news channels that sometimes tells you more about what's going on in the world than you can bear to know. I expected the part about the wars, the "decency" vigilantes, the drug-addicted and AIDS-doomed babies born without a chance, being raised without a choice in places colder than the Leeside. Someone was always there to shake his head, and say what a great pity it was, and do nothing to make it better, and remind everyone that it was all for the best.

"Sad." The witch clucked over the flickering images, but she was smiling. "So sad. Is too deprassing. Is why I never watch tee-wee." She plucked a videocassette from the rack and popped it in. Pretty soon we were watching Bambi Yaga prancing in spandex to a selection of Madonna tunes while promising us *Thinner Thighs Through Thaumaturgy*.

She turned from the screen. "Not bad, if I am saying it mysalf. Is jost marketed to buy me borscht-money, but is already sold over meellion copies. Not bad, yes?" She killed the tape. "You see, dollink Dr. Faustus, is not so hard after all for me and my monstrous frands to be fitting in with this vorld. . In fact, is becoming urgent ve fit in sooner, batter. If ve do not hurry, is not going to be moch vork laft for monsters to do! Grabby leetle peegy mortals is alraddy nearly holding monopoly on being real sheets.''

"What's your point?" I asked.

She pinched my cheek. Hard. "So smart! Is so sharp, boychik is nearly cutting own throat, *da*? My point? I am glad you are asking. Ve are back, ve are here, and ve are going to take back everything you creeps ever took from us, in spades! Force now holds us close to place ve emerge from Leeside, but vunce ve have become part of this vorld, *nothing* holds us back! Brooklyn is only begeening. Terre Haute, here ve come!''

She flung her slender arms high above her head, and peals of exultant laughter filled the cottage. Another snap of her fingers and the TV/VCR combo winked away; the computer was back. If the witching game ever gave out, Bambi Yaga had a great future with a moving company. Then she sat down at the keyboard again and cocked an eyebrow at Faustus. "So? Is signing post-duel agreement or not?''

He signed. So did I. Bambi Yaga put her John Hancock—or should I call it her John Dee?—on the agreement too, then summoned Ilya to witness it. The bannik's tongue protruded from the corner of his mouth as his thick fingers inexpertly guided the pen into forming a Happy Face. (Making an X came a bit too close to a cross for the witch's comfort.) One blank space remained for the signature of a second witness.

"How about Yaroslav?" I suggested.

"Oho." Bambi Yaga got a canny look in her eye. "Trying to pool fast one on me, sugar-shorts? Yaroslav is guarding your mamma. Wampire has strict instroctions from me that if *any*-one tries rescue, he bites! From spell of sleep to life of ondead is not so far to go. One small neeble for a wampire, one giant sleep for her. *Forever!*''

I felt my face harden. I couldn't believe Yaroslav would ever do anything like that, no matter how strict his instructions. My refusal to believe must have showed, because the witch added:

"Transformation is complete. Is *full* wampire now. He disobeys, one tweetch of Wenetian blinds and sonlight slices him into leetsle beetsy motes of dost. Or is stake through heart, garlic, volfsbane, Duran Duran records, seelver boollet, you name it, I got it. So does Yaroslav. Onderstand, my leetle vand-vagger?''

Having suppressed any possible backstairs-dealing on my part—or so she assumed—Bambi Yaga returned to the problem at hand. "Let's see . . . a weetness . . .''

"Madam, allow me." Dr. Faustus scooped Bungay from his pocket and deposited the amber kitten on the table. The wizard's familiar regarded the agreement from several angles, then apparently nodded satisfaction. As we watched, Bungay found a large potted cactus, piddled in the soil, dabbled one paw in the resulting muck, limped carefully back to the outspread agreement, and planted his paw-print neatly, if none too fragrantly, right on the second witness's line. He then shook his paw off and vaulted onto Faustus' shoulder to see what happened next.

"*Clever* poosy cats!" Bambi Yaga was delighted. She tried to tickle Bungay under his chin and came away with a gouged finger. "*Bad* poosy cats," she snarled, and went back to typing at the keypad with a vengeance.

"What's she up to now?" I whispered to Faustus.

"What is won and lost by either party when the battle's done is already set," he replied. "Now we must officially register the place and time of battle, weapons legal and illegal to our use, and how the winner shall be known."

I watched the witch type furiously for a while. Then I said, "Uh . . . shouldn't you be putting in a couple of ideas?"

"What she enters now is mere boilerplate," the wizard told me. He sounded like he was lying.

The witch overheard and swiveled around. "Teemothy, is wanting to put your own two rubles-worth in?" Her hand swept the screen. "Be mine gast! All I am doing is calling op menu—*choices* we have for everything concerning battle. Vunce these are made-poof!—we prass ANTER and nothing in all the Mythological Continuum can change chosen conditions for duel."

I leaned nearer the screen. The characters were pixel-tiny, almost illegible to my eyes. Bambi Yaga tilted her head back and regarded Faust upside down. "Mages' code says both of us most have chance to sat terms of combat . . . onless we choose not to. So! Care to be making selaction, dollink?"

The good doctor peered helplessly at the screen. What he'd said about his eyesight was true. A gesture of his formed a huge magnifying lens, which an answering gesture of hers immediately shattered. "Ah, ah, ah. Selaction most be made without halp of any kind. Uf course, *I* vould be happy to settle all details, if you like forfeit choice." Only on Bambi Yaga could dimples look evil.

"*I'll* make our choices for him," I said. If I squinted real hard, I *thought* I could read some of the possibilities.

"*Nyet!* No minors."

I looked to Dr. Faustus for confirmation; he nodded. "I'm sorry, Tim. I fear I will have to permit the witch to make all the choices regarding this battle."

"*Try*, at least!" I protested. "Even if you just punch up some random keys, it's got to give you a fairer chance than if you quit and let her call all the shots."

Faustus just shook his head. Bambi Yaga's expression was a combination of raw triumph and great orthodonture. "That's right, Teemothy. Your frand is wise man, and wise man knows when to throw in the babushka." She flexed her fingers and poised them over the keys. "Hotcha," she remarked.

I don't know, there's just something about quitting without a fight that makes me mad. Stupid, too, but mostly mad. I always feel that *any* action's better than lying down and taking it. Some day maybe I'll be wrong, permanently.

For the moment, though, I felt the blood rush up behind my eyeballs. My hand tightened on the hilt of my wand. I raised it, summoning in all the power I could safely use and still keep Mom from harm.

That is to say: none.

But that didn't mean I couldn't use the wand magic-free, and you bet I did. Right on Bungay's fuzzy little bottom.

The kitten yowled and rose a foot off Faustus' shoulder. He landed on Bambi Yaga's naked back. The witch leaped from her seat, spitting obscenities. Bungay launched himself again, and I was there, using the wand to parry him gently right onto the keyboard. I don't know how many keys he trampled before scrabbling off. Bambi Yaga was strieking that her tan was ruined. I took advantage of the confusion to step in and scoop up the culprit. First, though, I pressed ENTER.

By the time the witch had calmed down enough to reclaim her place at the terminal, it was done. She stared at the display.

"Hoboy," she said. Then, to the rhythm of "The Volga Boatman," she banged her head repeatedly against the screen.

24

Shall We Dance?

COUPLES ONLY? *ALL the allies either side wants so long as they're couples only? Are you sure Bungay's a kitten? I think he's a refugee from* The Dating Game. *How in heck could you trust something as important as this battle to the random key-jumps of a kitten, you dipstick?*

I crumpled up T'ing's note as soon as I read it and began composing my reply under cover of my *Hablemos Español Ahora Mismo, Estudiantes, Por Favor* textbook. I folded the paper carefully and slipped it into the good old dependable hand-to-hand classroom postal system. As a method of communication, note-passing had the U.S. Snail beat on points. There was just one disadvantage, though. . . .

"Well, well, well," said Mr. Richter, snatching the note from T'ing's hand. "What have we here? Something we can share with the whole class, Ms. Kaplan?"

It was a rhetorical question of the sarcastic kind my Spanish teacher delighted in. He made a great business of unfolding the paper and clearing his throat before beginning to read the contents aloud.

"Hrhm! 'The menu didn't say "couples only," it said, "sword-brothers," which was a perfectly acceptable and common arrangement in lots of historical military situations. Considering *where* we've got to have this battle, we all agreed on the "couples only" interpretation. As for Bungay, *any* action, no matter how random, is better than *no* action, that's why! And don't call me a dipstick.' "

Hardly the high drama of teen passion he had been expect-

ing, was it? The class exploded with subversive laughter. Mr.
Richter glared doom all around, to no avail. The note wasn't
signed, and I'd taken the precaution of printing, so he couldn't
play guess-who on the basis of my handwriting. A few fruitless
interrogations by Mr. Richter as to the identity of the note's
sender went unanswered. T'ing swore up, down, and sideways
that she had only picked it up from the floor out of curiosity.
It must have been left from the previous class. Surely Mr.
Richter never thought that members of *this* class would do
something so vicious, reprehensible, and foul as note-passing?
No, no, we lived but to have him fill our eager, upturned faces
with the *imperfecto del subjunctivo* of the verb *estudiar*.

Later, as she and I entered Doc Ox's office, she said, "A
little more b.s. and he would've believed me. I don't know
why you had to confess and ruin everything."

"A little more amateur-level b.s. like you were dishing out
and you'd be going home with a plump 'n' juicy suspension.
Try bouncing *that* off your mother's collection of parenting
books."

T'ing shuddered. She knew whereof I spoke. Mrs. Kaplan
was a ruthlessly results-oriented parent, one who collected her
children's achievements the way Tamerlane piled up the skulls
of his enemies. Even though T'ing was the Kaplan's adopted
child, they expected as much of her as they did of their own
flesh and blood, Daniela. Daniela was now safely married,
which left Mrs. Kaplan free to hover over T'ing like Dracula
over an untasted throat.

"I still bet I could've done it," T'ing said weakly.

"You're too honest to sell a lie, T'ing, and it shows."

She gave me one of her sweetest smiles. "Well, if you say
so. Anyway, it was nice of you to throw yourself to *los lobos*
like that."

"Hey, I wrote the note."

"I know you did. Dipstick." She was still smiling.

"And if you get into big trouble now, no way your mother's
gonna let you go to the prom with me. 'Couples only,' remember?"

The smile was gone. "Why, you—!"

"Yes, children? May I help you?"

A voice—hard, sharp, and cold—cut short T'ing's rising cry
of outrage. The door to Dr. Oxenstierna's office stood open,
though no one was near enough to have turned the knob. In-

side, guarding the way to the inner room where our beloved
Doc Ox lurked, was a desk with a small tank, and at the con-
trols was a woman whose nameplate identified her as Ms.
Stone.

My heart chilled. It didn't matter that Eleziane had spoken
well of the lady in question. There are people in this world
born to give others the creeps, for no apparent reason. That
wasn't the case with Ms. Stone. She inspired me on sight with
a textbook attack of the clammy-skin shudders and the reason
was glaring apparent. Granted, there was nothing really terrifying about her pale gray blouse, no hint of horror resting on
her too-brightly rouged cheeks. When she stood up and came
toward us I could regard her black twill skirt, thick support-
stockings, and battered white athletic shoes without thinking
of nameless, gibbering abominations from the nethermost
abyss.

Then again, there was her hair. It hissed.

Very carefully she adjusted the huge scarf covering her head,
a precise gesture primly echoed in the way she settled the pair
of wide-screen wraparound shades on her nose. Between the
sunglasses and the scarf, three-quarters of Ms. Stone's head
was hidden from sight. Considering my suspicions, this was
very considerate of her.

"Have you an appointment with Dr. Oxenstierna?" she inquired. Something wriggled under the scarf.

"No, Ms. Stone," T'ing replied, with remarkable self-
possession. Her eyes were as good as mine; she'd seen the
wriggling going on under cover of Mr. Stone's headwrap, she'd
read up on Greek Mythology, and she had too much experience
in the front trenches of a leaky Mythological Continuum to
pass off all that hidden shimmying as the work of energetic
dandruff.

A kindly smile softened Ms. Stone's rough-chiseled mouth.
"Get into trouble in class, dear?" Her voice sounded like pebbles shaken in a velvet sack.

"Yes, Ms. Stone. We were caught passing notes."

"Oh, you poor darlings." She ushered us over to the long,
cold bench just outside Doc Ox's inner sanctum. "To send you
down here for such a silly trifle! Well, I'm sure Dr. Oxenstierna
won't be too hard on you. Please wait."

I couldn't see Ms. Stone's eyes—for which I was grateful—
but the warmth in her voice led me to imagine that she was

not one of those adults who believe that the proper place for
Young Love is chained up in separate kennels. I stole a peek
at her desktop and had my suspicions confirmed. Face down,
spine cracked, lay a much-thumbed copy of *Passion's Cats-
paw*.

"This one'll be easy," I whispered to T'ing.

"No." She wasn't contradicting me. The way she rolled her
eyes heavenward meant she was using that single word to dis-
sociate herself entirely from my lunatic notions.

"Come *on*, you know it'll work. It's not like we've got all
that much time. And she's a *gorgon*! Think what a feather in
our cap that'll be if we show up with her on our side!"

"Statues don't wear caps," T'ing returned. "And a pigeon's
restroom is what you'll be if you fool around with that monster."

"Aw, she's not so bad." I folded my arms and observed
Ms. Stone as she did various bits of office work. Once upon a
time, before the monsters came pouring out of the Leeside,
there had been three other people employed in this office. Since
Ms. Stone's advent, no one knew where they'd gone. *Oh, well,*
I thought. *When we get rid of the monsters again, I bet all the
changes they've caused on the Outside will go back to normal.*

As we waited, I caught a glimpse of a wee figure climbing
into the office by way of the open window. Outside it was a
fine morning in May. The forsythia in front of Glenwood High
had gone nuts and there were even some doggedly determined
tulips doing their best to bloom under a load of soot and all
the empty Big Mac containers that just "happened" to fall out
the windows.

The creature that now came crawling over the sill wasn't a
monster. Very few of them are so neatly turned out. Small and
roly-poly, our blond-haired, blue-eyed caller was dressed in
bright colors and had a fiddle strapped to his back. The fiddle
was the tip-off: a *tomte*. The *tomten* are Swedish sprites who
are pretty handy to have around, as domestic spirits go. They
don't just do the dusting, they take over household finances
and will even do a little thievery on the side for their masters,
all of which comes in mighty handy when April fifteenth rolls
around. All they ask in return is tidiness, peace, and a little
extra *lutefisk* on Thursdays.

The tomte paused on the sill, his wide nostrils flaring. I
knew what he was up to: Hot on a scent, he was, and that

scent highly Scandinavian. The little spirits of hearth and home were born to help mortals—more, they *lived* to serve—but only mortals whose blood sprang from the same culture as had spawned each particular sprite. I'm mostly Irish-American, so I found a banshee on my doorstep. My mother's more Russian-American, and that attracted Ilya Mikulovich, the bannik, like catnip draws tabbies.

When there's a man with a name like Oxenstierna in the vicinity, three guesses who the tomte was after. Doc Ox was no prize, but household spirits aren't fussy. The tomte's whole reason for existence was to hitch up with a human, and I suppose Doc Ox was the best culture-compatible one he could find this side of Minneapolis/St. Paul. One last twitch of the nostrils, a satisfied smile, and the tomte leaped from the windowsill and high-tailed it for the principal's closed door.

Ms. Stone casually swiveled her chair until her back was to us. With two fingers she slid her sunglasses off and uttered a sharp, shrill, guaranteed-attention-getting whistle. The tomte stopped in his tracks and jerked his head around.

The sound of flesh turning into granite is dry, harsh, and scratchy.

Ms. Stone pushed her sunglasses back on and turned towards us, smiling. "I didn't think Dr. Oxenstierna wanted to be disturbed just now. Don't you agree?"

Boy, did we.

Doc Ox was pretty lenient with us. "*Ja*, sure, kids yoost bayn kids." His accent had gotten thicker, surely the by-product of his association with the frost-giant. "You go tell your teacher you not bayn passing love notes anymore, *ja*?" There was a kindly twinkle in his eye. A *twinkle*! This, from the principal voted most likely to approve flaying as an acceptable punishment for breaking the school dress code.

Thoughts of Ms. Stone tingled in my mind as I determined to take advantage of Doc Ox's unnatural affability. "Oh, it wasn't exactly a love note, sir."

"No? Vot den?"

Avuncular. I swear he looked *avuncular* when he said that. Hey, look it up. It could show up on your SATs.

An actor prepares. My expression was a meld of Mickey Rooney playing young Andy Hardy in love, Jerry Mathers as the Beaver, and William Shatner as Captain Kirk attempting to convince the girl that he's still a virgin.

"It was an invitation to the prom"—my voice trembled like naked Jell-O with poorly suppressed Tragic Significance—"if there *is* a prom."

"Lord, you're good." T'ing gazed at me with undisguised admiration. I liked it.

Still, a man has to put up a modest front. I tried to shrug, but it was difficult while toting a petrified tomte around under one arm. "No big thing. I don't know what Doc Ox and his overgrown Popsicle pal have been up to, but he's lost touch with the school. It was even odds he'd believe me when I said they were going to cancel the prom for lack of chaperones."

"Yeah, but then getting him to ask Ms. Stone to go with him—"

"A snap. I told him that she volunteered to chaperone, but the poor woman lives in a neighborhood where she's afraid to go out alone at night. You know, too many punks hanging out on the street corners getting stoned."

T'ing giggled. "Especially if they try messing with *her*." She watched me try to cram the tomte into my locker. "So what are you going to do with it?"

I looked down at the poor little fella. "*Him*, not it. I don't know. Pop by the Agency after school, see if someone there's got the power to help him. If not, I'll pick up a few more allies for the battle while I'm in there, collect money to buy enough prom tickets to go around, like that."

"And *him*?"

"Stick him in someone's garden, I guess. If we win, he might be among the automatically cured. If we lose, at least he'll have steady work."

"Tim . . . what happens if we lose?"

She didn't sound scared; she made the inquiry sound off-handed, a second thought. There was a sliver of fear in her eyes, but she kept it out of her voice. Times like this, I could understand why T'ing Hau Kaplan was the preferred hauntee of her mad Mongol ancestor, Yang, User of Yorkshire Terriers for Toilet Paper. She was a fighter.

I determined to meet her show of courage with my own. "Well, for one, the monsters get to stay on the Outside. My mother stays asleep. Eleziane stays ugly. Benjamin Kipnis stays on ice, wherever he is, and the demon that's taken his place at Feidelstein's Deli stays on duty, letting even more monsters come out of the Leeside whenever they want. Any of our allies who are magic-users forfeit all their powers to Baba—*Bambi* Yaga. She'll have enchantment coming out the wazoo, sorcery enough to do whatever she wants with the world." There was more, but I didn't feel like saying it.

T'ing knew me too well. "And—?" she prompted.

What the hell. "Since I co-signed as Dr. Faustus' second, I've got to offer the kind of collateral that's recognized by all parties as irrevocably binding in an agreement of this magnitude."

"Cut the lawyerese. What does it mean?"

"If we lose, I lose: My soul."

Her mouth opened to speak, but no sound came out. I tried to reply to her unasked questions, her unvoiced protests, only I was just as tongue-tied as she. I was only able to begin, "T'ing, it's not—" when I felt a tapping on my shoulder.

"They want you," Yang said. He was wearing his official security guard cap, but the rest of his outfit was pure skins-'n'-stink. No one at Glenwood High seemed to notice or care anymore, certainly not Doc Ox. "Downstairs." He didn't look happy.

"Who wants him?" T'ing had found her voice again, and it had a dangerous edge to it. She stepped between Yang and me as if her normal position in life was to protect me from any and all perils, real or implied.

"Honored Granddaughter, mind your own beeswax. I got no time to explain. When *they* say they want to see somebody, they mean *now*."

T'ing folded her arms. "*They* can wait, whoever *they* are. Tim and I don't go anywhere blind."

Yang sucked air through his teeth. "Listen, beloved nincompoop, I don't know from blind. *Deaf* I know, because you're it. They don't want you, they just want him, got that? Him *now*, and they sent me to get him. Why don't you go somewhere, shop for prom dress, get your hair done, buy shoes. Yeah, buy lotsa shoes. That's what you women do instead of sex, right?" He got a hold of me by the shirt-collar and tried hustling me down the hall. "Don't call us, we'll call you."

When two dogs squabble over a bone, I bet the bone gets fed up fast. I didn't mind Yang's highhanded abduction as much as T'ing's constant stance as my brave defender. Jeez, didn't she think I could stand up for myself? Now I knew how all those fairy-tale princesses must've felt. After Prince Charming saved them from the tower, or the man-eating ogre, or the dragon, it's a wonder they didn't clop him one with a loose stone, a well-gnawed thighbone, or a handful of dragon-doo.

I got one arm up and broke Yang's grip. "I've got all the shoes I need. Tell *me* where we're going, or I don't go."

Yang looked at the ceiling and shook his head. "Kids," he sighed. "Alla time questions, questions, no respect for the wishes of their elders. Whaddaya gonna do with 'em?"

He clasped both hands firmly together and brought the resulting double fist up smartly under my chin. I hit the corridor wall and slid down it nice and slow. As I watched the pretty lights whirl and twinkle before they blurred to a nice, uniform black, I heard him say, "It's a damn good thing I know how to talk to the younger generation!"

25

Triple Play

I AWOKE IN a cloud of steam that smelled like tuna casserole. *School cafeteria* tuna casserole.

You can imagine my feelings.

"Dear boy, if you must throw up, do try not to get any on the dragon's paws. It makes him a trifle skittish, and then we're all at sixes and sevens for the rest of the day."

The voice, warm and maternal, made me feel like I was sinking headfirst into an apple pie. I looked around, but the only thing I could see was a dragon. Well, of course. And here I'd been thinking that big green thing I was leaning against was a boiler. Boilers do not smell like tuna fish casserole, as a rule.

Lucky for me, the dragon was just as peaceable as a well-maintained boiler. Either the creature was of an easygoing disposition or I wasn't worth troubling his taste buds about. Still, I resolved to keep an eye on him; you never could tell. I rested one hand on his forepaw, trying to look as if I did stuff like this every day, and regained enough self-control to seek whoever had spoken to me. It wasn't easy.

The dragon snorted another fishy gust in my face, to no effect this time. Baleful eyes the color of creamed corn followed me as I got to my feet and wiped cold sweat off my face. It was difficult to see anything except the dragon, what with all the steam the beast was generating. Thick geysers spouted from its silver-rimmed nostrils at regular intervals, beads of condensing water slicked its emerald hide. When I gave it a mistrustful look, its sides pulsed with reptilian chuckles.

"Oh, do leave Bubbles alone, Mr. Desmond. He hasn't the slightest intention of eating *you*." A second voice, drier and more acerbic than the first, cut right to the heart of my dragon-watching thoughts. Whoever this person was, she made me sound downright unappetizing.

"Where are you?" I called into the mist.

"Where do you think we are?" A third distinct voice joined the party, this one flighty and teasing. "Shall we give him to the count of three to find us, and if he does, he gets a kiss?" Musical merriment echoed through the dragon-generated fog, although musical or not, I have to admit it sounded about as honest as a laugh-track.

A cavernous sigh made the mist swirl. "Not that again. He'll only trip over the chimera, and if the lion head doesn't rend him open, raw and bloody, the goat head'll eat him. Goats will eat *anything*." I couldn't see the speaker shudder, but I knew she had. You could cut the distaste in her voice with a chain saw.

"Sisters, sisters, please." Super-Mom was back, sounding plummier than ever. "We really must get down to business. Mr. Desmond, if you wouldn't mind, kindly step over to the leeward side of Bubbles."

"Leew—?"

There must be a practical way to tell the leeward side of a dragon from the windward, but I never got the chance to learn it. A blast of tepid air roared out of nowhere and on to somewhere else, attempting to peel the skin from my face in transit. The gale picked me up off my feet and walloped me against Bubbles' scaly flank. The dragon bawled like a frightened calf and bolted for parts unknown, leaving me to do a bearskin-rug imitation on the floor.

Then all was calm. The wind dropped, I rolled over onto my back, and there I lay staring up at a logjam of plumbing, a multilane motorway of pipes. I sat up and saw the great, green bulk of a boiler. A real boiler, this time. Above, a high window showed sunlight and the underside of a forsythia bush.

"I'm in the school basement?" I said, making a question out of a pretty solid certainty.

"On the floor of it. Comfy?"

The first one of the Three I saw was Miss Personality personified—if you believe lemons have personalities. Skinny and sharp-tongued, she loomed over me like the iron skeleton of a skyscraper. The black jumpsuit she wore tried to fake some flesh onto her bones, but good luck on that project. Her long, knife-straight white hair was pulled back until every edge of her wintry face was starkly plain.

"Honestly, you *might* help the poor child up."

The grinning hag shrieked as a plump hip gave her a deft body-check clear across the boiler-room floor. I expected to hear bones rattle when she hit the wall, but I was disappointed. Cushiony hands smelling of chocolate-chip cookies patted my face as the motherly one of the Three knelt before me, burbling tell-me-where-it-hurts noises.

I closed my eyes, enjoying the fuss. I was in familiar territory here, even if I could never recall my own mother wearing such a perfectly starched and frilled June Cleaver apron, complete with the requisite pearl choker. The—whaddayacallit— the *gestalt* was the same, though. Since Bambi Yaga had slapped Mom into the depths of slumber, I hadn't once had to tell a grown woman to knock it off, leave me alone, I was all right, I could take care of myself. I never realized I'd missed it so much.

The pampering stopped without warning. I opened my eyes to bosom. Much bosom and very little leopard-print cloth containing it. "Are you going to sit there forever, like a zit?" I recognized the third voice straight off, without waiting for the inevitable trill of phony giggles to confirm it. Besides the Jungle Girl outfit, the lady had no other adornments except a curling fall of bright red hair and blue eyes big as golf balls, though not so googly.

Now they all Three massed in front of me, each one extending a hand. I hesitated. I knew I was in the presence of power— no, make that Power, or Yang wouldn't have been so jittery—and I didn't want to offend any one of them by refusing her help up. Since I only had two hands, this was going to be a tricky bit of diplomacy.

They saw my predicament and they laughed. Then, as I watched, I saw the three hands—bony, pudgy, slim—blend into a single one. I gaped—who wouldn't—but there was little time for wonder. The hand made an impatient "let's get on with it" gesture and I took it automatically. One yank later I was standing up and surrounded by the Three.

"No, dear, we are not the Norns," said the motherly one. A frown line showed between her heavily plucked and penciled brows. "Unless you're Norse. You're not Norse, are you, dear?"

I wasn't. "Then you're what?" I asked. "The Fates? The—what's the Greek word?"

"*Moirae*, darling." Jungle Girl purred up at me. We were all sitting on a row of packing crates, only she had decided that the proper place for her was on the floor making like a boa constrictor around my legs. It made it kind of hard to enjoy the milk and cookies Super-Mom was pushing on me when my mouth kept going dry.

"Unless he means the *Eumenides*, dear," Super-Mom suggested. "The Furies. We do those for the Greeks, too."

"Doesn't matter." Bones sat stiff as an ancient Egyptian funerary statue, leering at me nastily. "We're not them either. Not unless you're Greek. Which you're not."

Jungle Girl pouted. "I wish we knew what he *is*. If I've got to change iconography, I'll have to wash my hair."

Super-Mom's rosy cheeks dimpled over the knitting in her lap. "Why should that matter to us any more than our identity must matter to him? The old boundaries have long since broken, in this land. *If* they were ever firm from the beginning, which I doubt. He is what he is, and we are the Three. That ought to suffice all around, don't you think?"

"Okay, so no names. But if you can't tell me who you are, at least you want to tell me *what* you are?" I never had learned when to quit. I looked from side to side, but wedges of impenetrable blackness had been set up all around our packing cases, as if someone had sliced a starless night into portable screens. From behind the dark, I heard muffled roars, snorts, and howlings.

"Well, ladies, I do suppose he's entitled to *that* much." Super-Mom tucked her knitting aside where I couldn't see it. Her two companions rose as if on cue and took their places to either side of her. The black behind them shimmered. So did they.

"We are what you think we are," said Bones.

"More," Jungle Girl twittered.

"Or less," Super-Mom finished. Taking dainty steps, they wove the figures of a dance.

"If you think that Three of us are too many, we can accommodate your fancy."

"Remodel to suit."

"Refurbish, redesign, rethink." A pirouette, and they were a single female form, but with three faces. A leap, and they were the Three again.

"We are what you believe."

"We are what you think."

"We are what you need."

"What *everything* needs, if it's to make sense."

"A beginning, a middle, and an end."

"And then a beginning again."

"Well, dear, it *does* make for steady work, having it that way." Super-Mom tried to execute a bit of complex footwork and stumbled into Bones. "Whoopsy! Excuse me."

Bones glared. "Sometime," she growled, "we ought to consider whether there are worse things than unemployment. An end, a *final* end with no new start to follow might be just the restful change the world desires. The ceaseless round can be quite tiresome."

"Now you're talking like those wicked things we left behind us in the Leeside." Super-Mom gave her gruesome colleague a severe stare.

"Oh, pooh!" Jungle Girl waved away Bones's distasteful notion. "If the world wants a once-and-for-all ending, good thing the world doesn't always get its own way, then. Silly old world!"

I followed their dance better than I followed their explanation. "I still don't understand!" I cried. "What are you? You're speaking in riddles!"

"Oh no, dear, that would be poaching on someone else's territory." Super-Mom pinched my cheek as she whirled past. "Although we have been known to dabble."

"We played at beauty pageants with Paris of Troy."

"We had a fine round of blindman's bluff with Perseus when we were the Gray Ones, although having just one eye to go around strikes me as rather stingy dealings."

"Babd, Maeve, and Morrigan."

"Artemis, Cynthia, and Hecate."

"Life, Liberty, and the Pursuit of Happiness."

"Larry, Moe, and Curly Joe!"

"Who said that?"

All of them tried looking innocent.

Bones paused in her part of the dance to clamp steely fingers into my shoulder and hiss in my ear, "We are *so* fond of games, we Three."

Her breath had an unpleasantly moldy tang to it. I jumped away and landed between the other two. They never missed a beat, so I had to shout my questions at them on the fly-by.

"But whatever you are, you're not monsters! Why were you trapped in the Leeside?"

"Not monsters? Isn't he a dear to say that!" Super-Mom took my hands and dragged me into her arms, where we did a waltz. In perfect Three-quarter time, of course.

Jungle Girl cut in and had me doing the cha-cha-cha before I knew it. "*I* don't think we're monsters. We're just the Three. We know an awful lot, and we do have this itsy-bitsy smidgy-widge of power . . . or so I've heard."

Again cold claws dug into my arms and wrenched me away from my partner. Willing or not, I was caught up in Bones's unyielding grip and prancing out a polka. "Legends name us the controllers of man's fate, the guardians of man's knowledge, the possessors of answers to all the questions man might wish to know. We decree the beginning, the middle and the end of every life, if you believe all that's ever been said of us."

I struggled to get away, but Bones was a loyal partner. The one-two-THREE-*and*-one-two-THREE of the polka sped up, until I could only pant, "That doesn't make you monstrous!"

All at once, the unheard music seemed to stop. Bones dropped me, to stand again with her sisters. Now Jungle Girl was robed in maiden white and held a golden spindle in her hands. Super-Mom wore the blue of heaven as her fingers played out the thread, and Bones, face hidden in a deep cowl, dipped into the folds of her black gown to bring out the shining ivory shears. They looked at me, all Three, incredulous.

"We spin, we measure, we cut short the life of every man."

"We hold more wisdom than any man will ever learn."

"We *are* the start, the quickening, the death, and still the new birth after for all men."

"But we are *women*."

Bones drew back her cowl, and there was no more skin to veil the smiling skull. "For some men," she said, "to bear the insult of such power in such vessels makes us monstrous enough."

She held the strand taut and by some passing enchantment the filament widened before my eyes until I saw each fiber of it heavy with my own lifetime. Chalky teeth parted in glee as she opened the shears and laid their hungry blades against the thread.

Just as the pale blades met, a blinding blue flash dazzled me. When I blinked away the after-spots, we were back on the packing crates again.

"Uh . . . I guess that answered my question about what you are, all right," I said.

"Well, yessss." Super-Mom tapped her lips thoughtfully. "I suppose you *could* see it that way."

"We just like to think of ourselves as the Boss." Bones showed me more of her dental work than I cared to inspect.

Super-Mom gave her another of those hefty pokes. "Don't get too big for your britches, my girl, and go claiming to be more than you are. Or have you forgotten the Leeside so soon?"

It was weird seeing someone as white as Bones go paler yet. Upset or no, she covered by getting stubborn and saying, "Who cares how he sees it? What counts is that as far as he's concerned, we *are* the Boss." Her eyes slued in my direction. It was like suddenly having a rattlesnake decide to take a personal interest in your every move. "Perhaps he's wondering why we asked him here?"

" 'Cause he's *cute*!" Jungle Girl wrinkled her nose at me. Super-Mom just sighed.

"Well, yeah, that would be nice," I said, playing it cool. Somewhere behind the screens of night something roared loud enough to made me jump. So much for cool.

"We asked you here, dear, because we've been following you rather closely." Super-Mom had her knitting out again. I eyed it warily. Now that I knew where she got the stuff, I didn't want my life being made into a cardigan.

Jungle Girl nuzzled my knee. "Or do you think a mere kitten's random leaps came up with the terms of your battle?"

"You mean you—?"

"We had a hand in it." Jungle Girl inspected her pearly polished nails, playing coy. "Or Three."

"Why?" I asked. "Does this mean you're on my side?"

Bones smashed a scone to crumbs with one vicious bite. "The only side we take's our own. And we don't like being cheated." For a heartbeat, her eyes blanked out into empty sockets in whose depths I saw Bambi Yaga's face. "Talk about getting too big for one's britches," she grated.

Super-Mom reached across her knitting to pat my hand. "Even the rankest amateur spinner knows that there's only so much weight a strand will bear. Put too much on it, and it snaps. If he loses to the witch, Dr. Faustus' forfeited sorcery will be but a small addition to her power. Unfortunately, if you lose as well, she will possess enough magic to strain the web-work of the world to the breaking point." She sat back and resumed knitting. "We wouldn't like that at all, dear."

"Huh? If she gets *my* magic she'll be—? I don't have any magic! Nothing to write home about, anyway."

"Yes, dear." Super-Mom wrassled with a snarl. "Whatever you say, dear."

"Listen, all I have I got from Eleziane's father, Lord Pala-mon. My wand—my father's sword—both together, but it isn't working—it can't—my mother—"

"Shut up," said Bones. "We know."

Jungle Girl ran her fingernail up the inseam of my jeans until I squirmed. Hey, she got my attention.

"We Three are whatever you mortals believe us to be. Just so you are to yourselves. Does magic's symbol bestow power, or merely wake it where it lies? When greed fights goodness, does it matter whether the battle-plain is the borderland of empires or the Glenwood High School gym?" A weird, foggy look came over her. She began to sway on her haunches, chanting: "Armies gather, if you can the armies see. Who claims them for his own, owns victory. Sword-brothers stand together in the fray, heart to heart, and win the day. Magician, wisely choose your friends! Strange allies rule when battle ends."

"There she goes again." Super-Mom shook her head indulgently. "You'll have to excuse her, dear. She *will* get these attacks of prophecy. You know how it is with virgins."

"I do not," I grumped.

"Well, pay attention anyway. There might be something important for you in what she says."

Pay attention? Important? *Now* she tells me! While Super-Mom had been speaking I'd missed a good stretch of doggerel revelation.

Desperate to salvage something, I patted my pockets and turned up a leaky ball-point stick pen and a wadded-up receipt from Record City. As I scribbled down as much as I could remember of her babblings, Jungle Girl cried out: "She wakes to see the frog be crowned a queen!"

And quit.

"Oh, goody," said Super-Mom. "Peace at last."

"Wait! Hold it!" I gasped. "I didn't get all that. What comes after 'Seek heroes'?"

Bones plucked pen and paper from my hands and stuffed a bunch of folding money into my shirt pocket.

"Just buy the prom tickets for us, kid. We'll see how much of your butt we can save for you there, okay?"

I was making my stunned and silent way up the basement steps when I heard Three voices call as one:

"—and when you're lining up our dates, be sure to tell them we've got *great* personalities!"

26

Save the Last Dance for Me

"TRUST ME: SHE'S got a *great* personality," I wheedled.

"But does she like dogs?" Gorm of the Shining Helm replied.

"Sure she does," Neil said briskly, swaddling the hero in a rented cummerbund. "Crazy about 'em. Why don't you trade those two whatever-the-hells for a coupla dogs yourself some day?"

Zisi and Zasu, the Hounds from Heck, growled ineffectively at us from their place under Neil's bed.

"I still don't like this whole setup," said Perseus, fiddling with his bow tie. "By rights, the Mythological Continuum should've been set ass-over-amphora the minute we stepped out of the Back Room."

"But it wasn't," I hastened to remind him. "Which means *de facto* that this is something you heroes are not only permitted to get away with, it's something you're *supposed* to do. Perseus, this is your *mission*!"

I waited for him to get the "hero-look" in his eyes when I said *mission*. You know, that bright-eyed, simpleminded, oblivious stare you see in every picture of Sir Galahad beholding the Grail. I'd seen it first when Neil and I, accompanied by T'ing and Teleri, entered the Back Room of Feidelstein's to do our heavy-duty recruiting. The heroes were reluctant, to begin with. A few of them were downright truculent. Mostly we garnered a lot of I-gave-at-the-human-sacrifice responses.

Then Teleri played hardball. "Glory," she said. "Battle. Death. Blood. Havoc. Girls. Free beer."

Bingo. The "hero-look" in spades. Which was how we managed to scrape together the ten happy souls (not counting the dogs) presently crowding Neil's bedroom. Our task now was to get this pack of yahoos zipped into their rented tuxes, introduced to their dates, and over to the Glenwood High School gymnasium before Neil's father came home and discovered all of his six-packs were missing.

It had been a long afternoon. Even thoughts of impending immortality-through-bloodshed lose some of their glamour for the staunchest of heroes. Perseus wasn't buying any.

"Our mission?" he repeated with all the fiery passion of a life insurance actuary. "So you said. So it seemed when you unmasked the fiend who had usurped our noble host's place."

Fat lot of good that had done. I'd stepped up to the monster who'd been playing Ben Kipnis' part at the deli counter and pulled a Perry Mason sudden-death accusation on him. It was pure bluff, but it worked. The critter got the wind up, panicked, and tried to make a dash for it. Siegfried (or Siegmund) leaped in and made like a Germanic Cuisinart.

"Would've been nice if we could've asked him where he stowed Mr. Kipnis," I mumbled. "It's mighty hard to cross-examine a pile of fiend purée."

"Fear not," said Perseus. "Once we have triumphed over the witch and her minions, we shall undertake the . . . *Quest for Kipnis*!" Whoa! The Q-word! The "hero-look" flickered alive, then died quickly. He gave the bow tie another futile twitch. "Speaking of fiends, who in Hades created this sadistic frippery?"

"Probably the the same asshole whose only social skill is knowing how to tie one of them," Siegfried suggested. He had dealt with the problem of bow ties with his usual heroic directness, by ripping the one I gave him off his neck and chopping it into cole slaw with his sword Nothung.

"I still don't like this," an Aztec hero said. We gave up trying to call him by his given name as soon as he gave it— something like Hzulptlzpotecatlieeatl. "All this stealth, these ruses, this obnoxious clothing. Why can't we just show up and bust heads? I am morally opposed to skulduggery."

"Unless it involves real skulls," said Cuchulain.

"Celts who live in huts with niches for displaying severed heads shouldn't throw stones," the Aztec shot back.

The Irish hero stopped carving CUCHULAIN + EMER 4EVER

in Neil's bedroom wall long enough to ask, "Why not? Throw one big enough and the job's done."

There was an urgent knocking at the door. T'ing came in without bothering to wait for a by-your-leave. Our token knight, Sir Edgar Dragonslayer, let out a yip of outraged modesty and clutched his cast-off hauberk to his massive chest. "Woman, people are changing in here!" he bellowed.

T'ing didn't look like she was in the mood to coddle anyone's propriety, least of all that of a warrior who augmented his basic armor with accessories made from the tanned hide of a slain dragon's—uh—Well, *he* said it made a pretty good sleeping bag.

"What's the holdup?" she demanded. "The girls will be here any second, and the four heroes you guys *have* gotten dressed are starting to get antsy."

"So, keep 'em busy."

"*You* keep them busy. I tried teaching them some card games, but Yoshitsune threatened to commit *seppuku* if anyone accused him of cheating—which he *does* do—and the big Russian just looks at his cards, sighs, and tells us another endless story about winter on the steppes, and did you know that Heitsi-Ebib—you know, the Hottentot—is both a hero *and* a sorcerer? *Try* keeping the game honest with that bunch."

"What about the Roman?" Neil inquired. "Square jaw, clear eye, good posture, virtue to burn? I bet he plays an honest hand of poker."

"Maybe. But all Horatius wants to do is play bridge! If we don't get some help out here in two seconds—"

I got behind our Aztec friend and propelled him past her, out the door. "That's five, okay? We're almost done with Gorm, too. Neil! Give Perseus a hand with his tie. T'ing! Check in the garment bags to see if there's a spare tie for Siegfried and *don't let him try tying it on himself*! Do it out in the kitchen. Sir Edgar! What the heck is that thing you're trying to squeeze into your trousers?"

Neil raised one eyebrow. "Looks like an athletic supporter to me."

"My sword has grown rather heavy with the weight of legend," Sir Edgar explained. With a discreet cough he added: "Rather than do myself a mischief when I heft the blade, I thought that an ounce of prevention, etcetera. And it's made of only the finest dragonhide, removed exclusively from the fire-worm's—''

"Never mind! It won't fit under a pair of tux pants. Put on those BVDs.''

"BVDs, sirrah?''

"Beaten Vicious Dragonskins," Neil said smoothly. "See how white? That's the color the beast turned when he saw Tim the Terrible was about to slay his ass.''

"So?'' Sir Edgar picked up the underwear reverently and gazed at me with new respect. He was dressed in two shakes of a big lizard's death-throes.

Cuchulain was the last of the bunch, and he almost didn't make it because Teleri came in and kept pestering him for an autograph. My banshee looked more delectable than ever, in a frothy prom gown the color of a summer sky. I saw her making goo-goo eyes at the great hero of Ireland, but she might as well have saved her efforts.

I was trying to get my own bow tie to lie down and play dead when she tugged at my arms. "Tim, darlin', might I be asking ye a wee favor?''

"Stinking rotten loathsome walleyed slippery . . .'' I paused in my Litany to the Bow Tie and gave her my attention. "Yeah? Like what?''

She twiddled her fingers demurely. "Ohhh, not such of a much at all, at all. Only that when ye've to pair off these fine gentlemen as ye've rallied t' yer cause with such ladies as ye've likewise conscripted, if ye'd but see yer way clear t' having me own humble self on the arm o' yon Cuchulain, 'twould be ever so obliged t' ye I'd be until me dyin' day.''

"I see," I said. "No," I added.

"And would ye be tellin' me why the devil not, while ye've still a throat in working order?'' Teleri inquired.

"Well, for one, you've already had your dying day. For another, it's not in my hands. I can't have the last word on the fix-ups. Only those who are meant to fight together, as a team, will pair off, and only those who find their sword-brother will be able to fight. If Cuchulain isn't responding to you, it's because you're not the one he's waiting for.''

"Hmph.'' Teleri tugged her tulle skirt. "That's as may be. I, fer one, will be after seeing what it is that *Cosmopolitan* has t' say about this!''

She flounced out of the bedroom just as the doorbell rang.

Neil was there before me to welcome Brendan, Ibrahim, and Gaspar, three of his onetime Rawbone Kings cronies. All of them were arrayed in cheap rental tuxes of various grades of bad taste. They traded high-fives and knuckle-knotting secret handshakes along with the traditional Rawbone King greeting: ''So where's the brew?''

''In them.'' Neil jerked a thumb at the assembled heroes. We had finally gotten them all ready and rounded up in the kitchen. Stuffed into their monkey suits and cranky as camels with heat rash, they scowled doom and dismemberment at the newcomers.

It takes a lot to give a Rawbone King pause, but that did it. Gaspar ran a finger around the inside of his shirt collar and managed to say, ''Err . . . We all going in one car or what?''

Ibrahim slugged him one. ''Sure we are, butthead. And where's our dates gonna ride?'' He checked out the talent, which at the moment was T'ing and Teleri, period. T'ing had her Yang-face on and Teleri had her nose buried in the latest *Cosmo*. If you listened carefully, you could just hear her muttering, '' 'When all else fails, greet Mr. Yummy at the door wearing nothing but carefully selected pages of the *Wall Street Journal* wetted down with Perrier.' ''

I steered them away from the ladies. ''Your dates are coming any second. You'll like them. They've got—''

Brendan unraveled my bow tie with one tiny yank. ''If you say 'great personalities,' I walk, freebie prom or no freebie prom. I don't dog-sit for nobody.''

''They ain't dogs, are they, Desmond?'' Gaspar cozied up to me like a friendly hammerhead shark. ''I mean, it's real nice of you to give us prom tickets, pick up the tab for our tuxes, the whole nine yards, but if it's dogs . . . We wouldn't be happy campers if you're fixing us up with dogs.''

''Dogs? Who? Them? Naaaaaah.''

''So they're what? Your cousins?''

''Welllll, nooooo. What they are is—'' The doorbell rang, greatly to my relief. ''What they are is *here*,'' I said, running to answer it and praying I'd guessed right.

My luck was sweet, for once. ''Hello, Tim,'' said Super-Mom. Even in a gown of royal blue satin she looked like she was puttering around a kitchen.

Jungle Girl had swapped her leopard-print bikini for a strapless sheath made of red aluminum foil. "Where's the men?" she asked, trying to steal a peek inside the apartment.

Bones took the direct route, elbowing her way in without awaiting an invitation. Her chicken-wire body was camouflaged in a welter of black sequins, until she resembled the ideal mourner for Liberace's funeral. Her sisters came teetering after on sling-back heels.

It was simple arithmetic: Three plus three. It didn't take a genius for the Rawbone Kings to understand that these were their dates.

"Dibs on the bimbo in red!" they cried with one voice.

It took a little backdoor diplomacy on my part, Super-Mom's surprise offer of a batch of homemade fudge for her date, and coldblooded intimidation from Bones, but we got them paired off.

"They don't look happy," I whispered to Neil.

"Ibrahim does."

"Yeah, sure, he got the one in red, but the other guys aren't thrilled. I was hoping it'd work out. The Kings are good plain dirty fighters, and we could use the Three on our side. We can't, if they're not paired. I mean *really* matched to their escorts. Only couples can fight."

"Know whatya mean. I remember how it was when Mom lived here."

"Come on, Neil, you know we need more allies. I matched up Doc Ox and Ms. Stone—not that he knows it yet—but he's no warrior; he's dead weight. Jeez, I don't even know if Faustus is going to be able to get in on this!"

"You can pair off a gorgon and you can't find *anyone* for our pal the wizard? Hell, Desmond, he's not even half bad looking. So he's five hundred years old. You couldn't fix him up with one of the chaperones?"

I gave up trying to explain. Magic didn't do things by simple mathematics. One plus one equalled much more than two in the equation of power that sword-brothers made. To enter the battle of wizard and witch you needed a partner, but to fight your best you needed a friend. I had T'ing to stand beside me and lend me strength, but who would be there to augment Faustus' sorcery?

"Don't sweat it, Desmond, he'll be there." Neil clapped me on the back. The doorbell rang again. "I'll get it. Maybe it's the rest of the girls."

I saw him go to the door. I saw him open it. I heard him whine a curse and back up fast, but not fast enough. Big hands fell on his shoulders and threw him against the nearest wall. Mr. Fitzsimmons had come home early tonight.

"What the fuck is going on here?" He was bigger than I remembered from when I occupied Neil's body. Point of view at work, I guess, though even then I recall being cowed by the sheer size of the man and all the anger in him. He reached for Neil and grabbed him by the front of his rented tux. "Who in hell are these sons of bitches? What do you think you're doing, turning my house into a crash pad for all your rotten 'friends'?" His eyes were bleary and red with liquor, and they burned as he looked at us. "Get the fuck out," he growled.

T'ing tried playing by the rules. "We're sorry, Mr. Fitzsimmons. We were just on our way to the school prom. We'll be going n—"

"You shut up." His finger shook as he pointed at her. He stank of stale tobacco, sweat, and booze. "Hear that, slant? I got nothing to say to you, so you just get your yellow ass out of here before I kick it out."

I don't think he should've said that.

A lot of people agreed with me. That's the funny thing about heroes: They don't bathe too early or too often, but they know when something smells worse than dirt and they do something about it. Also, for good or bad, most of them have never heard of Alan Alda or of letting a woman fight her own battles.

It wasn't a fair fight; just a fast one. Nine against one are lousy odds, and that's not even counting Zisi and Zasu, who leaped right in. Now that I think of it, the odds Mr. Fitzsimmons gave his kid all those years weren't what you'd call sporting. It would've been ten-to-one, only the Rawbone Kings and I had to bench Siegfried by sitting on him, or he would've treated Neil's father like another contrary bow tie. The other heroes had the class not to use steel against an unarmed man. It didn't take them long to fell him, truss him, and plop him down at the kitchen table, where Zisi wet on his shoes.

Super-Mom shooed Neil into the chair opposite. "I really think you boys need to talk. I'll just go whip up some milk and cookies, hm?"

Mr. Fitzsimmons talked. The air was blue afterwards. Jungle Girl covered her ears and squealed, "Ew, ew, *ewww*! That's *not* what we want to hear."

Mr. Fitzsimmons repeated most of it and played variations on a theme by Lenny Bruce, just in case we missed it the first time through. When he was done, even the Rawbone Kings were impressed. Sir Edgar said he hadn't heard the like, although he came close the time he tried sneaking up behind a Wiltshire dragon that had eaten too many ripe plums.

"Ah, forget it." Neil pushed his chair away. "That's all you're gonna get from him. That's all *I* ever get. Let's go wait for the girls downstairs. I don't want to be near him any more than I have to."

He tried to go, but Super-Mom was suddenly in the doorway, looking stern. "That is not what we want to hear either, young man."

Jungle Girl slithered up his back. "He is your father."

"So what? That's not my fault. I wish he never—"

"Be careful what you wish for, boy." Bones trailed a black-gloved forefinger down his cheek. "You might get it."

They returned him to the table and shoved him back into his seat. Super-Mom snapped her fingers. All at once Jungle Girl and Bones were holding two knit garments. I couldn't tell whether they were sweaters, shawls, scarves, or what. Light and shadow teased my eyes across them, making them seem to change shape every second. One thing I could see: One of them looked considerably bigger than the other; older too. The colors were more drab, the yarn sagged more wearily. Bones stood behind Mr. Fitzsimmons and shook the bigger garment out, gloating over how close in size it was to the man.

Neil frowned, then looked behind him just in time to catch Jungle Girl going through the same motions with the smaller garment. He tried to snatch the cloth away and failed. She made coquettish "naughty-naughty" faces at him and danced over to Bones's side of the table. Neil would have followed, but Super-Mom was there.

"Young man, sit *down*." He sat.

We all saw Bones come slinking around the table to take her sister's place. Another sign from Super-Mom and the garments fell across the shoulders of father and son. It was a poor fit, but it was one try-on neither of them would ever forget.

I don't know what they saw, wrapped in the folds of each other's lives. I can only imagine, and tell you how it looked from outside. Neil shook, froze, shook again. Names stammered from his lips: *Saigon, Hue, Da Nang, Hanoi.* Others: *Frank, David, Allen, Phil, Larry*! And there were screams.

His face became a mirror for horrors until his spirit snapped with the weight of everything he witnessed. Until his soul had no more room for fear or grief, only the white-hot fire of rage. We'd read about Vietnam, his father's war; Neil lived it. One sentence in a textbook skimmed over the count of the dead like a skater over ice; Neil plunged beneath the cold, clean surface to number each torn and emptied body as a friend.

Opposite him, Mr. Fitzsimmons walked another road. What he experienced brought no screams, just tears. They ran down his face without making a sound, without a single sob to shake his broad shoulders. He looked like a rock in the rain.

Then he did move. Nothing fast, nothing spectacular: his hand, that's all. It was gently struggling to escape its bonds. I saw Super-Mom nod, and Bones snipped the ropes with an ordinary pair of kitchen shears. Released, Mr. Fitzsimmons' hand traveled across the table to clasp his son's. When the Three removed the garments, the two at the kitchen table didn't notice at first. When they realized they were free, they overturned the table between them and fell into each other's arms.

While the rest of us stood there in silence, Gaspar cautiously approached Super-Mom and put his arm around her. "That was cool, y'know?"

"Yeah," said Ibrahim, taking his place with Jungle Girl. "Something else, babe." She giggled.

Brendan edged up to Bones, but said nothing. "What's the matter?" she asked sardonically. "Don't you think what *I* did was cool?"

"Dunno," he replied. Then he swept her off her feet and gave her the biggest, wettest kiss I'd ever seen, short of a Saint Bernard slobber. "Yeah, I guess you are pretty cool," he admitted.

Breathless, Bones hailed her sisters: "I think this means we're popular."

"Are we?" Super-Mom beamed. "How nice." She got the drop on Gaspar, slung him over one shoulder before he could let out a peep, and cheerfully announced, "All right, everyone. Let's party."

27

Matchmaker, Matchmaker

WE LEANED AGAINST the parked cars, polishing their dented hoods with the seats of our rented pants. We could hear the sound of loud music throbbing from the gym and watch the couples as they arrived for the prom. The girls' skirts made this rich, rustly noise that left my skin warm and tingling, don't ask me why. Some things don't need the wizard's touch to make them magical.

"What are we waiting for?" The Aztec slapped the handle of his obsidian sword into his palm. By street-lamp light the blade shimmered silver. Here was a man who liked his job. He wasn't going to like what I had to tell him.

No sense rushing into an unpleasant scene. "The girls," I said. "We're waiting for your dates."

"Why weren't they delivered to Sir Neil's hold?" Sir Edgar asked. He had given all of us honorific knighthoods, in view of our impending brotherhood-of-combat, and promised to send the survivors some handmade dragonskin wallets when it was all over.

"That's a toughie," I admitted. My hair still prickled at the memory of T'ing's expression when the phone rang and Neil called her over to take it. She'd volunteered to be our scout for females willing to partner our corps of heroes, but until that moment I didn't know how she'd planned to do it, nor had I asked.

Now I knew without asking. Only one thing could turn T'ing's normally smooth, pale, serene face into a cross be-tween a stoplight, a prune, and Three Mile Island about to go

"Uh-oh": Yang, Leveler of Cities! Yang, Slaughterer of Innocent Bystanders! Yang, Brief-but-efficient Consoler of Widows!

Yang, Purveyor of Pork Rinds?

That was what it said on the side of the van he drove up in, right under the painting of a happy piggy dressed up like Genghis Khan about to lop the head off a not-so-happy piggy garbed like a Chinese peasant. Yang beeped the horn and yelled out the window, "Hey! I brought snacks!"

T'ing waded into the street and got him by the left-hand moustache. "Wasn't there something *else* you were supposed to be bringing along, honored Grandfather?"

"Lay off the lip-spinach, beloved Granddaughter. You know how long it takes to grow one of these?" She released her grip, leaving him to fuss over the wounded whiskers. "All right, so I'm late and you're pissed. Gimme a break, huh? Last time I ravished anyone I was a coupla centuries younger. Also, I had a horse. Those were the days! See a nice woman, grab her, haul her up across the withers, gallop away to the nearest yurt, eat a sheep afterward—cooked, if she was in a good mood—You can't haul anything up across the withers of a Volkswagon!"

Yang's canter down Memory Lane ended in a shrill *ouch* when T'ing recaptured his moustache and twisted. "Where . . . are . . . they?"

"Imma bag. *Imma bag!*" Yang waved his hands wildly, then took the cheap way out and dematerialized. As an ancestral spirit, he was entitled. He reappeared standing behind T'ing and nursing a sore upper lip. "In the back," he repeated, peeved.

T'ing marched the heroes to the rear of the pork rind van and had them stand so that the street light was shining full on them. With her hand on the door handle, she made a last-minute check. "Ready, gentlemen?"

"Verily."

"Jawohl."

"You bet your sweet—"

"Hai!"

A couple of them howled at the moon, and T'ing had to remind them that only Zisi and Zasu had drooling privileges.

"These are nice girls," she said. "My revered ancestor—may he someday get the lobotomy he deserves—has gone to a great deal of trouble to select those classmates of mine most likely to be open-minded and compatible enough to get you into the prom. Be nice."

"We're *always* nice," said Perseus. Then he looked down, saw what Zasu had done on his winged sandal, and cut the hound's head off with his sword. The beast instantly reassembled itself without losing a beat of its idiot panting.

"That's another thing," I said, deciding it was now or never. "Before you meet the girls, we're going to have to take your swords."

Gee, you'd think they'd all read Freud from the way they reacted.

"You'll get them back," I said, trying to calm them. "Later. Inside. I'm going to sneak them into the gym by a secret way and return them to you as fast as I can. But you can't get into the prom carrying serious steel."

"Why not?"

"Because you'd be too conspicuous."

Neil nudged me and nodded at the heroes. "Perseus is wearing open-toed sandals with wings, the Russian won't lose his riding boots, Siegfried never *did* take a shower, Gorm's got that dumb Shining Helm *and* the Bobbsey Mutts with him, and *you're* telling them it's the swords that'll make them conspicuous?"

"Look, back me up on this, okay?" I shot back. To the heroes I said, "The swords?"

Bones came up behind me and smiled at them over my shoulder. Something about the lady's look always inspired co-operation. My arms were soon weighted down with edged steel and toothed obsidian. Neil took the load from me before I collapsed. "Good," I said. "Swords collected. Flowers?" Teleri passed among the heroes, distributing supermarket-bought corsages and squandering melting looks on Cuchulain. "Flowers, check. Okay. *Now* the girls."

T'ing opened the back door of the van. I held my breath. I didn't know who Yang had tapped or how he'd "persuaded" them to join our merry band. With the door open, the girls might imitate the big pigeon-release at the Olympics. They might scream. They might use pork rinds on us in a markedly unfriendly manner. I held my breath and peered into the unlit van, trying to glean some hint of what was to come from the shadows within.

"Oooooh, look, Tiffany! They're like, *hunks*!"

Like circus clowns, only dressed funnier, the Glenwood High cheerleaders came tumbling out of the van and all over the waiting heroes.

* * *

T'ing passed Yang a cup of watery pink punch, head bowed.
"Honored Grandfather, I owe you an apology."

"You also owe me thirty-five bucks for the pork rinds those pom-pom ass-pains ate." He swigged down the punch and spewed it right back out in a thin stream that shot down several yards of mango-gold crepe paper from the walls. "Giving honest men horse urine to drink—this is another trial to see whether I get to stay at this cruddy orgy?"

"Yes," I said. (He never would've believed that sane people actually drink prom punch because they want to.) "You passed with flying colors. If you want, I'll get you something decent to drink from one of the vending machines. I really owe you for what you did about getting those girls."

"How did you know they wouldn't run away the first chance they got?" T'ing asked.

Yang laughed so loudly he attracted the attention of every chaperone in the room. This included Ms. Stone, looking radiant in a sheath of white pebbled silk with matching (and wriggling) mantilla. "I saw what those heroes looked like! Swinging swords is *really* pumping iron. They got sturdy backs. Strong shoulders. Buttock muscles you can bounce medium-sized rocks off. I think, *Yang, some of them look like they'd be almost as good to have sex with as you. Almost. Barely. If you squint.* But then I figure, these modern women, they don't got anything decent to choose from, they'll jump at the chance to get a real man."

"I don't think that holds true for all modern women," I said, my politically correct knee jerking so fast I almost fell over. "It sure looks like it worked that way for the pep squad, though." I'll say it did. Yang had done a straight sweep of our cheerleaders—minus the harpies—and they'd not only jumped at the chance, they'd done cartwheels. Not even Kirsten had balked. She was across the dance floor, draped over Cuchulain's arm, all thoughts of her previous passion for Goliath obviously forgotten. Teleri slouched near the bandstand, glaring poisoned daggers at her rival. "Looks aren't all that important in a *real* relationship," I finished.

Yang condescended to pat me on the back. "Tim, anyone ever tell you you can be one pretentious little snot? Looks aren't important . . . Pfui! Tom Cruise is starving, huh?" The friendly pat turned into an imperious shove. "Bring me back a Pepsi and cut the crap."

The nearest vending machines were in the hall near the cafeteria, a good distance away from the gym. Maybe I shouldn't have left the battle site, but I *did* owe Yang a favor for getting the heroes dates. Anyhow, neither of the two major combatants had arrived yet.

And when Dr. Faustus came, would he be alone? He seemed to have vanished since our last meeting. No one had seen him. Now I thought of it, the naturalized monster population in the halls of Glenwood High was apparently down, too, or at least a whole lot less visible. Had poor Krito the minotaur perished of hunger while seeking his minimum daily requirement of virgins? Had the EPA slapped a writ on Shiko, the blue oni, for not filing an environmental impact statement about his supernatural exhalations? Were his six goblin henchmen hidden in some dim corner of the school, trying to get a rap act together?

Not all of the horrors were gone. I accidentally stepped on Danforth's foot on my way out of the gym.

"Lord, Desmond, watch where you're going! If you break my toe, how ever am I to lambada with any *real* feeling?" The ogre only pretended to be hurt. It would take a pile-driver to do his toes a genuine injury.

"Gee, I'm sorry, Danforth." I tried getting past him, but the ogre was in a chummy mood.

"Don't give it another thought, dear fellow. *Noblesse oblige.* I forgive you utterly and entirely if you'll just be kind enough to give me your uncensored opinion of the *mise en scène.* I *was* rather influential on the decorating committee, you know."

I made a big show of looking around and evaluating the gymnasium. Our prom theme was Beautiful Hawaii. After the committee got all the usual jokes about poi-meets-girl-gets-lei'd out of their system, they set out to buy up every honeycomb paper-pineapple, palm tree, angelfish, and flower garland in Brooklyn. Cardboard hula dancers plastered the walls. Paper tiki masks grimaced down from the basketball backboards. The refreshment table was heaped with tissue-paper carnations, which weren't very Hawaiian, but I think there's some kind of Federal law that says you can't hold a prom without tissue-paper carnations.

"Nice," I told Danforth. "Real—um—aloha-y."

"Do you really think so?" The ogre blushed with pleasure.

"I only did my poor best. There *was* a certain disruptive element on the committee that *insisted* we use only the Glenwood High school-colors, but we soon squashed *that* silly notion."

I'll bet. Along with the proponents of said notion.

"They did a neat job," I said, and made another attempt to get away. He blocked me.

"They?" Danforth laid a hand to the pleated bosom of his shirt. "One mustn't hide one's light under one's bushel, must one? I confess: *I* was the one who saw this room as a veritable *riot* of color. We could have had pastels, but the occasion and the setting simply *screamed* 'primaries, primaries, primaries!' It makes a more unified statement, don't you agree?"

You bet. And the statement was: Bad taste kills.

"Too bad none of your buddies are here to see it. Where's Kirkwood? How come I don't see that frost-giant Sweyn hanging out with the principal tonight?"

Danforth made a face. "Oh, I don't know. Something about a summons to prepare for battle. They all went scurrying off, like good little abominations. *I* should've gone, I suppose, but I decided I'd sat in on quite enough committee meetings already, thank you, and my *first* obligation was of course to see that my decorating concepts were faithfully carried out here."

"Well, you did great. Super. You've got a marvelous future in the arts. I gotta go." I faked left, darted right, and almost got driven six inches into the floor when Danforth's hand fell on my shoulder.

"So kind of you to say so, Desmond. I love a man who appreciates artistic integrity." He lowered his head until we were eye-to-eye. He reeked of Old Spice aftershave, nachos, and a minty mouthwash that was *not* living up to its advertising. "Which makes it so much easier for me to ask you to remove that *icky* piece of statuary you so rudely parked on the central refreshment table."

I followed where his taloned finger pointed to the petrified tomte, who now stood surrounded by platters of rapidly browning sliced pineapple, several plastic leis around his neck. He looked about as authentically Hawaiian as Arnold Schwarzenegger in a grass skirt.

A little while later, as I was lugging the unlucky tomte back to my locker, I heard crying. It was coming from the girls' room. The lockers were pretty far from the gym, and most of the girls were using the facilities closer to the action. Whoever was in there wanted to be alone with her misery.

Knowing the score has never stopped me from trying to change the game. Hadn't I had the brainstorm of putting the tomte out as part of the prom décor, so that if we won the day, the little sprite wouldn't wake up shut away in my locker and panic? Meddling is my life. Still carrying the tomte, I opened the girls' room door.

Eleziane sat in the middle of the floor, her vast gown spread around her like a sea of white lace. At least fifty assorted lipsticks, eyeshadows, mascaras, and whatever else girls inflict on their faces lay scattered over the tiles.

"Want to tell me about this?" I asked.

"Drop dead."

"Sooner than you think, if Bambi Yaga has it her way. What are you doing in here? We need you."

Eleziane lifted a face covered with a clashing color-war of makeup. Blots of red, peach, and pink smeared her cheeks and lips. Smudges of blue, gold, green, purple, and iridescent white spread wings from lashes to eyebrows, nose to temples. Streaks of black and blue mascara trickled down to her chin with her tears. "You're out of luck, then. Couples only, remember? And I'm alone. I've been in here, trying to do something— anything to trick someone's eye long enough for him to think I'm—not beautiful, but not as revolting as I really am. It's no use." She doubled over with fresh tears.

Every time I opened my mouth to say the perfect words that would make her stop crying, nothing came out. I tried kneeling beside her for a hug and was told to back off if I didn't want a mascara wand up my nose. I decided this was *not* a job for the Grand and Puissant Champion of the Fey.

This was a job for . . . Super-Mom!

Great. Only I couldn't find her. When I stuck my head back in the gym, none of the Three were anywhere to be seen. I ignored Yang, who called me several different kinds of musk-ox body fluid for forgetting his Pepsi, and cornered Neil. "Seen the Kings?"

"Well, Ibrahim's over there, dancing with Muffy."

"*Muffy?*" I finally spotted Jungle Girl, who was doing an energetic bump-and-slither on the dance floor.

"That's what she said her name was."

"And the other two?"

"The one with the fudge is Buffy—"

"I should've known."

"—and Snuffy. They're not here."

"I gathered. Where are they?"

Neil got a how-shall-I-phrase-this-delicately? look on his face. "You know, Desmond, contrary to common sense and the laws of physics, some people can really get somewhere in a parked car." Talk about embracing your fate. For my solace he added, "At least this guarantees they qualify for the fight."

"Great, just great. I still have to go fetch the swords, Faustus is God knows where, and I've got a princess of the Fey in the girls' room near the lockers who's ready to go into the back yard and eat worms because she thinks she's repulsive!"

"Who? Eleziane?" Neil's expression changed radically. "She may not look like a cover girl right now, but I always thought she was—"

I missed the rest of his words. I'd spied the man of the hour. Handsomely decked out in a conventional black tux with a sprinkling of alchemical signs on the lapels, Dr. Faustus was arguing with the kids taking tickets at the door.

I got over there fast. He was happy to see me. "Ah, Tim! Would you kindly explain to these urchins that the fate of the mortal world depends upon my presence here?"

"Yo, Desmond!" Billy "No Neck" Klauser leaned over the table. "You wanna explain to this bozo that he can stick the fate of the mortal world the same place he left his prom tickets?"

"It's okay, Billy, I was carrying his tickets for him." I handed them over, then started to drag the wizard inside. "We're in luck. We've got ten genuine heroes backing us, plus the Three—if we can get two of them hosed down in time—and the witch isn't even here yet. We can plan—"

"Wait, Tim, please." He pulled free, smiling. "You're forgetting something."

"Like what?"

"Like my date." He ducked out past Billy Klauser and returned an instant later pushing a wheelchair.

The kitten Bungay was so deeply asleep on Mom's lap that even my loudest holler of protest didn't wake him.

28

Save the Last Dance for Me

"STOP ARGUING IN there!" T'ing shouted through the boys' room door. "They can hear you over the band!"

"Let them!" I shouted back. "It's better than listening to another zydeco arrangement of 'Tiny Bubbles'!"

"Tim, you're being unreasonable," Faustus said softly.

"Oh yeah? What was so reasonable about you kidnapping my mother?" I kicked the mound of swords between us viciously. My own sword-wand slid from the top of the pile and I grabbed it. Waggling it at the wizard, I shouted, "And you probably had to kill poor old Yaroslav to pull off the job, too. *Murder* is reasonable?"

A squeaky voice came from inside one of the stalls: "I am not too sure that murder applies to the undead." A flutter of leathery wings, and a small bat flew over the top of the stall to perch on the point of my sword.

"Yaroslav?"

There was a Las Vegas-style spangled poof of smoke, and the golden-haired vampire stood before me. "In the flesh. More or less." He flourished his cape.

"You're in on this? But—when the witch finds out, she'll kill you. And don't tell me you're already dead. You know damn good and well what I mean."

Yaroslav brushed off my qualms. "A time comes when a man must banish fear. To die—fully, finally—is something the priests tell us to prepare for. I have had more time than most for such preparation. And who knows? The witch may not

discover my complicity until . . . until there is no more witch!
This I am willing to chance.''

I still had my doubts about how things would work out tonight, but Yaroslav looked so confident I couldn't bring myself
to dishearten him. ''You're a brave man, Yaroslav,'' I said.

''Bah.'' He turned self-effacing on me. ''I am just—how you
say?—sucker for a happy ending.''

''Tim,'' Faustus said, ''we *will* win, I know it. Bringing
your mother with me was the wisest thing I've ever done. Ever
since the terms of battle were set, I have been pondering
whether it was mere wild chance that decreed each contender
must seek strength in partnership, or whether it was fate at
work.''

''It was fate at work overtime, okay? That still doesn't make
it a good idea for you to start messing with my mother.''

He acted as if he never heard me. ''I've done what's right,
I'm sure of it. Don't ask me to explain, but I feel that she is
the one for whom I have searched all my long life. She is the
one who can make life sweet enough for me that losing it
would be sorrow, not relief. Yet if she were mine for however
brief a time, I would lose my life gladly, sooner than trade it
for a life without her. She completes me. She lends the strength
of love to my humble magics.''

''She's someone you've never said two words to, and I don't
want to know how you managed to get her changed into the
gown she's wearing now! How can she complete you? She
doesn't even know you're alive!''

''I see.'' The wizard's brow was dark. ''So there is only one
acceptable form of love abroad in the world these days? The
heart cannot *know* unless its knowledge receives the psycho-
babble seal of approval? What is the approved procedure? Have
her personhood call my personhood so that they can do lunch?
Or do we share personal ecospace until we either make a com-
mitment—no strings attached, of course!—or follow the next
different drummer out of town?''

''Ha, ha. Cute. One look tells you she's the love of your
life? Gosh, I guess I'd better call up the foldout from last
month's *Playboy* and tell her that our story was meant to be.''

The boys' room door banged open as T'ing came dragging
Mom's wheelchair in backwards. ''Look, guys—'' she began.

''T'ing! Just who I want.'' I pulled her away from the chair
and made her face Dr. Faustus. ''Tell him why you love me.''

"I never said—I mean, what are you—"

"I could tell him why I love you, but he'll only claim I'm cutting my reasons to fit the argument. That's why you've got to be the one to tell him."

"You love me?"

"Yeah, yeah, yeah. You know I do. For years."

"You mean *love* love? I thought you just *like* loved me. Sort of."

"*Love* love. The real thing. The grand passion. When Neil was using my body and I thought he was getting places with you, I wanted to rip his face off and feed it to shrews. Anyone gets anyplace with anyone else it's us, together, or the trip's canceled. I want to be there when you get your first gray hair, so I can tell you it just makes you more beautiful. I want to learn how to play a musical instrument and buy a rhyming dictionary so I can write songs about you." I was gaining momentum at about the same rate I was losing restraint. "If you claim you see Elvis buying toothpaste at K-Mart, I want to be there to tell the shrinks I saw him too so they lock us up together. I want to call you mine. I want to hold your hand. I want to bear your young!"

I realized that she wasn't saying anything, and *then* what I wanted was a large rock to crawl under and die.

All of a sudden she said, "Me, too."

"Children," said Faustus, trying to break us apart. "Children, we ought to get back to the dance."

"No more kissy-kissy, Tim. Your mamma is watching," Yaroslav teased.

Breathless but happy, T'ing said, "Faustus is right. We should get back."

"Not so fast," I said. "First you have to tell him what made you fall in love with me. You know, intelligence, personality, sensitivity . . ."

"All right." She turned to Faustus. "It was his looks."

"My *looks*?"

"Your face. Just by looking at your face, I knew."

I was nonplused. "If I'd known I was that handsome—"

"You're not." She kissed me again. "There's more ways to look at a person than stopping on the surface. It's like reading a mystery: There are lots of clues to pick up on, if you're patient. For starters, you smile a lot—"

"I saw the lines of kindness and joy on her face," Faustus interjected, gazing tenderly at my mother.

"—and when someone else was hurting, you couldn't hide the way you shared their pain—"

"I read the lines of sorrow there too," said the wizard, brushing his fingers across my mother's brow. "Yet I saw no trace of bitterness."

"—but especially I'm crazy for the way you always cross your eyes, stick your finger down your throat, and make fake gagging moves like some kind of nut-case whenever we had a pop quiz in English class. I love a man with a good sense of humor."

Faustus refrained from commenting on whether he'd observed evidence of either humor or inherent insanity in Mom's face, but T'ing had made her point. I could only give in.

"Dr. Faustus, if you say you're in love with my mother, that's fine with me."

His closely trimmed moustache lifted with a wistful half-smile. "For that I thank you. But will it be fine with her? That is something I cannot read in her face, and I may not read her heart without her own permission."

"Permission later. Swords now," I directed. We split up the pile of weapons and followed T'ing as she wheeled Mom back to the dance. The plan for rearming our heroes was simple yet elegant: We'd stand the swords up in the hall, behind Mom's wheelchair, then go into the gym and send each hero out by turns to pick up his blade.

What happened to conspicuous? Circumstances alter cases. An action that would make people gawk when the dance was just revving up tended to lose its shock-value the further we got into the festivities. The prom was at its peak of pandemonium, with different clumps of kids sneaking in and out to share a controlled substance or two on the Q.T. If any of them saw a man go by packing steel, they'd be too stoned to be believed if they reported it to a chaperone. Anyhow, kids who are stoned prefer to steer clear of chaperones. As for the clean-and-sober part of the student body, their attention was divided between the dance contest, the last-minute campaigning and voting for Prom Queen, and seeing who could flip the most macadamia nuts down the front of Ms. Cecilia "Sine Curve" Fine's excellent strapless formal.

The simpler the plan, the simpler the execution. Also the simpler the flop.

Neil came running up to me just as I set the plan in motion by sending Siegfried out of the room to collect his blade. "Desmond! We've got a big problem. Eleziane won't listen to me."

"She wouldn't listen to me either." My mind was too full, worrying about how soon Bambi Yaga would show up and how heavily backed she'd be, to spare a subsidiary worry for a princess of the Fey's poor self-image. "You want to cheer her up about not having a partner? Tell her what with the heroes on our side, we may not even need her magic."

"Yeah. Being told I'm dispensable always cheers me right up. You dork. What *I* was trying to tell her was that the reason *I* don't have my own prom date is that I was kinda hoping that she'd—Well, that maybe we could—" He dug into his cummerbund and showed me a carnation and satin-ribbon pancake that was a corsage before it died.

"You? You and Eleziane?"

"So we're from different religious backgrounds. We can work it out."

"Elves." I threw up my hands. "First it was Andraste, the *lhiannan sidhe* with a real thirst for poets, now it's Eleziane. The man's got a taste for dating elves."

"At least this one won't taste me back." Neil got a quirky smile on his face. "Too bad." Then the smile was gone. "Desmond, I know who she is and what she is and what she looks like now, which doesn't matter. Only I can't make her *believe* it doesn't matter to me. She's strong. She's a fighter. She's been fighting for us, but she's had enough." He looked dead serious. "She borrowed a quarter from me and she's gone to call her daddy."

"God, that's all we need: Lord Palamon and his roadshow barging in, and he probably won't let them fight with anything not given the Middle Earth seal of approval. Which puts them right out of the running in a battle of sorcery, because I don't remember the Tolkien elves mucking around with anything but conventional weapons in battle. Talk about cannon fodder!"

"I'm going back to her." Neil looked resolute. "Maybe I can convince her I was telling the truth. If it works, she can call off Daddy."

"If it doesn't?"

"Then I'll try to join you in the fight if I can." It was a good lie, and we both let it pass. I knew that he meant it when he said he'd have Eleziane for his partner or no one. He knew the rules and he'd spent enough time among the Seely Court to understand that if a sorcerous agreement only admitted paired fighters, I shouldn't count on him being there for our side.

"Hey!" I called after him. "Make sure you got the right area code for Elfland!"

Someone poked me urgently in the back. It was Siegfried. "My sword is Nothung," he announced without preamble, standing there like a kid in a declamation contest, both hands behind his back. "It was my father's sword, the gift of Odin Allfather. Once it was shattered, and though the wicked dwarf Mimir labored long at the task, none but I might make it whole again. With Nothung I slew the dragon Fafnir. With Nothung I killed the treacherous Mimir. With Nothung in my hand I dared the fire that ringed the fair Brünnhilde!" He brought his hands out where I could see them. He was holding something that looked like the front bumper of a sports car that had lost an argument with a brick wall. "This is Nothung," he said. "Now it's crap."

She was leaning against Mom's wheelchair when I burst into the hall, all ten of the heroes with me. Dr. Faustus stood on the other side of the chair, unable to do more than glower at her, his power already a crackling aura around him. However much he yearned to throw the first bolt, by the terms of the agreement only the gymnasium proper was the accepted battleground. Behind her I spied the cyclops, the frost-giant Goliath, the harpies, Shiko the oni, and an assortment of monsters with whom I wasn't on a first-name basis.

The witch had undergone a further metamorphosis since I'd seen her last. Now she looked like a Barbie doll. Her escort, Glenwood's former *numero uno* hunk Glendon Essex, didn't seem to mind dating plastic.

"Hallo, dollink," Bambi Yaga greeted me. "You are maybe looking for something?" She gave the high sign and the goblins Doggo, Skeffins, Gwimcur, Ving, Luthenard, and Stalker-of-Deadmen paraded out from around the back of the chair. I saw that the witch had taken the arbitrary route when it came to signing up her paired fighters. Three of the goblins wore tattered tuxes, the other three were dressed in drag and looked grouchy about it. All six carried the twisted, shattered, blunted chunks of metal and obsidian that used to be the swords of heroes.

There was a collective gasp from our side when the little buggers dumped their cargo at my feet.

"Tsk, tsk." The witch twiddled her satin-gloved fingers. "Such pity. But is maybe good in long run, *da?* Swords of legend, these are always slaying ten times ten thousand foes, causing monsters to flee in terror, not even show up for fight sometimes jost because sword has raputation. Is always screwing op betting odds, this raputation. I speet on raputation." She did. Glendon was right there to pass her a Kleenex for blotting her lipstick.

Her smile didn't involve her eyes at all. Behind the perfect makeup they remained as cold and hard as a pair of pebbles. "Ah, so sad you are! Cheer op. Is no swords for you, but is also no swords for us."

"Who needs a sword when you're born with fangs, claws, and five times your opponent's muscle?" the Aztec muttered.

Bambi Yaga primped her curls and made one final adjustment to the scarlet crinoline of her minidress. Linking arms with Glendon, she flounced towards the gym. "Well?" she tossed back over one naked shoulder. "Coming, sockers?"

29

Lost Soul Train

THE LAST THING I remember seeing before all hell broke loose was Yang, Flinger of Musk Ox Body Fluid Epithets, standing under the big papier-mâché Hawaiian war canoe the decorating committee had hung from the ceiling. He was feeding pork rinds to his date, Crazy Nadine Dunlop, who had finally caught on to the fact that her escort wasn't going to pick her up at her home, so she came to the prom under her own steam. That didn't bother Crazy Nadine. Nothing bothered Crazy Nadine, except the time someone told her they were going to take all the Star Trek reruns off the air.

She wasn't even bothered when ten heroes, grim but earnest, strode past her and arranged themselves in a variety of fighting crouches on the dance floor. The maneuver did bother their dates. Unlike Crazy Nadine, the Glenwood High cheerleaders had come to expect a modicum of undivided attention from any male lucky enough to share their company. A good date does *not* march past you as if you weren't there and hunker down for a fight. Not after you spent all that money on your hair. Looking equally grim but earnest, the girls waded onto the dance floor to have it out with their men.

I suppose there was going to be some kind of signal from Bambi Yaga to decree the start of battle. I gathered as much when she pulled a flare gun out of her sequined evening bag.

She never got to use it. From the ranks of the monsters, Goliath saw Kirsten—maybe not the love of his life, but to his eyes his property of the moment—and he called to her, "Hey, babe! What say after we get this mopped up, you and me go catch a 'za?''

Kirsten pouted. "I already *have* a date." And she went back to nagging Cuchulain to tell her why he was flaring his nostrils, flexing his muscles, and in general acting like a dweeb.

"Raaaaarh!" said Cuchulain.

"La! 'Tis the battle-frenzy on him." Teleri was beside me, eyes brimming with hero worship. "When he fights, all his body shakes, his legs from the knees down turn back to front, one eye creeps back into his head, th' other swells up fiercely big and red. Every hair o' his head bristles out wondrous, blood at the tip, and 'tis a great gout o' blood rushes up from th' top o' his head fer all to see!''

"What? In the middle of the gym?" I shook my head. "The chaperones are never going to stand for it."

We didn't have to wait for the chaperones. All at the same time, Kirsten told Cuchulain to "stop acting like, you know, weird" and gave him a kiss as incentive; Goliath saw, let out a ululating battle cry and charged his rival, picking up a chair in passing with which to make his point; the other monsters took this as the go-ahead and broke ranks, emitting their various yips, howls, shrieks, and grunts of joy-through-rampage; and Bambi Yaga witnessed her total loss of generalship, made a face, and threw the flare gun into the punch bowl, saying "The fock with eet," before zamming Faustus with a bolt of power.

It was the prom to remember.

The noncombatant innocent bystanders were too stunned to run. That was probably a good thing, or they'd have trampled each other. The chaperones stepped in, seeing a world-shaking battle between the forces of Good and Evil as just another silly "gang thing." Mrs. Fiorelli, our all-purpose school aide with the four-by-four body, began herding some of the students out in an orderly fashion.

"But I just saw a dragon!" one of my more open-minded classmates exclaimed.

"You don't do what I say, you'll have worse to worry about than dragons!" Mrs. Fiorelli snapped. "That was a stray dog that got into the school building somehow, *entirely* against the rules, and when I catch whoever let it in, he'll burn in hell if he's lucky." The "dog" in question sat up on its leathery haunches and puffed out tiny licks of fire in amusement.

I wasn't so amused. After leaving Mom in T'ing's able care, Dr. Faustus had taken the middle of the dance floor with Bambi Yaga to begin their duel of magics. Multicolored strands of enchantment swirled around them, thicker and thicker, sparks leaping from the forming shell. Holding tight to my wand—the only sword which had escaped the witch's wholesale disarmament action—I tried to get into the heart of the sorcerous combat.

A blast of sizzling air threw me halfway to the refreshment table. From the quickly closing sphere of power I heard Faustus call, "No, Tim, this is not your fight!" My magic and my soul on the line, and it wasn't my fight? But I had no argument strong enough to crack the shell that witch and wizard had pulled closed around their solitary struggle.

I looked around. The gym was a sea of little islands of battle. The one calm atoll was the corner where Yoshitsune and the blue oni Shiko were seated facing one another, each armed with an exquisite lacquerware brush. Two pieces of paper lay between them, the fine whiteness becoming swiftly covered with a pretty pattern of ink marks.

"Haiku," the oni replied when I asked.

"To the death," Yoshitsune added. He picked up his paper and read his latest creation. Shiko sucked air between his teeth and turned pastel. Then he seized his own sheet and rattled off a response. The Japanese warrior flinched. Wounded but not down, both sides attacked their papers with renewed zeal.

This time, the oni struck first, only without the desired effect. Yoshitsune clapped his hands to his knees and laughed. "Ha! Too many syllables! And you call a bullfrog *ineffable*? Where did you learn Zen, in a barn?"

Shiko dropped his horned head. "It is so. I have disgraced myself. For this, there is only one expiation." Fascinated, I watched as the blue oni prepared to commit *seppuku*. When the sword appeared in his paws, Yoshitsune lodged a complaint.

"The witch said no swords!"

With a mild look of apology, Shiko responded, "I do not think even she would expect me to join my honorable ancestors without access to the proper hardware. *Sayonara*." He closed his eyes and we lowered ours out of respect.

Suddenly we were looking at the beautifully honed edge of the oni's blade. Robes in disarray, Shiko stood over us and gloated, "Nor do I think she would mind were I to take a few of our mutual enemies along with me to meet my honorable ancestors."

"Oh yeah?" a well-known voice interjected. "Well, *I'm* an honorable ancestor and I say the hell you will!" With that, Yang made a neat sideways chop with his own blade and Shiko's head rolled across the floor like a melon.

Yang was sopping up Yoshitsune's fulsome thanks with a spoon when his own continued spectral health came into question. Screaming a whole lot of unnecessary personal remarks, the three goblins in tuxes leaped on him from behind and knocked him facedown. His sword skittered away, to be seized by Doggo and snapped into bite-sized pieces.

"Kill our old chum, would 'ee?" Great was the wrath of Skeffins as he and the other two pummeled the prone Mongol.

"You get offa my date, you creeps!" Hands made terrible by combat-length press-on nails took the goblins by surprise. Crazy Nadine Dunlop hauled them off Yang, pushed them into a compact unit, yelled, "Three to beam up, Scotty!" and clonked a half-empty punch bowl down over their heads.

For a second they stood there, punch and fruit bits dribbling down, nothing visible but their six little legs making the upended punch bowl look like a high-class cockroach. Then wails of pain leaked out from beneath the rim as the punch did its fiendish work. Inch by ugly inch, the goblins were dissolving. Soon there was nothing there but the bowl and three empty tuxedos.

Yang picked one up. "I wonder if we can get the deposit back on this one?"

A dragon the size of a bulldog barreled past us, knocking Yang sideways. Hot behind it came Sir Edgar Dragonslayer, only without a sword he wasn't likely to be doing much slaying. On second glance, I saw that the little serpent was just one of many nuisance-value dragons in Bambi Yaga's army. Their heads were long and narrow, probably holding brains the size of Brussels sprouts, but they didn't need much intelligence to run around the gym, biting and butting anyone who smelled like a good guy.

"Come back, sir! Back, back I say!" Lacking his sword, Sir Edgar had opted to audition for the title of Dragonswatter. The rolled-up prom poster in his hand looked deadly. "Heel!

Heel, sir!'' His date, Shana, trotted after him making smoochy ''Here-puppy'' sounds at the worm. I had to smile.

A hoarse shriek from on high tore the smile from my face. The three harpies had taken to the air. Already they were swooping low, swiping at our men with their talons. It was hard enough for heroes to fight monsters swordless, but the added distraction of aerial attack really set the odds against them. The harpies cawed with glee and massed for another strafing run.

They reckoned without the Code of Glenwood High—the great unwritten body of traditional law that rules us all, except maybe Crazy Nadine. And one of the keystone tenets of the law was that family and friends are expendable, but a girl who doesn't defend her date deserves to spend Saturday night washing her hair.

Call it instinct. Call it reflex. Call it the famous Glenwood High cheerleading squad pyramid, because that's what it was. Prom gowns be damned, the girls still managed to stack themselves up floor-to-ceiling in record time. The startled harpies fluttered too near and Kirsten grabbed two of them by their necks and banged their heads together. The birdwomen plummeted to the hardwood floor, where the heroes meted out some barnyard-style executions.

The third harpy swore at everyone in Greek. (I don't know Greek, but I do know she wasn't thanking us for killing her sisters.) She soared out of reach and scowled at us from the rafters. Then her eye lit on the refreshments table.

The cheerleaders knew that look, even if they didn't know Greek mythology. Fouling food was like a warm-up exercise for a harpy before she started fouling people. They'd seen what the harpies had done to the Desiderius fans at the soccer game, and they weren't going to wait around for the same treatment. The pyramid self-destructed to a chorus of ''Ew, ew, *ewwwww*!'' as the girls decided to let their dates protect them for a change.

As the harpy began her descent, I saw the Hottentot warrior-mage Heitsi-Ebib comforting a cowering Courtney. She pointed at the circling harpy and shuddered. She must have told him what to expect, because he put her to one side, stepped up to the refreshments table, and waited. A shriek of jubilation sounded from the harpy as she went into her dive, marking him for an easy target. Heitsi-Ebib didn't move. Only when the creature was almost upon him did he murmur a few strange words, then spring out of the way.

The harpy frowned to lose her prey, but she never lost her momentum. The air-show must go on, and she was going to teach us a thing or two, both of them smelly. At just the proper moment she let fly on the refreshments table, then pulled up into a climb.

So did everything on the table, including her own unsanitary additions. As soon as the harpy's fifteen-megaton bird-splats hit it, the whole table bowed like a giant rubber band and, with a rubber band's elasticity, launched its entire burden after her. She was struck down in mid-wingbeat by a mix of pineapple, punch, and poo-poo. She died disgusted.

Too bad. At least the harpies had shown some solidarity. You couldn't say the same for the giants. The witch had worked her will on the monsters when it came to pairing them up, yet all of her matches were superficial. Shiko might have arrived with a partner, but you'd never know it by the way he operated solo. Maybe his ''date'' was the odd harpy out. For the giants, Bambi Yaga had dressed them in matching colored tuxedos to keep them paired. For instance, Goliath and the cyclops both wore blue.

They could have come as a crazy quilt for all the teamwork they exhibited. Goliath was still trying to kill Cuchulain for stealing Kirsten, leaving the cyclops to go hang. Horatius marked the one-eyed giant for his own and closed in. He recovered the empty punch bowl Crazy Nadine had used on the goblins and flung it with deadly accuracy. It landed dead on the cyclops' eye and stuck there like a huge, opaque contact lens. Blinded, the beast lunged about until the Aztec stuck out a leg to trip him. When he hit, Zisi and Zasu were waiting for him. It wasn't pretty.

Meantime, Goliath wasn't making much progress at murdering the great Irish hero. They were still at the circle-and-snarl stage. Deep in his battle-frenzy, Cuchulain looked like every plastic surgeon's greatest challenge. His date observed these physical alterations, somewhat perplexed and not a little grossed out. Teleri sidled up to her, a sly smile at the ready.

''Faith, 'tis a sight he is, is he not?''

''Totally,'' Kirsten agreed.

''Not what ye expected o' the lad, is it?''

''For real.''

Very much the canny bargainer, with great casualness Teleri now said, "Then I don't suppose ye'll be continuin' t' permit him the pleasure o' yer company this night?"

Kirsten's eyes flashed. "No *way*! I mean, what kind of girl do you think I am? Give up my prom date just because he gets a little faced, right. It's not like he barfed on my shoes or anything."

My banshee suffered a great revelation. "D'ye mean t'say ye'll cleave t'him yet, woman?" Kirsten nodded. Teleri shook her hand. " 'Tis a grand thing, loyalty is, and a banshee knows how best t'honor it. Then it's by yer side I'll fight this day, and both o' us fer th' life of Cuchulain!"

"Okay," Kirsten agreed. "Only, like, I think we'd better move it if we want any of his life left, you know?"

Right she was. The fighters had left off name-calling and started swinging. Goliath still had the chair and was landing one blow after another on Cuchulain's unshielded ribs. Heroes are built to take punishment, but there are limits. The Irish champion was starting to fold.

Together, Teleri and Kirsten raced from the gym. They returned quickly enough, breathing figurative fire, and carrying something I couldn't quite see. Splendidly defiant, they placed themselves between the giant and their man.

"Move it or lose it, toots," the Philistine bellowed.

"How rude," Kirsten riposted. "Okay, Teleri, load her up."

I saw what they had. It was a bra. Please don't ask me whose. All I could positively identify were their purses, which they loaded into the cups. I recalled the time I'd picked up Mom's purse and asked her whether she had rocks in it. Evening bags are smaller, but still . . . I felt really sorry for Goliath. Teleri gave the nod and Kirsten twirled the improvised sling rapidly overhead and let fly.

I heard Goliath grumble, "Oh, shit, not again," just before he took the two hits and toppled across a table.

It happened to be the table holding the ballot box for Prom Queen. Goliath smashed down on one end and the seesaw effect sent the box soaring off the other. It was solid wood and didn't break on impact. Neil saw it and scrambled in to pull it out of harm's way. "Terrible if anything was to happen to it," he gasped at me as he ran out of the gym, hugging the box to his chest.

I had other things to think about than Neil's abrupt eruption of school spirit. The three goblins forced into dresses were taking out their resentment on Siegfried, Perseus, and Yoshitsune. They had tapped a pack of werewolves to help them harry the heroes, whose spiffy tuxedos already showed the signs of tearing teeth.

"Oh my *Gawd*, would you look at *them*?" Brooke, Ashley, and Summer, the beset heroes' dates, stood staring at the goblins, arms folded, lips curled.

"Here! What's wrong with the way we look?" Luthenard wanted to know. For answer, the ladies snickered. Then, chapter and verse, they proceeded to dissect the goblins' appearance.

It was awful. Years of training as the merciless arbiters of fashion, taste, and school "cool" had honed the cheerleaders' tongues to scalpels. Their scorn was precisely tuned, their disdain devastating. The three goblins had arrived believing there was nothing worse than being forced to dress like girls. Now they learned that, yes, there was: being forced to dress like *tacky* girls.

"—and that shade of lipstick with that dress? Ew."

"Oi!" Ving came stomping over. "Who asked you?"

The girls just turned and walked away. Summer took the trouble to turn her head for a parting shot: "Where'd you get those shoes, Imelda? The supermarket have a special on banana boxes?"

A werewolf laughed. Another one waggled his furry hips and remarked that even a cub knows better than to wear pearlized green eyeshadow with a complexion like *that*. It was the last straw. With howls of sorely abraded pride, the goblins flung themselves on their allies. The three heroes had the leisure to break themselves off some table-leg cudgels, station themselves on the periphery of the brawl, and pick off the wounded.

I moved to the other end of the gym, where there was still one refreshments table left standing. The band platform was abandoned, and those chaperones with less grit than Mrs. Fiorelli were huddled behind it. There were still plenty of students left to watch the fight. I wondered how many of them thought it was part of the entertainment and how many thought it was almost as good as a video game. I spied Eleziane among them. The princess of the Fey was standing with Doc Ox and the gorgon. "Ms. Stone" had been kind to Eleziane once, and now she was having a friendly chat with the bewitched elf-maiden. Eleziane still looked sad, but not as despairing as before. I prayed Neil had managed to convince her of his sincerity before she called home. One person we didn't need here tonight was Lord Palamon.

I had my thoughts scattered when the Russian hero went loping past the bandstand, pursued by the frost-giant Sweyn. Evidently all those winters of running away from or after wolf packs had done him good. He had Sweyn sweating sleet. The frost-giant was so caught up in the drama of the chase that he didn't watch where he was going.

"OW!" Doc Ox jumped up and down, clutching his foot. When he could stand again, he gave Ms. Stone a sheepish grin and said, "I'm afraid this means we yoost have to bayn having a rain check on that dance I bayn promised you, *ja?*"

"A rain check?" The gorgon was not pleased. Soon the two-man chase back and forth across the floor picked up a third runner. "Stop!" she shouted at Sweyn. "You big clumsy iceberg, I was looking forward to that dance all evening! Now you've spoiled everything! Stop this minute, you lousy party pooper!"

Sweyn paused to sneer at her. "Why should I care?" She removed her sunglasses and her mantilla and showed him why. The sneer froze on his lips. His lips froze on his face. His face froze on—Well, you follow it. When he fell, he shattered. Some of the more pragmatic and devoted prom committee members gathered up the ice fragments and dumped them in the punch bowl.

The Russian hero and several others in the area came over to thank Ms. Stone for her help as soon as she had her eyes and hair safely hidden. One of these well-wishers was Perseus. He really should have known better. After all, he'd had dealings with gorgons before: fatal dealings. It didn't do to glad-hand one of those snake-tressed ladies when your sword had once been wet with her sister's blood; especially when you didn't have that sword with you at the moment.

Well, maybe this gorgon was no relation, or didn't bear grudges, or wouldn't remember—

"Don't I know you from somewhere?" Ms. Stone asked.

Perseus froze, though only metaphorically. He tried to back away from his error, but the gorgon was relentless. "Does the name Medusa ring a bell? Hmmmm?'' Her hand was on her sunglasses again.

Just as she jerked them off, Gorm of the Shining Helm thrust himself between her and Perseus to shake her by her free hand. Through his spotlessly polished lowered visor he effused, ''By Glyph and Sifwa, I must thank you for aiding my comrade in arms! Had not my trusty blade, the fiery Sword of Tagobel, been reduced to a twist of metal, I would lay it even now at your feet in token of—of—'' He stopped, tongue-tied by the coldness and rigidity of the hand he clasped.

Perseus steered him away from the granite-faced gorgon. ''Have I ever told you how much I admire that Shining Helm of yours, Gorm?'' he was saying.

Doc Ox stood there, blinking like a lizard. With the fall of the frost-giant, maybe the spell on him had lifted. As each of the monsters perished, I thought I detected an almost imperceptible lightening of the air, as if each departing creature took with it a layer of enchantment as it returned to the place of legends. I wondered whether I was going to miss them.

I didn't have much time for reflection. T'ing screamed. My eyes flew to Mom's chair, which T'ing was supposed to be minding. T'ing was gone, but Mom slept on undisturbed. A second scream for help and I saw the woman I loved—not *like* loved—in the grip of an ogre.

It was Kirkwood. He was crouched on his hams just under the suspended war canoe. Strings of slaver dripped from the corners of his mouth as he watched T'ing's useless struggles to break out of his grip.

''T'ing!'' I came running. So did Sir Edgar, only his path lay perpendicular to mine. He was in pursuit of a chubby yellow dragonling. The varmint faked left, went right, and I tripped over it. Kirkwood guffawed. His fellow ogre, Danforth, also thought my pratfall was mildly amusing. He was engaged in some offhanded fisticuffs with the Aztec warrior, a trifling occupation that allowed him to spare me a few genteel sniggers.

From where I lay, I watched Sir Edgar continue his dash after the froward dragon. He had already rounded up most of the beasties, and Shana had them sitting in mannerly rows over in a quiet corner. The man had what it takes to teach good manners to animals. He could either become a successful preschool teacher or pen the guaranteed best seller, *No Bad Drag-*

ons, if he so chose. That yellow one, though, was leading him a jolly chase. I waited until the plump little reptile was right where I wanted it, drew my wand up to my eye, sighted along the sword-hilt, and fired.

I could have cheered. Not only did I manage to get off a blast of arcane energy, but it landed at just the desired angle right in front of the dragon. The beast jumped as the power crackled past its left flank to singe its snout, veered sharply to the right, and tore off blindly straight for the squatting ogre.

The dragon was small. It passed between Kirkwood's legs undetected. Sir Edgar was a strapping man, and tall. He didn't quite duck low enough as he ran through. The bump to his head was negligible. I doubt he even felt it.

Kirkwood felt it, though. He rose up howling with pain. T'ing got away. The royal Hawaiian war canoe didn't.

Danforth saw what happened. He carelessly flicked the Aztec warrior unconscious and came over to stare at the broken decoration. "Kirkwood," he said, with a suspicious undertone of restraint in his voice. "Kirkwood, that was *not* a piñata, you know."

Kirkwood just rubbed his head and other afflicted areas, snarling.

"That canoe was the result of long hours of creatively exhausting labor for the entire decorations committee, although the project concept itself was exclusively mine. It was my *vision*. We did not merely construct it of common papier-mâché. In the interests of aesthetic purity, I directed that the only paper used come from Ivy League and Seven Sisters college catalogues. You have ruined my masterpiece, Kirkwood. I trust you have something to say?"

Kirkwood said it. It was ugly.

"I see," said Danforth, and he killed him with the air of a fabulously well-paid commodities broker who still must flea-dip the family Labrador retriever on Saturday.

I approached him while he was wiping his hands on one of the tablecloths. I was accompanied by nine of the heroes, Sir Edgar still being occupied with trying to make the fat yellow dragonling respond to hand signals. The ogre looked at us, then at the small bat that flittered down onto his shoulder and became a full-grown vampire.

"Oh dear," said Danforth.

"This is correct," Yaroslav agreed. "Is now being suggested that if you have someplace else to be, and you are giving us your word of honor to cause no further damage to mortal society, you should go and be there."

"You'll—you'll let me live?" We all nodded.

"You just slew an ogre," I told him. "That sort of makes you unofficially one of us. We can live with that if you can."

"I can, but—but what if your—*our* side doesn't win?"

"Then none of us are going to have to live with anything for long." I shrugged. "I don't think that's going to be the case, though. Look over there." I gestured with my wand to the center of the dance floor.

The shell of magics was thinning away. In the heart of it we could see the witch held prisoner by bright chains of energy pouring from Faustus' fingertips like water. Twist and turn as she did, they remained unbreakable. The lesser monsters she had brought with her to the battle saw how things were going and escaped.

"See? It's done, Danforth. We—" I became aware of an ogre-sized absence. He had made a break for it with the rest. *Let him run*, I thought. *Once Faustus concludes his conquest, all true monsters will be banished with their leader, the witch. It's a matter of minutes, now.*

It was actually a matter of seconds. The wizard's face clouded as he forged one last shackle to hold his captive. It took the form of a golden cage, the bars joined with purple stars. Door wide, it glided toward the witch. Her whole body stiffened with fear as it neared her, and she filled her lungs with air for a final scream.

No scream came out, but a spell. The gym shook with the force of it. Then came the rending sound. Plaster fell in chunks as the whole ceiling of the gymnasium was peeled back like the top of a sardine can to let in the night. By the magical illumination of the battle-locked witch and wizard we all saw Bambi Yaga's chicken-legged cottage step primly in among us. The witch barked a command. The cottage lowered its front window shades once in acknowledgment. Then it turned, balanced on one foot, and painstakingly leveled a yard-long talon at my mother's heart.

30

Next Stop, Topeka

KRITO THE MINOTAUR crept into the gym with his tail between his legs. I was the first familiar face he saw, so he came over to me and said, "Hi, I'm sorry I'm late, but I couldn't find my way out of this mall, and then I took the subway and I *really* got lost. Did I miss anything?"

I lifted my arm as far as the handcuffs would let me and pointed to the chained string of heroes on the other side of Mom's wheelchair. Dr. Faustus was anchored to the left arm-rest of the chair just as I was attached to the right. "We won," I told him.

Krito mulled over this information and added to it the brightly illuminated transparent dome presently covering the gym, the vampire spread-eagled against the dome's centermost point, Bambi Yaga enthroned near the bandstand with Glendon Essex hand-feeding her bits of egg roll, the mournful howls and hisses of Zisi, Zasu, and Bungay, whose cage she was using as a footstool, and the chicken-legged cottage hovering above all in sinister fashion.

At length he said, "It may be that like the dog in Aesop's fable I'm losing the substance by grasping the shadow, but frankly . . . don't you have this backwards?"

"We won," I repeated, "and then we surrendered."

The bull's horns swayed slowly from side to side. "I'm going back to the mall, where things make sense." So saying, the minotaur left.

Bambi Yaga ate the last morsel of egg roll and sent Glendon after more. While waiting for his return, she studied us. "Why such long faces?'' the witch exclaimed. ''Is time for celebration! Jost one leetsle beetsy bit of nasty business to handle and then—poof! Off come the chains! We drink! We dance! We boogie down!''

The heroes remained glum, the Russian glummest of all.

This piqued the witch. She deserted her throne, the better to question him individually. ''*Tovarisch*, this sad you are—Is ethnic or is the real thing?''

''The wind howls across the steppes,'' the Russian intoned. ''Snow covers the bodies of the slain. The bright god hides his face. The women weep.''

''*Da, da, da*. I hear them till here, yowling in bathroom like cats. They be back when they get on fresh mascara. So you lose a fight because I play dirty? Beeg deal! You're not the one going to lose nothing.''

''The warrior's bond is to his brother, the brothers' great bond is to their lord.'' Cold contempt drove out the misery in his blue eyes as he stared at her. ''To save his beloved, the magician yielded to you. Your own powers were not enough to beat him. For this nobility he has lost the magic that should have been your doom. Let this be enough for you! Leave the boy alone.''

Bambi Yaga's smile spread over her face like an oil-slick. ''Not on your tintype, Comrade buckaroo.'' She strolled down the line and chucked me under the chin. ''This keed got beegtime power. Why should I not take it?''

''Take it, then, but let him keep his soul!''

''Eh!'' The witch snapped her fingers. ''Why bother? But look, sweetsy, jost because I like to make you happy, I am telling you what I am going to be doing: Wizard surrenders to save life of boy's mamma, *da?* Least I can do is lift spell of sleep on her now.''

''You will?'' I couldn't stop myself from sounding surprised.

She pinched my cheek. ''Of course, dollink. I am wanting her wide awake to say bye-bye when I take your soul.'' Her hands formed a softly pulsing turquoise sphere that floated up over Mom's head. ''Is only one catch. Sleep spell is strong like bool! Is not easy to break, can only *lift*''—she wafted the ball of light higher—''with a kiss.'' The witch slued a shrewd look at Faustus. ''Once lifted, spell has to go to some other host.

So! Any takers? Sleep for thousand years . . . Think of all the dentist's appointments you can miss!''

''A thousand years . . .'' The weight of all the centuries he had lived already seemed to press down on the wizard. Then he looked at Mom. ''When I wake, she will be gone.''

''Dad like doornail, you betcha. But if you don't take this offer, she sleeps on. Your choice, poosy-cats. I don't got all night.'' Bambi Yaga folded her arms. ''What's it going to be, ha?'' The ball was descending. ''Tan, nine, eight, saven, seex—''

Faustus was in agony. He looked from my mother to the witch, then to me. For the first time I understood what he and T'ing had said about reading faces. In his, I could see the love he felt for Mom, the willingness to do anything for her, and the fear that making the sacrifice would condemn him to awakening in a world where she was only dust.

''—fife, four, three, two—''

Over her head he spoke to me. ''I do love her. But I'm afraid. I do—''

''—one—''

She was my mother. If I did this, we'd never speak or see each other again. If I didn't, what would she wake to? The loss of my soul? If she waked at all.

If I acted, I would sleep, but at least she would have someone who loved her to be her consolation.

''—zero!''

My lips hit her right cheek at the same instant that Faustus bent to kiss her left. The turquoise ball exploded into a shower of harmless sparks.

Mom yawned. Then she took in the wreckage of the prom. ''What am I doing in a Polynesian restaurant?''

''Why can't you just say 'Where am I?' like normal people?'' I replied, grinning. Then I caught Faustus' imploring look. Solemnly I said, ''Mom, I'd like to introduce you to a very good friend of the family, Dr. Johannes Faustus.''

''Is he?'' She took his hand and looked up at him. I recalled him getting that same blitzed look when he'd first studied her sleeping face. ''I'm so glad.'' This would be interesting, if we lived.

The chances of that were dwindling. Bambi Yaga was not pleased by the inadvertent shattering of her sleep spell. When Glendon came back with a fresh plate of tidbits, she smacked it out of his hands. "This is only way you peasants can celebrate? Eating like peegs?"

"Well—"

"What is this, prom or prayer meeting? Where is music? Where is laughter? Where is whoop-de-do?" She gave me the gimlet eye. "When I take soul from this rotten keed, I want him to go out knowing what he is going to be missing."

The witch's wish was everyone's command. The band had run away, but they did manage to locate the saxophone player hiding under the platform. He blatted his way through half a chorus of "Sunrise, Sunset" before the witch materialized a hedgehog and crammed it into the bell of his instrument.

Drumming her fingers on the arm of the throne, she growled, "There had batter be more than that, peoples."

Glendon cleared his throat, overawed by his date's transformation to Ivana the Terrible. "We—we haven't had the crowning of the Prom Queen yet, angel." He cupped his hands to his mouth and asked the remaining attendees to divulge the whereabouts of the prom committee. Most of them were still present, and good old Neil was on the spot to hand over the carefully guarded ballot box.

Bambi Yaga passed the time while they tallied the votes by throwing flaming paper airplanes at Yaroslav. She decreed her intention to have everyone dance until dawn, at which point the rays of the rising sun coming in through the dome would bring both the prom and the turncoat vampire to a spectacular end.

She had just ordered Doc Ox to rustle up some decent music and a record player from the media room, when Glendon presented her with the election results. He had helped add up the votes and his expression was inscrutable. I checked out the other committee members and saw that they were all whispering, rolling their eyes, and shrugging at a fantastic rate.

Mom tugged at my sleeve. "Probably a big write-in vote for Pee Wee Herman," she suggested. As good a guess as any.

"So, dollink? You have got Prom Czarina?" The magic word drew the cheerleaders back into the gym like sugar draws ants. Each cuddled nearer to her chained hero, but not close enough to mess her hair. "Read, read!"

Glendon straightened the fateful slip of paper. "The winner is—" And he announced a name.

In the stupefied silence that followed, Neil came to take

Eleziane's hand tenderly. "Didn't you hear what the man said, milady? It's not polite to keep your subjects waiting."

"No." Eleziane didn't move. "It's a mistake. It has to be."

"You heard him," Neil insisted. "It just sounded funny to you because you're not used to hearing your mortal alias. The decision of the judges is final. No refunds, no exchanges. Look, there's the prom chairman on the bandstand, waiting to crown you."

She took a few steps toward the platform and stopped again. "You did this," she said. "I saw you bring in the ballot box. You stuffed it. You cheated so I'd win. Why?"

He winked. "The noble explanation is that I think you've got more claim to the Prom Queen's crown than some bimbette whose good looks are all on the surface. The truth is I was hoping to con you into naming me Prom King. So how's about it, baby?"

The joy that broke over her ungainly mortal features made them beautiful. "You've got a deal." All her regal bearing flowed back into her as she mounted the bandstand. When the prom chairman set the crown on her head, you'd have thought she was the one doing him an honor. He handed her the Prom King's crown and Neil was there before she could even motion him up.

"You are too bold, Your Majesty," she told him.

"I'm worse than that," he said, "when the lady's as gorgeous as you." And he kissed her.

"No!" The witch's shout counted for nothing. A spell once cast is cast entire and can't be modified. A spell is a cell of the greater magics, and its immutable DNA carries the information that tells how the spell may be broken. There's nothing anyone can do about that, so Bambi Yaga discovered.

"Wow," said Neil, gazing at the freed princess.

"You find me more beautiful now, I assume."

"Nah. It's just weird to start kissing a girl with braces and have them melt out on you right in the middle. It kinda breaks up the, you know, poetic unity of the kiss."

"Then by all means we must encourage poetic unity." She kissed him again so intensely that she knocked his paper crown off.

"No!" Bambi Yaga repeated, stamping her foot. "No, no, no! This is not how it most be! They are happy! The spell I cast on nasty rotten cheepy who attacked me in my own house, it breaks with true love's kiss! Why should she find true love? Why not me? Is not fair. I *won*!''

Have you?

We all looked up. Three faces filled the dome. I thought that two of them were still out in the parking lot. Then it struck me that I hadn't seen Jungle Girl since the commencement of the great battle.

Wherever the Three might be in the flesh, their phantoms were above us. Bambi Yaga's flying cottage could not block their faces.

The prophecy is accomplished, Jungle Girl crooned.

The frog is crowned a queen, the lady wakes.

True victory remains in the hands of those who earned it righteously.

What is ill-won shall be restored.

''Bah! Robbish!'' The witch shook her fist at the Three. ''*I* have won! *Mine* is the wictory! You cannot take this from me!''

If so, then why does your deepest heart tell you that you have lost?

We take nothing that is not ours to reap.

Just as you may chain these folk of fey or mortal or mythic blood, yet never may you take from them the one treasure you will never have, for all your magic.

Someone touched my hand. It was T'ing. I saw Mom reach out to Faustus. The heroes shifted in their chains to let the ladies of their hearts stand by them. Even Yang threw his arm around Crazy Nadine Dunlop and passed her an open bag of pork rinds. On the platform, Neil and Eleziane moved closer.

Our actions spelled out a message that the witch understood and hated. ''Love? Is that it? I have that! You! Come here.'' She motioned for Glendon to embrace her. He did it with the enthusiasm of a man climbing the gallows. She jerked her lips from his and spat, pushing him away.

''I vill show you vhat I have!'' she shouted, storming from her throne to mount the bandstand. She tore the Prom Queen crown from Eleziane's head and shoved the elfin princess off the platform. Neil leaped after her while the witch placed the pasteboard diadem on her own head. ''You see?'' She scowled up at the Three, her chicken-legged cottage circling loyally overhead. ''All is mine, all! Vhat I vant, I take, your foolish mouthings of love be cursed. Do you think I envy them? Ha!

Vhen love is somesing I can grasp with my own two hands, *then* I vill have it jost as I have all else I desire."

She spread her arms wide and tossed her head back, cackling. Her body became the center of a vortex of greed, sucking in all power, all beauty. I felt my own magic start to slip from me, and still she laughed.

"Where is being fool enough to think he can reclaim vhat I have taken as mine?"

"Yoo hoo! Here I am!" That voice! That voice connected to a brain with the retentive properties of cheesecloth! Could it be? "Eleziane I—Oh, I say, what a smashing bit of luck! There's one of the buggers now!"

Twang!

The arrow soared straight and true, right through the front door of the flying cottage. I never heard a piece of real estate utter a death-cry before. Bambi Yaga gawked, then ran. She might have made it if she hadn't lost the Prom Queen crown and doubled back to get it.

How to describe the sound of several tons of poultry and masonry smashing one witch into a blin? You had to be there.

Our savior ambled up to the ruined cottage and stared at it. "Ouf! My error. Thought I'd bagged a ringwraith, don'tcha know. Frightfully sorry." He turned to the suite of elves that had followed him into our world via the invisible web paths of the Fey. "What *is* this thing?"

"*Daddy!*" Eleziane squealed, and threw herself at the longbow-toting Lord of the Fey.

"Oh, hullo, love." Lord Palamon disentangled himself from his little girl and regarded her critically at arm's length. "You don't *look* miserable and heartbroken and repulsive and ready to die, the way you told me you were on the telephone, m'dear."

"I'm not, Daddy." She beckoned Neil and took his hand. "I'm in love." The happy pair exchanged dopey looks.

"Ah?" The elf-lord's brows rose. "Hm. Rather. Easy to see how I'd get the two messages confused, then. Well, water under the bridge and all that." He slung one leg up onto the fallen cottage and struck a proud Great White Hunter pose. "At least I bagged a proper little trophy from this venture into the Dark Lord's domain, what?"

Eleziane hugged her father fondly. "I'm sorry it's not a ringwraith, Daddy."

"So I see. Appears to be a bird of some kind."

"It was a chicken. Partly. Just the legs, see?"

"Ah yes. Quite. Never had the Dark Lord pegged for a fowl-fancier. Wonders never cease. Well." Lord Palamon prodded the cottage's avian underpinnings with the toe of his boot. "Anyone here fond of dark meat, then?"

I stopped my rooting through the wreck of the witch's cottage to ask Yang, "What are you doing with those pantyhose?"

"I found 'em sticking out from under the foundations," he said, proud of the trophy. "Her legs used to be in 'em, but they wrinkled up and vanished. I let Nadine keep the shoes. What should I do with these?"

I considered letting him in on the No-Place-Like-Home flight plan, but I decided that Mongolia had enough troubles. Anyway, it wouldn't be worth having to stand the sight of Yang in pantyhose, however transient. "Toss them," I said, "and help me dig. There's someone alive in here."

We burrowed into the thatch, helped in our search by the party of elves who had accompanied Lord Palamon on his mission of fatherly mercy. We nearly had an ugly incident with Andraste, who had tagged along. The *lhiannan sidhe* was peeved to the marrow to discover her former lover Neil now her younger half-sister's swain.

Our good luck, T'ing was there. "Excuse me," she said just as Andraste's white eyes were growing perilously hot. "There's someone here I'd like you to meet." Smoothly she brought the recently rescued Yaroslav to the fore. From that point on, it was a matter of moments for those two to discover how much they had in common. The fact that Andraste's elfin home was a place where the sun don't shine was sheer icing on the vampire's cake. As they wandered away arm-in-arm, I heard her ask him if he were fond of poetry.

" 'There once was a bat from Nantucket—' " he began.

Back at the thatch, it didn't take us long until we found first the bannik Ilya Mikulovich, then the deli-man Ben Kipnis. They were both unharmed. Mom would have welcomed Ilya into our home again, but before we left the school that night the bannik struck up a friendship with the melancholy Russian hero. When Mr. Kipnis announced that he and all the heroes were heading back to Feidelstein's and the Back Room, little Ilya decided to go with his new pal for awhile.

"No hard feelings?" he asked Mom.

"Not a one. I'll miss you, but if you can get just one of these heroes to take regular baths, I'll know I did the right thing." She hugged him. "Go with God."

"Stay ninety-nine and forty-four one-hundredths per cent pure," he returned.

Mom looked at Faustus. "I'll try—" His face fell. "—but not *that* hard."

This time when he kissed her it wasn't on the cheek and it wasn't with me for a partner.

"Ain't love grand?" Neil sighed, batting his eyelashes at me like an idiot.

"Almost as grand as a tidy school," said Dr. Oxenstierna. He had lost his bizarre accent and regained every ounce of his icy demeanor. He handed us each a broom and indicated the devastation that was our gym. The prom committee was already busy trash-bagging Beautiful Hawaii, and the chaperones were arguing about whether to call the city morgue or the ASPCA about the disposal of the dead harpies.

I heard Mrs. Fiorelli yelling, "But they're *dogs*, I tell you! What, you blind?"

How hard would it be to clean up the whole mess with magic? I put aside the broom and held my sword-wand up straight before my face, concentrating. Its crystal heart began to throb with focused energy. An emanation of rainbow splendor fanned out from the blade. Many who saw it fell to their knees, ravished by so much beauty and power.

Doc Ox confiscated it as being a potentially dangerous object not specifically cleared for student possession in the school handbook. "You may pick this up from my office Monday morning. In the meantime—" He urged the broom back into my hands. "Gentlemen?"

It takes five and a half dumpsters to hold the remains of one completely dismantled chicken-legged cottage.

Or did you already know that?

Epilogue

THE SEMIFINALS FOR the arm-wrestling championship of the Mythological Continuum had reached their peak of excitement when Ben Kipnis strolled into the Back Room and accosted the occupants of a private table for Three.

"Someone to see you," he said.

"Tell him to drop dead," replied the skinny white-haired one whose few friends called her Snuffy.

"Now, now," motherly Buffy chided. "Not nice."

Muffy didn't even bother looking away from the contest. She wriggled her tightly sheathed hips and cooed, "Oooooh, don't you just love the way they get all *sweaty*?"

Kipnis remained his phlegmatic self. "It's the kid. Remember him? With the wand? He's got his punk friend with him. You know, the big, good-looking yutz."

"Them again?" Snuffy looked disgusted. "Ah, hell, bring 'em in." Kipnis did so.

"Well, dear hearts," said Buffy when the boys had pulled up a couple of chairs to crowd the little table. "What can we do for you?"

Tim slapped a thick, crumpled oblong of paper onto the tabletop. "Do you know what this is?" he demanded.

"Should we?"

"It's a college acceptance letter, that's what! From Princeton University! It's only what I've been waiting for my whole life!"

"Oh, I don't think it's that, dear." Buffy produced a loosely knit scarf and began counting off rows. "No, it isn't. See?

Princeton acceptance is right up here, and all the way down
here is what you've been waiting for all—''

"And it's ruined!"

The arm-wrestling semifinalists paused in mid-grunt to stare
at the person who dared interrupt their combat.

The Three herded their mortal guests out of the deli and into
the street. "Perhaps you're calmer now?" Buffy inquired.

Tim slumped against the supportive bulk of a mailbox, even
though the July sun had made it an uncomfortably warm brace.
"My life is over."

"Don't call us," Snuffy smiled. "We'll call you."

"Look, this is all my fault," Neil broke in. "That letter
came to Tim's house back in April, while I was taking his
place. Even if I was in his body, I didn't think it was right to
open his mail, so I just put it somewhere—"

"Crammed into the pocket of a crummy pair of jeans I never
wear," Tim muttered, his face in his hands. "Until today,
because Mom's too busy to do as much laundry as before, so
they were the only clean pants I had left. That's how I found
it."

Buffy patted him on the back. "And how is your dear
mother?"

"Grrf." It was an unintelligible mumble.

"Oh, Mrs. Desmond's great!" Neil was eager to change the
subject.

"She and Faustus still an item?" Muffy asked, fairly trembling with prurient ignorance.

"You bet. And ever since she sold that comic strip of hers—
you know, *Mister Mephisto*?—to this newspaper syndicate, she's
been doing swell, quit the job at McDonald's, the whole thing.
See, it's about this wizard and this demon and they go around
with this fat orange kitten that thinks all these funny things and
eats lasagna and—"

"Tim, darling," Muffy said, pressing her nubile body to his
back like a second skin. "If you're accepted at Princeton, why
is it bad news?"

Tim lifted his head. "Because this came in April with a
deadline attached. If I didn't respond by May, they released
my place in the freshman class for another applicant who was
on the waiting list. By *May*, got that?" His eyes flashed. "It
is now July."

"You were busy in May," Muffy pointed out. "Just write

and tell them that you had to save the world from monsters. They'll understand."

Snuffy peeled her youngest sister off of Tim. "He wants to go to Princeton, kid, not Bellevue." She turned to the maternal one of the Three. "But *we* understand what he did. We couldn't be there to interfere firsthand, but he handled it fine."

"Not alone," Tim put in. "I had help; plenty of it. Lord Palamon—"

"—just stepped in to fire the final shot. Don't minimize your part in what happened, boy, or the selflessness that freed your mother."

"Or *your* role in this, Poet." Buffy inclined her head to Neil. "The two of you have passed through much together. We and the Balance are in your debt. It would not do for us to stand by indifferent and permit *that*"—she pointed to the battered envelope still in Tim's hand—"to come between you."

The Three took hands in a circle around Tim and Neil and the mailbox. "Shall we?" asked Muffy, bouncing on her toes.

"Let's."

Their hands parted. Again Buffy materialized the trailing scarf with all its snarls and wrinkles and swaths of glorious color. Muffy held it taut and Snuffy took hold of the long thread dangling from the end. Slowly, carefully, she began to pull.

"Hey, take it easy with that!" Tim cautioned. "That's my life you're—"

"We are trained professionals," Snuffy assured him. "Kid, don't try this on your own."

The scarf unravated. The hot sun of July paled and cooled. A stiff breeze, still not free of winter's frost, raised goose bumps on the boys' bare arms and legs. People passing on the street wore heavier clothing. A sign saying "Special After-Taxes Sale" appeared in the window of a store across the street.

Snuffy stopped pulling and held up the tight little ball of yarn she'd accumulated. "Well? Why are you just standing there, Tim? I think my sister is eager to get this knitted back into the pattern. What's the holdup? Don't you want to put that in the box before pickup time?" She pointed to the envelope.

Tim looked at it. It was no longer addressed to him, but to Princeton. "You told them yes," Muffy said, giggling. "Now mail it." He did.

"Good boy."

* * *

"Well, we *did* owe him," Muffy said later, over the tuna-salad plate Ben Kipnis set in front of her. "We couldn't just leave the world overrun with monsters."

"It's not like he got them all swept away," Snuffy complained, tearing big mouthfuls out of her bagel and lox.

"Oh, one or two monsters on the Outside won't make that much of a difference." Buffy picked at her cherry blintzes and dismissed her sister's gripes. "It happens all the time. Just read *The National Enquirer*. It's not the end of the world."

"And Tim is such a nice—Bad doggie! *Bad* doggie! Shoo! Stop that! Go away!" Muffy reached under the table to give Zasu a firm lesson in respecting a lady's personal space. The chastened hound snorted and trotted off in search of other interesting smells.

There was one scent that was especially intriguing. Zasu followed it down to an unoccupied corner of the Back Room where disused chairs and tables obscured the growing gap in the wall. Something was in there. Something almost doggy, by the smell of it. Zasu stuck his head in, sniffing madly.

The Fenris wolf snapped it off with one bite. Leeside exile had made him ornery, and since he was a creature whose whole existence was geared to bringing about the end of the world, he was pretty ornery to begin with.

He noticed that the dog he had decapitated was already growing a new head back, and decided to be on his way before his resurrected foe could retaliate. Vicious, massive, and merciless as he was, the Fenris wolf was not fond of a fair fight.

He passed through the hole. He saw the massed populace of the Back Room, all of them too caught up in the competitive spirit of the arm-wrestling contest to notice whether it was a hound or a wolf who went sauntering by. On the threshold of the Back Room he paused to sniff the rich and varied air of the world Outside, the world whose ultimate destruction he was fated to be. His jaws hung open and his tongue lolled in a lupine grin.

This was going to be fun.